Truth & Betrayal

K.C. WELLS

Truth & Betrayal

This is a work of fiction. Names, characters, places, and incidents either are the product of the author's imagination or are used fictitiously, and any resemblance to actual persons, living or dead, business establishments, events, or locales is entirely coincidental.

Truth & Betrayal
Copyright © 2018 by K.C. Wells
Cover Design by Meredith Russell

Cover content is being used for illustrative purposes only and any person depicted on the cover is a model.

The trademarked products mentioned in this book are the property of their respective owners, and are recognized as such.

All Rights Reserved. No part of this book may be reproduced or transmitted in any form or by any means, including electronic or mechanical, including photocopying, recording, or by any information storage and retrieval system without the written permission of the Publisher, except where permitted by law.

By K.C. Wells

Acknowledgments

A huge thank you to my AWESOME betas,
Jason, Daniel, Helena, Debra, Sharon, Mardee & Will.

Jason Mitchell, my wonderful Alpha and chief Plotter.
Thanks for those hours in Ontario, talking about this book.

Thank you to Ed Davies, who finally helped me to come up with an ending.
Thanks also to Zac Richarmé, for the advice re Atlanta.

Thanks to all those Facebook friends who shared their first experiences of going into a sex shop. You might find yours in here somewhere.

And a HUGE THANK YOU
to Cammey Kelley, Megan Turngren and Becca Waldrop.
Y'all made sure this book was firmly rooted in the South.

By K.C. Wells

Chapter One

May 5, 2017

Jake Greenwood pulled off the thick gloves he'd worn to protect his hands from the lumber, and threw them into the back of his daddy's truck. Right then he could almost hear the hot shower that was practically hollering at him, promising to ease away his aches. It had been a long day, but thank God, the weekend had arrived at long last. Not that it brought the prospect of anything new, but the thought of hanging out with Pete, Dan and the rest of his little group of friends made him smile.

Of course, the one person he wanted—needed—to hang out with was about two hundred fifty miles, or a four-hour drive, away.

Maybe he'll visit soon.

Even as the thought left him, Jake began his habitual process of denying the possibility. It made for less hurt in the long run.

Maybe I jus' need to accept that this is how things are now.
Yeah. Like *that* was gonna happen.

"Don't you wanna go home?"

His daddy's amused tone pierced through the multiple layers of Jake's hopes, fears and internal turmoil. Jake arched his eyebrows. "Are you in such a hurry to get home to Mama's fried catfish, slaw an' hush puppies? Because it *is* Friday, right?" He snickered. Mama sure loved her routines.

His daddy narrowed his gaze. "Your mama is goin' to go to her grave believin' I love her fried catfish just as much as her hot chicken an' biscuits an' her banana pudding. Just 'cause you know different does *not* mean you're gonna be sharin' that piece of information. Do that, an' I'll tan your hide, nineteen or not."

Jake crossed his heart. "Mama will be happier than a pig in mud, I swear."

His daddy bit his lip, his eyes gleaming. "An' don't think you can get around me by using one of my sayin's." He climbed behind the wheel of the truck. "But please, Jacob, take your own sweet time. I'm sure your mama won't mind if we're late." He gave Jake an innocent smile.

That was enough to have Jake dive into the passenger seat. Mama in a mood was *not* something he wanted to contemplate. It would screw his whole weekend.

His daddy switched on the engine and pulled away from the house on West Fir Street where they'd just started a new renovation. It was going to be a lot of hard work, and it would take time, but Jake didn't mind that. He loved working with his daddy. It was nearly two years since he'd graduated from LaFollette High School and begun working full-time. Before that, he'd worked every summer vacation since he was twelve years old.

Of course, throwing himself into tasks that kept him occupied might have had *something* to do with trying not to miss Caleb. Like *that* worked.

As they turned right onto South Tennessee Avenue, his dad cleared his throat. "So, wanna tell me what's wrong?"

Jake kept his face straight. "Nothin's wrong." When his daddy reacted with a snort, Jake sighed internally. There were times when he forgot how much his daddy saw.

"You don't fool me none. You've been wound tighter than a clock all week. An' I don't think work is the cause, so why don't you tell me what's on your mind?"

The truth sounded childish, so Jake kept silent.

His daddy sighed. "I miss him too, alright?"

There was no way Jake could remain silent after that. "I guess I'm still not used to the idea that he's left home." Not that he hadn't had enough time to grow accustomed to it. Caleb's visits had become increasingly rare from the time he started college. The ache in Jake's heart had lessened a little with each year, but initially it had been painful for the eleven-year-old boy who'd lost his best friend.

"Can't think what he finds so fascinatin' in Atlanta that it keeps him from visitin' his folks. An' it's not like I don't call him an' tell him to git his ass back home once in a while."

"You do?" Jake gave his daddy a startled glance.

Daddy huffed. "Don't matter. He pays me no mind. But it's not me I'm thinkin' 'bout, it's your mama. It's not enough to come home once in a blue moon." He sighed heavily. "I guess I'm not used to the idea either. When I was Caleb's age, I lived about an hour from your grandparents. Your mama an' me, we were in church with 'em every Sunday mornin', an' we'd stay until late afternoon. Times change, huh?" Daddy gave a weary smile. "I'm still proud of him, for goin' to college an' gettin' a good job in Atlanta."

"Why don't you an' Mama go see him instead?" It was something that had bothered Jake for the longest time. He had no clue about where his brother lived, what Atlanta was like.

There had been no invitations, and that had hurt.

Another snort. "Lord knows, your mama leaves enough hints, but he never says a word." He paused. "Sometimes I git the idea that he doesn't want his friends to meet his folks."

It came as a shock for Jake to realize that his daddy was hurting too. He wanted to say something, *anything*, to let his dad know that he got it, he really did, but the words stuck in his throat.

They turned onto Shoreline Circle, and soon reached the turnoff for the house. Jake loved how you couldn't see their home from the road. Trees surrounded it, casting their shadows over the roof and walls. He pointed along the driveway. "We got visitors." A police car was pulling up in front of the house.

Oh Lord.

His daddy pierced him with a look. "Okay, what have you gone an' done now?"

Jake groaned. "I haven't done anything! An' that was two years ago, alright? An' it was *one joint*." Not that his daddy was going to let him forget it. His mama certainly wouldn't. Which was why the less they knew about how he spent his weekends, the better.

He'd learned to be more careful about who he hung out with. One call from a friend's daddy to his had been enough to make him wary.

Daddy switched off the engine and they got out of the truck, just as two police officers approached the front door. He cleared his throat. "Can I help you?"

The officers turned, and Jake was struck by their expressions.

This is not gonna be good.

"Good evenin'. Do you know Caleb Greenwood?"

And just like that, an icy hand closed around Jake's heart.

Daddy froze. "He's my son. I'm Hank Greenwood."

The officer gestured toward the house. "Can we step inside, sir?"

It was as if the world abruptly changed speed, and everything shifted into slow motion. His daddy walking over to the door, the officers following, removing their caps… Even the wind through the trees was reduced to a distorted whispering as he followed them into the house.

Mama stood by the fireplace, her eyes wide, all the color drained from her face, her hand to her chest. "What's happened?"

"Ma'am, how 'bout you sit down?" The older officer pointed to the armchair.

"How 'bout you tell me why you're here?" she flung back at him.

"Maggie, do as the officer says, alright?" Daddy moved to her side, put his arm around her waist, and guided her toward the chair. He glanced at the officers. "This is my wife, Maggie, an' our other son, Jacob." When Mama was eventually seated, he straightened. "All right. Now s'ppose you tell us what's goin' on."

Jake sank onto the couch, perched on the edge of the seat cushion, his heart still constricted.

The officers remained standing, their caps in their hands. The older one took the lead. "I'm officer Abernathy, an' this is officer Cox. There's been an accident, an' we're sorry to inform you that Caleb didn't make it."

The fear that had been building ever since he'd seen the police car flooded through Jake in a wild surge, and he was grateful to be sitting down. "What kind of accident?" he choked out.

Cox, who had to be in his mid-twenties, gave him a compassionate glance. "His car was involved in a traffic accident on the I-20 near Greensboro, Georgia. The paramedics weren't able to help him."

Daddy made a strangled noise, then composed himself, his face pale. "You're positive it was Caleb?"

Abernathy nodded. "He was the passenger. The driver identified him at the scene, an' Caleb had his ID on him. I'm sorry, sir. Is there someone we can contact to be here with ya?"

Mama stared at Daddy with anguished eyes. "Rev. Hubbert? Would you call him?"

Daddy nodded, before turning to face Abernathy. "So… what happens now?"

"You'll get a call from the medical examiner soon, I reckon. Then when you've decided on a funeral home, they'll contact McCommon's in Greensboro. That's the funeral home that has Caleb." Abernathy's voice softened. "Arrangements will be made to bring him home."

Mama finally broke with a wail, and Jake held onto every ounce of strength he possessed not to join her. The two officers held themselves still, and Daddy knelt on the rug in front of Mama, grasping her hands so tightly that the skin across his knuckles was white. "I gotcha, Maggie." His voice quavered, and his shoulders shook.

"Would you like us to wait until the preacher arrives?" Cox asked, his tone kind.

Daddy shook his head. He wiped his eyes. "Thank you, but there's nothing more you can do here. Jacob, would you see the officers out?"

Jake didn't know if he could even stand.

"Sure, Daddy." He pushed himself up off the couch, his legs trembling, and walked over to the door, the officers close behind him. He stepped outside with them and pulled the door to.

"Y'all stick together now," Cox said gently. "Your mama will need you, but you'll need them too. We're sorry to have delivered such terrible news."

"Thank you again." Though it seemed plain wrong to thank the people who'd just brought Jake's whole world to a standstill. He stood by the door as the officers got into their car, pulled past the house, turned in the clearing, then drove slowly past the truck.

Jake waited until they were out of sight, then dropped onto his knees, hardly feeling the pain when they connected with the hard ground. He bent over, holding his head in his hands, and cried for his brother, hot tears spilling over his cheeks and spattering on the solid earth.

It didn't matter what the officer had said.

Caleb was never coming home.

Chapter Two

Jake passed through the three weeks that followed the police visit, enveloped in a numbing fog. The time was marked not in days, but in episodes, and each one brought fresh jabs of pain that opened up the wound once more, until he retreated into himself, seeking the numbness again.

Episode #1 was the call from the medical examiner. Jake had sat holding his mama's hand while his daddy talked in that flat tone Jake had never heard before, but which had become more prevalent lately. It had felt like the examiner had done all the talking, because his daddy had asked few questions, and when it was over, he replaced the phone in its cradle, walked over to the window, and stared out for what seemed like ages. Subsequently, he'd turned to them, and carefully, *so* carefully, relayed how Caleb had lost his life.

It appeared he and another man had been on the freeway, when a tractor trailer going in the opposite direction had shed its load of tires, which had bounced their way across the lanes. One of them bounced over the divider, and right into the windshield. Caleb's injuries were such that he died not long after, but the driver sustained facial bruising and a broken right arm.

The knowledge that the car's other occupant has escaped with so little burned Jake, tightening his chest until he couldn't breathe. It was only his mama's harsh, staccato gasps that reminded him he wasn't the only one suffering, and he'd gripped her hand more tightly, as though that would help.

Nothing would help, *ever*, and all those platitudes that

friends and neighbors dished out about time being a healer? Well, they could take all of their well-meaning crap and shove it. And that went double for the Rev. Hubbert, who wasn't so much an Episode, more like an ongoing occurrence.

Jake didn't have anything against the preacher personally. He wasn't a fire-and-brimstone kinda guy, but he'd said a couple of things in church on occasion that had sent icy fingers crawling under Jake's skin, creeping their way to his heart where they squeezed and squeezed. But now? It seemed like he was living with them, he was there so often. Jake didn't mind that so much—what hurt was what he said. How Caleb was in a better place. How he was with the Lord.

How the fuck do you know that? Jake wanted to scream. This guy didn't know his brother. He knew nothing of the Caleb who'd snuck comic books into church in his bible when Jake was six or seven. The Caleb who cussed when he and Jake were alone by Ollis Creek, and made Jake swear not tell their mama. If Caleb had believed, he'd have gone with Mama and Daddy every Sunday when he was a teenager. Mama hadn't pushed when he'd asked to stay at home, but it was plain to all concerned that she wasn't happy about it.

So while Reverend Hubbert was in the house, Jake buttoned his lip and kept the peace, for his mama's sake. He smiled politely every time the preacher turned up on their doorstep, poured him glasses of sweet tea, and then ducked out of the way. He couldn't deny those visits did Mama some good, however, and for that reason alone he was prepared to bite his tongue when the reverend got going on his theories as to Caleb's eternal resting place.

Jake knew exactly where that was gonna be—in the family plot in the Woodlawn Cemetery. Anyone who claimed any different was deluded.

Only, with the good Reverend came all the ladies from the United Methodist Church, clucking sympathetically, bearing gifts of casseroles, fried chicken, corn bread, country ham, and enough mac and cheese to feed an army. Not that Mama took all these neighborly offerings as an excuse to rest. She set about cooking up a storm, until the freezer lid groaned in protest when you tried to close it, and you couldn't find an inch of space in the refrigerator. When the ladies descended, Jake stuck to pouring out countless glasses of iced tea, and did his best to avoid the cloying sympathy and heartfelt remarks.

Is there a book for all this crap they keep comin' out with? Because I swear, every single last one of 'em says exactly the same thing.

Daddy was nowhere to be found when they came around, of course. He got into his truck and went off to work, leaving Jake with his mama, claiming she needed him.

Jake didn't think Mama even knew he was there.

Episode #4 was a harsh reminder that yeah, this had really happened. A week or so after their first visit, the same two officers turned up again, only this time they brought with them a box containing Caleb's personal effects, that had been sent on from Georgia. Daddy signed for it, and when the officers had left, he placed it on the coffee table and just… stared at it. When neither he nor Mama made any move to open it, Jake took matters into his own hands. Not that there was much in there. No clothing apart from a pair of sneakers, but Jake had seen enough emergency room dramas to expect that. Caleb's wallet and key chain were there, along with a couple of leather bracelets and a gold chain. One of the keys was clearly for Caleb's apartment, and Jake put the chain in a drawer.

There would be time enough after the funeral to think about the apartment, and the rest of Caleb's stuff. Right then, getting through the funeral was the only goal in sight, and the closer it got, the more painful the prospect became.

Episode #5 nearly broke all three of them; Cliff Dawson from the Martin Wilson Funeral Home called. Jake could still hear Cliff's voice, his way of talking softly, see him nodding gently, a cup and saucer balanced on his knee, while he tried to take notes unobtrusively. What cut them all to the bone was the discovery that it was to be a closed casket.

The look on Mama's face when Cliff told her…

The news conjured up images in Jake's head that he did *not* want to contemplate, and judging by his daddy's pallor and sharp intake of breath, he wasn't the only one having a hard time of it. And when Mama clutched the gold cross around her neck, her eyes wide, her lips parted, and that familiar staccato beat as she tried to drag air into her lungs, all Jake wanted was to curl up under his comforter and shut out the world.

Of course, Cliff had moved on quickly, wanting to talk about the obituary that would appear in the LaFollette Press, Campbell County's weekly newspaper, both in paper and digitally. That was when Jake had gotten up and left the room, unable to bear a second more.

Whenever he thought about those three weeks, what came to mind was the sweet, heady perfume from the many bouquets and arrangements of flowers that filled the house. Jake couldn't deny that people were being kind, and their reaction to Caleb's passing overwhelmed him, but he would have traded all those episodes for *one more minute* with his brother.

Jake held on tight to his emotions and reined in his grief, for his parents' sake. They didn't need him falling apart on them, not when they were so close to breaking point themselves. So Jake became the son they needed, the one who did everything he was asked without question, who supported them and loved them.

They didn't get to see the Jake who shut his bedroom door each night and cried into his pillow to muffle the sound. Or the Jake who found himself welling up at the slightest provocation, and had to quickly seek privacy until he'd gotten himself under control. They had no clue as to how many times Jake sobbed in the shower where he knew they'd never hear. But maintaining such a tight grip on himself was something that couldn't last.

The evening before the funeral, he reached his breaking point.

As soon as he'd cleared away the dishes, Jake grabbed his

phone and snuck out into the back yard. The last rays of the sun lit up the tree tops, and the temperature had dropped low enough that he was shivering. He walked briskly to the fence that marked the boundary of the property, and scrolled through his contacts for Pete's number.

"Jake?" Pete sounded almost cautious.

"Hey." Jake kept a wary eye trained on the back porch, making sure his folks were still inside the house.

"Didn't think I'd hear from ya. Kinda thought you'd be dealin' with shit right now."

"Yeah, well, I've dealt with enough shit to last a lifetime, an' I'm goin' stir crazy. You doin' anythin' tonight?" Jake crossed his fingers.

There was a pause. "Well…"

"Jesus, it's not a trick question. I need to get outta here." He needed more than that, but if he knew Pete and his friends, his other requirements would be taken care of.

"Dan an' me were gonna go to Mike's place later. His parents are visitin' his grandma, an' they won't be back till tomorrow afternoon." Confidence crept into Pete's voice. "Mike's got somethin' you might like."

"It'd better be booze or weed." Either would do at that point.

"How does a bottle of vodka grab ya?" Pete snickered. "Yeah, dumb question."

"What time?" Some questions weren't even worth answering.

"I'll be there in an hour, soon as I finish my chores here. Dan's meetin' me there." After a moment's pause, his voice grew more hesitant. "Are you sure you're—"

"See you in an hour then." Jake disconnected. He wasn't about to let Pete talk him out of it.

"Jacob?" Mama called from the porch.

He knew what *that* was about. "I'm comin' in right now to do the dishes, Mama." He didn't want to give her any reason to complain later when he announced his intention to go see his friends. After three weeks of being house-bound, he figured he deserved a break.

More than that, he needed some anesthetic to combat the pain inside him, and alcohol was the perfect solution.

Jake parked his truck on Mike's driveway, directly behind Pete's Honda, and by the time he reached for the doorbell, Pete was already there. "Hey. Dan'll be here in a sec."

Jake smacked the back of his hand against Pete's, their usual greeting, before stepping into the house. "Okay, where's the booze?" he called out.

Mike appeared in the doorway to the kitchen. "Jeez, tell everyone, why don'tcha, asshole? That ol' bitch next door can hear a mouse fart from twenty feet. We don't want her to come marchin' in here, 'specially when she knows the olds are away." He peered closely at Jake. "You look like crap."

Jake rolled his eyes. "Well fuck, my brother got his head caved in by a bouncin' tire. How'd you think *you'd* deal with that? Maybe you could sleep at night, but me? Every time I close my eyes, I keep imaginin' how bad he has to look for them to insist on a *closed fuckin' casket*. An' if all you wanna do is ask questions about Cal, then I might as well leave *right fuckin' now*."

Mike gaped at him, his mouth open.

From behind Jake, Pete snorted. "Wow. Three weeks with no one but your folks. You're just gonna get all your cussin' in' at once, ain't ya? Get it outta your system?"

It took a second to register the humor in Pete's words. Jake huffed. "I think they need to pin a goddamn medal on my chest, that's what *I* think. Three weeks an' not a single fuck has passed my lips." He sighed and gave Mike an apologetic glance. "Sorry. I didn't mean to stomp all over ya. I'm a little... raw, what with tomorrow an' all."

Mike nodded, his expression softer. He held out a nearly fully bottle. "Then you prob'ly need a slug of this."

Jake stilled. "Like you wouldn't believe." The numbness that had cocooned him since that awful day was dissipating, and in its place was pain, sinking its sharp claws into his flesh, piercing its way through his sternum and right into his heart. He gave Mike a frank stare. "We only got the one?" Because the way he was feeling, one was not gonna be enough.

Not by a long shot.

Mike passed him the bottle, and Jake opened it, tipped it up, and drank two huge gulps of it, before handing it back, coughing harshly. "Where'd you get that?"

"Snuck it out of my dad's truck when he got back from the liquor store." Mike's eyes gleamed. "I figured he'd bought that much booze, he wouldn't miss one bottle. I stashed it under my bed. Even my mama's not brave enough to peek under there." He snickered. "She'd prob'ly get attacked by rabid dust bunnies."

"An' as to your question?" Pete held up a joint. "What the vodka don't cure, this will."

Jake could have kissed him. "Then what are we waitin' for? Let the party begin." So what if he ended up three sheets to the wind drunk and high as a fucking kite?

Anything was better than *feeling*.

"If you're gonna smoke, do it outside. Bottles I can get rid of. The smell of weed? Hell no. My mama has a nose like a bloodhound." Mike pushed past Pete, heading for the back porch and handing him the bottle as he went by. "I'll get the bonfire goin'. We can sit around it."

Pete grinned. "Besides, once we get this inside us? Who's gonna notice if it gets cold?"

Jake nodded. *Good deal.* And with any luck, he'd end up with such a massive hangover that he wouldn't be able to recall a single detail of the next day.

Which was exactly how he wanted it.

Truth & Betrayal

By K.C. Wells

Chapter Three

"What time is it?" Dan asked, peering up at the night sky.

Jake was past caring. They'd finished the vodka, plus two six-packs that Dan had brought with him, and the rest of Pete's stash. He was at the stage where he moved his head an inch, and the world moved six feet. A weird sensation, but Jake would rather have that than the way he'd felt on arriving.

Pete giggled. "You know what I'd kill for right now? My mama's corn bread, drippin' in butter."

Jake cackled. "Christ, you say that every time you get high." He poked Mike's arm. "You got any chips? You know what he's like when he gets the munchies."

Mike snorted. "He ate the last bag half an hour ago."

"Jake?" Dan stared at him across the dying flames of the bonfire. "If I ask you somethin', will you promise not to bite my head off?"

Jake shrugged. "Depends. Try me."

"Was there a reason Cal didn't wanna come home so often? I mean, once he left for college, he was never here." Dan's brows knitted together. "I'm askin' cos you never talk about him. Fuck, the two of you were like… like…." His frown deepened.

"Like *brothers*, you drunken asshole?" Pete suggested. "An' why're you talkin' 'bout Caleb now? Are you such a fuckin' moron? They're *buryin'* him tomorrow, for Christ's sake. Jake don't wanna talk about 'im."

"He changed, alright?" Jake blurted out.

His friends fell silent, and the only sound to be heard was

the crackling of the fire.

Jake took a second or two to breathe deeply. "He didn't talk so much anymore. I noticed it the first few times he came home. Before, we'd jaw for hours about pretty much anythin', but once he'd left…" Caleb had been less inclined to get into conversation. Whenever Jake had tried to talk to him, it seemed Caleb always found something for them to do. And it had gotten worse after Caleb's graduation, when he'd announced he'd got a job in Atlanta. Jake had wanted to talk to him so fucking badly on those rare occasions when he visited, but each time he got the feeling Caleb was avoiding him, and that had fucking *stung*.

He didn't want to *think* about Caleb, let alone talk about him.

Jake staggered to his feet, fumbling in his pocket for his keys. "Y'know what? I'm goin' home."

Pete blinked. "You wanna call someone to take you home? Someone sober?"

Jake shook his head and instantly regretted the action when the back yard swam before his eyes. "I'll be careful."

Mike got to his feet too. "Jus' stick to the speed limit. You don't want the cops callin' on your folks just now."

And that right there was a sobering thought.

"I'll be fine," he assured them. "I'm only ten minutes away, right?" To his surprise, Mike gave him a firm hug.

"We'll be there tomorrow, alright?" His voice softened. "We're here for ya, Jake."

Jake's throat tightened. "Thanks," he managed to croak out. Before the others could say something else to bring on the tears that threatened, he lurched across the yard to the gate that led to the front of the house. Once in the truck, he backed out of the driveway and onto the quiet, deserted street.

Jake tried to concentrate on the darkened roads, but his mind kept going back to Dan's question. *Was* there some reason for Caleb's continued absence? There hadn't been any falling out between him and their parents, at least none that Jake knew of.

Lord knew, Jake had asked himself a hundred times if there'd been anything he'd done to upset his brother, but he'd drawn a blank.

Whatever Caleb's reasons were, he'd never know. They'd died with him.

It took a second or two for him to register that the flashing blue lights in the rear-view mirror were for him.

Well fuck.

Jake pulled into the curb on the empty street and waited as the police car pulled in behind him. *Daddy is gonna kill me this time.* A car door opened and closed, then came the sound of boot heels on tarmac, slow and steady. Jake wound down the window with a sigh. "Evenin', officer." He kept his breathing slow and even, determined to bluff his way out of this mess if he possibly could.

A flashlight momentarily blinded him. "License, identification, an' proof of insurance please." The voice was young and vaguely familiar.

Jake reached up to the sun visor where he kept them and handed them over. "I wasn't speedin', was I?" He was positive he'd kept below thirty. Of course, in his present state, he couldn't be sure of anything. He could've driven over a deer and he'd never have noticed.

"You were drivin' a little erratically." There was a pause. "Jacob?" The flashlight lowered, and the officer leaned on the sill.

Jake stared at him, and just like that it came to him. "Officer… Cox?" Of all the cops to pull him over, why did it have to be one of the two that had been to the house?

The officer nodded. "Get out of the truck, please." He opened the door for Jake, who got out, carefully. Officer Cox regarded him steadily. "Have you been drinkin'?"

Jake bit his lip. "I had a couple o' beers."

Officer Cox arched his eyebrows. "A couple?"

Yeah, he didn't believe a fucking word of it.

Jake's heart pounded. "Look, if you're gonna take me in, *please*, don't let my mama an' daddy know 'bout this, alright?

They've got enough on their plate right now."

Officer Cox tilted his head to one side. "The funeral's tomorrow, isn't it?" he said softly.

What the fuck? Jake swallowed hard. "Yeah."

Cox nodded. "Yeah. If I was in your shoes, I'd want to tie one on as well." He paused. "I was a couple of years behind Caleb in high school. I remember him." He sighed. "I couldn't say anythin' that day we came by the house, but…" Cox switched off his flashlight. "Okay, here's what we're gonna do. Lock up the truck, an' I'll take you home. You can come back for it tomorrow. It'll be safe enough here."

Panic bubbled up inside him. "But—"

Cox held up his hand. "Relax. I'm not takin' you to your door. I'm just makin' sure you reach it. I won't be comin' inside." He gave Jake a firm stare. "But if I catch you drivin' in this state again, I won't be so lenient. An' don't let your folks see you like this. Because yeah, they don't need this."

"Thank you." Jake wanted to say something else, words that conveyed the depth of his gratitude, but to his horror, what came out were hot tears that spilled over his cheeks.

"Hey." Cox's voice was gentle. "It's okay, Jacob. I can only imagine what you're goin' through right now. But you gotta be strong tomorrow, for your parents' sake."

Jake wiped his eyes savagely on the sleeve of his jacket. Crying like some goddamn snot-nosed little kid. "Yeah." He hiccupped. "It's Jake, by the way. Only my folks call me Jacob. An' thanks again."

Cox patted his arm. "Like I said. I get it." He hesitated. "Look, I know you don't know me from Adam, but… drinkin' makes things a little easier, I won't deny that. I wouldn't have gotten through some truly awful times without a couple of stiff drinks. But… don't let it become a crutch, is all I'm sayin'. An' that's without even mentionin' the fact that you're underage. I promise, it does get easier." He reached into his breast pocket and pulled out a notepad and pen, then scribbled on a page. Cox tore it out and handed it to Jake. "Here's my cell. If you ever need someone to talk to, just to let it all out, please, call me, okay? I can't promise to make it better, but I'm a damn good listener." He put the notepad and pen back in his pocket.

Jake swallowed, fighting back the tears that had become so commonplace during the last three weeks.

Cox's eyes were full of compassion. "I know. You don't have to say anythin', alright? It's just in case you need a friend. Now let's get you home—Jake." He patted him on the back.

Jake followed him to the police car, and Cox gestured to the passenger seat. They drove in silence for a minute or two, and then Cox pulled up at the entrance to the driveway. Jake hesitated a moment before getting out, his heartbeat returning to normal.

Cox cleared his throat. "I'll be there tomorrow, by the way. I asked if I could go."

That was enough to have the tears pricking the corners of his eyes again. "Thank you." Jake couldn't stand it a second longer. He got out of the car and hurried along the drive, his feet stumbling over the gravel. He was dimly aware of the police car moving off, but he didn't look back. The lights were out inside, the only illumination coming from the porch.

They left the light on for me. The thought warmed him. Using every ounce of stealth he possessed, Jake opened the door as noiselessly as possible, taking his time to close it with just as much care. He took off his sneakers and crept through the house, taking extra special care in the hallway where that one floorboard always squeaked. Mama was a light sleeper. When he reached his room without incident, Jake closed the door behind him and flopped down onto the bed on his front, burying his face in his pillow.

His last thought before falling into sleep was that the following day was going to be the worst one ever.

Reverend Hubbert rested his hands on the pulpit, speaking in a low voice about Caleb the son and brother, Caleb the student, Caleb the athlete…

Jake wanted to scream. *But you didn't even know him!*

Behind him, the church was full. Apart from the usual members of the congregation, there was a large contingent of people roughly Caleb's age, so Jake figured they'd known him from high school. Most high school graduates in LaFollette tended to stick around, going into local industries and businesses, or in some cases, doing very little. Going to college wasn't unheard of, but those who did were in a tiny minority. Mama had been so proud of Caleb, Daddy too, when Caleb got his scholarship. His graduation photo took pride of place on the shelf above the fireplace, and Mama dusted it religiously every week.

"Caleb was a popular young man, with a sense of humor," Reverend Hubbert intoned. "A young man who loved the Lord. An' now the Lord has taken Caleb to be with him. Let us hope that we too will see the Lord one day, providin' that we have been saved."

That was it. Jake had had just about as much of the reverend's drivel as he could stand. He raised his hand, waiting until the reverend noticed and stared at him. "Yes, Jacob?"

He got to his feet. "I'd like to say a few words about… about Caleb." Beside him, his mama caught her breath, but said nothing. Daddy remained silent, his eyes locked on the coffin before them, covered in white carnations, white waxflower and greenery. Yet more flower arrangements stood on either side, a mixture of white roses, snapdragons and blue delphiniums.

The preacher cleared his throat, then nodded. "Of course," he said, his tone deferential.

Jake eased past his parents and made his way to the front, his throat tight as he walked by the coffin. He tried not to think that it was *Caleb* in there, Caleb who he'd never see again.

Reverend Hubbert stepped aside for him, and Jake stepped up onto the wooden platform. He stared out at the gathered throng,

By K.C. Wells

and for a moment, his nerve left him.

Then he caught sight of a few familiar faces. Pete, Dan and Mike sat half-way down on the right, their gazes fixed on him. Pete gave him a small nod of encouragement. Two rows behind them, Officer Cox sat, wearing a black suit. He too gazed at Jake, his expression full of compassion and sympathy.

I can do this.

Jake took a deep breath and gripped the sides of the pulpit. "Caleb was… awesome. An' I'm sure I'm not the only one who thinks so. He was real good with people, an' he knew how to make 'em laugh." Nods from the younger mourners eased the constriction in his chest, and Jake breathed easier. "He was hilarious when he got drunk." Jake ignored his mama's gasp. "Anyone here remember that time he wanted to make himself a pair of wings, so he could jump off the roof of the school gym?" Muffled snickers and chuckles greeted his ears, and someone guffawed. Jake smiled. "An' how about the time he an' some friends went skinny-dippin' in Ollis Creek?"

There was no missing his mama's choked response, but Jake didn't give a shit.

He scanned the congregation, noting the smiles where before there had been only sorrow.

"I know we're grievin', but we have to remember the good times." His stomach clenched. "Caleb was the best brother a guy could have, an' as long as he's in *here*…" He covered his heart and put a hand to his temple. "Then he ain't really gone. Sure, there are gonna be times when I'll wish I had my brother to talk to." Raw pain surged through him. "There are things that are gonna go unsaid, stuff I can never share with him. But I'll always be grateful I got to have him in my life, even if that time was cut short." He pushed down hard on the tears that threatened to overwhelm him. "The world is a sorrier place without him."

The truth of that final statement undid him, and Jake let go of his tight rein on his emotions. "That's all I wanna say," he choked out, before stumbling off the platform. He stopped by the coffin and laid his hand on the varnished surface. "Love ya, bro," he whispered.

Daddy got up from his seat and joined him, putting his arm around him. "You done good, Jacob," he said in a low voice. "Time to let him go, son." He released him and stood aside to let him sit down. Mama was crying into her handkerchief, but she reached across and took hold of Jake's hand.

Reverend Hubbert cleared his throat. "Thank you, Jacob, for those… heartfelt words. An' now it is time to commit Caleb to his final restin' place, safe in the knowledge that we shall see him again, in a far, far better place." Everyone rose, and Daddy joined the pallbearers who carefully lifted the coffin up onto their shoulders.

Jake followed them, Mama's arm through his, as they walked solemnly out of the church to watch them load the coffin into the hearse, ready for Caleb's last journey.

He locked his gaze on the flower-covered coffin, until it was no longer in sight when the doors closed. Daddy joined them as they climbed into another car to follow the hearse to the cemetery on the other side of town.

Time to let his brother go.

Chapter Four

Jake clutched his mama's hand tightly as the coffin was carefully lowered into the gaping earth, the edges of the hole disguised by AstroTurf, the same substance that lay beneath their feet and those of the other mourners. Daddy stood next to them, his jaw set as though he was doing his damnedest not to weep. Reverend Hubbert was speaking again, only this time Jake tuned him out, focusing his attention on the coffin that was disappearing from view.

What filled his sorrowful heart was regret.

So much I wanted to tell ya, bro. The timing had never been right, and on those rare occasions when he could have seized the opportunity, his courage deserted him. What came to mind as he watched his brother's slow descent, were his grandpa's wise words.

You always regret not doing somethin'.

Yeah, Grandpa had nailed it.

Jake snuck a glance at his parents. He swore there was more gray in Mama's curly hair, what he could see of it from beneath her hat. There were more lines on her face too. His daddy stared into the grave, his eyes so like Caleb's had been, but it was like he was looking past it somehow.

Then he realized Reverend Hubbert had stopped talking. More importantly, something was happening. Jake scanned the people standing at the graveside for some clue as to why the silence had swiftly become oppressive. Then the whispers began, growing in volume as the older citizens pointed blatantly toward the outer edge of the mourners.

The explanation for such behavior was shockingly apparent.

A stranger stood at the back of the crowd. He wore a black jacket over a white shirt, open at the collar, and black jeans. What made him stand out was the fact that he was black, a single dark face in a sea of white.

Jake listened as those around him voiced their suspicions at the stranger's sudden appearance. He couldn't entirely understand the reactions, but he could see why his arrival would cause a stir. Less than two percent of LaFollette's inhabitants were non-Caucasian. He caught sight of Pete, Dan, and some of his other friends, who appeared unfazed by the decidedly un-Christian comments and whispers around them.

"Who are you?" Mrs. Talbot, their neighbor who lived in the house next door, and not known for her subtlety, called out to the stranger. "This is a private ceremony. You can't just stroll in here." Her elderly voice cracked.

The man stilled. "I'm sorry. I came here to pay my respects, as I'm sure y'all did." His rich, deep voice carried across the mutterings of the assembled mourners. Haltingly he came forward, stepping carefully through the crowd, until he reached the graveside. "My name's Liam Miller. My condolences on your loss. I don't mean to intrude. I'm here because I knew Caleb," he explained, addressing Jake and his parents.

It was only then that Jake noticed his right arm, held up in a black sling. A cast was visible, covering part of his hand. Jake looked him up and down. Liam was handsome, with high cheekbones, and dark brown eyes. Then Jake looked closer. Liam's face bore a few scars, recent ones by the look of them.

Facial injuries. A possible broken arm.

Jake might not have gone to college like his brother, but that didn't mean he was stupid. A wave of ice surged through him as he realized exactly who was standing before him.

Fuck no.

"Oh, my God. You… you're the driver."

Liam blinked, his eyes widening. Then he regained his

composure. "I was drivin' the car, yes. I wanted to—"

That was as far as Jake was prepared to allow him to go. The only thought consuming him was that the person responsible for Caleb's death was standing right in front of him. He balled his hands into tight fists, his arms rigid at his sides.

"You've got a fuckin' nerve, showin' up here." The words came out strained as he battled to hold onto his rage. "Haven't ya done enough? Why in the hell would we want *you* here? It's all your fault Caleb's dead, you son of a bitch."

"I don't understand." Mama's voice quavered. "Why're you yellin' at this man? What's he done?" It was as if Jake's furious words had roused her from the unfathomable depths of her grief.

"He was drivin' the car that killed Caleb, Mama." Even as he uttered the words, some part of Jake knew they weren't all together true, but he was too far gone to give a flying fuck about logic. All he knew was *right there* was someone to blame for Caleb's light going out of the world, and he was about to vent his rage and despair and heartache, everything he'd kept bottled up inside him for the last three weeks.

Jake finally had a target, and he aimed to let loose with every ounce of bile and vitriol within him.

Liam straightened. "You know that's not true," he said, his voice firm. "It could just as easily have been me who died that day. Caleb happened to be in the path of that tire. There was nothin' I could've done to avoid it. It came right at us."

"But you're still here, an' Caleb's gone! Why should *you* be the one to live, instead of him?" Jake yelled, barely conscious of his daddy stepping toward Liam.

"I think you need to leave, boy." Daddy's voice was deep. "Cos it's plain you're not welcome here." Murmurs of agreement rippled through the crowd, and several of the men shifted closer as menace laced the atmosphere.

Liam opened his mouth, obviously to protest, but glanced around him, his face tightening as the whispers grew louder. Finally he heaved a sigh. "I'm sorry y'all feel this way. I only wanted to say goodbye to Caleb, same as you. But I guess I can understand why you might feel like this."

"We don't give a fuck if you understand," Jake retorted. "We just want you to go. Now." He was past caring about cussing in front of his mama. He just wanted Liam out of his sight.

Liam gave a single nod. "Then... I'll go." He turned and walked slowly through the crowd, who parted to give him space. Jake couldn't tear his gaze away from the retreating figure, and when he subsequently got into a waiting taxi that drove off, only then would Jake allow his muscles to relax. He sagged, stumbling into his daddy who supported him, his arm around Jake's back.

"It's okay, son. He's gone. You were right to say what you did." Daddy pressed a kiss to his hair. "An' he had no right to be here."

Gradually the chatter and murmurs died down, and Reverend Hubbert took control of the proceedings once again. Not that there was much more to be done. The last words were uttered, a prayer offered up, and at long last it was over and Caleb was in the ground. Jake stood with his parents as the mourners filed past them, offering their condolences. He barely heard a single word. All he could think about was Liam.

I shouldn't have made him leave. I should've kept him there, until I'd thrown every last bit of grief an' suff'rin' at him. I should've kept him there until he finally understood the pain an' anguish we've been through.

But it was too late. Jake had let Liam escape, and that would probably be the last opportunity he'd ever have.

Lucky for him. Because if I ever do see him again, it'll be Liam that'll regret it.

"Mama? You got a sec?" Jake closed the kitchen door behind him, dimming the voices that came from the living room. Several members of the church and a few neighbors were still in

By K.C. Wells

there, talking amongst themselves, drinking tea and eating the food that seemed to keep on coming.

She looked up from her task of making yet more sandwiches. "Do you need somethin'?" There were dark smudges under her eyes, but her expression was a little brighter than it had been that morning.

He snickered. "Yeah. I need to get outta here. I wish someone would remind all your ladies from the church that I'm nineteen, an' that pinchin' my cheek is *not* appropriate."

His humorous note struck a chord, and she smiled. "It's their way."

Most of the people who'd joined them at the house after the funeral were the same age as his parents, or older. His friends and Caleb's had stayed away, which Jake totally got. It wasn't his idea of a fun time either, but he didn't have a choice in the matter. He'd stood it as long as he could, before ultimately deciding to appeal to his mama's better nature.

"So… can I leave, please?"

Mama let out a sigh. "You want to go out now?"

"It's not like I can do anythin' here. I just need a bit of time to myself."

She narrowed her gaze. "Where were you thinkin' of going? An' for how long? Because if you crawl home late again like last night, we *will* have words, Jacob John Greenwood. An' don't even bother lyin' to me about that either, because your daddy heard you come in." Her face tightened. "He jus' cut you some slack because of… today."

Oh shit. "I'm sorry, Mama. I jus' lost track o' the time, that's all. An' I was only gonna wander down to the creek. Not for long, I swear." He needed some peace, and he sure wasn't going to get it at home.

She put down the butter knife and held out her arms. "Come here." Jake walked into them, and she enfolded him in a hug, her cheek pressed against his. "I know today wasn't easy for any of us. Sayin' goodbye never is. But I just wanted to tell ya that what you said during the service… well, it was… beautiful." She released him, her lips twitching. "Apart from you tellin' everyone Caleb went skinny-dippin'."

"Trust me, Mama, they already knew." LaFollette was a small town.

She gave him a mock glare. "Not all of them. But yeah, they sure do now." Mama kissed his cheek. "Go on, get outta here. But be back in time for supper."

Jake bit his lip. "That's if they leave us anythin' to eat."

That brought a laugh. "There's still mac an' cheese in the freezer. I reckon we've got enough to last us 'til Rapture." She picked up the butter knife and resumed her task. "Mind what I said now about gettin' back late."

He didn't wait around for her to change her mind. He grabbed his jacket from a hook by the back door, went out onto the porch, and drew in a lungful of crisp, fresh air.

Thank God. For the last few hours, he'd done nothing but inhale several different perfumes, some heavily floral, others just plain heavy. Add to that the heady scent of the flowers Mama had brought from the church, and Jake hardly dared draw a breath.

He walked down to the end of the yard, hunkered down to climb through the gap in the fence, then picked his way through the dense foliage that grew past knee height on both sides of the creek. He could remember being six or seven years old, the first time Caleb had taken him there.

Caleb, his big brother who had officially become a teenager. Caleb, who had led the way, hacking at the undergrowth with an imaginary sword, making Jake giggle, like they were on some great adventure in the middle of a jungle.

Lord, it feels like it was just yesterday.

Jake climbed over tree trunks that had fallen during the early Spring, and when he reached the creek, he paused. Before him flowed slow-moving waters, receding in parts to leave drifts of hardened mud where the creek had dried up. The creek was bathed in shade, the trees forming a canopy above it, and only now and then the sunlight poked through, glinting on the water's surface. Left would take him past the LaFollette Wastewater plant, eventually becoming the Ollis Creek trail that led to the reservoir. Right would take him to the Wishing Seat.

It was a no-brainer. Jake went right.

He recalled the first time Caleb had shown him the large boulder that squatted beside the creek. It was just an ordinary lump of rock, but that wasn't how Jake saw it, no sir. Caleb had pointed to a spot near the top where the stone had worn away to form a dent, just big enough to sit in. He'd told Jake in hushed tones that it was a magical spot.

Jake could still hear his voice.

"Mind, you can't tell Mama an' Daddy I showed you this, alright? This is a secret place."

"Why?" Jake had stared at the grey stone in disbelief. It was just a lump of rock.

Caleb lifted him up and placed him almost reverentially on the worn spot. "You're sittin' in the Wishin' Seat. All you have to do is close your eyes, make a wish, an' it'll come true. But you have to believe, truly believe, cos if you don't, the only thing you'll get is a numb ass from sittin' here too long." Jake gaped at him, and Caleb narrowed his gaze. "An' you are *not* gonna tell Mama or Daddy that you heard me say ass, you got that?"

Like Jake would've ratted out Caleb. He worshipped his brother's every step. Jake crossed his heart. "I swear, I won't tell."

Caleb had smiled. "Well okay then. I guess it's time for you to make your first wish."

Jake had closed his eyes, knowing with all the certainty of a seven-year-old boy *exactly* what he would wish for. "Do I tell ya my wish?"

"Lord, no. That's a surefire way of wastin' a wish. You don't tell anyone, Chuck. It's *your* wish."

Jake opened his eyes and glared at Caleb. "I told you, don't call me that."

Caleb snickered. "Aw, but you're my little woodchuck.

You're so cute, the way you burrow in the dirt under the back porch."

Jake didn't mind the nickname all that much. It made him feel special.

"Now, close your eyes an' make a wish."

Once more, Jake closed his eyes, determined to believe and send his wish out into the ether. *I want to grow up like my brother Caleb.*

And just like that, Jake was hurled back into the present, his hand resting on the familiar boulder. Tears welled in his eyes, and he clambered onto the rock, his vision blurred. He sat on the cold, hard stone and closed his eyes.

"I wish you were here, Caleb."

No sooner had he whispered his wish, than reality crashed over him, and he groaned aloud to hear that inner monotone voice, so bereft of all hope.

It don't matter how much you believe, you know that, right? Caleb's not comin' back.

Jake drew his legs up, lowered his head onto his arms, and wept unrestrainedly, letting his grief overwhelm him. When his tears eventually abated, leaving him wrung out and weak, he wiped his eyes on his shirt sleeve, then raised his head to gaze at the creek.

What came to mind in the stillness was not his brother, however, but Liam.

"I don't know where you are, Cal, an' I sure as hell don't know if you can hear me, but I tried to do right by you today. I swear, when I saw him there, saw the sheer nerve of the guy, I wanted to flatten him, to grind him to a pulp." He swallowed. "I jus' didn't try hard enough, I guess." His failure felt like a betrayal, and Jake's chest tightened. "I'm sorry. I let you down. I promise, if I ever get the chance again, he won't escape without a bruisin'."

It felt like a vow, and that was fine by Jake.

Liam had stolen his brother right when Jake needed him the most. The number of times during the last two or three years when he'd been on the verge of calling Caleb, but his nerve had failed him. Those few times when Caleb did visit, Jake had yearned to take him down to this secret place of theirs, with the intention of pouring his heart out…

He'd needed Caleb's advice so badly, and now it was too late.

And it was all Liam's fault. Never mind the idea that Jake might have overreacted a smidge back at the cemetery. With hindsight, it was clear he hadn't been thinking straight then. But now? Hell yes, he was seeing how it all was, with 20/20 vision.

The more he thought about Liam's sudden appearance, the more his grief was shoved aside, to be replaced with the familiar anger that had been prevalent since Caleb's death.

Jake could handle that. Rage was better than grief any day. And unlike before, now he had a focus for that rage.

Liam.

Truth & Betrayal

Chapter Five

June arrived, and with it came the rise in temperature. The lighter evenings didn't bring a lightening in Jake's spirit, however. He'd never felt so lost.

Everything had changed.

The church had almost become his mama's new home, she was there that often. Only now she was arranging the flowers, visiting those who were house-bound, and attending the twice-weekly prayer meetings. Jake had a feeling that what lay at the heart of the matter was not a newfound devotion to the Lord, but rather an interest that kept her out of the house.

Too many memories lurked there.

His daddy was just the same. He and Jake had gone back to work the Monday following the funeral, and that was fine and dandy as far as Jake was concerned; keeping himself occupied was the best remedy for what ailed him. But Daddy was working longer hours. He let Jake get off home at the usual hour, while he stayed on to 'just do a little more.'

That usually amounted to a couple of hours.

Mama had complained at first, but after a couple days of similar timekeeping, she'd given up. Jake guessed she knew what was going on though. What troubled him was the distance between them.

Why aren't you helpin' each other out? He'd supposed they'd lean more on one another, but if anything, they seemed to exist in two separate bubbles. What brought it home to him with all the force of a sledgehammer had been the night Mama had sent him

Truth & Betrayal

to Daddy's woodshed, to call him in for dinner. Jake had gotten as far as the aging door when he'd caught the unmistakable sound of weeping from inside.

No child should hear such sounds from a parent. Jake had retreated back to the house, giving Mama some vague excuse that Daddy was doing something. She'd gazed at him for a moment, until he was convinced she knew exactly what was going on, and finally she'd nodded. When Daddy came in half an hour later, nothing was said.

Jake wasn't sure how much more of this he could take. His family was disintegrating, and there was fuck all he could do to stop it. Jake did the only thing he could to lessen the ache in his heart. He switched onto autopilot and did his best not to think, not to feel, slogging through the days with his focus on... existing.

Tedium became a daily way of life, and that was just fine. Days turned into weeks, and before he knew it, July was almost poking its head around the corner.

What changed everything was his daddy's tape measure.

"Jake, we got a spare tape measure anywhere?" Daddy called out as he came through the front door. "I broke mine just now, an' I don't have time to go to the store before work in the mornin'."

From her armchair beside the fireplace, Mama glanced up at the clock and her lips thinned. She got up and went into the kitchen. She and Jake had already eaten when it became clear Daddy wasn't going to be home at a reasonable hour.

When Daddy entered the living room, Jake switched off the TV, not bothering to hide his irritation. "That's all you can say? Daddy, it's nine o'clock. You didn't even call Mama to say you'd be late."

Daddy had the good grace to flush. "Shoot." He sighed

heavily. "I s'ppose I'd better get in there." He inclined his head toward the door. "She pitch a hissy fit?"

Jake gazed at him incredulously. "That surprises ya?" It was an odd sensation. For a moment, their roles were reversed, and Jake felt the more adult of the two. "Maybe a bunch of Mama's favorite flowers might be a good idea? Y'know, to smooth things over?"

Daddy nodded. "Yeah, that sounds about right. I'll get her some tomorrow." His eyes gleamed. "Well, *you'll* be the one buyin' 'em. I'll be workin'." He held up a single finger. "Let this be a lesson to ya, son. Keep on the sweet side of women. It makes everythin' easier in the long run. You need to know such things, cos one day, Lord willin', you'll have yourself a wife."

Jake changed the subject. "An' yeah, there's another tape measure 'round here someplace. Gimme a minute an' I'll find it." He got up from the couch and went over to the dresser. The top middle drawer was the repository for all the junk Mama found lying around the house. It had become the dumping ground for anything that didn't have a place of its own, but might come in handy one day.

He pulled open the drawer and quickly located the tape measure. As he was about to close it, Jake caught sight of something, and his stomach clenched.

It was Caleb's key chain.

He stood still, unable to tear his gaze from it. *Shit. How can we have just… forgotten?*

He knew how, of course. Dealing with such practical matters involved thinking about Caleb, and the pain was still too close to the surface. But it was clearly time for *someone* to think about those practicalities.

Somewhere in Atlanta, Caleb had rented an apartment, one that none of them had ever laid eyes on. An apartment that contained his clothes, his possessions. And that realization brought yet more questions bubbling to the surface. *Is the rent overdue?* Because that had implications. Had his landlord been informed of his death? His bank? Why had no one been in touch?

Jake figured it was time for them to deal with reality. He picked up the key chain and closed the drawer.

When he walked into the kitchen, Daddy was sitting at the table, demolishing the chicken and collard greens Mama had put aside for his dinner. Mama sat with him, sipping from a glass of tea. Jake pulled out a chair and joined them.

"There's somethin' we need to talk about." Before either of them could respond, he carefully placed the key chain on the table in front of him.

Mama's breathing hitched. "I see."

Daddy stared at the keys with a resigned expression. "Yeah, you're right. I've been fixin' to do somethin' about Caleb's place, only somethin' else always came up." He put down his knife and fork, and took a long drink of tea. "No point lollygaggin' around. You'll have to take your truck an' go get his stuff."

"Me?"

Daddy arched his eyebrows. "Well, I can't go, now, can I? I've got work to do. Besides, you can be there an' back in a day. It's only four hours or so to Atlanta. I can do without ya for a day." He leaned back and tore off the small page from the wall calendar behind him, then stretched higher for the pen that sat in a wall-mounted holder.

"You'll need to find out his bank details. There'll be statements somewhere. I know he used a bank in Atlanta. We can call the comp'ny where he worked to see about his salary. If you need boxes, find the nearest grocery store or liquor store. They'll have boxes stacked up 'round the back." Daddy scribbled on the paper, making notes, his brow furrowed. "I let this go on for far too long. Should've dealt with this weeks ago, but you know how it is."

Jake knew alright. Dealing with it meant thinking about Caleb, and he could easily understand why none of them had been keen to go down *that* road.

Mama touched his arm. "Maybe this is too big a job for one day. If Jacob needs to, he can find a hotel or someplace for the night. I don't want him drivin' if he's tired." Her gaze met Jake's.

"You hear me, Jacob?" The skin around her mouth tightened.

It didn't take a genius to know what was passing through her mind.

"Yes, ma'am. I'll be careful."

"You be sure you do." She glanced toward the kitchen clock. "In that case, maybe you'd better get along to bed. You'll need to be up awful early in the mornin', if you're gonna get a good start. I'll pack you some sandwiches an' a flask of sweet tea."

Jake heaved an internal sigh of relief. This was the mama he'd missed. "Thank you, Mama." He got up from the table and walked around it to kiss her cheek. "G'night."

She reached up and cupped his face. "Now, no chattin' with your friends all night on your phone. I'll be in early to wake you."

Jake was in no mood to chat with anyone.

He left the kitchen after saying goodnight to his daddy, then headed to his room, pausing at the door to Caleb's bedroom. He hadn't been in there since Caleb's passing. Somehow it felt... wrong. Jake was sure he wouldn't always feel like that, but for the time being, the door would remain closed, keeping his memories alive within.

Jake gave himself a rough mental shake. *Get a grip*. At least the following day would bring with it the opportunity for a little closure, maybe even the chance to mend. Because there was no denying it.

Since Caleb had gone, Jake felt broken.

His teeth brushed, he climbed into bed and lay there in the darkness, listening to the crickets. Jake rolled onto his side and stared at the wall that separated his room from Caleb's.

What would I give to hear Caleb's voice one more time? His muffled snorts cos he was talkin' with his friends when he should've been asleep? Then him goin' real quiet because that creaky floorboard was better than an alarm. Or how about him scratchin' on the wall when I was just a kid, tryin' to convince me it was mice?

So many memories.

Jake hugged his pillow, closed his eyes, and tried to sleep.

Jake glanced at his phone sitting in the console, recharging. Thank God, he was nearly there. The longest trip he usually made was as far as Knoxville, and that was only forty-five minutes away from LaFollette. He chuckled to himself.

"*Only* four hours, Daddy?" He guessed that amounted to peanuts in his daddy's book. Of course, Mama had awoken him at a quarter after five, just before the sunrise, and he'd still been yawning when he'd climbed behind the wheel of his truck at six. Thankfully, most of the trip had been on one highway, the I-75 S that had virtually landed him on Atlanta's doorstep. He'd stopped once in need of a restroom, but otherwise it had been a straight run with the AC set on *freeze your nuts off* to combat the temperature. When he spied Publix, he'd made the decision to stop and pick up any boxes he could find, throwing them into the back of the truck.

Piedmont Ave NE meant he was only five minutes away, and there was the whole day ahead of him. He peered through the windshield, sighing with relief when he saw the sign for Myrtle St. NE.

Made it.

Jake pulled over into a space and switched off the engine. The street was a quiet spot, with trees lining both sides. He unhooked his phone from the cable, got out of the truck and locked it. Black iron railings surrounded the two-story property, which comprised eight apartments, each with a dark green door. Caleb's was #8, and outside on the walkway sat two green canvas chairs, looking out over the street. Below was a small front yard, with a larger area to the side, filled with plants and shrubs.

Jake badly wished he'd been able to see this place before now.

He climbed the wrought iron staircase and went along the

walkway to the door of #8. His hand shaking a little, Jake removed the key chain from the pocket of his jeans. He selected the appropriate key and slid it into the lock. It stuck a little, so he tried jiggling it around until it decided it was going to open. Jake pushed open the door and stepped into a surprisingly cool interior.

No sooner was he indoors than he realized he wasn't alone. Noise was coming from somewhere.

"Hello?" he said cautiously. "Who's there?"

A door swung open, and—

Jake froze. "What the fuck're *you* doin' here?"

Liam stared at him, a phone in his hand. After a moment he sighed. "I guess I can cancel the call to 911. Although I should've figured someone robbin' the place wouldn't have a key."

"Of course I have a key. Caleb's key. An' you still haven't told me what you're doin' here." Jake's heartbeat raced.

Liam regarded him mildly. "I live here. Caleb and I were roommates." His eyes widened. "Oh my God. You didn't know."

"*'Course* I didn't know. *No one* knew back home because Caleb never once mentioned havin' a roommate. Now why exactly was that?" Jake was still reeling. Of all people…

Liam's face tightened. "Yeah, that'd be right," he muttered. He put down the phone on a nearby table.

"How long have you lived here?" It had to be a recent thing, because Jake couldn't believe Caleb would have kept this to himself.

Liam studied him for a moment before gesturing into the apartment. "How about I pour us some tea, an' then we can sit down an' talk?"

Jake set his jaw. "Fine, but you'll be the one doin' most of the talkin'."

Because Jake sure had a lot of questions.

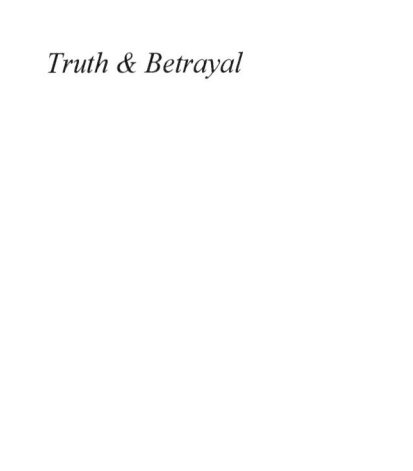

Chapter Six

Jake followed Liam into a small living room, where one wall was taken up by a large couch, with two armchairs facing it across a coffee table. He had to admit, the place had a sparse feel to it. Nothing like a home. A tall, slim bookcase stood empty, and apart from the TV, there was little else in the way of furniture.

It had the feel of an apartment that had just been let, with all the unpacking still to do.

Liam gestured to the couch. "Please, sit down. I'll go pour the tea. Sweet or unsweet?"

"Sweet, please." He waited until Liam had left the room, then glanced around him, taking in his surroundings. It didn't feel like a big apartment, but he supposed there was room for two. His gaze fell on the coffee table, and he caught his breath. A laptop sat there, the dark grey of its lid almost obliterated by numerous stickers of all kinds.

Oh my God. He was still using that? Jake had imagined it had died long ago.

Jake jumped when Liam placed a tall glass in front of him. "Christ."

"Sorry. I should've made more noise. You looked like you were miles away." He sat on the chair facing Jake, his legs crossed, his right arm resting on his thigh, his left on the arm of the chair, holding his glass.

An awkward silence fell, and that was fine with Jake. He was still reeling from walking in and finding Liam there. Jake took a sip of tea, surreptitiously taking in the guy facing him. Liam's eyes were a rich, dark brown verging on black, and his skin was dark brown, with a cool undertone to it. There was the faintest hint of a mustache above that full upper lip, matched by the scruff on his chin. His hair was cut close to his scalp, tapering away to almost nothing at the sides, with the look of soft, coarse wool. He wore a white T-shirt that clung to his slim torso, cut low at the neck, revealing wide shoulders and upper arms that had a bit of definition. The purple cast covered his right forearm from the elbow to past the wrist. The fingers wrapped around his glass were long and slim.

"So, have you been to Atlanta before?"

Jake blinked, then flushed, hoping to God Liam hadn't been aware of Jake checking him out. Then his words registered. Jake gave him an incredulous stare. "Really? That's how you wanna start? Fine. No, this is my first time here. Yes, from what I saw on the way here, it's impressive. Yes, this is the biggest place I've ever seen. There. We all done with the small talk now? Can we get onto the important stuff?"

Liam took a sip of tea, then set down his glass, his face impassive. "D'ya think you could lose the attitude? Because I think I was remarkably polite when you came in here, considerin' the way you spoke to me. You did just march into my home, remember?"

Jake stiffened at the slight rebuke, but he knew Liam was in the right. "Sorry."

Liam's expression softened. "Okay. I'd assumed you knew Caleb had a roommate. There was no reason for him to hide the fact."

"Just how long did you an' Caleb share an apartment?" Jake couldn't get his head around that either. Then he reasoned that Caleb never talked about where he lived. They knew only the bare facts about his job, that he worked for a large insurance company.

"Since we graduated. We met in college. When we realized we were both lookin' for jobs here, it made sense to share."

Four years? Jake frowned. *This is nuts.* "You're not from 'round here?"

Liam shook his head. "My family lives in Wilmington, North Carolina." He leaned forward, his elbows on his knees, his left hand supporting his right, encased in its cast. "Look, Jake... Is it okay if I call ya Jake? That was how Caleb... always referred to ya. Well, most of the time."

Jake stared. "An' what did he call me the rest of the time?"

Liam's lips twitched. "Chuck. He said it was short for—"

"Yeah, I know what it's short for." The familiar term of endearment made his chest tighten, but he was determined not to let it derail him. "You sounded like you had somethin' to say."

"Yeah... About what you said to me at the funeral."

Jake tensed. "What about it?"

Liam sat so still. "Do you really blame me for what happened?"

Fuck. Jake's scalp prickled, and his stomach quivered. "Look, I—"

Liam sprang to his feet and rubbed his hand over his head. "Okay. I can understand ya feelin' the need to have a target right now, but trust me, you're aimin' at the *wrong guy*. There was *nothin'* I could've done that would've changed the outcome. I wasn't drivin' erratically, I was payin' attention... An' let's be totally logical for a minute. If the police thought I was responsible in *any way whatsoever*, they'd have charged me, right? If you're gonna blame anyone, blame the guy who loaded up the tractor trailer, because he must've done *somethin'* to make that load unsafe." He shivered. "That tire just came straight for us, an' we couldn't move out of its path." Liam walked over to the window and leaned against it, his forehead pressed against the glass.

The pain in Liam's voice cut through Jake's low-boiling anger. Jake hated to admit it, but his words made sense, especially the reference to the police. "Okay. Okay. You're right." Deep down, hadn't he always known that? But it had been easier to ignore logic and focus on blame.

Only, when he tried to see past his own rage, Jake knew he

hadn't been fair toward Liam. Which only served to fill him with shame.

He had to do the right thing.

"I'm sorry. I shouldn't have said all those things." Jake rubbed his nose. "Caleb used to say I fired first an' asked questions later."

Liam came over to the armchair and sat down. "I can understand why you said what you did. If it had been my brother? Hell, I'd have done exactly the same." He held out his left hand. "Wanna start again?"

Considering the vitriol Jake had flung at him, it was a generous gesture. He took Liam's outstretched hand and shook it awkwardly. "Hey. Pleased ta meetcha. I'm Jake, an' I'm an asshole. Some of the time."

Liam smiled. "You're allowed. You're nineteen. An' I've had my share of similar moments." He cleared his throat, his expression more serious. "One of them was showin' up to the funeral without lettin' you know I was comin'. But then, you didn't have a clue who I was in the first place, so that would only have caused more confusion."

"An' that's the one thing 'bout all this that don't hunt." Jake frowned. "If you an' Caleb knew each other since college, why did he never mention you? I mean, not once."

Liam's mouth tightened. "No clue. So let me ask *you* somethin'. When he came home on visits, did he ever mention *anyone* from Atlanta? Did he talk about any part of his life here?"

Jake's gut roiled. "He didn't talk much, to tell the truth. An' when he did, it was never to share personal stuff." There was a familiar ache in his chest, and a heaviness that seeped into his limbs. "I guess the answer's no. It was like his whole life here was one big secret." His eyelids grew hot. Since when had Caleb kept secrets from him? Sure, Jake had secrets, but…

Jake had yearned to share the one thing that was eating him up inside, but he'd never gotten the chance. He certainly wasn't about to spill his guts to any of his friends. There had only been

Caleb whom he'd have trusted to react the way Jake needed.

"I s'ppose you came for Caleb's things?"

Jake welcomed the change of subject. "Yeah. I got boxes in the truck." He had no idea how much stuff Caleb had in the apartment, but he aimed to pack it all up as fast as possible, and be on his way home long before nightfall.

Liam got to his feet. "You won't need 'em." When Jake gave him a quizzical stare, he beckoned with his left hand. "Come on, I'll show ya."

Jake followed him through the apartment, noting the tiny kitchen. There wasn't much in the way of countertops, and what there was already contained the microwave oven and the coffee machine. A stove stood in the corner, its stainless-steel surfaces gleaming.

Liam followed his gaze. "Neither of us were any great shakes when it came to cookin'. Apart from breakfast, we ate out most of the time."

Jake had to snicker. "That don't surprise me none. Mama wouldn't let Caleb anywhere near her pots an' pans, after he burnt one so badly, she had to throw it in the trash." Beyond the kitchen, there were only three doors in sight.

Liam pointed to the nearest, which stood open. "That's the bathroom, such as it is. It's tiny." The door next to it was shut. "My room." He led Jake to the remaining door and pushed it open. "This was Caleb's room."

Jake blinked. "You've already packed up his things." A queen-sized bed stood beneath the window, stripped of bedding. On it sat several boxes with varied labels. The walls were bare, as was the table, and beneath it were more boxes.

"Yeah. I knew someone would turn up eventually to collect 'em, but to be honest, when it got to mid-June an' I hadn't heard a peep out of anyone, I decided to pack up everythin' an' have it all shipped to Tennessee." Liam gazed around the room with a distant stare. "That was gonna be on my To Do list for the weekend."

He looked so lost for a second that Jake's heart went out to him. Jake had lost his brother, and Liam had lost a friend. Then Liam turned to him. "Was there anythin' else you needed?"

Jake remembered his daddy's list. He pulled it from his pocket and peered at it. "Bank statements. Rent information. Any details about his job."

Liam pointed to a box. "There's a folder in there that has all his statements. I'm assumin' his final salary an' any money owed him has been paid. Don't worry 'bout the rent. That's taken care of. So basically, all his ties to Atlanta are cut." He let out a sigh of resignation. "How 'bout I help ya carry all this stuff to your truck?"

"I'd appreciate that." Jake smiled. "After I finish my tea."

Liam chuckled. "Yeah, sorry. I wasn't tryin' to run you outta here, honest. I jus' figured you had a long trip home ahead of ya." He left the bedroom, Jake following, and they went back to the living room. As they passed through the hallway, Liam picked up his phone. "Just a thought," he said as they sat down. "Why don't we swap numbers? That way, if there's somethin' particular you can't lay your hands on, or if I find somethin' I missed, we can get in touch."

"That makes sense." Jake handed over his phone, and took Liam's in return. He punched in the number and saved it to Contacts. That done, he leaned back, his glass in hand. There was an uncomfortable feeling in his belly. "About the funeral…"

Liam waved a wand. "It's okay. We're past that now."

"No, we're not." Jake put down his glass. "I wanna apologize for the way some people reacted to ya. They were outta line. In case you didn't notice, LaFollette ain't exactly…" He searched for the politest turn of phrase.

"Yeah, I felt like a sheep that had stumbled into a wolf convention." Liam shrugged. "That wasn't any surprise, b'lieve me. Caleb did talk about his home town. Mine's not that different, to be fair. Maybe a higher proportion of African-Americans, but less than twenty percent." His eyes gleamed. "That said, there *was* a moment back there at the funeral when I expected someone to start handin' out pitchforks. I could almost hear 'em. 'You ain't from 'round here, are ya—?' Insert racial slur of choice."

Jake stilled. "You noticed that?" He shook his head. "I don't get it. These folks are meant to be Christians, an' that… display was anythin' but."

Liam tilted his head to one side. "I take it you don't feel the same way?"

Lord, now *there* was a question. Jake picked up his glass and drained half of it. "Let me put it this way. In my class in high school, everyone was white. In fact, the school had around a thousand students, an' only a handful were anythin' other than Caucasian. Two kids were African-American, an' me, well, I felt sorry for 'em."

"Why?"

Jake sighed. "They'd been recruited to come play basketball for the Cougars. That's the school team. Now, I'm not sayin' the other kids treated 'em with hostility, no sir. They just… weren't included."

"An' you felt that was wrong," Liam said softly.

"Yeah." Totally wrong. "Seems to me the younger generation is gettin' there, but as for people in LaFollette? It don't matter what's happenin' in the rest of the country—they haven't caught up yet."

"Give it time. There's hope."

Jake had kinda been all out of hope lately. "I'm not so sure."

"You said it yourself. The younger generation is gettin' there. Well, they're the future. *You* are the future."

Jake had to smile. "So're you. I'm assumin' you're the same age as Caleb, so that makes you what, twenty-six, twenty-seven? Seems to me you got time to make some changes too." His gaze alighted on the laptop, and he leaned forward to run a hand over its sticker-covered surface. "I didn't think I'd see this again. My parents gave it to Caleb when he was in twelfth grade. I felt sure it would've been stepped on, broken, whatever, by now."

"I told him so many times that he needed to upgrade, but

nope. Caleb insisted on keepin' it, even though it works slower than molasses. The number of times he's deleted a load of files or programs, just to keep it tickin' over."

Jake picked it up and put it on his knee. "I was ten or eleven when he got this. He used to get madder'n a wet hen every time he found me tryin' to work out his password. An' I never did." He stroked it almost fondly. "I guess I might have more luck now."

"You're takin' it with you?"

An edge to Liam's voice intrigued Jake, and he jerked his head up to look at Liam. "Sure. I mean, it's Caleb's, right? I was hopin' to use it myself, now that I know it still works." He gave Liam a speculative glance. "Did *you* want it, or somethin'?" Jake couldn't think why.

Liam smiled. "No, of course not. I think it's probably on its last legs anyhow."

Even if it died the moment he got it home, there was no way Jake could ever get rid of it. This was part of Caleb, part of Jake's childhood. "I'll take real good care of it." He placed it almost reverentially on the couch next to him. "Okay, how about you an' me get to work on these boxes? That way I might get home in daylight."

"Sure." Liam got to his feet. "It won't take us all that long." He glanced down at his arm. "Then again… Thank God the cast comes off next week."

"Don't you go hurtin' yourself," Jake hurled at him.

"Look, you can't carry all those boxes on your—"

"I can manage on my own." Jake stuck out his chin.

Liam bit his lip. "Just for a second there, it was like I was listenin' to Caleb. He could be a stubborn asshole too."

Jake could live with that.

"That's everythin'," Liam said as Jake came through the

front door. "I've refilled your flask with sweet tea, an' there's chips an' snacks too."

Jake's stomach clenched. "You didn't have to do that."

"Sure I did." Liam's eyes were warm. "You're Caleb's little brother."

Jake hit him on his good arm. "Hey. Less of the little." What a difference a few hours had made. He recalled with shame the rage and hostility he'd shown Liam on first arriving. "I'm sorry 'bout the way I spoke to you earlier. I—"

"You really need to stop apologizin'," Liam said with a scowl. "Seriously. I thought we were good."

"We are," Jake protested. Liam had turned out to be an alright guy.

"Then this is where we say goodbye. I'm only sorry we got to meet like this." Liam held out his left hand, and Jake shook it. "Take care of yourself, an' a safe trip back to Tennessee. You could do me one favor though."

"Sure, what?"

"You've got my number. Text me when you get there? Jus' so I know you got home okay."

Liam's words were an uncanny reflection of his mama's, laced with the same concern—and the same unspoken fear.

Jake swallowed. "I promise." He picked up the bag containing the flask and snacks, and turned to leave. As his feet touched the threshold, he froze. "Wait. Caleb's laptop."

"I'll get it." Liam went back into the living room, returning with the precious item. "Take care of that too. I still say it'll be a miracle if it keeps on workin', so don't get your hopes up on keepin' it for too long. An' it can be a little… temperamental. One option to consider might be takin' it someplace an' gettin' its memory wiped. Maybe settin' it back to its factory state might extend its life a bit longer."

Jake tucked it under one arm. "That's a way to go, I suppose." Privately he wasn't that keen on the idea. Who knew what information the laptop's memory contained? He gave Liam a single nod and walked out onto the covered walkway. When he reached the street, he looked back. Liam stood by the railings, watching him. Jake raised his hand and Liam returned the gesture.

Jake climbed into the truck and placed the laptop carefully on the passenger seat, covering it with his jacket.

Time to go home.

Chapter Seven

By the time Jake switched off the engine, Mama was already at the door. She walked over to greet him, smiling.

"I didn't expect to see you this early." She gave him a tight hug. "So glad you're home. Was everythin' alright?" Before Jake could reply, she released him and peered into the back of the truck. "Oh my. I guess this can all go in Caleb's room for the time bein'."

Jake stretched. He'd only stopped the once to take a leak, anxious to get home. "I'll do that after supper."

"You will not." Mama gave him a hard stare. "Your daddy'll take care of the boxes. You're gonna get inside an' eat. There's fried chicken in the oven, an' I made a fresh batch of cornbread this mornin'."

Jake's mouth watered. "Aw, Mama. Was that for me?"

Mama kissed his cheek. "Any boy who drives for more than eight hours in one day deserves a treat when he gets home." She ruffled his short hair. "I was worried, y'know. 'Bout you drivin' all that way."

Jake ducked out of the reach of her hand. "Come on. Caleb used to do it, didn't he? An' it wasn't so bad. I had the radio playin' the whole time." Except he *was* tired. He reached through the window of the passenger side to pick up his jacket and the laptop. No way was he leaving *that* in the truck.

By the time he'd eaten a plateful of fried chicken, mashed potatoes, greens and several pieces of cornbread, Jake felt more human, even if he was as full as a tick. Daddy saw to the unloading, joining him and Mama in the kitchen when he was done.

"So, what was his place like?" Mama asked as she poured out three glasses of sweet tea.

"It looked like a nice neighborhood. Quiet, with lots of trees. Kinda peaceful. An' the apartment was okay." Jake demolished his last mouthful of cornbread before speaking. "Caleb had a roommate."

His parents froze, their mouths open.

"He sure kept that quiet," Daddy muttered. "Who was he sharin' with?"

"A guy called Liam. Seemed an okay guy." Jake met his daddy's gaze. "You met him at the funeral."

Daddy's eyes widened. "That… that fella?" He flushed. "I see."

"I don't understand. How come he never mentioned this… Liam?" Mama bit her lip. "Did he move in recently? Is that why?"

Jake drew in a deep breath. "Mama, Liam was there from the beginnin'. They were in college together. That's how they met."

There was no disguising the hurt in her eyes. "An' he didn't tell us. You think you know a person, an' then…"

Jake knew where she was coming from. "I know. I didn't get it either. But then I thought about it some more. Caleb didn't share a whole lot about his life in Atlanta, did he? With any of us." He'd thought about this during the ride home. "Maybe he jus' wanted to keep the two parts of his life separate. Not sure why, mind you. An' it's not like we'll ever know the reason."

"Well, that part's over n' done with now," Daddy declared. "We're jus' gonna have to git on with our lives. It's not like Caleb's ever gonna be far from our thoughts." His face tightened. "'Scuse me. I gotta go check on somethin' in the woodshed." He got up from the table and left them, moving swiftly.

Jake stared after him, his heart heavy. Like they could ever forget Caleb. He figured it would be a long time before the pain of Caleb's passing eased in any of them.

Mama's hand covered his. "Are you alright?"

Jake pasted on a smile. "I'm fine, Mama. Jus' dog-tired. Think I might go to bed." A wave of fatigue rolled over him, seeping into his bones. He got up and went to pick up his plate, but Mama stopped him.

"I'll take care o' that. You jus' go n' sleep. You'll feel better in the morning. Your daddy'll be expectin' you to work tomorrow."

Which was probably the best thing he could do right then.

Jake kissed her cheek and went to his room. Once he was cleaned up and under the sheets, he glanced over to the nightstand where he'd left the laptop. He was too exhausted, physically and mentally, to contemplate doing anything with it.

That could wait until he was more alert. He'd need to be, if he was going to crack the password. Because if the past was anything to go on, Caleb wouldn't have made it an obvious one. The thought made him smile, and he hugged his pillow as he dropped instantly into a deep sleep.

"Goddamn it, Caleb, what is so all-fired important in that fuckin' laptop?"

Jake was at the point of tearing his hair out. Two weeks since he'd brought the fucking hunk of metal home, and he was still no closer to working out the password. He'd tried the obvious ones, birthdays, but no luck there. Memorable dates, like Caleb passing his driving test, or graduating, were equally unsuccessful. That left favorite bands, TV shows, the names of girls he'd dated in high school… Nothing.

It was becoming an obsession.

Jake knew exactly what was driving him. *What was Caleb doin' all the time he was away from home? Is there some clue to why he changed? Why he stayed away?* Damn it, Jake wanted to *know*. And all the time these questions remained unanswered, Jake felt like he couldn't let it rest. It wasn't until Saturday evening that he had a flash of inspiration.

What if Liam knows the password?

No sooner had the thought occurred to him, than Jake dismissed it. If Liam had known, he would have shared it.

Another thought struck him, so fast it was like someone was playing ping-pong inside his head. *Oh yeah? Think about that. He didn't seem real keen for you to get it workin, now did he? Even suggested wipin' the memory.* It hadn't seemed a big deal at the time, but looking back...

Jake reached for his phone, scrolled through his contacts, and sent a message.

Hey. U got a sec?

Liam's reply was swift. *Sure. U OK?*

Jake's thumbs flew over the screen. *Do u have the password to Caleb's laptop?* He waited for Liam's response. Nothing. Jake started to type another text, but was interrupted when the phone rang. It was Liam.

"Hey. Can I ask you somethin'?" Liam sounded almost subdued.

"Sure."

"Why is it so important to you to get into the laptop?"

Not the response Jake had expected, and for a moment he was flummoxed as to how to reply. "Isn't it obvious?"

"Not really. It was Caleb's. Whatever he has on there was important to *him,* an' no one else. It's like... tryin' to read someone's journal."

Jake's chest constricted. "Okay, fair enough, but..." He struggled to phrase what lay on his heart. "It feels like there's this... hole, an' I have to fill it. Ever since Caleb went off to college, it's been like..." Fuck, this was difficult. Jake took a deep breath. "I want to see what I've missed out on. All these years since he left, an' I have *no clue* what he was doin' all that time, how he was findin' his studies, his job..." Jake swallowed, his throat tight.

"Look, Liam, I don't give a rat's ass what's on there. Right now, not knowin' is… well, it's keepin' me from findin' any real closure. Does that make any sense at all?"

For a moment, there was only silence, then Jake caught Liam's sigh. "Got a pen? You'll need to write this down."

Jake's gaze went to his desk under the window, where a jar sat, full of pens and pencils. He dove across the room and grabbed a pencil, along with a notepad, before returning to sit on his bed, his back against the pillows. "Okay, got it."

"It's a series of letters. Ready? I-A-B-W-W-T-2011."

Jake scribbled them down, then stared at them, frowning. "What does it mean?"

"Caleb was forever changin' his passwords. Not because he was particularly security-conscious, mind you. He just had a terrible memory, that's all. In the end, he used to take a line from a favorite song, an' use the first letter of each word, along with a memorable date."

"So what's the line?" Jake reread the password, trying to fathom it out.

Another short pause. "You don't need to know that. You've got the password. So go ahead an' fill in your hole." Before Jake could respond, the line went dead.

What's eatin' him? Liam's abrupt manner seemed nothing like the pleasant man he'd met in Atlanta, and the sharp contrast sent a shiver down Jake's spine. Then he pushed his unease aside. *Finally*, a password.

"Jacob? Supper time."

Jake suppressed his groan. *Talk about timin'…*

The laptop would have to wait.

Jake waited until the house was quiet, and there would be no likelihood of either of his parents knocking on his door, before reaching for the laptop, the notepad lying on its lid. He opened it up, surprised to find his heartbeat racing.

What is it you think you're gonna find in there?

Just like on his previous attempts, the login screen took an age to load, and Jake realized Liam hadn't been joking when he'd said it was slow. When the login box eventually made an appearance, Jake carefully typed in the password, his breathing quickening—and stopped at the last digit.

For some reason, he was scared. Of what, he had no idea.

Jake knew his fear was illogical. He told himself it was the late hour that prevented him from continuing, that he should be starting this when he had sufficient time, and no likelihood of interruptions.

He knew they were just excuses, but they were enough to make him hit the power button.

Tomorrow. When Mama and Daddy go to church. I'll open it then.

Jake placed the laptop on the nightstand, along with the notepad, and clicked off the light next to his bed. He lay back against the pillows and closed his eyes, aware of the scent of night blooming jasmine, carried in from the yard on the warm night breeze.

Two things made falling asleep difficult, however—the puzzle of the password, and Liam's odd behavior. Song lyrics flitted through his brain, until he grabbed the pillow and folded it over his head, as though that would somehow stop the constant flow.

It did—eventually.

Jake watched through the living room window as Daddy headed up the driveway, Mama beside him in her Sunday best hat. When the truck was no longer in sight, he went into his room, closed the door, and sat on the bed. He opened up the laptop and waited for it to load the login screen. His heartbeat pounding, he typed in the password.

The desktop appeared eventually, and Jake scanned the icons. The screen was covered with them, hardly any of the wallpaper showing through. Jake chuckled, his nerves dissipating. *No wonder the damn thing is slow.* There were the usual programs, and a load of folders, one of which caught his eye immediately. *Pictures.*

There ya go. He clicked on the folder, and was greeted by the sight of at least twenty more folders. Some had labels, while others were merely numbered. When Jake saw *Family*, he opened it quickly, smiling when he saw photos of himself and Caleb, taken during the holidays when Jake was only a baby. *Aw.* It warmed him that Caleb had kept such images.

Then he saw one that puzzled him, and he clicked on it. Everyone in it was black. The photo showed a group of people sitting around a dining table, all smiling for the camera. Jake wondered who in the hell they were, until he took a closer look at one of the diners.

It was Liam.

What in the Sam Hill is he *doin' in here?*

There were more such photos, and then Jake saw yet another gathering, only this time, Caleb was present too. And in another. And another.

Wait a sec. Maybe he visited Liam's family. Not so weird, right? I mean, how long were they friends? It didn't answer his question as to what the photos were doing in that particular folder. It wasn't a mistake, a couple of photos copied there accidentally. There were too many of them for that.

Jake came out of it and peered at the rest. *Trips, College, Projects...* and a folder labeled *US*. That only added to Jake's confusion. As far as he knew, Caleb had had little opportunity to visit places outside of Tennessee and Atlanta. Then he reasoned that his knowledge was sadly lacking; he had no clue where Caleb might have visited in the States during the eight years since he'd left home.

More secrets. The thought made his heart ache. He opened the folder to discover more—and froze.

What the fuck?

The hairs on the back of Jake's neck stood on end as realization hit him right between the eyes.

It's not US as in the U.S.—it's US as in capital us.

He was looking at countless photos of Caleb—and Liam.

At the zoo. At the Aquarium. At the beach. Both of them happy. So many photos.

Wow. They really were close, weren't they?

When he saw a folder labeled with a smiley, Jake knew he had to look. His hand trembled as he clicked on it, and saw—

Liam in bed, lying on his side, looking toward the camera with sleepy eyes, and smiling.

Liam on his back in bed, his chest bare, laughing, staring up at the camera above his head.

And…

Jake stared in disbelief at the photo of his brother and Liam, in bed together, naked from the waist up, Caleb's head resting on Liam's chest, his arm stretched up as he took a selfie, the contrast of Caleb's light brown hair against Liam's rich brown skin tone…

Caleb—and Liam. Looking as comfortable as could be, looking so goddamn happy.

And there were more of them. Not just selfies, but shots of them obviously taken on a timer. Holding each other. Gazing at each other.

There was no other way to interpret those photos, barring the obvious one. The intimacy between the two men couldn't be ignored.

Caleb, you son of a bitch. Why didn't you fucking tell *me?*

Chapter Eight

I'm not readin' this all wrong, am I? I mean, look at 'em!
Talk about fucking irony.

Jake exited the folder, scanning the desk top. He wasn't sure why he needed more proof of what his own eyes were telling him, but he knew he wasn't gonna settle for just the photos. Then he saw it.

Journal.

Hallefuckinlujah.

Jake didn't give a shit that this was Caleb's, it was private, whatever. He had to know. He clicked on the folder, and one Word document appeared. Jake took a moment to breathe before opening it. One glance at the date told him Caleb had started it in twelfth grade, about five months after he'd received the laptop.

The journal didn't seem all that long. He scrolled through it, noting that the entries were sporadic and not that long. It didn't surprise him none. Caleb had never been one for writing much. He scrolled back to the beginning, and started to read.

May 10, 2008

Never thought I'd want to keep a journal. It's what girls do, right? Some little thing with a lock they keep under their pillow and hide from their pain in the ass brother, or worse, their folks.

I guess I'm doing just that, right? Only, my lock is a password, and the only person I'm keeping out of here is Chuck. Because Mama and Daddy and technology? Yeah right. It took me years to convince him to put together a web page for his business.

And why start a journal now?

Because I want to remember how I'm feeling <u>right now</u>.

In church, the preacher read once about Paul going someplace, and falling down, and this big-assed light shining down on him. And that's when he knew he had to stop running down Christ's followers, and became one himself.

Now, there was no white light. And it wasn't one moment, more a series of them, starting off as nothing more than a feeling. Gotta say, first time I felt this way?

I ran from it. Nope. Not me. No fucking way.

Only, it wouldn't go away. It kept coming back, and every time it was stronger.

Fuck it scared me. I did not want to be that person. I hid this feeling, because I had to. Can't let anyone see. But I know now it's not going away. This is who I am.

I'm not gonna tell anyone. Hell no. Not here anyway. Things will be different later, when I go to school in Atlanta. When no one who knows me will see me.

Christ, I want to type the words, but that feels like something... final.

Gotta do it, right?

Here goes.

I don't like girls. I like boys.

Just reading that last line is huge. First time I let it out. But it feels good. Right. Like I can breathe again.

Hear that, world? Did you miss it?

Caleb Greenwood is gay. And NO ONE in this town is ever gonna know that. That goes double for Chuck. Thank fuck he's too young to know what that means.

Jake stared at the screen, his heartbeat racing. *Christ...* Coldness hit him right at his core, spreading icy tendrils throughout his body.

It could have been him writing. Word for fucking word.

Memories bombarded him. The way he'd felt that day three

years ago, that big-ass momentous day, when he'd glanced across the crowded study hall and caught Dylan Torrance staring at him. The thought that had flitted so fast through Jake's head he'd almost missed it.

Lord, I wanna kiss that mouth.

His skin had tingled all over, and he'd felt out of breath. He'd lowered his gaze, his face burning up, praying his reaction wasn't noticed. He hadn't once dared to raise his head to find out. He didn't want to know.

In the weeks and months that followed, Jake had truly struggled. That one line of Caleb's was a solid fit for his own reaction. *I ran from it.* He'd ached to call Caleb, to talk about it, but one thing held him back—the silence he'd feared would fall on the other end. There was no one else he could trust not to react with disgust and loathing. So he ignored it. Pushed it aside, hoping against hope that it had been a moment of mental aberration.

No such luck.

Caleb's words eerily mirrored Jake's confusion and messed-up emotions, but that only brought home to him the whole fucked-up situation.

He got it that Caleb wouldn't have said a word back then, but later? *Christ, if he knew he was gay when he was fuckin' seventeen, why in the hell didn't he say anythin' all these years? Didn't he fuckin' trust me* at all? Jake went back to the journal, anxious to learn more.

June

That's it! High school is OVER.

A whole load of us went to McDonald's last night, and after we hung out in the old quarry off West Central. Trey and Corey brought beer, and we got totally wasted. I slept at Corey's – his folks put him in the room over the garage, and I got a mattress on the floor. Better than going home.

Lots of kids from school at McDonald's. There's this one

kid in tenth grade, I've seen him a lot around the halls. He's got the kinda face that stays with you. Never thought I'd think of a guy as beautiful, but God, it fits him.

Not gonna go there. Don't shit where you eat, right? Wait until Atlanta.

I went online last week to look up some stuff about Atlanta. OMG. There are neighborhoods that are totally gay. Stores, bars… This is gonna be AWESOME.

Jake stared at the words, stunned. The similarities were uncanny. Hadn't he begun to notice the faces of guys who up until that year had been just that—faces? Only, all of a sudden, he was seeing them with different eyes. And yeah, the eyes were what Jake noticed most of all.

And once he'd started on that road, *fuck*, talk about the floodgates opening…

That last part drew him back to the journal. He'd witnessed an excitement in Caleb those months before he went off to college, and had taken it as his reaction to leaving LaFollette, making new friends, anticipating the start of an adventure. Except now he saw it for what it was. A closeted young man, anxious to throw off the constraints of a small town in Tennessee, and live life as he really was. The chance to finally be himself.

Jake had never thought he and Caleb were all that alike. Why would he? He'd been eleven when Caleb had left, and in the years since they didn't see all that much of each other. Too little time spent together to notice their similarities. But seeing Caleb's innermost thoughts and feelings in stark print on the screen brought home to Jake just how much he'd lost.

Just how similar he and Caleb had been.

He glanced at the screen. June's entry continued, and something caught his eye that made his stomach turn over. Something about his daddy.

Saw pictures of a Pride parade in NYC on TV. Daddy made

some comment under his breath that turned my stomach, something about pansy-assed fags, and switched channels. Pansy-assed? Does that even make sense? No matter. It's the thought that counts, right? Mama heard him. She looked like she was sucking on a lemon. Jake was in bed, thank God. That kid misses nothing. And he would see something. Only last week, he asked Mama if she knew anyone who was gay. How does he pick up these things? At school? God knows. One thing's for sure. He's not gonna know about his big brother.

Caleb's depiction of his daddy only echoed what Jake had already seen for himself. Wasn't *that* what had kept him silent these last two years? A fragment of conversation between his daddy and Mrs. Talbot next door had solidified his fears. She'd appeared on their doorstep one weekend with a box of eggs from her chickens, and Daddy had answered the door. Jake had been in the living room, and part of their conversation made him prick up his ears. Some well-meaning friend of Mrs. Talbot's, bless her heart, had called to say she'd seen Mrs. Talbot's great-nephew Lance going into a gay bar in Knoxville. Mrs. Talbot had retorted that she'd rather he was gay than marry out of his race.

Daddy had snorted, and made some remark about how there'd be no rainbow flags flying outside *his* house, thank you very much.

Jake's heart had sunk. It was only later that night when he lay in his bed that the rest of Mrs. Talbot's words truly hit home. *There's a gay bar in Knoxville?* That was only forty miles away. His heart pounded, and his palms grew clammy at the thought of walking into such a place. Then he dismissed it. He'd never have the nerve to go there alone.

With an effort he dragged his attention back to the journal. He wanted to finish reading it well before his parents got home. It was such a weird feeling, seeing his own thoughts and experiences reflected in Caleb's words.

Got my dorm sorted. I'm gonna be sharing with four other guys. TBH, I can't wait to get out of LaFollette. Lately it feels like I can't be me. I'm always watching what I say or do, even around Chuck, and that hurts. When I hang out with my friends, it's like I'm hiding the whole time. Last night was just…fucked up. We were all at Burger King out on Jacksboro Pike, and Vaughan showed up with a couple of girls. A shit-ton of make-up and overdone on the perfume, no change there. Well, one of them – Becca, I think – starts coming on to me. I mean, she was all over me like a rash. I felt trapped. It was obvious what she wanted, and then Corey said his folks were away, and did I want to use his room?

Everyone was grinning, like they totally expected me to take her off someplace so we could fuck. Yeah, like I've ever fucked a girl before. But they didn't need to know that. I'd gotten through high school by lying my ass off. To listen to my friends, they're fucking every chance they get. Fine. Chance is they don't have parents like mine. God, I can still hear Mama in my head, jawing about abstinence. Saving yourself for marriage. Respecting girls.

What's really weird? I bought all that. I believed it. I lived it.

Plus there was zero opportunity.

Oh my fucking God. Caleb was a virgin?

Jake shook his head. *Nope. Not buying it.* Okay, so there hadn't been many girls that he could recall, but the idea that Caleb hadn't gotten past first base with any of 'em? Yet that bit about Mama and The Talk… that rang so true. And then he reconsidered. Caleb had been seventeen when he'd written those words. It wasn't so hard to believe that he'd abstained up to that point. Because that part about zero opportunity? Yeah, Jake knew all about that, not to mention the fear of disappointing his mama.

An' what about me? How can I not believe his words when I'm in the same state, an' I'm nineteen, *for Christ's sake?* All those times when Pete, Dan, Mike, any of them, had bragged about who they were fucking, and how hot she was…. Hadn't he lied his ass off? He'd acted all secretive, like he couldn't reveal her name, and they'd responded with snickers and winks, and digs to the arm. And the part about hiding all the time… *Jesus.*

A little further down the page, Jake caught sight of his nickname.

I'm ticking off the days until college. Can't come soon enough. Until then, I'm just gonna keep busy. Chuck wants a treehouse in the back yard, so I'm gonna help Daddy put it together. That's one thing I will miss when I leave here – spending time with the little squirt. I see him with Daddy in the woodshed sometimes. Talk about cute. Daddy bought him a set of toy tools one Christmas, and watching him pretending to saw a piece of wood, copying Daddy, was hilarious. Guess it's in his genes.

Tears pricked Jake's eyes, and he wiped them away. *God, I remember that summer.* A wave of sorrow rolled over him, so acute that it made his heart ache. Long, hot, sunny days. Going down to the creek with him, squealing when Caleb dripped water down his back. Caleb squeezing into the treehouse with him, listening as Jake read aloud from one of his books. What felt like a thousand other memories, each bringing with them a sharp prick of pain, until he could no longer hold back the tears that spilled over his cheeks. A glance at the following entry only made matters worse.

September.
Can't believe I'm finally here!
Daddy surprised the hell out of me this morning. I got up at dawn to put all my stuff in his truck – and there was a car in our driveway, a Chevy. Nowhere near new, of course, and I don't wanna think about how many miles she's got on here, but she's mine. A present from Mama and Daddy. I teared up.
Gave Jake a big hug before I left. I promised to write him letters, but I know it's just not gonna happen. How many times have I written in here, for one thing? Not a big writer. But I will

call him. He was so upset when I left. Gonna miss my little brother.

Jake couldn't take any more. He scrolled through the document with blurred eyes, dipping in here and there, thankful for the mundane entries about his classes, parties, and everyday shit. The style grew more rambling, and Jake skimmed over most parts. *I can always come back an' read it another time.* Right then he was too excited to give it the attention it deserved. He was looking for answers. There were references to gay bars and clubs in Atlanta, and evidence that Caleb loved his newfound freedom. There was even the briefest indication that he'd subsequently gotten laid, but in true Caleb style, it amounted to a guy's name, followed a series of exclamation marks and smileys.

Jake was thankful for small mercies. The last thing he wanted to read was a full-blown account of his brother fucking. He was perfectly capable of reading between the lines, and besides, there was some things he *really* didn't need to know.

About halfway through the journal, Jake saw Liam's name mentioned for the first time, a passing remark about meeting him at a party. Caleb referred to Liam as stubborn, which made Jake snicker. *Pot... meet kettle*. It wasn't until his third year in college that Liam's name popped up again, only this time, it was obvious they'd gone on a couple of dates. Jake slowed down, reading intently. Caleb didn't give much away, but judging by the increasing number of mentions Liam got, things were becoming serious.

And then one line stood out above all the rest.

It was an entry just before the end of his third year. Only one line, but so powerful that Jake couldn't read past it.

June 26, 2011.
I think I love him.

Jake sagged against the pillows. *Then it's true.*
He closed his eyes, his energy gone. *Caleb, you could've*

told me. He kicked himself for not reaching out sooner, for not making more of an effort to get in touch. For just accepting the situation instead of fighting it. All the anger he'd succeeded in tempering, was once again on a slow boil, as he reasoned that he really wasn't the one at fault here.

Caleb hadn't said a word.

Not *One. Fucking. Word.*

Not only that, he'd stayed away. Deserted Jake when he'd needed his big brother most.

How could he fucking DO THAT?

In a surge of heated rage, memories surfaced. Those times when Caleb did make it home—not that he stayed all that long, only a few days—always ended the same way. Caleb would throw his bag into the car, then turn to Jake, arms outstretched. There'd be a hug that almost took his breath away, and then those words. The same words, every visit.

"If you ever need me, just call, okay? I'm always here for ya."

Jake slammed down the lid of the laptop and tossed it onto the comforter. "But you weren't, were ya? You weren't here for me, an' fuck, I *needed* you. Why, Caleb? Why'd you stay away?" His voice rebounded off the walls.

The sound of tires crunching on gravel put paid to any more questions flung into the ether. Mama and Daddy were home. Jake shoved the laptop under his pillow, not bothering to shut it down. It was only as he was struggling to calm down that he realized he'd left the charger in Atlanta.

Damn it. He'd have to call Liam, or else buy a new one. If they still made a charger for a laptop that was at least ten years old. Not that he needed an excuse to call Liam.

He wanted answers that only Liam could provide.

Chapter Nine

By Wednesday, Jake was beyond pissed.
Why won't he answer a single fuckin' call?
Three days of texts, more texts, calls, only to be greeted with silence. Liam apparently didn't want to talk, and the longer this went on, the more angry and emotional Jake became. He reread Caleb's journal from start to finish, until he knew it by heart. Working with his daddy didn't provide enough of a distraction. He couldn't stop thinking about it.
Caleb couldn't have been gay. I'd have known.
He told himself the journal was an exaggeration, not that it gave a shitload of details anyway. He likened it to how some teenage girls wrote in *their* journals, where they built up this fantasy of loving someone.

Except Jake knew deep down this was a bullshit theory. He wasn't even sure why he wanted to talk to Liam in the first place. Initially, Jake had had some lame-ass idea of confronting him, of forcing him to admit it was all fabrication on Caleb's part.
Who am I kiddin'? That just don't hold water.
Jake had to do something. Judging by the looks he caught his daddy giving him, his behavior was erratic enough to have been noted. The last thing Jake wanted was for him to start asking questions, because it wouldn't take much for him to break.

It was no good. He had to talk to Liam.

Wednesday evening after supper, Jake went out into the back yard, heading for his tree house. It had been years since he'd played in there. Sometimes Pete or Dan or some other friends would come visit, and Mama brought them all sodas and chips. They'd bring comics, cards, whatever they felt like, and hide up in there, away from the prying eyes of adults.

For a little boy who was missing his brother, those days were precious.

Jake sat at the foot of the tree, his back against the solid trunk, and got out his phone.

Come on, Liam. Answer me. Just once. Jake hung on, listening to it ring, unwilling to give up, as though perseverance would eventually have its reward.

Apparently, he was right.

Liam sighed into his ear. "Jus' why do you have this burnin' need to call me, Jake? I'm pretty sure you have all your answers by now." He sounded bone-tired.

Whatever opening Jake had planned flew out the window. "This isn't true," he blurted out, and as soon as his words were out there, he realized how foolish he sounded.

There was a moment's silence. "Oh. My. God. If that's all you have to say to me, I'm endin' this call right now."

"Wait!" Panic rose up inside him, his heart racing. To his intense relief, Liam did as he'd asked, and before Jake could properly frame his thoughts, his mouth took over. "Caleb was gay? You an' Caleb… you were really together?"

Another sigh. "You've got the laptop. I don't know what you found, believe it or not, but if you've worked that much out, you know you're not the only one suff'rin' here."

Holy fuck. Then it *was* true. A numbness crept through him, leaving him weak. "Why didn't he tell me?" Jake whispered.

For a moment, he thought they'd been cut off, the silence was so profound. "We could talk all night about that one."

Not good enough. "I need to know. Didn't he trust me? Was he scared of how Mama an' Daddy would react if he came out?" Jake hesitated, but it had to be said. "Was it because of you?"

"What about me?" There was a sharp edge to Liam's voice.

Jake snorted. "Oh, for Pete's sake. You were at the funeral.

You saw everyone who was there. You even mentioned their reaction yourself. Was Caleb scared to tell 'em because you're black?"

Liam huffed. "Well, that's better than I anticipated. Goin' by all the stuff Caleb told me about your town, I half expected you to say 'colored'. I guess you an' he were more alike than he thought." Another pause. "I'm sorry. I can't help ya."

"Now wait just one minute!" Jake's anger began to bubble up once more.

"No, *you* wait!" Liam's breathing was harsh. "I get that you're goin' through all this emotional turmoil. Well, here's a newsflash for ya—so am I. You lost your brother, an' yeah, I know that hurts like fuck, but guess what? I jus' lost the man I love. He fuckin' *died* next to me. So forgive me if I don't invest in your pity party. Right now I have enough problems dealin' with my own." And with that he disconnected.

Jake stared at the screen, dizzy and disorientated. *What the fuck?* No *way* was he gonna let Liam end it like that, not when he had so many questions left answered. *An' he says I have an attitude?*

"Jacob? Come inside, please," Daddy hollered from the back porch.

Aw, crap. Jake knew that tone of voice. Something was up. "Comin'!" He hoisted himself to his feet and shoved his phone into the pocket of his jeans. As he neared the house, he saw his daddy waiting on him, and the sight was enough to have him move a little faster.

Daddy gestured inside. "Go on into the livin' room. Mama an' me, we wanna talk to ya."

Not now, he groaned internally. He had no clue what was about to come at him, but it wasn't gonna be good. Dutifully, he walked through the house, to where Mama was sitting in her chair beside the fireplace. Jake sat on the couch, his pulse speeding up. *What is all this?*

Daddy came in and took the other chair. "Okay. Wanna tell

us what's goin' on?"

Jake blinked. "'Scuse me?"

Daddy pierced him with a hard stare. "Jacob John Greenwood, don't you think I know you by now? Your head ain't been straight since you went to Atlanta. So s'ppose you tell us what's botherin' ya? An' don't give me some guff about you still grievin' for Caleb. 'Course you are, same as us. But I *know* you, boy. This ain't the same thing. You've got somethin' goin' on in that head of your's, an' it's drivin' you to distraction."

Before Jake could tell him he was wrong, Mama piped up. "You hardly talk these days. I always thought if you had a problem, you'd come to me." She pressed her lips together. "It's like I don't know you anymore."

Lord, the pain in his chest right then. Jake's throat thickened, and he lowered his gaze. There was no way he could share his thoughts, but he had to find a way through this. "I think…," he began, but the words dried up.

"Jacob?" He raised his head to meet his mama's gaze. "If you can't confide in us, is there anyone else you *can* talk to? 'Cause it seems to me you're just bottlin' everythin' up, an' that's not good for the soul. Maybe if I asked Reverend Hubbert to stop by?"

Hell no. Jake's breathing quickened. "S'alright, Mama. Don't you go botherin' the good reverend." An idea glimmered in his head, and lightness suffused his body. "There *is* someone I could talk to… Only thing is, he's not from 'round here. It'd mean a trip to see him."

Mama gave him a speculative glance. "He live in Atlanta by any chance?"

God bless Mama and her intuition.

Jake smiled, relief flooding through him. "Yes, ma'am."

"Who you talkin' 'bout?" Daddy looked from Mama to Jake, his brows knitted.

"Caleb's roommate." She nodded knowingly. "Stands to reason he'd be a good person to talk to. An' if it would help, then of course you need to go there." She glared at Daddy. "Don't you think so?"

Daddy cleared his throat. "Sure thing. Only, can he leave it 'till the weekend? I really need Jacob right now. There's too much to be done, an' I can't do it alone."

"'Course I can." Jake gave his daddy a reassuring smile. "I won't let you down, sir. I'll go early Saturday, like last time."

Daddy's face glowed. "You're a good boy." He glanced over to the fireplace, and his face tightened a little. "God blessed us with two wonderful sons."

Jake followed his gaze, and he suddenly had difficulty swallowing. On the ledge above the fire stood a series of framed photos, one of which was of Caleb in his high school graduation robes, Jake standing in front of him, barely up to his shoulder. Caleb's hands rested on Jake's shoulders, and Jake was staring up adoringly at his big brother.

Jake wasn't surprised when Daddy got to his feet and left the room.

Mama's eyes were full of dismay. "Seems like you're not the only one who's talkin' less these days." It was such an unexpected remark that Jake stilled. In that moment she was more than just his mama—she was his daddy's wife, his soulmate. Then she blinked, and the moment passed. "Now, if I go into that kitchen, am I gonna find all the dishes washed an' put away?" The twinkle in her eyes was a welcome sight after the seriousness of the last few minutes.

Jake bit his lip. "I'll get right on it, Mama."

"You do that." She picked up her cross stitch. "An' bring me a glass of sweet tea when you're done? You might take one to your daddy too."

"Sure, Mama." Jake left the room and hastened to the kitchen. He got on with his task, his mind already dwelling on his trip to Atlanta. Not that Liam was going to know of his intended visit. No sir. Jake wasn't going to give him the chance of making an excuse not to be there. A weekend was a safe enough bet that he'd be home.

An' then we're gonna talk.

Jake had wanted the laptop to achieve some closure, and he'd gotten anything but. What he'd seen created more questions than before, and Liam was the only person who might be able to answer them—providing he let Jake cross the threshold.

Jake switched off the engine and yawned. Thank God he'd stopped to pick up a couple of cans of energy drink. His sleep the previous night had been pitiful, and he'd been barely awake when he'd climbed into his truck. Mama was no fool. It wasn't as if she could miss the dark smudges under his eyes that he'd seen in the mirror that morning, but she'd said nothing, simply handing him a bag containing sweet tea and a hunk of a sandwich.

Driving that distance second time around had been a little easier, and once more the radio had proved a godsend. Anything was better than silence. It only made him think.

Jake got out of the truck and walked around to the stairs that led up to the covered walkway. He got to the door of #8 and knocked loudly. Liam had kept Caleb's key, naturally. Jake pasted on a smile that he certainly didn't feel as the door opened. "Mornin'. I—"

A young woman faced him, a baby held in one arm. "Hey. Can I help ya with somethin'?" Behind her, a young man with a scruffy beard appeared, gazing at him inquiringly.

Jake frowned. "Excuse me. I came here to see Liam. He lives here." He stared past the couple into the hall, where boxes stood piled up against the wall. *What in the hell?*

The young man's brow smoothed out. "Ah, was he the guy who lived here before? He moved out a week ago. We've only just moved in ourselves. We jumped real fast when this place became available." He gestured to the boxes. "It's chaos, but we're gettin' there, aren't we, sugah?" He put his arm around the young woman.

Jake thought fast. "Would you have a forwardin' address for him?"

She shook her head. "The landlord said to put all his mail together, an' he'd collect it an' send it on. Sorry."

Jake thanked them, and said goodbye. He wandered along the walkway in a daze.

How in hell did he move so fast? Then he considered the sparse state of the apartment when he'd seen it last. *Well fuck.* He'd been close, he'd just got it the wrong way 'round. It wasn't the look of someone who'd just moved in—it was someone who was all packed up and about to move *out*.

An' he didn't say a word about it. Liam had to have known. *But then why would he mention it? It wasn't as if he thought he'd see me again.*

The laptop had changed all that.

Jake got into his truck and pulled out his phone. He scrolled through and called Liam.

No answer.

He tried again with a text. *U got a minute? Need 2 talk 2 U.*
No answer.

Jake let out a low growl. "Not again, you don't." He called Liam again, redialing several times, before resorting to hanging on. It had worked before, so why the hell not?

After ten minutes, Liam answered. "You're persistent, I'll give you that."

Jake ignored him. "Where in tarnation are ya? An' *don't* tell me you're in your apartment, 'cause we both know that's a fuckin' lie."

Several seconds passed before Liam's heavy sigh greeted his ears. "What do you want from me, Jake?"

It was a good question. Only thing was, Jake didn't know the answer.

Truth & Betrayal

Chapter Ten

"So where are you? An' how come you didn't say you were movin' out?" Jake answered Liam's question with a few of his own.

"I'm sorry, I didn't realize it was any of your goddamn business!" Liam drew in an audible breath. "Look, I'd already made plans to move in with my folks for a while by the time you turned up to collect Caleb's stuff. I couldn't stay there anymore. Too many memories. I quit my job too. There's no way I can live in Atlanta now. Every time I walked down the street, or went past our favorite restaurant, whatever, I was aware of this… space beside me. Because he's not there, so I can't be there either. An' it's not so bad bein' home again. I'm lookin' for a job here." Liam paused, and his voice softened. "Which brings us back to you. You know everythin' now. Why are you still callin' me? Why can't you let this drop?"

Pain lanced through his heart. "Because he shouldn't have died, not before I had the chance to talk to him." Jake swallowed hard. "God, if you only knew how long I'd been waitin' to talk to him."

"All you had to do was pick up the phone, right?"

"Uh-uh. Not for this conversation. This was somethin' that had to be discussed face-to-face, an' now I'll never get the chance to tell him…" His throat seized, and the words died there.

"Tell him what?"

"That… we were more alike than I'd thought. In a way I'd never have believed." Jake choked back his tears. He was not gonna lose it, not on the phone to Liam, sitting in his truck.

"What way, Jake?" Liam's voice was whisper-soft. "What was so important that you had to share with him?"

There was no backing out now, not when he'd gotten this far. And he knew he had nothing to fear from Liam. "That I'm… gay." Jake held his breath, not really sure why.

"Well, I'll be—" Liam expelled his breath in a soft stream of air. "Does anyone know?"

Despite his fucked-up emotions, Jake had to smile. "Well, yeah—you." His sigh echoed Liam's. "I was waitin' for the right opportunity to tell Caleb, but there never seemed to be one. An' when I *could've* said somethin', I chickened out. Too afraid, I guess."

"What of?"

"How he'd react."

Liam let out a wry chuckle. "Boy, you two really were alike. Caleb wanted to tell ya, so badly, but what held him back was the fear you'd react like your daddy. I kinda got the impression he wouldn't have been all that keen on the prospect of a gay son. Caleb said you an' your daddy were so alike, an'—"

"Oh." *An' I thought Caleb knew me.* "We're alike in many ways, but not that one."

"You must have so many things buzzin' through your head right now."

"You have *no* idea." Then Jake let out a wry chuckle. "Well, maybe you do." If he'd thought the situation was messed-up before…

"Is there anyone you can talk to?"

And there it was, the heart of what ailed Jake. "No one I can trust to react the way I need them to." He'd seen enough of what went on in the school halls not to be one hundred percent positive his friends would support him. Their family environments were just like his own. It was hard to avoid such perceptions, not when you lived and breathed them every day.

"Look… do you want to talk to me?"

Jake blinked back the tears that welled up, and his face grew warm. "You mean that?" Not that he was sure he could impose like that. Liam didn't know him from Adam.

"It's just a suggestion. I take it you're at the apartment?"

"Yeah."

"So what's your plan?"

"I was gonna go home." There was nothing to keep him there.

"If you're gonna do that, go before it gets too late. You've been through a lot emotionally, an' I imagine you're exhausted. An' if you're too tired to drive, *please*, Jake, get a bed for the night. There's a cheap place on Pine Street NE that's not far from there. You mustn't drive if you're tired."

He's lookin' out for me. The thought sent warmth spreading through Jake. He knew at the heart of Liam's concern was Caleb. Add to that his invitation for Jake to talk to him, and Jake knew his brother had got a good man.

"I'll be jus' fine. I'll make a few stops an' grab a little sleep if I get tired." As much as he welcomed the idea of having someone to confide in, Jake wasn't about to act selfishly. "Are you sure it's okay to call ya? Because if it's too much for ya, I'd understand." He reckoned it would be painful, so close to losing Caleb.

"I would never let Caleb's little brother go through this by himself. You've got my number. An' I promise, next time I'll answer right away. Any time, Jake, okay?" Sincerity rang out with every word.

"Thanks."

"An' if you still have questions about Caleb, just ask. I might not have all the answers, but I'll do my best."

"Can't ask more than that, can I?" Jake breathed easily for the first time since he'd called. "I'm gonna leave now."

"Text me when you get there, alright?"

Jake assured Liam he would, then finished the call. Four hours on the road awaited him, but he felt a damn sight better than he had on the way down there. It comforted him to know that for the first time, he wasn't alone.

It was a good feeling.

By the time Jake reached the outskirts of LaFollette, Liam's assessment proved correct: he was physically and emotionally exhausted. The one emotion that had plagued him more than any other all the way home was regret. Wishing Caleb had said something. Wishing *he'd* said something. Then he was reminded of a saying his tenth grade English teacher had been fond of sharing on many occasions: *Make it a rule of life never to regret and never to look back.*

Yeah, easier said than done.

Jake pulled into the driveway and parked his truck behind his daddy's. He was dog-tired, and more than ready to eat something. Mama opened the door before he'd even reached for the handle, and drew him into a hug. Jake held onto her, breathing in her familiar scent, a mixture of perfume, fresh cotton, and the aroma of baking.

"Did you find what you were lookin' for?" she whispered, her arms still around him.

Jake had to be honest. "Yes an' no. Talkin' with Liam did help a little, but…" He pulled free of her embrace and looked her in the eye. "Would you understand if I said maybe some time I'd like to go back there?" She didn't have to know Liam was now in North Carolina. It wasn't that he envisaged going back there either, but he wanted to get an idea of the lay of the land. At least if she was receptive to the idea, that gave him the option should he need it.

Mama regarded him steadily for a moment. She cupped his face with both hands. "We're all fumblin' through this on our own, but you mustn't be afraid to ask for help if you need it." She paused, her expression thoughtful. "I was talkin' 'bout you with Reverend Hubbert this mornin'. I think you should come to church with us tomorrow."

Jake suppressed the urge to sigh. "I go there once in a while, an' it's never for my benefit, Mama, but yours. So… I don't think so." He didn't want to stomp all over her suggestion, but it was better she knew the truth.

Mama nodded. "I might not be happy 'bout that decision, but I do understand. Your daddy copes by throwin' himself into his work. I find the church gives me what I need." She paused. "If… connectin' with Caleb's friend in Atlanta helps ya… if you need time away from work to do that…. Then we'll support ya." She grinned. "An' I'll make sure your daddy understands that too."

He hugged her tightly. "You're the best Mama ever."

Mama chuckled and pushed him away. "Flatterer. You jus' want what I got waitin' for ya in the oven."

He rolled his eyes. "Well *duh*." Jake followed her into the house, feeling more optimistic despite his fatigue.

The phone conversation with Liam, while not answering all his questions, had at least provided a glimmer of light at the end of the tunnel. Not to mention a confidant.

Jake had just finished breakfast when his phone rang. He smiled when he saw Pete's name. It had been on his mind to see what his friends were up to. "Hey, whassup?"

"Whatcha doin' Tuesday? Got any plans?"

The apparent randomness of the question stumped him for a moment. "Why Tuesday?"

Pete snorted. "Are you awake? Can you see a calendar? Then look at it, dumbass!"

Amused, Jake stared across the kitchen. "Really?" How could he have lost track of time so badly, not to know Tuesday was the Fourth of July?

A derisive snicker filled his ears. "So? You doin' anythin' with your folks?"

"I doubt it." The fact that nothing had been said thus far was a good indication. "Why? You got an idea?" Jake wasn't really in the mood to celebrate.

"Me, Dan, an' Mike are goin' to Knoxville. Everything kicks off around four, but we figured on makin' a day of it. Wanna come along?"

"I'd have to ask Mama 'n' Daddy."

"Ask us what?" Mama walked into the kitchen, Daddy not far behind her.

"Pete asked if I wanted to go to Knoxville on the Fourth with him an' a couple others."

Mama narrowed her gaze, but Daddy nodded enthusiastically. "Sounds like a great idea. You don't spend enough time with those friends of yours. It's not like you'll be missin' work, right? An' we weren't plannin' on doin' nothin' special, was we, sugah?"

"No, but..." Mama pursed her lips before speaking. "As long as you boys aren't plannin' on drinkin' an' drivin'. An' don't give me that 'but we're too young to drink' routine. I may've been born at night, but it wasn't last night."

"I heard that," Pete said with a chuckle. "Tell your mama there's no alcohol allowed."

Jake repeated his words, although knowing his friends like he did, he suspected alcohol was gonna make an appearance at some point. But what Mama didn't know, wouldn't hurt her none.

Mama gave a reluctant nod. "Fine. Jus' make sure you come straight home once the fireworks are done. You'll need to be up early the next mornin'."

"Of course, Mama." Inside, Jake was buzzing at the chance to visit Knoxville without his parents. LaFollette, with its inhabitants numbering just under seven thousand, was like an ant next to Knoxville. Why, there had to be at least two hundred thousand people there.

Spending the Fourth of July in a large, hopefully more diverse city…

By K.C. Wells

Jake couldn't wait.

Chapter Eleven

Pete tapped out a rhythm on the steering wheel. "Don't know 'bout *you* boys, but I sure am ready to have a good time."

From behind him, Mike cackled. "Oh, I think *I* can help there." He held aloft his backpack, grinning.

In the passenger seat, Jake regarded him suspiciously. "Okay, what're you up to? What you got in there?"

Mike opened up the pack and pulled out a large bottle of orange Gatorade. "I got four of 'em. We jus' can't take 'em into the Park, is all."

"Why not?" Jake rolled his eyes when both Pete and Dan erupted into childish giggles. "Really? You brought spiked Gatorade?"

Mike elbowed Dan in the ribs. "The way Jake talks, you'd think he didn't know us at all." Another cackle burst from him, and Dan joined him. "*'Course* it's spiked. You don't think I'd drink it when it isn't, do ya?" He prodded Pete's shoulder. "We nearly there yet?"

"Not far now." Pete peered through the windshield, watching the road signs.

Dan chuckled. "I've bin lookin' forward to this for weeks."

An alarm bell started ringing in Jake's head. No *way* would Dan be *this* excited over a couple of bands, the Knoxville Symphony Orchestra, and twenty minutes of fireworks. "Lookin' forward to *what*, exactly?"

Dan beamed. "The Love Shack."

Jake groaned. "Oh, Lord." He might have known.

"Will you fellas stop jawin' for a sec?" Pete growled. "I gotta concentrate, or we'll end up back in LaFollette."

Jake glanced ahead at the confusing tangle of roads. "Tell me what you're lookin' for, an' I'll direct ya."

"Henley Street. I think it's dead ahead, but there's so many exits."

Jake scanned the signs above the highway and pointed. "There."

"Gotcha." It wasn't long before they were on the right road. "Now we're gonna take a right onto Cumberland Avenue. It's a straight run from there to the Love Shack." He grinned. "In case you haven't guessed, it's a sex shop."

Mike cleared his throat. "Adult Entertainment store, if you don't mind."

Pete snorted. "Whatever. It's got videos, toys, everythin' a horny boy needs. There's a strip club too, not far from there."

"When are we gonna have time to go to a strip club?" Jake demanded. "I don't know 'bout you guys, but my mama said to come straight home."

"Lord, you've turned into such a goody two shoes," Mike said with wide eyes. "You didn't *really* think we were here to watch fireworks, did ya?" The other two laughed.

Jake ignored the comments. "An' of course you checked to see if these places are open today, right?" His heart was pounding. He did *not* wanna look at a load of naked girls.

"Yup. Openin' times are slightly different, but yeah, they're open." Mike reached over to hand Jake his phone. "Looky here." He leered. "Says they're naked, but you can't touch."

Thankfully the girls in the images were clothed, albeit in the skimpiest of costumes. "Nice of you to let me know what we're doin'," he joked as he handed back the phone, ignoring his racing pulse. Then it occurred to him that one of their destinations might actually work in his favor.

An Adult Entertainment store ain't jus' for straight people, right? An' if there's a gay bar in Knoxville, stands to reason there'll be gay stuff at the store.

"Don't forget to clear your browsin' history before you get home," Peter told Mike. "You know what your mama's like."

"Yeah, a nosy ol' bitch," Mike grumbled. "I swear, the number of things I have to hide from her is nobody's business." He laid a gentle hand on Jake's shoulder. "I know we should've said somethin', but we jus' thought you needed cheerin' up. You've had quite a time of it lately."

Like Jake could be annoyed after that. "Thanks, guys. I don't mind goin' to the store, but to be honest…" He thought quickly. "I'm not so sure 'bout the strip club. Maybe a few months down the line, yeah, but right now?" Jake let out a purposefully heavy sigh. "Sorry, fellas, I've just gotta lot on my mind, an' I don't think oglin' naked ladies is gonna help that much." He mentally crossed his fingers, praying at least one of them had an ounce of sensitivity to them.

Pete came through for him, God bless him. "Listen, if you don't feel like it, that's fine. We'll leave you to watch the fireworks, if you like, an' pick you up after. We've gotta come by there anyhow to get back on the 275."

"Thanks. I 'preciate that." Jake pointed off to the right. "There it is." It wasn't as if you could miss it. The sign was bright blue, with little red cupids on either side, the black lettering loudly proclaiming it to be the 'Love Shack Couples Intimacy Store.'

Oh Lord.

Pete pulled into one of the few parking spaces, and switched off the engine. "Fuck, it's tiny," he said, gazing at the building clad in dark brown timber, with pale blue trim that stood out a mile. "It really *is* a shack."

They piled out of the truck, and Pete led the way, pointing at a bright pink sign by the door. *Smile - You're on Candid Camera.* "Now, no lickin' the plastic video cases, boys." And before Jake had time to draw breath, they were inside.

Christ, it was small. Definitely not what he'd expected.

"Fuck, would you look at that," Dan breathed, pointing

toward an extremely large and very realistic-looking dick in flesh-colored silicone.

    Jake didn't want to look, especially at the sales clerk who stood behind the counter, a pretty young thing with red hair. She gave him a warm smile, and he quickly averted his gaze, convinced his face was as red as a tomato. One look at the wall of dildos had him struggling between suppressing his giggles, and trying to adjust his jeans surreptitiously so his hard-on was less noticeable. Because the mere thought of sliding one of those up his ass...

    Then he turned the corner around a display stand and tried not to choke at the sight of a giant poster depicting a woman with her legs spread. Holy Mother of God. Jake swallowed hard, his erection wilting. He felt certain that the girl behind the counter was watching him, judging him, and he sought refuge in the lube section.

    Holy mackerel. Who knew there were so many different types of lube, for God's sake? Not to mention vibrators, plugs, handcuffs... Handcuffs? *What the fuck?*

    Jake didn't want to buy *anything*. He just wanted out of there before his face exploded. Lord, he'd never been such a mess of contradictory emotions all at once; curious yet repulsed, surprised and frightened, and totally overwhelmed. He'd read about such places, of course, and was relieved to find there wasn't some dirty, dark little room at the rear of the store, with booths where you could watch pornos, or—thank heaven for small mercies—holes cut out of the wall, for someone to poke their dick through.

    There was a book stand, and a couple of titles leaped out at him, but *no way* was Jake gonna pick up a book on gay sex with those guys hanging around. It was infinitely worse when he found the DVDs. At the end of the shelf was a small selection of gay movies, and he was dying to take a closer look, but he didn't dare. Jake escaped from the tempting array and sought refuge in the sex toys. He pretended to look at the row upon row of toys, catching the boys' laughter now and then.

    At least someone *is havin' a good time.*

Jake strolled around the small store, anxiously waiting for the moment when it would be time to leave. He rounded the corner of the stand to find himself back with the dildos and vibrators. To his horror, the sales clerk was standing there.

"You might like this one," she said, pulling a dildo from off its peg and removing it from its packaging. "It's a good size, and there's a suction cup on the bottom if she wants some fun when you're not around." She grinned. "Or maybe you do. Either way, it's nice an' thick, an' it feels real soft to the touch. Here. Try it an' see." She held out the veiny dildo.

Jake did. Not. Dare.

"Now, why should he need one of those?" Dan said, coming from behind him. "Jake here has somethin' of his own that's *much* better, I'll bet, an' she'll prob'ly enjoy it a whole lot more." He winked at Jake. "Ain't that right?" Dan pointed to a cock ring with a vibrating protrusion. "Now *that* is more like it."

"You seen anythin' you wanna buy?" Pete asked Jake, his hands full of DVDs, a blindfold, and a pair of handcuffs.

Mike guffawed at the sight. "Well, whaddaya know? Pete's a kinky little bastard."

Pete grinned. "Gotta spice things up now an' then, right? Don't want her gettin' bored."

Jake attempted a smile. "Not seen anythin' that's screamed '*buy me*'." He smiled at the sales clerk. "Thanks for the demo, but I think I'll pass." He stood to one side while the boys paid for their purchases.

Jus' get me outta here.

"That's the best thing about festivals," Mike remarked as he dropped the paper napkin that had contained his hot dog into the trash bin. "Junk food. You can't beat a hot dog with all the fixin's." He rubbed his hands on his jeans. "What next?"

Dan gave him an innocent look. "There's Lego buildin', if

that's what you're into." That earned him a whack on the arm. "Hey, dumbass! I nearly dropped my burger, an' I ain't finished with it yet!"

From the park came the strains of a band playing something that clearly had its roots in the Blues. Jake would happily have sat in the park and listened, but he knew there wasn't a cat in hell's chance of *that* happening.

Pete was peering at his phone. "Jus' seeing what else there is 'round here." He grinned. "Hey, fellas? Did you know there's a Gay Street in Knoxville?"

"No shit." Dan cackled. "We'd better not buy anythin' on *that* street. You never know—you might end up with more than you bargained for, know what I'm sayin'?"

Mike scowled. "Fuckin' fags," he said under his breath. "Yeah, don't drop your wallets, boys. You don't wanna have to bend over to pick 'em up, right?"

Pete hooted. "Too right. 'Course, you know what gay stands for, don'tcha?" He lowered his voice. "Got AIDS Yet?" The other two erupted into coarse laughter.

Jake's stomach heaved, and the back of his throat burned. His flesh crawled. Any hopes he'd had that he could confide in them lay smashed to pieces.

"You know what?" Jake's voice cracked a little. "I think I'd like to go listen to that US Air Force brass band that's on next. They're not gonna play for all that long."

Pete gave a slow nod. "I could go for that. Then we can go back to the car an' finish the Gatorade. I want a nice buzz on by the time I get to watch girls take their clothes off." He leered. "Got me a wad of singles jus' for the occasion."

They headed back to the park, and while the others laughed and chatted, Jake couldn't join in. His heart had never felt so heavy. Despite knowing those boys all his life, he'd never realized just how full of hate they were. Sure, he'd had his suspicions, but it wasn't as if it had been a regular topic of conversation: they just *didn't talk* about stuff like that. Why would they? There was no one in high school who had come out as gay—but then *why the fuck would they*? In *LaFollette*? Jesus, it would be like cutting your own throat.

Fuck. I really am on my own in that fuckin' town.
Thank God he had Liam to talk to.

Nine o'clock found Jake standing across the street from Club XYZ. An honest-to-goodness gay bar that hadn't been difficult to find. *God bless Google maps.*

The others were safely out of the way, doubtless handing singles to scantily-clad girls wearing only high heels. The image made him shudder. At least it gave him the opportunity to check out the bar. When the Knoxville Symphony Orchestra came on stage, that was Pete's cue to leave, apparently, and they'd headed for the car, waving at Jake, laughing and joking among themselves.

Thank fuck for that. Jake finally had some breathing space.

He gazed at Club XYZ. It was the tiniest bar he'd ever seen, yet it appeared to be full to bursting. The front comprised two windows covered in grilles, and a single glass door between them. Outwardly, there was no indication it was a gay bar. Loud music burst out every time the door opened, and more guys arrived, disappearing from view.

Jake knew he couldn't go in, of course. What struck him was the confidence the men exuded. They weren't scared to be seen going in there. They were out and proud. And all kind of men, all shapes and sizes.

I could never be like that. Not in LaFollette. It was a dismal thought

Jake began the slow trek back to the park. The firework display kicked off at nine-forty, and he needed to make sure he was there when the boys turned up to collect him. What saddened his heart was that it might have been the Fourth of July, but Jake had nothing to celebrate.

Chapter Twelve

The house was quiet. Jake lay in bed, listening to the usual night sounds that filtered through his open window. Out in the hallway, he heard the steady slow tick of the clock Grandpa had left his Mama. She always said the sound reminded her of her childhood.

An' what sounds remind me *of mine?*

That was easy—Caleb's laughter. He had one of the sunniest natures Jake had ever encountered.

He closed his eyes, and behind his eyelids swam the words from Caleb's journal. So much that Jake didn't know, because the journal gave no indication. Had he ever wanted to tell Mama and Daddy? How did it feel to walk into his first gay bar? To be attracted to a guy, and *finally* be able to do something about it?

So many holes in his knowledge that Caleb couldn't fill.

He glanced across at the clock beside his bed. Five to midnight: the Fourth was almost over. On impulse, he grabbed his phone from the nightstand and composed a text to Liam.

Happy 4th. Thought I'd get it in there while it still is.

A minute later he got a reply. *LOL You just made it. Same to you.*

Jake smiled. A minute later his phone vibrated again. *You have a good one?*

Lord, how to answer *that* in one message. *Not really. Didn't feel much like celebrating.* He wanted to be straight with Liam. That made him smile even more. Straight. Yeah right.

I gotcha. Same here.

Those few words said it all. They served as a reminder that Jake wasn't the only one grieving. *He must miss Caleb so much.* In the hall, the clock made its customary on-the-hour click, and Jake felt a pang of guilt. He typed quickly. *Sorry. It's late.*

Liam's response was swift. *Don't be sorry. Can't sleep anyhow. I guess you can't neither.*

In a rush, Jake knew what he needed, some positivity to counteract the sour taste still in his mouth from that hateful exchange. *Saw my first gay bar tonight in Knoxville. From the outside.*

?? Oh, right, you're not 21. How did it look?

Jake thought for a minute. *Small. Like U could maybe fit 10 guys in there in a pinch.*

LMAO. Yeah, that sounds about right. Caleb mentioned a bar there. Guess it's the same one. Can't be that many gay bars in Knoxville. LOL.

Liam's reaction lessened the ache inside him, and the idea that Caleb had been to that same bar made him feel somehow connected. *I like that. He was there too.* An idea came to him. *Hey... can I ask u something?*

Sure. Got nothing else to do but lie here & count sheep. LOL

Jake's fingers flew over the keypad. *How old were u when u came out?*

When Liam's reply wasn't instantaneous, Jake figured he'd gone too far. But a couple of minutes later, he responded. *16. I'd known for longer, but it took me a year to get up enough nerve to tell my parents.*

U knew at 15? Wow. I was a late developer then. Didn't know til I was 17.

What gave it away? LOL

Jake smiled. *Dylan Torrance smile. I wanted to kiss those lips.* It was weird, but sharing what had been a very intimate realization felt... right.

Terry Allbright. Jock. Dumb as a bucket of rocks but SO

gorgeous.

Jake laughed, then abruptly covered his mouth. It wouldn't do to wake up his parents. And speaking of parents… *How did your folks react when you told them?*

Another pause. Jake had half begun to give up on him, but then a message arrived. *Sorry. Dozed off. Those sheep are finally getting their act together. Can we continue this another time?*

Sure. Jake yawned, and realized he wouldn't be all that far behind Liam. *Tomorrow?*

Yup. TTYL :-)

Jake attached his phone to the cable from the charger, set it down on the nightstand, and curled up on his side, hugging his pillow as usual. For the first time in weeks, he fell into a deep, dreamless sleep.

By the time they got home Wednesday evening, Jake ached like a son of a bitch. It seemed like his daddy had tried to cram two days' work into one, to make up for the holiday, and Jake was in sore need of a shower to relieve his aching body, not to mention removing the layer of sweat he'd built up. He knew he'd spent way too long in the shower when Mama banged on the door, telling him 'other people have a right to a shower too, y'know.' When he emerged, a towel wrapped around his hips, he felt almost human again.

Jake went into his room to get dressed. He sat on the edge of the bed, reached into his jeans pocket, and pulled out his phone. As a rule, he kept it on silent during working hours. Daddy tended to frown if it went off while they were doing something.

When he saw a message from Liam, he smiled. *So it wasn't an excuse last night.* He sat back against the pillows and opened the text.

You asked about my parents. I lucked out when it came to mine. They told me they'd support me 100%. Even suggested I take a boy to the prom. LMAO Bless em. They had no clue.

Jake couldn't imagine getting such a response from Mama and Daddy. *Wow. They sound awesome.* Liam's words brought up another thought, however. *Were u living in NC then?*

Yup. New Hanover County. Born here.

What's it like being gay there?

There was a minute before his response. *You don't wanna know. About the same as it is being black, I guess. But according to Caleb, we have it good compared to Campbell County.* Another pause. *God bless the South, right? Feel free to discriminate against the gays, y'all. Don't let 'em marry. And don't forget that sodomy law that you can't enforce but haven't repealed yet.*

Fuck. To Jake's mind it sounded just as bad. *How did your friends react? Did they know you were gay?*

Lord. I can still hear them. 'You're black. Ain't that bad enough without being a fag too?'

Jake scowled. *So much for the younger generation.*

Sorry. I'm not being fair. Not all of them were like that, just most. And there were more AA kids than in your high school. Good ol' John T. Hoggard, bless it. preparing its students for a 'democratic, diverse, global environment.' And give them their due, they did their best. Can't help human nature though.

For a moment there, Jake was confused as hell. *AA? Why is he talkin' 'bout Alcoholics Anonymous?* Then it hit him. *African-American, you dumbass. Jeez.* It wasn't as if he didn't know the term. Hell, he'd used it himself, the time he'd met Liam at the apartment.

"Jacob? Aren't you ready yet? Supper's on the table."

Shit. Mama. *Sorry. Gotta go. Later?*

Liam's response was swift. *Sure. Probably tonight when neither of us can sleep.*

Yeah. Jake knew *that* feeling.

Jake waited until he was sure Mama and Daddy were sound asleep before reaching for his phone. It had vibrated in his pocket that evening after supper, but he knew better than to take it out. Mama disapproved of him being on his phone when he was sitting with them in the living room, calling it antisocial.

He lay back against the pillows and read Liam's latest text. *You sure there's no one you can trust? Not even a couple of close friends?*

Jake's throat tightened. *Sure. Especially after yesterday. Why? What happened? You alright?*

It was like he could hear Liam's concern. *I just discovered they are hateful assholes. All u need to know. I'm fine.*

Liam sent an emoji, a red-face scowl. *People suck.*

Like we didn't already know that. He recalled Caleb's descriptions from the journal. *Atlanta was better though, right?*

A thumbs up this time. *Way better. Still Georgia, so not that much different from TN or NC, but there's a whole gayborhood.*

Okay, that made him chuckle. *LOL* The idea of such an area brought a smile to his face.

Liam went quiet again, and Jake figured he'd fallen asleep like last time. But then… *Too late to call?*

That was unexpected, not to mention intriguing, and Jake found he wanted to know what was on Liam's mind. *Gimme a sec.* He got out of bed, pulled on a pair of shorts, and gradually, so gradually, he opened the window to its fullest extent. Jake squeezed through the gap, almost hobbling himself when he stepped on a pile of bricks Daddy had left under his window. He pushed the window to almost shut, then carefully made his way further into the yard.

The sky was like dark velvet, and the moon was nearly full, bathing the trees in its ethereal light. Jake scrolled through his contacts and called up Liam's number. "Hey," he whispered when they connected.

"Where are ya?" Jake could just about hear him.

He laughed quietly. "Do you have to whisper too? I'm in the back yard. I climbed out the window."

"Seriously?"

He snickered. "Trust me. It was the best option. That squeaky floorboard catches me out every time. You'd think by now I'd know how to avoid it. So... what's up?"

"I had an idea that I wanted to share with ya. All these texts back an' forth..." Liam paused. "Could you meet me in Atlanta this weekend?"

"What for? You don't live there anymore."

Liam sighed. "Look. I just want to show you Atlanta, that's all. Show you places me an' Caleb went to. Introduce you to some of our friends. He had this whole life you know nothin' about, an' I guess I wanted to share that with ya. Might even help ya, give you an idea of what he got up to all that time." He paused for a moment. "Think of it as a chance to reconnect with him. Lord knows, it might help me too."

God, it was tempting. Just the way Liam described it made Jake yearn to go. Of course, he'd have to run it past Mama and Daddy, but something told him Mama would be all for it.

"Okay," he said hesitantly.

"You don't sound too convinced." A pause. "Jake. You don't have to say yes, okay? It was just an idea."

Jake was only just listening. He was too busy going over the practicalities in his head. "We talkin' a day there?"

"Nope, that's not enough, 'specially for what I have in mind. I was thinkin' you could get there early, like last time, an' stay the night."

"Where? That motel you mentioned?" Jake could afford somewhere as long as it wasn't too expensive.

"I was thinkin' more along the lines of stayin' with friends of mine. They've got a spare room an' a couch that folds out into a bed. I'll have to check with them in the mornin', but I can't see it bein' a problem." Another pause. "So... if I can sort us out somewhere to sleep... you interested?"

Damn straight he was interested. "Yeah. Sounds like a good idea."

"Great." Jake heard the note of relief in Liam's voice, and it struck him that this meant a lot to Liam too. "I'll text you when I know the details. I'm guessin' you'll need to talk to your folks too."

"Yeah, but I think Mama'll go for it. I'll let you know if it's gonna be a bust."

"Sure. I guess we'd both better get some sleep." Liam chuckled. "I'll let you go, so's you can climb back through the window. Just don't break anythin', okay?"

Jake snickered. "Night." He disconnected the call, and crept toward the house. He was still smiling to himself as he hoisted one leg over the window sill. The act brought back a memory of Caleb tapping on his window late one night when Jake was maybe nine or ten. Caleb had gone out with his friends, gotten a little drunk, and had arrived home to discover he'd forgotten his key. Coming in that way showed a lot more sense than waking up Daddy.

Of course, Caleb had spoiled it by tripping over Jake's sneakers and falling head first into the dresser.

That little escapade had gotten him grounded for a month.

Jake got back into bed and put his phone on charge. He lay on his side, staring out at the moonlit sky.

Wonder what I'm gonna learn about you, Caleb?

He couldn't wait to find out.

Chapter Thirteen

Mama paused mid-pour, steam rising from the coffee jug. "Atlanta?"

"Yes, Mama. It wasn't my idea, but I kinda like the sound of seein' places where Caleb went with his friends." He crossed his fingers beneath the table. After spending so much time anticipating the prospect, he didn't want to contemplate her saying no.

"What's this about Atlanta?" Daddy asked as he came into the kitchen. "You're not wantin' to go off gallivantin' again, are ya?" He pulled out a chair and sat down heavily. "We got too much work, boy."

Mama gave him a stern glance as she placed a mug of coffee in front of him. "Jacob is talkin' 'bout going early Saturday, an' comin' home Sunday, so there'll be no need to miss work. An' I can do without him 'round the house for a weekend."

Daddy poured sausage gravy liberally over his biscuits. "I see. You've already told him he can go, I s'ppose."

Mama arched her eyebrows. "Was there somethin' you needed him for this weekend? Some urgent job that can't wait?" Her innocent tone made Jake fight the urge to smile. She knew full well there was nothing.

Daddy scrunched up his forehead. "I'll think about it."

Mama gave him a sweet smile. "Fine. You do that." Her gaze met Jake's, and his lips twitched. Lord, he loved his mama. She handed him a mug of coffee. "More bacon, Jacob?"

He nodded, helping himself, no longer worried. Mama had everything in hand.

By the time Jake walked out of the house to join his daddy at the truck, he knew he'd been right. Daddy gave him a thoughtful look. "'Bin talkin' with your mama. She thinks spendin' time with Caleb's friends will be good for ya. Well, as long as it don't interfere none with your work, I'm okay with that. Lord knows, if you can find *somethin'* that helps you get through this…"

Jake's throat thickened. Daddy never spoke about his own grief, but Jake knew it had to be tearing him apart too. "Thank you, sir."

Daddy gave a single nod. "Well alright then." His voice was gruff. "We'd best be on our way. Got a lot to get done before supper time."

That was as much as Jake was gonna get. He climbed into the truck next to his daddy, his mind already speeding ahead to the weekend. As they pulled out of the driveway, he composed a quick text to Liam.

Okay for the weekend :-)

It wasn't long before a reply pinged back. *Great. I'll text you with details tonight.*

Jake smiled to himself as he put his phone on silent and shoved it into the pocket of his jeans. Less than forty-eight hours to go before he'd be on his way to Atlanta. Inside he was a mixture of emotions. The thought of learning more about Caleb was what pulled him the most, but there was an undercurrent of excitement. To be in a part of the city where being gay was… normal?

He couldn't wait to experience that.

It wasn't until Jake looked closely at the map on his phone, that he realized Liam's friends only lived a stone's throw from their former apartment. He'd set off a bit later than he'd intended, but that was no one's fault but his–Mama couldn't get him to haul his ass out of bed. It was almost eleven by the time he pulled into the parking space Liam had told him to use on Juniper St. NE. Liam was already there, sitting in a dark blue Ford Fusion. He got out of the car as Jake switched off his engine.

"I'm sorry," Jake began, but Liam waved his hand.

"S'okay. I only just got here myself." He yawned. "An' that was due to two coffee stops. Took me seven hours to get here."

Jake gaped. "Lord, what time did you set off?"

Liam grinned. "No idea. It was too dark to see my watch. Got a bag in there?"

Jake nodded, and reached down to pick it up. "So, who're we stayin' with again?" he asked as he got out of the truck and slung his backpack over one shoulder.

"Dev an' Pauli. They're good guys. We met them in a bar not long after we moved here." Liam's eyes sparkled. "Watch out for Pauli when he's tipsy. That man is a wicked flirt."

Jake didn't like the sound of them drinking when he couldn't. "So long as y'all remember I'm not twenty-one, alright? If we're drinkin' in their apartment, that's okay." He followed Liam from the parking space to an odd shaped, three story apartment building, a central door surrounded by a white stone frontage, with two blocks framing it. A long, paved path led up to the door, flanked by deep purple flowers and luscious green grass. "Someone sure takes care of this place."

"Well, it isn't them, that's for damn sure." Liam chuckled. "Dev kills every green thing he touches." He pressed the buzzer to the right of the door, and a tinny voice trickled out of the intercom.

"'Bout time you got here. Drinkin' time's wastin'." A metallic click later, the door opened, and they stepped into the cool interior. Liam headed for the stairs, his long legs taking them two steps at a time. As they reached the top floor, Jake heard laughter. A man with black hair and a thick black beard was leaning over the bannister, grinning at them. "C'mon, boys. You've only driven, what, over six hundred miles between you to get here? That's a mere hop, skip an' a jump, right?"

Liam flipped him the bird. "Dev, you shit. You only have to

drive an hour to see your folks."

Dev straightened and pushed open the door behind him. "In you go, boys. I'll give you the five-cent tour, Jake." He paused as Jake stepped past him into the apartment. "Hey," he said softly. "I'm really happy to meet you, finally. Your brother was somethin' special."

Jake blinked back tears. "Thank you." He found himself in a light, sunny open space, most of which was taken up by two couches, backing onto a kitchen area with granite countertops. It wasn't a large apartment, but it had a homey feel to it, filled with splashes of color and some outrageous things, like the tall flamingo that stood in the corner.

Dev obviously caught him looking. "That was a present from Caleb. Pauli's a Florida boy, an' Cal thought he needed a reminder of home. Pauli! Get yer ass out here."

A door opened, and a slim guy with dark brown hair came out, glaring at Dev. "Hush your mouth, unless you'd rather clean the bathroom? Because I think we *both* know that's not gonna happen this side of the Second Coming." He went over to Liam and flung his arms around him. "God, we've missed you. And you've only been gone a couple of weeks."

Liam hugged him back. "Yeah, I know."

Pauli pulled back a little and regarded him closely. "How are you doing, sweetheart?" He cupped Liam's cheek. "You're still not sleeping, are you?"

Liam gave a slight shrug. "You know that line about a bed bein' too big?" His face tightened, and Pauli's eyes glistened. Liam gripped his shoulders. "Hey, you stop that right now, y'hear? Else you'll have me bawlin' my eyes out, an' I don't want Jake here thinkin' I'm a big softie."

Pauli snickered. "Why the hell not? We all know it's the truth." He released Liam and held out his hand to Jake. "Welcome, Jake. It's great to have you here." He studied him for a moment. "You an' Caleb weren't alike, were you?"

Jake had to smile. "Caleb used to joke that I was found on

the front porch, an' Mama took pity on me."

Dev cackled. "Yeah, that sounds like Cal. Well, you two can toss a coin to decide who gets the bed an' who sleeps on the couch."

There was no way Jake was gonna let Liam sleep on the couch, not after he'd gone to the trouble of organizing the weekend. "I'm on the couch," he said promptly. When Liam opened his mouth, obviously to argue the point, Jake shook his head. "Don't bother. I'm not gonna change my mind."

Pauli snickered. "Well, he may not look like Cal, but he's certainly got Cal's stubborn streak."

"Yeah, I've noticed," Liam muttered.

Dev rubbed his hands together briskly. "Okay, you boys do what you have to in the bathroom, because we're goin' for brunch at Joe's. An' that's just the start." When Liam gazed at him quizzically, Dev gave him an innocent look. "Relax. I've been thinkin' 'bout this ever since you called Thursday. We've thought of a couple of places to take young Jake here."

Liam narrowed his gaze, but before he could say anything, Jake blurted out, "Hey, less of the young, alright? I'm twenty soon."

Dev lifted his eyebrows. "An' that makes you young, okay?" He grinned. "'Specially compared to Pauli. He's pushin' on thirty, the ol' bastard." Pauli was close enough to whack him on the arm, and he rubbed it dramatically. "What have I said about not hittin' the driver?"

Pauli chuckled. "Well, you're not driving right this second, are you?"

Liam cleared his throat. "The thought of you two puttin' together a schedule makes me nervous. I know ya, remember?"

Dev patted his arm. "Look, you said Jake's only just come out, right?" He peered at Jake. "That right?"

"Yes." Jake's heartbeat sped up.

"Okay then. We thought he'd like to see how gay boys live in Atlanta. *And* get to see some of Caleb's favorite haunts too."

Dev's eyes sparkled. "He needs to see what life is like on the other side of the church."

Liam shook his head and met Jake's gaze. "Be afraid. Be *very* afraid." His lips twitched, however, and Jake's pulse climbed down a little. Liam leaned in close. "Don't worry. Whatever these two have in mind, I'll be right there with ya, okay?"

"Thanks," Jake whispered.

"An' now that we've got *that* all sorted, let's get goin'. We've got a lot to cram into one day." Dev pointed toward the bathroom door. "If you're gonna pee, be quick."

"Jake, have you got something with you that you can swim in?" Pauli asked abruptly.

He blinked. "Er, no. Should I have?" Liam appeared clueless too, his forehead creased into faint lines, but then his eyes widened.

Pauli waved his hand. "Don't worry. I got a pair of shorts that'll fit you." He walked across the room to another door, Dev following.

Jake turned to Liam. "Where're we goin' where I might need shorts?"

Liam scowled. "I got an idea, but if I'm right, I'm gonna kick both their asses. They should know better."

What the hell? "You gonna share?"

Liam shook his head. "Let's see if I'm right first. I reckon you'll love brunch. Joe's on Juniper is—was—one of our favorite restaurants."

Something about his expression touched Jake, and he laid his hand gently on Liam's arm. "You sure you're okay with this?"

Liam drew in a deep breath. "I'm sure. Besides, I want you to have a good time, an' Joe's is a good way to start." He glanced toward the closed door. "If those two ever get their asses in gear." Liam looked back at him, rolling his eyes.

Jake liked Dev and Pauli. It was easy to warm to them. He couldn't help wondering about their plans—and why they could possibly make Liam nervous.

Chapter Fourteen

"Are you gonna eat those sweet potato fries?" Dev asked innocently.

Jake held out his fork. "Yes. Touch one an' you're a dead man." He grinned. "You've already had five of my fried pickles—or did ya think I didn't see ya sneak 'em off my plate while Pauli distracted me?"

Dev gave Liam an approving glance. "He's quick, ain't he?"

Pauli snorted. "And more observant than Cal. I swear, the number of times I snuck food off that boy's plate…"

Jake laughed. Brunch had turned out to be a lot of fun, and that was all down to Dev, Pauli and Liam. They regaled him with stories about Caleb, some of which made him gasp. The tricks he got up to in college…

"I never knew he was such a prankster."

Liam widened his gaze. "Seriously? He an' his dorm buddies had this whole feud goin' on with the guys in the next dorm house. So Caleb decided to prove once an' for all that they were the best. Late one night, he was walkin' back to the dorm when he spied an open window next door. He rushed back to tell 'em all. Well, he got every bucket he could lay his hands on, an' filled 'em up with soapy water. Then he poured all of it through the open window, quiet as you please. Took him forever! The next mornin', all hell broke loose. The water had seeped under every door, ruining rugs, clothing, anything that had lain in its path. They suspected it was Caleb, but they couldn't prove a thing. Caleb said they made damn sure after that to lock all the windows at night."

"What about that time three years ago, during Pride, when he did himself all up in drag?" Dev shook his head. "I almost didn't recognize him."

Pauli huffed. "I could have killed him for those legs of his, especially when he wore the—"

"Ruby slippers!" Liam and Dev chimed together.

Pauli nodded. "He made the best Dorothy ever, even down to that little toy puppy dog in a basket."

"Caleb—in drag?" Jake's mind couldn't compute.

Dev cackled. "Oh Lord. You never saw him in a dress? Man, he had this gold sequin-covered number that he just—" His words tailed off, and he swallowed. "I guess you had to be there."

Pauli reached over and covered Dev's hand with his, his brown eyes filled with warmth. "I know, babe. I know."

It wasn't until that moment that something struck Jake so forcefully that it truly rocked him. He was with three gay men, and he felt… relaxed, at ease with the love Dev and Pauli shared. And that in turn opened his eyes to Caleb's situation. The reason why he'd seemed so different once he started college. Why he'd rarely come home. "I think I get it now," he said in a low voice, his appetite fled.

"You okay?" Liam's hand covered his, and concern laced his voice.

Jake attempted a smile. "Not really. I jus' realized that all those times Caleb did make it home, he must've felt so uncomfortable, because he was… hidin' who he truly was. An' after listenin' to y'all talk about him? It's like you're talkin' 'bout a different person, not the brother I knew." He sighed heavily. "You're describin' the brother I never knew I had."

"Aw, sweetheart." Pauli stretched his hand across the table to join Liam's. "I know it must be hard on you, but at least you know he was happy here."

Dev coughed. "How 'bout we take you to one of his favorite stores? Not that there's any shortage of them. Cal loved the

Ansley Mall."

"It's kind of a gay shopping center," Liam explained.

"Really?"

Liam chuckled at his expression. "Yep. Caleb used to flirt with the cute guys at Boy Next Door. 'Course, he liked to pretend I didn't notice." He snorted. "Like you could miss Caleb in full Flirt Mode." Pauli's snicker echoed his.

"I was thinkin' Jake would like Brushstrokes."

Jake was a fast learner. He knew by Dev's innocent expression that Brushstrokes wasn't gonna be a paint shop. He threw down his napkin and smiled. "Then let's go."

He also knew whatever Dev had planned would be fun, and he could use a little of that right then.

Jake got out of the car and smiled when he peered at the window of the store. "It's a bookstore." Now *that* was the Caleb he remembered. He'd always had his nose in a book.

Behind him, Liam cleared his throat. "Yes…an' no."

Before Jake could question what he meant, Pauli grabbed hold of his hand and led him to the door. "Now, you can look all you want. Touch, even. We won't mind." And with that, he pushed open the door and propelled Jake inside.

Oh. My. God. Jake was in a sex shop. Again.

"To the left is the bookstore," Liam said quietly. "To the right is the underwear, and… what you see right there."

Jake recovered quickly. "This is *not* my first time in a place like this." Except Knoxville was something he'd rather forget. This was a totally different experience. No one was gonna judge him. No one was gonna laugh or deride him for looking at the merchandise.

He was in a safe place.

Jake wandered over to the wall of dildos and vibrators, much the same as the ones he'd seen previously, but most of these had semi-naked boys on the packaging. Then there were the flashlights—only, they weren't…

"Oh, Lord," he murmured, staring at the replica of some porn star's butthole, fashioned in pink silicone.

"They feel amazing," Liam whispered. "And every gay boy needs a toy—or two."

Jake's resultant coughing fit had everyone in the store looking in his direction. The sales clerk snickered, then winked at him.

"Kinda spoiled for choice, right?"

Jake turned to Liam beside him, his eyes wide. "There is *no freakin' way* on God's green Earth that I can take *anythin'* like that home with me. Imagine if my mama found it." He couldn't even contemplate the conniption fit she'd have.

"Then you need a secure place. Even if it's a drawer with a padlock. Caleb managed it."

"Say what?" Jake gaped at him.

Liam grinned. "He told me he went to Knoxville one time, an' came back with some gay magazines. He hid 'em somewhere in his bedroom. Far as I know, they're still there." He pointed to the dildos. "So… wanna take a look?"

"I… couldn't." Except inside Jake's head, a voice was hollering, 'Sure you can!' Because the thought, the wonderfully *illicit* thought, of sliding a silicone dick into his ass was just as seductive as it had been back in Knoxville. *Jus' to know how it feels…* His mind was already mentally picturing his bedroom, searching for a hidey hole.

"I gotcha. You don't want one."

"No, I do!" Jake blurted out before he had time to put his brain into gear. His face bloomed with heat. "I mean… yeah, I do, it's just…"

Liam reached out and plucked a package from its hook on the wall. "How about this one? Not too long, not too thick. Sort of a trainer dick."

Jake was positive his face was all the shades of red on the

spectrum. "Maybe I'll come back an' look some more before we leave here." He had a sudden urge to look at books.

Books were safe.

It wasn't until he saw the covers that he realized not *all* books were safe.

"Y'all gonna tell me where we're goin'?" Jake peered through the car window at the passing scenery.

"Seein' as it's such a beautiful day, we thought you might like to hang out by a pool. There's gonna be a hot tub too." Dev glanced over his shoulder. "Does that sound like somethin' you might like?"

Jake beamed. "A hot tub? Cool." *Now* he got the shorts part.

"An' where exactly are we goin'?" Liam leaned forward. "Because it looks to me like you're headin' for Flex. An' if you *are*, I—"

"Relax," Pauli interjected, his voice soothing. "Just the pool and hot tub, okay? Dev's right, it's a perfect day to chill out by the pool."

Liam sagged back into the seat. "Okay." He didn't look happy about the prospect, however, and Jake was dying to ask what was bothering him.

As they pulled into a parking lot, Jake caught sight of a large sign. "What's a bathhouse?"

Liam, Dev and Pauli simultaneously broke into coughing fits.

Liam recovered first. "I'll tell ya later. Not that it'll matter." He glared at Dev's reflection in the rear-view mirror.

They got out of the car, and Pauli went around to the trunk to grab the shorts he'd brought along. He grinned when he saw the Brushstrokes bag Jake had tucked in there. "I see. Someone went shopping after all." Jake held his breath, but Pauli didn't open it.

Truth & Betrayal

Instead, he gave Jake a pat on the arm. "What you buy is your business, and no one else's." He thrust a pair of red shorts into Jake's hands. "Now, don't go diving into the pool and losing these. Because then you *will* have a face like a tomato."

Jake didn't doubt that for a second.

The locker room was full of guys in various stages of undress, and Jake had a hard time keeping his gaze averted, because damn, the temptation to just *stare*... Once he was in his shorts and lying on a towel-covered chair by the side of a pool filled with sparkling blue water, his embarrassment receded, and he started to relax. Liam was next to him, wearing a pair of white shorts borrowed from Dev. Jake liked the contrast of the white cotton against his skin.

Dev and Pauli were nowhere to be seen.

Jake took a sip from the bottle of water Pauli had left for him. "If I ask you somethin' personal, will you promise not to be offended?"

Liam rolled onto his side, regarding him with mild surprise. "Well, that depends on what you're about to ask."

Jake took another drink. "Do... do you tan?"

Liam blinked, then smiled. "Yes, I jus' go a darker shade, that's all."

"Okay." Jake expelled a long breath. "'M sorry, it's jus' that..."

"It's okay," Liam assured him. "I know. Black guys aren't exactly abundant in LaFollette, right? An' I'm not offended." He tilted his head to one side. "Any more burnin' questions while we're at it?" Liam seemed amused, which relieved Jake no end.

"Why weren't you happy 'bout comin' here? An' what *is* a bathhouse, exactly?"

Liam sighed. "Okay. A lot of gay men come here to do jus' what we're doin' right now—chill out by the pool, an' use the hot tub an' sauna. That's what Caleb an' me used to do here all the time. But..." He paused and took a drink from his own bottle. "It's also the type of place where, if you're lookin' for it, you can find a casual hookup."

"Seriously?" Jake propped himself up on his elbows and stared at the men lounging by the pool. Everyone was soaking up the sun, talking in low tones, or standing in the water, chatting or swimming.

Liam chuckled. "I'll admit, the first time I came here, I expected to see naked guys walkin' around everywhere, an' men havin' sex all over the place. Except when I finally got up the nerve to come here, it was actually a laid back, relaxin' kinda place." He cleared his throat. "But yeah, there are also times when the atmosphere here is totally different."

"How?"

Liam lowered his voice. "Raunchy. Intense. It can depend on what day of the week it is, or if there's an event goin' on." He grinned. "Sort of a 'choose your own adventure game' kinda place. Sometimes you do see a little light action out here. Like over there." He gestured with his head to a point over Jake's shoulder.

As casually as he could manage, Jake snuck a peek. Two guys were on the same sun lounger, making out, and he stared at them, mesmerized, as they kissed and stroked each other, nothing too graphic, but *Lord…*

"Jake. Jake!"

Liam's voice broke through, and with a supreme effort, he tore his gaze away. Liam's eyes twinkled. "You won't see anythin' too heavy, 'cause the staff try to keep that sorta thing indoors, in the rooms you can rent."

"Why would you wanna rent a room in—oh." Jake swallowed. "I see."

"Nope, you don't see, an' you're not gonna either. An' I sure as hell won't let you anywhere near the open dungeon—which is *not* what is sounds like, alright? It's just a big ol' room where anythin' goes, an' everythin's public."

Jake reflected on Liam's words. "That's why you didn't wanna come here? Because of what I might see?"

Liam gave a gentle laugh. "Look at it from my perspective.

You're nineteen, a virgin, with absolutely no experience of bein' with a lotta gay guys, in a place which is basically where guys meet up to fuck." He arched his eyebrows. "You can see why I might be a tad unhappy about the idea?"

Jake saw, alright. "You were protectin' me, weren'tcha?"

Liam nodded. "If I thought those two brought you here to find you a guy to... well, I'd have torn them both new assholes." He set his jaw.

Jake liked that Liam was looking out for him. Sorta made him feel... special. Cared for.

He glanced around them. The two guys who'd been making out had gone, and it didn't take a genius to work out why. Then a thought occurred to him. "Where are Dev an' Pauli?"

Liam's gaze met his. "In the dungeon."

Jake stared at him, his stomach clenching. "Then they—"

"They like to play, let's leave it at that."

Jake gave him a speculative glance. "How 'bout you an' Caleb? Did you ever... play?"

Liam wiped off the sweat that glistened on his lean torso. "Occasionally, but never on our own. We did share a guy now an' then."

What the fuck? Jake wasn't sure how he felt about that.

Liam glanced over at Jake. "That shocks you, doesn't it? An' you don't have to answer. I know what it's like at home. I listened to Caleb often enough. You an' him were brought up to believe sex is for marriage, right? An' when you find someone, that's it, no more foolin' around with anyone else?" He sighed. "Sorry, Jake, but that's not how it goes. Like I said, Caleb and me, we were here for what we're doin' right now—*most* of the time. But yeah, not gonna lie to ya, we had threeways." Liam locked gazes with him. "An' the only reason I'm *sharin'* this is because I happen to think it's important you see things as they really are. Monogamy is fine—if that's what you both want." He shrugged. "We didn't, an' we were both happy with that. An' in the end, that's what matters."

"Okay." Jake was over his initial shock, but he couldn't deny it felt… strange. *If they loved each other, how could they do… that?*

Liam smiled. "Your lips say okay, your face says somethin' else. I'm sorry. I should've kept my mouth shut." He drank some water, letting some of it trickle down over his chest. "You havin fun?"

"I am now." It wasn't entirely true, but Jake's stomach was on its way to settling down, and he lay back and closed his eyes. *Hey, I can't complain. He was honest with me.* Jake had wanted to know what it was like to be gay, hadn't he? Well, now he knew how a lot of gay guys lived their lives. Liam wasn't sugarcoating anything. He was being straight.

Well… not *exactly* straight.

Having Liam there made him feel safe. No matter what else Dev and Pauli had planned for the weekend, Jake knew Liam would put his foot down if he felt Jake couldn't cope.

I can see why Caleb was with him. It was a comforting thought.

Truth & Betrayal

By K.C. Wells

Chapter Fifteen

Atlanta was a damn sight noisier than LaFollette, Jake decided. It was a hot night, and with the AC being on the fritz, the window to the living room was open, and the drone of traffic was constant, even though it was past midnight. He knew it was an excuse. It could have been as silent as a grave out there, and Jake still wouldn't be asleep. The couch folded out into a comfortable bed, and Jake shoved the cushions behind his head to stare out the window at the night sky beyond.

So much to think about.

It had been a day of revelations, that was for sure.

Dinner had been pizza, accompanied by several cans of beer. Jake had drunk until the point where he was feeling pleasantly muzzy. He'd caught Liam flicking a glance now and then at the number of empty cans on the coffee table in front of him, but Jake hadn't overdone it. And thankfully, Pauli seemed in no mood to flirt, preferring to cuddle up with Dev on the other couch. More talking about Caleb, about a vacation the four of them had taken to Florida to see Pauli's family, where they'd spent day after day on the beach.

What struck him most was that Caleb had had this whole other life Jake had known nothing about.

Noise filtered through to his tired brain, and Jake tensed, trying to locate its source. He craned his neck to peer over the back of the couch. A moment later, Liam shuffled into the kitchen area, rubbing his hand over his head, a glass held in the other. He held it up to the door of the refrigerator and poured himself some water.

The blue emergency light on the wall above it bathed his white shorts in a ghostly light.

"Can't sleep neither, huh?" Jake whispered.

Liam gave a start. "Christ. Give a guy some warnin', why don'tcha? Nearly gave me a friggin' heart attack."

"I'll have some while you're over there."

Liam put down his glass, reached into the cabinet above the sink, and pulled out another. He filled it, then carried it along with his own to the couch. "Here ya go."

Jake took it. With the couch opened up, there was nowhere to sit. He patted the sheet. "Sit here if you want." He kept his voice low, for fear of waking Dev and Pauli.

Liam joined him, chuckling faintly. "Relax. You won't wake those two. Besides, can't you hear their snores from here?" He grabbed another cushion and stuffed it behind him, stretching out his long legs on the bed, crossed at the ankles. "So, why aren't you asleep?"

"It's too hot," Jake lied. That much was true. The AC being bust hadn't helped matters.

"Mm-hmm." Liam drank from his glass. "Okay, seein' as it's just us... what *did* you buy from Brushstrokes? Because you were awful sneaky about it." Before Jake could reply, he held up one hand. "'S'okay. Forget I asked. None of my business."

Jake laughed quietly. "I don't mind, seein' as it's jus' you. I bought a Fleshjack, a dildo, and some lube."

Liam didn't laugh. "Looks like you've covered all options then. Jus' make sure you do find somewhere safe for 'em. The lube, not so much. I mean, you're a guy, for Christ's sake. Even your mama must know what guys do, right?"

Jake almost choked on his water. "Would you want to explain to *your* mama what you need lube for?"

Liam snorted. "Hell no."

"You know what the worst thing was about buyin' 'em? They cost a shitload!" Thankfully Jake had brought along enough cash. Working with Daddy meant he got regular money, and some of it went right back to Mama, which was only right. But what else did he have to spend it on? Hell, the only times he went anywhere were to meet up with Pete and the others, and get wasted. Still, the price tags on the sex toys had given him pause.

Only for a second or two, mind.

Liam snickered. "I remember buyin' my first toy. I was eighteen, an' believe it or not, I bought it in Brushstrokes." He set his glass down on the floor, then stretched out again on top of the sheet. "God, this heat is oppressive, an' we're not even into August. Looks like it's gonna be a hot one."

Jake rolled onto his side, shifting his legs beneath the sheet, searching for a cool spot. "Tell me about you an' Caleb," he said softly.

A sigh passed Liam's lips, so slight that Jake only just caught it. Liam shifted onto his side, his head resting on his arm. "I s'ppose I'd better start at the beginnin'.

Jake snickered. "As long as this doesn't turn out to be as long as Lord of the Rings, or we'll still be talkin' when dawn comes."

Liam didn't react, however. "We met sometime in late spring of our first year, at a party, an' at some point durin' the evening we got into a heated debate. I thought he was an opinionated asshole. Apparently, he thought the same of me."

"Wow. What on earth were you talkin' 'bout?"

Liam chuckled. "Politics. Whether or not our troops should pull out of Iraq."

Jake frowned. "You fell out over that?"

"Fallin' out kinda implies we were friends to begin with. Plus, Sweden had just legalized same-sex marriage that May."

"Lord, surely you both agreed on that one."

Liam rolled his shoulder in as much of a shrug as he could manage lying down. "I asked him if he thought it'd ever happen here. Turned out he thought marriage was invented by straights for straights, an' he had no need of it." He laughed again. "Back then, we'd argue 'bout the least little thing."

Jake couldn't imagine how they ever got together. "How long did you stay mad at each other?"

Liam smiled. "Not sure. I mean, we ran into each other at parties, on campus… We kinda avoided each other. Then one night, a friend pointed out how similar we were. What he meant was, we were both stubborn an' argumentative."

Jake had to smile at that. "Yeah, I remember that glint in your eye when you were talkin' to Dev earlier… I could believe that 'bout you. An' as for Caleb? Not even gonna bother denyin' it."

Liam cackled. "Yeah. By this time, we were in our third year. Caleb's friends had been tellin' him I was perfect for him, an' so one day, he had enough. He marched across to me an' asked me out for a drink that night. I was so stunned, I almost fell over. Then I said yes. Caleb told me later he only did it to get 'em to shut the hell up."

"So you dated, fell in love, an' the rest is history?"

Liam fell silent, not meeting Jake's gaze.

Jake tried another tack. "D'you think you an' Caleb would've gotten married one day?" He snickered. "Unless he still had strong views about it."

Another sigh fell from Liam's lips. "No, I don't think we would've gotten married. An' that was somethin' we both felt."

Liam's words were like an electric shock to Jake's system. "But… why not? You loved each other, right?" It felt like everything he'd come to believe about his brother was suddenly vanishing into thin air, and the ground beneath his feet trembled, as if it was about to give way at any second. "I *know* you loved him. You said so, damn it, that day on the phone, remember? 'I just lost the man I loved.' Remember?"

Liam rolled onto his back, staring at the ceiling. "Fuck, this is hard."

Jake propped himself up on one elbow and gazed down at Liam in consternation. "No, it's not. Either you loved each other, or you didn't. Simple as that."

Liam reared up into a sitting position, his elbows on his knees, his head in his hands. "God, you're so fuckin' *young*. You have *no idea* what love is like outside the limits of your own experience."

"Then you didn't lo—"

"Yes, I loved Caleb, alright? I loved him, but…" Liam drew in a deep breath. "It wasn't as if we wanted to spend the rest of our lives together, declarin' undyin' love for each other. It wasn't like that at all."

Jake's heart quaked. "Then tell me the truth. What was it like?"

Liam twisted on the bed and turned to face him, sitting cross-legged, hands laced together. "Every New Year's Eve, we'd drink a toast to the comin' year, an' we'd always add… 'If we're still together.' It got to be kind of a standin' joke between us. See, we enjoyed bein' together, we loved our life together, but…. deep down, both of us were lookin' for some earth-shatterin' love we believed was out there, waitin' for us. Don't get me wrong, we had no plans to go our separate ways, because we did love each other."

"Just not enough to want to be together forever," Jake said bitterly.

To his surprise, Liam took hold of his hand. "I'm sorry if I've shattered your illusions, Jake. But that's all they were, b'lieve me. If you're lucky enough to find your soulmate, the One who completes you, then you're a lucky son of a bitch."

Jake pulled his hand free, noting the fleeting hurt that crossed Liam's face. "Did you ever read Caleb's journal?"

Liam shook his head. "That was his. That was private. Nothing to do with me. Why'd you ask?"

Jake lifted his chin and locked gazes with him. "One line from that journal has stuck with me. I can't shake it."

Liam's breathing hitched. "Tell me."

Jake focused on the words, seeing them in his head. "June 26, 2011. I think I love him."

Liam's lips parted, but no sound came out. He swallowed,

and the light from the kitchen was reflected in the tears that spilled over his cheeks.

"Liam?"

He wiped his cheeks with the back of his hand. "Pride. We'd gone to New York for Pride. We were standin' on 5th Avenue, watchin' the parade, listenin' to the lesbian and gay marchin' band, both of us lustin' after the hunky sousaphone player, and…." His eyes met Jake's. "Caleb turned to me, smiled, an' said, 'I love ya.' That was the first time he'd ever said those words to me."

Jake nodded knowingly. "An' now it makes sense. Why he wrote 'I *think* I love him.' You were right. He wasn't sure either, was he?"

Liam gulped. "Oh, God, I did love him. Just not enough." Fresh tears sparkled in his eyes, and he fell back onto the couch, his arm across his face, harsh sobs racking his body.

That was more than Jake could stand. He lay next to Liam and held him, both of them shaking, and then he too was crying, for Caleb, for Liam, for the loss that bound him and Liam together. The grief he'd held inside for so long, poured out of him in a flood that would not be stopped, and in the midst of it all, Liam reached for him too, and clung to him, both of them lost to everything but the emotional sea that tossed them back and forth.

Jake had no idea how long they stayed like that. He only knew that at some point exhaustion overcame him, and he sank deep into a dreamless sleep.

Chapter Sixteen

"Okay, this is… awkward."

Liam opened his eyes gradually as Dev's words penetrated the fog that enveloped his brain. "Huh?"

Dev stood at the foot of the sofa bed, arms folded across his chest, eyebrows arched, staring pointedly at…

Oh God. Jake was lying in Liam's arms, fast asleep, both of them beneath the sheet. *How the hell did that happen?*

Gingerly, Liam began the task of extricating himself from Jake's slumbering embrace, knowing full well Dev was watching the proceedings with a grin. Jake grumbled a little, rolling onto his side. Perfect. Liam eased himself out from under the sheet, and carefully got up from the bed.

Dev bit his lip. "Wow. I should've sold tickets."

Liam glared at him, now fully awake. "There had better be coffee on, or Pauli's gonna be wearin' black real soon," he hissed. One glance told him Jake was still sound asleep.

Dev narrowed his gaze. "I'd forgotten what a bitch you are before coffee. An' yes, it's on," he said in a whisper as he tiptoed his way around the couch.

Liam remained where he was for a moment, staring at the sleeping Jake who had since rolled onto his back again. Pauli had been correct—Jake and Caleb hadn't been physically alike. There hadn't been much to choose between Caleb's straggly, light brown hair, and Jake's dark brown hair, shorn close to his scalp, but there the similarities ended. Jake's mustache and barely-there beard, along with those striking pale green eyes, made him appear older than his nineteen years.

Nearly twenty, remember? Liam smiled. Jake obviously didn't want to be thought of as a teenager. And there were differences too in their facial structure. Caleb had been slightly rounder in the face, whereas Jake looked leaner, his cheekbones more defined. Liam stared down at Jake's face, peaceful in sleep. *Caleb was a good-lookin' dude, but you?* Jake was almost… beautiful.

"So, are you gonna let me in on whatever went down between you two?" Dev stood at the back of the couch, making an obscene gesture with his tongue in his cheek.

Liam glared and signaled for him to hush. He crept around the couch and joined Dev in the kitchen area. "Nothing happened, alright? We just…" He was momentarily lost for words as the memory of the previous night came flooding back. He hadn't meant to share any of it, but somehow his mouth had overridden his good sense. He recalled his own hot tears, trickling down his cheeks, and how they'd mingled with Jake's.

"You okay?" Dev's voice lost its humorous edge. He poured out three mugs of coffee. "Come on into our room. Sleepin' Beauty is already awake an' bitchin' for his coffee too. We can talk in there." He inclined his head toward the couch. "Let Jake sleep. He's got the drive home later. Let him rest while he can. It's not even six yet, anyway."

Liam picked up the mug Dev left him on the counter and followed Dev to their bedroom. Pauli was lying in bed, peering at his phone. He frowned when Liam entered the room, then his eyes lit up as he almost bounced into a sitting position. "Ooh, is this my lucky day? You finally agreed to a three way?"

Liam chuckled. It had been Pauli's regular joke ever since Liam and Caleb had become friends with them. All of them had known it was never going to happen: none of them wanted to ruin a perfectly good friendship.

It didn't stop Pauli from mentioning it, however.

Dev gave him his customary mock glare. "When you've

quite finished..." There was no real menace in him, and all three of them knew it. He handed Pauli a mug, then gestured to the bed. "You. Sit. Spill."

Liam sank onto the bed with a sigh of resignation. "I told you, nothin' happened," he repeated emphatically.

"Mm-hmm." Dev's eyebrows went sky high. "Wanna try that again, sugah?" He glanced at Pauli. "Him an' Jake were all cozied up in each other's arms in bed."

Pauli blinked. "O-*kay*."

"Don't listen to him, alright?" Liam blurted out. He drank a couple of mouthfuls of coffee, wincing at the heat, before telling them everything. They listened in silence, sipping coffee now and again. When he was done, Liam let out another sigh. "Heaven knows what he thinks of me now."

"Is that important? Jake's opinion of you?" Pauli's eyes gleamed.

It was, but for reasons Liam couldn't fathom. "I jus' get the feelin' he had this idyllic picture built up inside his head of how Caleb an' me were, an' I blew that all away." Like he hadn't already done that at Flex, when he'd mentioned their sex lives. *He probably thinks we were complete sluts*. They'd been far from that, of course, just ordinary gay guys with a healthy sexual appetite, who liked to spice things up occasionally.

Liam was pretty sure Jake didn't see it like that though.

"Which is better? Jake believing you and Cal were all white picket fences, a dog and a wedding in the future? Or him knowing what life is really like?" Pauli's smile was unexpectedly kind. "I know he's only nineteen, but—"

"Nearly twenty, remember?" Dev reminded him, his eyes twinkling. Liam bit back his snicker.

"Fine. But he's old enough to know the truth. Because one day he's going to meet some guy who will hopefully sweep him off his feet, and when the dust settles and he can breathe again, he needs to know the difference between reality and a fairy tale."

And with that, Liam was right back in that conversation.

"He reminded me of somethin' last night. I was twenty at the time, not much older'n' him, and a guy told me for the first time that he loved me. Back then? I wanted the fairy tale." His heart ached, but he kept hold of his emotions.

He'd cried enough.

"Caleb, right?" Dev said softly. When Liam merely nodded, Dev opened his arms, and Liam took the hug he badly needed right then. "I know, baby, I know. It's okay if you wanna let it all out."

Liam chuckled against his neck. "Trust me. I did that last night." He straightened.

Dev peered at him. "And? D'ya feel better for it?"

He ran a mental assessment and smiled. "You know what? I do."

"Cool. Now get your ass in the shower before Jake wakes up. Then we'll go for Sunday brunch at Cowtippers." He grinned. "It's the Heifer review."

Liam groaned. "You're gonna expose that innocent guy out there to drag queens?" He snorted. "He'll probably love it. He *is* Caleb's brother, after all. There have to be some similarities, right?"

Except he'd already noticed a couple. There was that thing with his hair, for one. And then there was the famous Greenwood stubborn streak for another.

Liam shook his head. What interested him more were the ways in which Jake was nothing like Caleb. The weekend had provided him with a glimpse, and he wanted to know more.

You were right, Caleb, all those times you said I'd like him. I really do.

Watching Jake's expression as he sat drinking root beer, his eyes glued to the drag queens' act, was vastly more entertaining than the review, Liam decided. From the minute the first act stepped out into the circle of chairs, he was mesmerized, his jaw dropping with regularity. Liam thought with that reaction, it was only a matter of time before one of the queens got Jake involved, but thankfully he was spared that. Liam thought Jake would probably spontaneously combust.

Pauli came back with another round of drinks. "It was quicker to do it myself. The servers are all run off their feet today." A huge crowd had turned up for the brunch, more than Liam had seen in a long while.

Applause broke out as one queen gave her final bow before exiting. Jake shook his head, his eyes bright.

"That was so much fun." He took a long pull on his straw, peering around the audience. Suddenly his eyes widened, and his mouth fell open. "Well, I'll be."

Liam twisted in his chair to see what the hell he was staring at. A guy was sitting on his own to the rear of the crowd, a glass of what looked like soda in front of him. Come to think of it, he seemed vaguely familiar. "Do you know him?"

The question was superfluous as the guy in question caught sight of Jake, and his jaw dropped. His gaze darted from side to side, as if he sought an escape route. There was no mistaking that reaction. Whoever he was, he was *not* happy about being spotted there.

"That's Officer Cox," Jake said.

"*Officer* Cox? He's a cop? I take it he's from LaFollette?" He glanced at Jake, who merely nodded. "Why do I think I've seen him someplace?"

"He was at Caleb's funeral. Said he knew Caleb from high school. An' one time he stopped me when I was drivin'... let's say I wasn't exactly sober, an' he didn't take me in or nothin'. Drove me home, in fact. *And* he didn't tell my parents."

"A good guy, then." Liam was intrigued. "I see. So he's enjoyin' a weekend in Atlanta, jus' like you."

Jake jerked his head in Liam's direction. "How *much* like me, I wonder?"

Liam knew what he was getting at, and there was only one way to solve that conundrum. "Let's go find out." Liam pushed back his chair and waited for Jake to follow suit. Dev raised his eyebrows, and Liam waved a hand. "We'll be right back." They picked their way through the tables and chairs to where the cop sat, gaping at them in undisguised horror.

"Hey," Liam said brightly. "Mind if we join ya?"

Officer Cox blinked. "Oh. Why, sure." He peered at Liam, a slight frown creasing his forehead. "Don't I know you from somewhere?" Then his eyes widened. "The funeral."

Jake gestured to Liam. "This is Liam, Caleb's… boyfriend."

Liam got Jake's hesitation. He had no way of knowing how the news would be received.

Liam had a hunch it wouldn't be an issue.

"Officer Cox, what're you—"

"Jake, you can't call me that. Not here. The name's Taylor, okay?" Taylor gave another furtive glance around them. "Look, we can't talk here. Is there somewhere else we could go? A little less crowded?"

Liam thought fast. "Smith Park is down the street. It's just a little green space, but there's a bench where we can sit an' talk. That do ya?"

Taylor nodded. "Sounds good to me." He dropped a couple of bills on the table and followed them outside. Liam got out his phone and sent a text to Dev.

BRB. Something cropped up. Do not leave without us, y'hear? He smiled to himself. That would drive Dev crazy with curiosity.

"Okay, park's over there, down Piedmont." He led them along the road to the intersection where the diamond-shaped park sat. They crossed the street and headed for the empty bench in the middle of the park. Taylor sat first, the sunlight glinting off his dark blond, cropped hair. Liam couldn't help the thought that crept into his head.

Oh my. Caleb would have loved you. Taylor was the type Caleb flirted with, especially when he was tipsy. And sometimes it got to more than flirting, especially when he turned puppy dog eyes on Liam, where he could read the unspoken question. *This one's cute. Can we?*

Like Liam could ever say no to that hopeful expression.

"What are you doin' in Atlanta?" Taylor asked Jake.

"He came to spend the weekend with me an' some friends. We all knew Caleb." Liam snickered. "But I guess you already knew that 'bout me, right?" He deliberately went for a humorous tone, because *Lord above,* Taylor seemed to be wound tighter than a clock spring. His shoulders and back were tense.

Apparently, his approach worked. Taylor relaxed a little. "Yeah. Boyfriend was a bit of a clue." He shook his head, smiling. "So Caleb was gay. Y'know, right now, God is somewhere laughin' His ass off at me."

"'Scuse me?" Jake frowned. "What's that s'pposed to mean?"

Liam had a pretty good idea what that meant, but there was no way he was about to out Taylor. That was his choice. "You don't have to answer that," he said discreetly.

Taylor regarded him with startled eyes, his lips parted. Then he sagged against the bench. "Yeah, I do. 'Bout time I told someone, right?" He gave Liam a half-smile.

Well fuck. Looks like there's nothing wrong with my *gaydar.*

Taylor addressed Jake. "It's just ironic that there I was in high school, thinkin' I was pinin' for a straight guy, an' he turns out to be gay." He paused and took a deep breath. "Jus' like me."

Liam said nothing, but patted Taylor's arm. Beside Liam, Jake gave the tiniest start, but then sat still. *Smart guy.* Taylor seemed skittish enough as it was.

Taylor let out a whoosh of air. "Whoa. That wasn't half as scary as I thought it would be." His breathing evened out a little.

"That's 'cause you know you're safe with us, right?" Liam

squeezed his arm.

Taylor gave him a grateful glance. "Yeah, I know."

Now that everything was out in the open, it all made sense. "Well, I can see why you'd come this far on a weekend off. Knoxville is too close to home, ain't it? Someone might recognize ya."

Another nod. "I figured I'd be safe here. I come here every couple of months, when I need to get away from…" He glanced at Jake. "Well, *you* know what's it's like back home."

"I surely do," Jake said with a sigh. He tilted his head to one side. "Wait a sec. You said you were pinin' for a straight guy. That was Caleb?"

Taylor was so still. "When I was maybe fifteen, I had the hugest crush on your brother. An' I mean, *huge*. I used to go places where I knew he'd be, just to watch him. The hardest part was makin' sure no one noticed me doin' it." He smiled, and just like that his face was transformed. "I even persuaded some friends to go to McDonalds the night of his graduation, 'cause I knew him an' his friends would end up there. We must've been there for two hours by the time they turned up. He looked so fine, laughin' an' jokin', not a care in the world. I couldn't take my eyes off of him."

Jake stirred beside him. "Oh my God. That was you?"

"Huh?" Taylor's brow furrowed.

Jake leaned forward, elbows on his knees, hands clasped between them. "In Caleb's journal. He wrote about that night." He gazed at Taylor. "Caleb noticed you. He thought you were beautiful."

Liam chuckled, and both Taylor and Jake stared at him. "Sorry, but you are *so* Caleb's type. Well, you were." That last thought sobered him a little.

Taylor's shoulders sagged. "I should've said somethin'."

Jake snorted. "Like what? You an' I both know what would've happened."

"True." Taylor sighed. "Don't know why I even thought of such a thing." He glanced at his watch. "Sorry, fellas, but I need to go. Got a long drive home ahead of me." He got to his feet.

"I hear ya." Jake did the same, Liam too. "I'll be heading that way soon myself." Taylor held out a hand to him, but to Liam's surprise, Jake gave him a quick hug. "Safe trip back, an' I guess I'll see you around, right?" He released Taylor, but then gripped his upper arms. Jake's breathing hitched, and Liam wondered what in the hell was coming. Because *something* surely was.

"I think it was real brave of ya to tell us. You didn't have to." Jake swallowed. "An' I'm not that far behind ya. Only Liam an' his friends know so far." His chest heaved. "An' you're right. It wasn't as scary as I thought it would be."

Taylor's eyes widened, and then he seized Jake in a fierce hug. Liam choked up for a second to see them connecting like that. When they parted, Liam hugged him too. "This is… I think this is awesome. I hated the idea of Jake havin' no one to confide in back home." Except that wasn't completely true. He'd sort of gotten used to the notion that Jake could confide in him.

Jake regarded him warmly. "But I'm not on my own anymore. I got you, right?"

After the emotional turmoil of the previous night, it was perhaps the best thing he could have said.

"You sure do."

Chapter Seventeen

Jake opened the front door, and the delicious aroma hit his nostrils almost immediately. He smiled to himself. Supper time. He'd texted Mama when he'd gotten to the outskirts of Knoxville, figuring she'd want some idea of when he'd arrive home.

"That you, Jacob?"

"Yes, Mama."

"Supper'll be ready in ten minutes. Go fetch your daddy, will ya? He's in his woodshed."

"Sure, Mama." He didn't go into the kitchen, however, but took his bag to his room. The thought of Mama going through it for laundry sent shivers tripping down his spine. "Be right with ya." He closed his bedroom door, and scanned the room, searching for a hiding place for his purchases. His drawers were a definite no-go area, and that went double for under the bed. That left his closet. He went inside and peered up at the shelves. There were boxes piled up to the ceiling, containing stuff from when he was a little kid, things he'd never looked at in years. His mama would never throw stuff out.

Then again, when was the last time she looked in any of 'em?

Jake stretched up on his toes, eased a box off the shelf, and carried it to his bed. Inside it were several different colored booties, a folded baby blanket, and lots of things that left him speechless. *Why in the hell would his mama keep a tooth, wrapped in tissue in a little matchbox?* Then he looked again at the cover. *Jacob's first tooth. Mama, really?* There was also a rattle in bright colors.

Thankfully, there was space inside for toys of a different kind.

Jake opened his backpack and pulled out the bag from Brushstrokes, tossing aside his clothes. He shoved it into the box, put the lid back on, and replaced it on the high shelf. No sooner had he closed the closet than his mama tapped on the bedroom door.

"Jacob, I thought I asked you to—"

Jake dove across the room and flung open the door. "Sorry, Mama. I was jus' puttin' my things in here. I figured you'd want my laundry." He went back to the bed and removed the rest of his clothing from the backpack.

Mama chuckled. "Since when do you do that without me hollerin' at ya? Your new friends in Atlanta are havin' a good influence on you." She peered at him. "How was your weekend?"

Jake took a moment to breathe. "It was awesome. Caleb's friends are good people, an' it was good to talk 'bout him."

Mama studied him carefully. "You look better." She hesitated before continuing. "D'you think you'll go there again?"

He'd been thinking about that all the long drive home. If the opportunity came up to spend time with Dev, Pauli and Liam in the future, Jake would jump at the chance. He'd felt comfortable around them.

Maybe that's because I could be me.

"As long as Daddy can spare me," he said, not wanting to appear too enthusiastic. He didn't want Mama asking lots of questions that he had no desire to answer.

"An' speakin' of your daddy..." Mama's eyes sparkled.

Jake snickered. "I'll go get him." He went toward the door, but Mama stopped him with a hand to his arm.

"Forgotten somethin'?" When he gave her a quizzical look, she grinned. "Laundry."

Damn. Jake scooped up his dirty clothes from the bed and stepped past Mama to take them into the utility room off the kitchen.

Next time you tell a lie, remember it? Not that he lied all that often, especially to his mama. She sensed untruth like a bat homing in on a bug, and it gave him an uneasy feeling in his belly that he was keeping something from her.

It's better this way. Finding out I'm gay would be like openin' up a hornets' nest.

No wonder Caleb stayed away.

Jake stepped out onto the back porch and took a moment to inhale the heady aroma of jasmine. Atlanta seemed like a different planet now that he was back home. Seeing guys walking hand in hand as they shopped had been a jolt at first, but one he'd quickly assimilated. Not only that—he envied them their freedom.

What stayed with him most was Saturday night, however.

Letting out the grief he'd fought so hard to restrain had been a cathartic experience. Sharing that moment with Liam had been…

Unforgettable.

He had a hazy recollection of waking during the night at some point, feeling safe. He wasn't sure if he'd imagined Liam lying with him beneath the sheet, holding him like he was something precious. If so, he had a vivid imagination, because he could still feel Liam's arms around him, the soft skin of his bare chest against Jake's cheek. He only knew that when he opened his eyes that morning and found himself alone in the bed, his first emotion had been one of having lost something.

What followed that was a hefty dose of guilt. Because no matter what their relationship had been exactly, Liam had still been Caleb's boyfriend, and enjoying being held by him felt… awkward.

Jake had watched Liam carefully throughout the morning and during lunch, but Liam hadn't acted any differently compared to the previous day, and after a while Jake became more convinced it had been a dream.

A really good dream, with an almost illicit feel to it.

Pull yourself together. Jake stepped off the porch and went in search of his daddy.

Back to reality.

Liam turned onto the driveway and drove up to the garage door. It was almost midnight, and he was surprised to see a light on in the kitchen. He collected his bag from the trunk, locked up, and made his way across the patio to the back porch. No sooner had he locked the door behind him, than he caught his mom's soft voice.

"Hey, baby." She was sitting at the breakfast bar, her laptop open in front of her, and a pile of folders beside her. Mom tilted her cheek to accept his kiss. "It's late. You must be tired." She nodded toward the coffee machine. "There's decaf if you're interested."

Liam peered into the mug sitting next to the laptop. "You need a top-up?"

She smiled. "I'm good. Besides, I should think about going to bed soon."

He dropped his bag beside the bar, poured himself a coffee, and sat on the high stool beside her. "Isn't this a little late for ya?" Mom was generally an early-to-bed kinda person.

She sighed. "It's this damn case. And no, I can't talk about it, so don't ask." She shivered. "Trust me, you wouldn't wanna know anyhow." She saved her file and closed the laptop, before removing her glasses and placing them on the countertop. Liam put his arm around her shoulders, and she put her head against his chest. "Lord, but there are some evil folks in this world."

He kissed her forehead. "That's why you work in Social Services. To stop those evil folks." Mom was the Child Protective Services Program Manager for New Hanover County.

She sighed again. "Yeah, but as soon as we nail one of 'em, another pops up, like that game you kids used to love in those amusement arcades when we went to the beach. What was it called?"

"Whack-a-mole." Liam gave her another kiss. "Jus' keep on hittin' 'em, Mom, that's the important thing."

She straightened. "Anyhow, never mind me. How was your weekend?" Her eyes twinkled. "Dev and Pauli missed you much yet?"

He laughed, keeping it low. "I guess. It was good to see them."

Mom inclined her head toward the coffee machine. "You know what? I *will* have some coffee. Just half a mug, mind you."

She didn't fool him none. Coffee at this hour meant only one thing in his mom's vocabulary—*let's talk*.

Liam got up and refilled her mug, then rejoined her. "Okay, what's on your mind?" He snickered when she widened her gaze. "Yeah, right. That look hasn't fooled me since I was in twelfth grade."

Mom chuckled, reached over to the letter rack on the wall, and handed him two long envelopes. "These came yesterday."

Liam tore open the first one and unfolded the stiff white paper. His heart sank as he took in the letter. "Well, shoot. Another rejection." He'd applied for a job at a bank in Wilmington—several banks, to tell the truth—and so far, he wasn't having much luck getting through the front door.

"There's something out there for ya," Mom assured him.

He was seriously starting to doubt that. Quitting his job and leaving Atlanta had been a wrench, but it had felt like the right thing to do. Only now he was beginning to regret that decision.

Liam opened the second envelope, and relief flooded through him. "Hey, I got an interview next week."

"Where?"

"Bank of America Financial Center on North 3rd Street." Maybe there was light at the end of the tunnel after all. At least it was a step in the right direction.

Mom chuckled. "You get *that* job, and maybe we need to talk about finding you a place of your own. You *know* I love having you at home, baby, but—"

"But you want your office back, I get it." Mom had turned his old room into her work space once he'd left home for good.

Bookcases lined one entire wall, and there was a large desk in front of the window. He was sleeping on the sofa bed but was conscious of disturbing her routine. The alternative would've been to share with his brother, Will, who was home from college for the summer.

Yeah, like Will would go for that *idea*. Not that Liam could blame him. Will was twenty, way too old to be sharing with his big brother. His sister Rachel was still at home too. She'd just graduated and was considering her options. Liam didn't think she'd stick around North Carolina, not when there were better opportunities further afield.

Mom took a sip of coffee. "So… want to tell me what was so all-fired important that you had to go back to Atlanta? 'Cause I doubt it was to hang out with your friends." She put down her mug and gazed at him. "I don't mean to pry, but you haven't talked much since…"

Since Caleb died. Mom might not have said the words, but they hung there in the air.

"I've been dealin' with it in my own way." Except Liam's way was to say as little as possible.

"Mm-hmm."

It always amused him how much his mom could convey with that particular reaction.

"Baby, I know you miss him. That's only natural."

Liam couldn't lie to her. "Yeah, I miss him, but not as much as I think I should."

Mom cocked her head. "Or do you mean as much as everyone *else* thinks you should?"

Damn it. Liam bit his tongue, choosing instead to drink his coffee.

"I'm not blind, honey. How many years did Caleb come here? Five, six? Enough for me to see how things were between ya."

"What do you mean?" Liam stared at her, aghast. *Just how much did she see?*

Mom gazed into her coffee mug. "I remember when I first

met your dad. We were nineteen, but he wasn't my first boyfriend, more like the third, I think. Anyhow, I can recall going out for dinner when we'd been together a year. He gazed at me across the table, and I swear, that look in his eyes left me humbled, amazed, and weak at the knees."

"That had to be some look," Liam commented.

Mom's smile reached her eyes. "It was. It told me in no uncertain terms that he loved me, heart, body and soul. That he'd do anything for me. It was a look I'd hadn't met in any of my previous beaux, and in that moment, I knew why."

"Why?" Liam was captivated by the expression on her face. Mom almost… glowed.

She lifted her chin and locked gazes with him. "Because I hadn't been in love with them, nor they with me. Not like your dad and me. I knew then that this was the real deal." Mom reached out and cupped Liam's cheek. "And I sort of got the idea that it wasn't the real deal for you and Caleb. That look was… missing, somehow." She stroked his cheek. "Now, I don't doubt for a minute that you loved him, baby, in your own way, but…"

"But I didn't look at him like he hung the moon, right?"

Mom slowly lowered her hand. "Yeah. That."

Liam sighed. "Saturday night, I was telling someone the very same thing."

"Who?"

Okay, confession time. "I finally met Jake, Caleb's little brother." *Only he's not so little, and a whole lot different to what I expected.*

Mom blinked. "This weekend? How did that come about? Did he happen to be in Atlanta?"

Liam put down his mug and held up his hands. "Whoa. One question at a time." He started at the beginning, telling her everything, from Caleb turning up at the apartment to arranging to meet him in Atlanta.

Mom narrowed her gaze. "You've had all this going on for over a month and you're only telling me now?"

"Like I said, I was… dealin' with stuff."

She gave him a speculative glance. "Well? What's he like? Is he like Caleb? Besides the being gay part."

"Not really, either in looks or personality. Except… he's as god-awful stubborn as Caleb, that's for sure." Liam let out a quiet chuckle.

"Oh Lord." She finished her coffee, then put down her mug. "So is that it then? You don't get to meet him again?"

"I don't think so." If he got this job, there'd be no time for gallivanting off to Atlanta, not when that meant a seven hour drive each way. The thought saddened him. He'd enjoyed spending time with Jake.

Mom straightened. "I have an idea." Her eyes sparkled.

"Oh, God help us, I know that look." Liam folded his arms. "Go on, lay it on me."

"Well, seeing as it's my birthday at the end of the month, and it's a… special one…"

He snickered. "I'd say the big 5-0 is pretty special."

Mom covered his mouth with her hand. "Do *not* say that out loud again, Liam Everett Miller. I'll own to it being special, but that is *all*." Slowly she removed her hand.

Liam tried to keep a straight face. "Go on with your idea."

"Invite Jake to spend my birthday weekend here."

Okay, he hadn't seen *that* coming. "Why would he do that?"

"His brother was a part of all our lives for the past six years. And judging by what you've told me, spending time with Jake has been good for you. Plus, I know why Caleb came here so often. I think we should provide Jake with the same… refuge." She peered at him. "Unless things have changed, and his parents have now decided they're happy to embrace a gay son?" When he remained silent, she nodded knowingly. "As I thought. Okay then. Invite him to stay."

"And where exactly will he sleep?"

She pointed to the den. "We *do* have another sofa bed, as

you well know, and it's pretty comfortable. Jake can sleep there."

"You've made your mind up, haven't you?"

Mom laughed. "You know me so well."

A cough startled him, and Liam turned his head toward the door. Dad stood there in his dark blue robe, arms folded, eyes heavy with sleep.

"Do you think this is a conversation that could keep until daylight? Because *you* may not have work tomorrow, but your mom certainly does. And I don't think she wants to be drinking several pots of coffee to keep awake." He gave Mom a mock glare. "And *you* should know better."

Mom rolled her eyes. "I just wanted to stay up until he got home safe, that's all."

Dad arched his eyebrows. "Well, your baby's home. He's goin' to bed. So are you. An' heaven help the pair of you if I'm bleary-eyed tomorrow. I'm meetin' with a new client, an' I want to sound enthusiastic about his exciting new project."

"Okay, okay, we got the message." Liam gave his dad an apologetic glance. "Sorry for disturbin' your beauty sleep."

Dad snorted. "Like any amount of sleep could improve *my* looks." He smiled wearily. "Glad you're home safe." He trudged out of the room, heading toward their bedroom.

Liam placed the mugs in the sink, then picked up his bag. "You go on to bed. I'll make sure everywhere's locked up here."

Mom kissed his cheek. "Night, baby. Sleep well. Pleasant dreams." She hesitated. "I suppose sleeping alone after all these years takes some getting used to."

Ain't that the truth? "Sometimes I wake up in the middle of the night, an' I think he's gone to the bathroom. Then I remember." Liam pasted on a half-smile. "At least I get to keep the covers now. An' it's a damn sight quieter."

Mom shook her head and covered her mouth, clearly biting back a chuckle. "Bad boy." She followed Dad, her shoulders shaking slightly.

Liam took a last glance around, checking the back door,

Truth & Betrayal

before creeping past Will's room to get to his mom's study. He knew there was no chance of disturbing his brother—waking Will was like trying to rouse a vampire during the hours of daylight. Once inside the room, he shucked off his clothes and crawled into the bed. There seemed little point in folding it away every morning, not when he was staying there indefinitely.

Liam pulled the sheet up over him and lay on his back, staring at the shadows that danced on the ceiling. He had to admit, he liked the idea of inviting Jake to his mom's birthday celebrations, if only because it gave him another opportunity to spend more time with him.

I hope he says yes.

It was then Liam realized just how big an impression Jake had made on him.

Chapter Eighteen

"Pass me that saw, will ya?"

Jake did as instructed, his heart heavy. Conversation with his daddy during the last week had amounted to little more than requests and instructions. Lord knew, Jake had tried to draw him out, talking about sports, local gossip, *anything* to get him talking, but Daddy hadn't taken the bait once.

Is this how it's gonna be from now on? Because Jake didn't think he could stand much more of this. When he got home every evening, things weren't much better there. Mama was usually at the church or doing something for the church. Jake knew it was her mechanism for coping, but what with his daddy's reluctance to talk, and her continued absence, it didn't feel like a home anymore.

Caleb's passing had stolen the life right out of it.

"Jacob!"

Jake gave a start. "Yes, sir." He pushed aside his reflections and concentrated on doing what his daddy paid him for.

When Saturday morning arrived, bringing with it a text from Pete, asking if Jake wanted to 'do something', he leaped at the chance. It didn't matter none that he knew what lay in Pete's heart. Jake wasn't about to come out to his friends, and he could hide how he felt as long as he needed to. But *Christ*, he needed an outlet, and in Pete's vocabulary, 'do something' amounted to weed, alcohol, or both.

Jake was fine with whatever Pete had in mind.

He went into the kitchen. It came as no surprise that Mama wasn't there. Instead, there was a note on the kitchen table. *Gone to the church. Back later.* Jake helped himself to a bowl of cereal, and sat down, eating mechanically. The house was silent, so he imagined Daddy was in his woodshed, or else he'd gone out.

Jake's birthday would be in a matter of weeks, but he felt in no mood to celebrate. It wasn't as if his parents would do much in the way of celebration anyhow, and twenty wasn't anything special. The most he could hope for was to spend some time with his friends.

And there was the heart of what ailed him.

Since the trip to Knoxville, he saw them in a completely different light. In Jake's mind, friends supported each other, rooted for one another. He couldn't picture a time where he would feel comfortable coming out to them, and if he couldn't share something so… vital with them, then how could he consider them friends?

Jake had never felt so alone in his life.

He washed his bowl, left it on the rack, and went out onto the back porch to see if his daddy needed any help. Not that he expected that to be the case. Daddy wasn't working in his woodshed—he was hiding. Or maybe 'avoiding' was a better way of putting it.

"Hey, Daddy? You need a hand?"

The only response to his holler was from the birds in the trees, who rose up into the air, flapping their wings in protest.

No Daddy.

Curious, Jake walked around to the front of the house. No truck either.

Guess I'm home alone. Far from saddening him, the news brought him some small relief. He could deal with his own company: tiptoeing around Mama and Daddy made for a tiring life sometimes. All he wanted was for things to return to normal, only he knew there wasn't a hope in hell of that happening. Things would never be normal again, even if the coming years worked their magic and dulled the sharpness of their grief.

There would always be a Caleb-shaped hole in there somewhere.

For some reason, his mind strayed to the bag safely hidden in his room. Jake hadn't even opened it since he'd returned from Atlanta. It wasn't that he was nervous about the prospect—well, not exactly—but it felt weird to consider playing with his new toys while Mama and Daddy were in the house. A situation that wasn't going to change anytime soon, unless he got a lot bolder, of course…

Well, they're not here now, are they?

Lord. He couldn't—could he?

Make your mind up. They could walk through that door any second now.

That was enough to put a burr up his ass. He ran to his room, went inside and bolted the door. Just in case. Mama had been known to walk right in, even after knocking.

His heart pounding, he hurried over to the closet, stretched up to reach the box, yanked off the lid, and retrieved his prize. Jake sat on the bed and stared at the two packages, plus the bottle of lube. His heartbeat didn't seem to want to climb down anytime soon.

Oh my. Which one do I try out first? Just looking at them made his balls tingle. *Okay, let's look at this logically.* Then he stopped himself. This was one crazy, fucked-up situation. What the hell did *logic* have to do with anything?

He thought about lubing up the dildo, and his nuts tightened. There was his answer. The Fleshjack first, then the dildo when he was relaxed enough to enjoy it.

Jake kicked off his sneakers, shucked off his shorts, and lay on the bed, his head on a pile of pillows. He thought briefly about propping a mirror at the foot of the bed, because *damn it*, he wanted to see what it looked like, but time was of the essence. He ripped the packaging apart, glancing at the instructions. *I mean, it's pretty obvious how to use it, right?*

Then he looked closer. Something about submerging it in warm water for fifteen minutes, so that it felt more like a real body. *Fuck that. I might not* have *fifteen minutes.* That luxury would have to wait for another time.

Jake removed the cap and stared at the smooth, pink silicone. He ran his fingers over it, pushing the tip of one inside. Oh *Lord*, that was tight. Soft too, almost like skin. It gave him a thrill to think of plunging his dick into that small opening, feeling it squeeze his cock with just the right amount of friction.

Then he laughed to himself. *If I ever doubted before now that I was gay...* Except wanting to slide into a tight ass didn't make him gay, right? It wasn't only gay guys who took it up the butt these days, after all. Lots of girls did too, if Pete and Mike were to be believed. Not that he had any desire to fuck a—

For fuck's sake, will you just get on with it?

Jake inserted a single finger into the opening—and encountered the hard edge of a plastic tube. *Yikes*. Well, *that* was coming out. No wonder it had felt tight. He removed it quickly and upended the bottle of lube, squeezing it generously into the orifice. Then he read the instructions again. 'It is not good to use too much lubricant.'

Well fuck.

Jake put the lube on the nightstand, then pumped his dick, staring at the pink hole he was about to penetrate. The combination of sight and imagination was enough to have him hard within a very short space of time, and his fingers trembled as he brought the pink silicone to kiss the head of his dick. A slow push inside, a feeling of cool slickness, and...

Jesus, Mary and Joseph. That felt *amazing*.

And *that* sounded like his daddy's truck.

I do not fuckin' believe this!

Jake pulled his dick free, which dripped lube all over his bed, and shoved the Fleshjack under his pillow. Cleaning it would have to wait until he knew he had privacy. His cock was shriveling with each passing second, and he hastily wiped it on the sheet before scrambling to put on his shorts. That icky feeling made him squirm, but there was no time for more of a clean-up.

"Jacob? Where are ya? I need a hand with the lumber."

Aw fuck. He'd only gone to the supply company. Jake took a glance in the mirror to check there were no stains anywhere, before heading to the door. One last look at his bed, however, had him diving across the room to stash the lube in the nightstand drawer.

I am not built for subterfuge. Now he understood Taylor Cox's remark about God laughing His ass off.

God sure has a twisted sense of humor.

Jake paused before unbolting his door, and sent a text to Pete. *Meet up later?*

The reply was swift. *U know it. Will pick u up at 8. Quarry? D has some good shit.*

At last, Jake's day was finally looking up.

So much for an afternoon to myself.

After helping his daddy shift lumber from the truck to the woodshed, Jake had been roped into helping him sort through all the chaos of tools, nails, screws, and odd pieces of wood that he'd accrued. He knew when his daddy got like this, the easiest thing was to go along with it.

When it came down to it, the afternoon wasn't so bad. He had to admit, he and Daddy worked well together. Lord knew, they'd been doing it for long enough. And if it made life easier, then so much the better. By the time they'd finished, Jake was dripping with sweat and in dire need of a shower.

"You did good, son." Daddy patted him on the back. "An' seein' as I'm in such a good mood, you can use the bathroom first." He grinned. "Jus' make sure you leave me some water?"

Jake laughed. "I'll think about it," he joked, then ducked to miss his daddy's arm swipe. He walked into the kitchen and gazed in surprise at the table. "Wow, Mama. Jus' how many of us are you expectin' for supper?" There was cold chicken, Mama's could-not-be-beaten potato salad, her homemade slaw, a bowl of tossed salad, and bread rolls that smelled like they'd just left the oven.

Mama beamed. "You boys bin workin' hard. Don't that deserve a reward?" Jake snuck a hand toward one of the bread rolls, and she slapped it hard. "Hands off. That's for supper. An' if you don't take a shower real soon, you won't be gettin' anywhere near it. You'll be drawin' flies an' bugs from miles around."

Jake gaped in mock surprise. "Why, Mama. Are you sayin' I smell like shit?"

She giggled. "Like twenty pounds of it, in a ten-pound bag. Now git." She flicked his ass with a towel, and he took a side step, neatly avoiding it. Laughing to himself, he headed for his room to divest himself of his offensive-smelling clothing. Once inside, however, he realized he had unfinished business to attend to.

There was a Fleshjack to clean up, plus sheets to be changed. *Damn.*

Jake stripped the bed, dumping the linen onto the floor, then went into his closet to grab clean sheets from the pile Mama left in there. He couldn't risk leaving the task until after the shower, for fear she'd come in.

That left his sex toy.

Jake stared at it, shaking his head. *You're gonna have to wait.* As for cleaning it...

He wrapped a towel around his hips, got another from the closet, and bundled the toy inside it. Thankfully there was no sign of either of his parents when he stepped out of his room, and he hurried to the bathroom.

You'd think with his skills, Daddy would've found a way to put another bath in this place, even if it meant turnin' a closet into a shower. Three adults plus one bathroom was a recipe for hell to his way of thinking.

Once he was under the warm water, soaping up his body, the thought did occur to him that this could be the perfect opportunity to try it out. Then he reconsidered. Even that first short experience had felt awesome, and the chances of him making himself come in the shower *and* not making too much noise?

Yeah, nonexistent.

Jake contented himself with cleaning the toy under the jets. All he had to do then was sneak it into his room again. He mentally crossed his fingers that his parents were nowhere near. He dried off quickly, then repeated the action with the spare towel, only just reaching his bedroom door as Daddy came into view. He closed the door behind him and bolted it, heaving a huge sigh of relief.

Nope. Definitely not cut out for subterfuge.

His room once again fit to pass his Mama's eagle-eyed inspection, Jake headed for the kitchen. Laughter stopped him as he passed the dining room, not that they used it as such. Mama had her sewing machine set up in there, and her dress form that had belonged to Grandma. He peered inside, intrigued, and—

What the hell?

Except Hell was definitely *not* the word to be using in the circumstances, not when Mama and Daddy were sitting at a fully laid-out dining table, chatting with Sarah Hubbert.

The eighteen-year-old daughter of Reverend Hubbert.

Who was apparently staying for supper.

Chapter Nineteen

"Jacob!" Mama beamed at him. "We have a guest for supper. Come an' say hi." Beside her, Sarah gave him a dazzling smile, and Daddy leaned back in his chair, looking… smug.

Okay, just what is goin' on here?

Jake stepped into the room, almost feeling like he was back at school, walking into a classroom to find there was a test he hadn't known was coming, one he sure as hell hadn't prepared for. He gave Sarah a polite nod, then pulled out a chair and sat down. Jake kept his features straight. "I'm sorry. I had no idea we were expectin' comp'ny."

"Well, it was sort of a last minute kinda thing." Mama looked awful pleased with herself for some reason. "I was at the church this mornin', an' Sarah was helpin' her daddy out, gettin' ready for the service tomorrow mornin'. She asked after you, an' said she hadn't seen much of you lately. So I thought it would nice if she came to share supper with us."

I'll just bet you did. For one brief moment it came to Jake that maybe he was being unfair, that it had happened exactly as Mama related. Then he realized his initial instincts were probably spot on. He was nineteen, nearly twenty, and hadn't brought home *one girl* to meet them. For LaFollette, that was an awfully late age to reach without having shown *some* interest in girls. Another thought sent cold shivers through him.

You tryin' to marry me off, Mama?

Not that he recalled her doing anything similar with Caleb. There hadn't been any mention of her doing such a thing in Caleb's journal either. *But Caleb wasn't around here enough, was he? A bit difficult to find your son a wife if he's never here, right?*

Whereas Jake was a sitting duck, about to be served up with orange sauce.

His gut clenching, Jake forced a smile. "It's good to see ya, Sarah. It has been a while." He reached for the plate of cold chicken and helped himself to a couple of pieces, before handing it over to her. "So, how are things?" He had no clue what she did with her days. Like a lot of LaFollette's youth, she hadn't gone to college, so he imagined she was living at home, spending her time practicing to be some good man's wife.

"Oh, you know. Mostly I help my mom at home, an' sometimes I go with her when she visits folks." Sarah flashed that dazzling smile again. "Mrs. Greenwood, this looks just delicious."

"You should try her potato salad," Daddy said, handing her the bowl. "It's her own recipe."

"Really?" Sarah took a large spoonful and tried it. "Oh my. This is awesome. You'll have to give me the recipe."

Mama just glowed. "Sorry, but that's a family secret. The only person who'll get to see that will be my future daughter-in-law."

Good Lord, Mama, could you make it any more obvious? A wicked thought snuck in, and Jake pushed it aside. Telling his mama that her secret recipe was gonna die with her would *not* be the way to go. Much as she was *aggravating the pants off of him* right that second, he would never willingly hurt her feelings. Instead, he went for handing Sarah the bowl of slaw. "This is just as good."

Sarah helped herself to a small portion, then put down the bowl, smiling as she surveyed the covered table. "This is real nice. An' what a lovely room."

Jake couldn't ignore *that* opening. "It is, isn't it? Usually you can't move in here for bolts of fabric, sewin' machines, paper patterns an' a huge dress form that hulks in that corner over there. You're honored. We normally eat on our knees in front of the TV, or else we're in the kitchen."

Yup, that got Mama glaring, but Jake was past caring. He hated being ambushed.

Daddy cleared his throat. "You'll have to forgive Jacob. Anyone would think he wasn't used to comp'ny." He leveled a firm stare in Jake's direction. "Maybe after supper you'd like to show Sarah our back yard. You know how proud your mama is of her flower beds."

Hell. No. "That's a great idea," Jake said smoothly, "but Pete is comin' by to pick me up at eight."

Mama's eyes widened. "You didn't say you were goin' out."

Jake shrugged. "Didn't I? Must've been a last minute kinda thing." Her gaze narrowed ever so slightly, and Jake knew he'd hit his mark. "An' it's not like I knew we were havin' Sarah 'round for supper, right?" Ordinarily he wouldn't have been this ornery, but being blindsided had left him feeling out of sorts and prickly as hell. So maybe they wouldn't have done this if they'd known he was gay. Maybe this was his fault for not sharing that vital piece of information.

Then again, maybe not. What burned him was the way they'd gone about it. And now that he thought about it, if they *had* known he was gay? They'd probably have gone and done it anyhow, in the belief that a good church girl would 'fix' everything.

Well, Jake Greenwood did *not* need fixing.

The rest of supper proved uneventful. Mama and Daddy were quieter, and Jake felt a little sorry for Sarah, who probably had no clue what was going on. Probably. She wasn't *that* stupid. Jake knew from listening to Pete and the others that a helluva lot of girls from their year were already married and starting families. There *were* a couple of them that had stuck their feet in and refused to be 'pushed' into marriage by their families, but that had only served to convince Dan and Mike that they were lesbians.

Talk about a narrow world view...

After supper, Jake took a moment to show Sarah the back yard, not wanting to come across as a *complete* asshole. She made the right noises about the flowers, and even praised the tree house, but when they were at some distance from the house, she reached out and caught Jake's hand.

"I'm sorry," she said softly.

"What for?" Jake glanced down at their joined hands, and she broke the contact.

"Your mama said you were havin' a bad time, that Caleb's… passin' had really taken its toll. She seemed to think some company would help that." Her cheeks flushed. "I jus' think she went about it—"

"Like a bull at a gate?" Jake suggested. Sarah covered her mouth and giggled, and he had to smile too. "Look, Sarah, I'm sure you're a nice girl an' all, but… I don't want to date ya. I don't wanna date *anybody*. Nothin' personal." He could barely keep track of his own emotions right then: the idea of adding someone *else's* into the equation freaked the shit out of him.

She sighed. "Yeah, I figured as much. Pity, because you are real cute." She bit her lip, and he sensed it wasn't out of some desire to appear coy. "To be honest, I did wonder at first if your reaction was anythin' to do with… my dad. You know, preacher's daughter? A lot of guys from high school found that a bit of a turn-off." Then she shuddered. "Of course, there *were* those who saw it as a challenge." Sarah stuck out her chin. "I soon showed *them* the door."

Jake laughed. "Wow. I'd pity any guy who crossed ya. An' for the record? It wouldn't matter who your daddy is, alright? I still wouldn't be interested." It was only a second or two later that he realized he'd come perilously close to outing himself. He prayed Sarah wasn't smart enough to read between the lines.

"Thanks for being so…"

"Blunt?" It was Jake's turn to sigh. "I'm sorry too. Mama rubbed me up the wrong way, an' I jus' fired without aimin'. I didn't mean to upset ya. Like I said, I'm sure you're a nice girl, but—"

"Can I quit while I'm ahead?" she asked, laughing.

"Sure." He shook her hand. "Thanks for comin' to supper. I'd ask you to come again, but Mama would definitely get the wrong idea."

"Yeah, I can see that." She glanced at the petite watch on her slim wrist. "Your friend will be here soon. Pete?" She frowned. "Would that be Pete Delaney?" When he nodded, her frowned deepened. "I see."

With a flash of insight, Jake knew the source of her discomfort. "Lemme guess. He's one of those guys who sees you as a challenge."

"Got it in one."

"Thank God not all of us are like Pete, then." Jake led her toward the house, where Mama was waiting on the back porch, watching their approach.

Sarah leaned in. "No. Some of y'all are perfect gentlemen," she said in a low voice. She gave Mama a winning smile as they drew near. "Thank you again for the invitation, Mrs. Greenwood. Supper was amazing, an' I had the best time."

Jake put his hand to the small of her back. "We were glad you could join us." Mama's eyes shone with approval, and he knew he'd made up a little for his earlier rudeness.

But it's not gonna go anywhere, Mama, so don't go gettin' any ideas.

The squeal of brakes and the sound of gravel flying told him Pete had arrived. He said goodbye to Sarah, then hugged Mama. "I won't be back late, I promise." He kissed her cheek, then ran around the side of the house to where Pete was tapping his fingers on the steering wheel, while Mike sat beside him, grinning, and Dan sat in the back of the truck, gesturing to him.

Jake clambered up onto the flatbed of the truck, which was covered by a worn, dirty mattress and several bits of sacking. Dan patted the backpack that sat in his lap.

"Ready for a good time?"

Jake rolled his eyes. "Could ya at *least* wait until we're out of earshot of my folks? I don't want 'em thinkin' I'm off doin' drugs."

Dan waited until the truck had hit the road before grinning at him. "But we *are* off doin' drugs, Jakey-boy!"

"Yeah, but they don't need to know that, right? An' while we're on the subject, neither does every person we pass, so jus' do me a favor an' shut the fuck up 'til we get to the quarry?"

"Jesus!" Dan gaped at him. "Who pissed *you* off?" Then he snorted. "Like I have to ask." Dan patted Jake's knee. "Don't worry. A little of what I got in here, an' soon all your worries will go floatin' off into the wind."

Jake could really do with a little of that right then.

"Damn."

Jake didn't bother to look at Dan, who was sitting on the roof of the truck's cab. He was too busy stargazing. "Whassup?" He lay on the flatbed, hands tucked behind his head, staring up at the beautiful night sky strewn with tiny pinpricks of light. The moon flooded the deserted quarry with a bluish light, providing plenty of illumination.

"We've run out of weed."

Beside Jake, Mike snorted. "Where you bin, dumbass? We ran out an hour ago."

"An' *you're* the main reason we ran out, fucker," Pete added.

"Hey! It is—well, it *was*—my weed, right? Didn't see *you* contributin' to the pot." Dan giggled. "Hey. I said pot."

Mike reached into his bag and pulled out a dark bottle with a cork shoved in it. "Okay, I was savin' this, but it looks like we're gonna have to break into the reserves."

Jake peered at it. "What you got in there?" Then he got it. "Oh, sweet Jesus. Not your granddaddy's moonshine?"

Mike beamed, nodding furiously. "I snuck it out of his barn the last time we visited. Lord knows why he keeps it in there." He shivered. "I made sure I got the right stuff this time."

Jake rolled onto his belly and gazed at him with interest. "Why? What's the wrong stuff, if there *is* such a thing?"

Mike clutched his chest. "One time, I tried to sneak some out, only he caught me, the ol' bastard. He made me swallow a teaspoon of it."

Pete cackled. "For real? A teaspoon? That all?"

Mike nodded again, only this time more slowly. "Yeah, but this was 180 proof."

"Holy shit." Dan scrambled down off the roof and landed with a thump on the flatbed. He didn't seem to notice. "What did it taste like?"

Mike chuckled. "How 'n' the hell would I know? I was too busy clutchin' my burnin' throat." That got all of them laughing. "Anyhoo, this is about 80 or 90 proof, so it's a whole lot smoother. Kinda tastes like vodka with a vanilla kick."

Jake held out a hand. "I'll give it a shot."

Dan fell over onto his side, still giggling. "He said shot."

"Oh, Lord, we've lost him." Jake sniffed the neck of the bottle. "Got a smell of corn about it."

Mike rolled his eyes. "Well, duh."

Jake took a hesitant sip, then grinned. "Hey, this ain't so bad."

"Well don't sound so surprised, you ass."

He took another mouthful and swallowed. "Wow. It really warms ya goin' down, don't it?" Jake handed Pete the bottle, who took a larger swig of it, followed by a fit of violent coughing. "See, thass' what you get for bein' greedy."

Pete wiped his mouth and handed the bottle back to Mike. He leaned against the truck cab, hands behind his head. "So. Wanna tell us what got *your* panties in a wad tonight?"

"That'd be my Mama, who decided to bring a girl home for supper."

"What did she taste like?" Dan cackled, kicking his legs into the air.

Pete shook his head. "Next time, one of us three'll be in charge of the weed." He regarded Jake with interest. "So? Who'd she bring?"

"Sarah Hubbert." He'd calmed down by that point, his initial anger numbed by the weed and alcohol.

Pete cracked up laughing. "Yeah, good luck gettin' into *her* panties. She thinks her pussy is made of gold, the way she guards it."

Jake's stomach roiled, and he pulled himself into a more upright position, leaning against the truck's side. "See, there ya go. No wonder you can't find a girl who'll stay with ya longer 'n' a couple of dates. You can't talk 'bout girls like that. It's… disrespectful."

Pete folded his arms casually. "Well looky here. We're talkin' 'bout respect? For a piece of *tail*?" He snorted derisively. "Oh, *now* I get the picture, an' it sure makes a lotta fuckin' sense."

"What you jabberin' on about?" Panic bubbled up inside Jake, reaching his throat and seizing it up. *Oh fuck no. Please, dear Lord, no.*

"Fellas? *Fellas?*" The urgent note in Mike's voice broke through, and Jake stilled. Mike pointed toward the entrance of the quarry, where a car's headlights had appeared, dipping now and then as it slowly covered the rough terrain, heading their way.

Jake squinted, trying to make out the vehicle. Then he froze.

"Fuck. It's a cop."

Daddy was gonna kill him for sure this time.

Chapter Twenty

Pete seemed to sober up real quick. "Mike? Stash that bottle, for chrissakes. Dan, hide your weed bags, you fucker. Everyone jus' act like we're hangin' out here, jawin'. Got it? An' let me do the talkin'."

Jake had no problem with that. He took several deep breaths, dragging air into his lungs in an effort to sober up, not that the approach of a cop car wasn't already having the same effect. He couldn't see who was driving, but he hoped to God it wasn't Officer Belmont. That was one mean-assed bastard, with a rep for being particularly hard on kids he caught drinking. Not that it mattered none. Once Daddy got to hear about this, that would be Jake grounded for the rest of the summer. And he could forget about any more trips to Atlanta.

The police car came to a stop. The door opened, and a uniformed figure got out, pointing a flashlight at them. "Get your ID ready, boys." The bright light bobbed as he approached them. "Hold 'em up so I can see. An' I'll need to see the license, registration, an' proof of insurance for whoever drives this truck."

Relief rushed through Jake in a wave as he recognized the familiar voice. It was Taylor Cox.

"Sure thing, officer. It's my truck, sir." Pete got down off the flatbed, motioning for the others to do likewise. "It's jus' the four of us. We like to hang out here 'cause we're not disturbin' anybody." The four of them stood along the back of the truck, Jake doing his best not to shake.

Taylor snorted. "Yeah, right. An' I was born yesterday. Do

you boys really think we don't know what you get up to here?" He went along the line, peering at their faces and ID. When the light flashed in Jake's face, he winced at its brightness. "Well well. Jake Greenwood. I'm real sorry to see *you* here. I thought we'd had this conversation last time we met." Jake blinked, unsure how to respond, but Taylor wasn't finished. "I took it easy on ya last time, what with your brother an' all, but if I find you've been drinkin' an' drivin' again…"

"Jake didn't drive here," Pete piped up. "I picked him up at his place, same as the others."

Taylor appeared amused. "Then it looks like *you* get to walk a straight line for me…" He took Pete's ID and perused it. "Mr. Delaney. Heel to toe, if you please. An' while you're doin' it, recite the alphabet. Backwards."

"Sure." Pete stepped away from the truck, looking at the ground where Taylor shone the light, and began to pace deliberately, muttering under his breath as he recited.

Jake was severely impressed. He doubted he'd be able to make a similar effort. Then he realized he felt a damn sight more sober than he had half an hour previous.

Apparently, Taylor was impressed too. "Okay, that'll do. I think it's time you boys were headin' off home, don't you?" He leveled a steady gaze at Pete. "As long as you're drivin'." Taylor glanced at the IDs again. "You three live close by one another, right? But Jake, you're on the far side of town. I'm goin' past your place, so I'll take you home. Besides, I think we're due another talk, don't you?"

Jake's heart sank. "Yes, sir." He was *so* busted.

Taylor lowered his flashlight. "Off you go then, boys. Once Mr. Delaney here has shown me his registration an' proof of insurance, of course."

Pete made a dash for the truck cab, while Mike and Dan piled onto the flatbed.

Taylor pointed to the police car. "Wait for me over there, please, Jake."

Jake trudged over to the vehicle. This was such a fuck-up. He leaned against the back of it, hands stuffed into the pockets of his shorts, head bowed, no longer interested in watching the others make their getaway.

He was too busy thinking about what was going to happen when he got home.

Pete pulled the truck around in a circle, and drove toward the quarry exit. Jake could hear Dan talking animatedly all the way there. He shook his head. That guy had no sense sometimes.

I need some new friends, because these *guys….*

Taylor opened the passenger door. "Get in."

Jake blinked. "Okay," he said haltingly. He climbed in and fastened his seat belt. Taylor got in beside him but didn't switch on the engine. Instead, he clicked on the light, and regarded Jake steadily. Eventually he let out a sigh of resignation.

"So what was the excuse this time?"

"Huh?"

Taylor snickered. "Jake, your clothin' reeks of weed. An' that probably wasn't all you guys were up to, right? I got it last time, Caleb's funeral an' all, but I thought you knew better. An' as for your choice of friends…" He grimaced. "Sorry, but they're bad news."

"They're not my friends," Jake blurted out. "They're more like… an outlet when things get bad an' I need to… let loose a little." He scowled. "Trust me. If those guys really knew me? They wouldn't spit on me if they passed me on the sidewalk an' I was on fire."

"Not the most enlightened souls, then." Taylor pressed his lips together, as if holding back a smirk, and Jake had to laugh.

"Yeah, you could say that. I got a taste once of how they view gay guys, an' I haven't ever been able to get rid of it."

Taylor gave him an inquiring glance. "So what made you go chargin' off in search of an outlet tonight?"

That was the last thing Jake wanted to talk about, not when there was a much more urgent matter to be dealt with. "Are you gonna tell my parents?" He didn't hold out much hope for leniency, not the second time around.

That careful scrutiny didn't alter. "Answer my question first, then I'll decide." When Jake didn't respond immediately, Taylor sighed. "What did your friend tell you? To confide in me?" He smiled. "I'm trustin' *you*, aren't I? I mean, you're the only person in this town who knows I'm gay, for one thing. Doesn't that tell you somethin'?"

It was only then that Jake realized here was the one person in LaFollette who would totally get where he was coming from. Before he could say anything, Taylor opened the glove box and took out a bottle of water. "Here. Have some of this. It's not cold, but it's better than nothin'. An' you could probably use some right now." His eyes twinkled.

Jake took it gratefully, drinking half the contents before he took a breath. "Damn. I needed that."

Taylor laughed. "Yeah. Like I thought. Now how about you tell me what's goin' on?"

"'S jus' my mama—an' maybe my daddy too, for all I know, 'cause he sure looked like he knew exactly what was goin' on, which was more than *I* did."

"Jake?" Taylor smirked. "You're ramblin'."

"Sorry." Jake related finding Sarah in their dining room and went from there. Taylor gaped when he got to some of the things he'd said to Mama.

"Oh my. I didn't think you were that… sassy."

Jake groaned. "Lord knows, I'm not, really. It's just… well, they sorta caught me off guard, an' I jus' shot my mouth off without thinkin'. I'm hopin' Mama will've calmed down by tomorrow."

"I'm sure she will," Taylor assured him. "Wanna know what's *really* funny 'bout all this? I'm kinda in the same position."

"What do you mean?"

Taylor leaned back against the head rest. "The Chief has had me over for supper two or three times durin' the last few weeks."

Jake's mouth dropped. "You don't mean… The Chief… I mean to say…"

Taylor burst out laughing. "Oh my God. No, Jake, the Chief of Police does *not* have the hots for me, alright?"

Jake's face grew hot. "I have no idea why I should even *think* that, let alone say it out loud."

Taylor smirked. "I do. You're stoned. An' don't bother denyin' it, because we've already been down *that* road. So, yeah, the Chief and I are *not* sharin' candle-lit suppers, but… he does have a daughter, Denise, who's twenty-two…" He peered intently at Jake. "Need I say more?"

Jake shook his head. "'Nuff said. If she's twenty-two an' not married yet, he must be gettin' desperate."

"Hey!" Taylor whacked him on the arm. "I'd be quite a catch, I'll have you know." He grinned. "Up-an'-comin' police officer, my own place, good prospects.…"

Jake smirked. "Sounds great, except for one eeny-weeny, teeny little fact."

"There *is* that, yeah."

He reflected on Taylor's earlier words. "Hey. Am I really the only one 'round here who knows?" he asked softly.

Taylor's smile faded. "Yup."

"Not… not even your mama?"

He sighed. "My momma still lives here. I moved to Nashville to train to be a cop, before stayin' on there in the police department, but after a year or two, she started makin' 'why can't you work in LaFollette?' noises. Now, ordinarily, I would've stayed put, because I'm more likely to get found out here than in Nashville, but… her health wasn't too good at the time. So I moved back home an' found a place. No plans to come out anytime soon. Not that I was out in Nashville either. I was too damn scared of it gettin' back to her somehow. So to answer your question, no, not even my momma."

"Would it really be that bad?" As soon as he'd said it, Jake knew it was a dumb question. *I live here too, right? I know what it's like.*

Taylor smiled. "Wanna hear something amazin'? A couple of years ago, Nashville PD had a gay cop. I mean, openly gay."

"Cool!"

He nodded. "I talked with him a lot, not that I told him I was gay, you understand. He told me how he'd thought it would change everythin'' when he came out, but when he did, it wasn't all that big a deal. Sure, there were fellow officers who weren't exactly… overjoyed at the idea of workin' with a gay cop, but he jus' tried to show 'em his sexuality didn't matter. What counted at the end of the day was being' someone they could rely on, someone who got the job done."

"Was he the only gay cop on the force there?"

"Yeah. I suppose I could've been the second, but…"

"You were always afraid of your momma findin' out," Jake surmised. "What about the Chief? What if he knew? D'you think he'd react badly?"

"I jus' don't know!" Jake couldn't miss the frustration in his voice. Taylor stared out of the windshield. "I mean, this is a man who gives speeches for the Boy Scouts of America, for God's sake. I guess in the end, what holds me back is fear. So, as to your question about would it really be that bad? I have no clue, an' I'm too damn scared to find out. I get it that attitudes are changin'. Hell, you only have to see how many police departments now have an LGBT liaison officer to know that."

"For all you know, the Chief might be real supportive." Jake grinned. "'Course, he'd lose a prospective son-in-law, but gain LaFollette's first openly gay cop. Sounds like a good exchange to me. It'd sure put LaFollette on the map."

"An' what about Jake Greenwood? Any sign of *him* comin' out to the good citizens of LaFollette?" Taylor gave him an easy smile.

Jake snorted. "LaFollette ain't Nashville. Smaller town, even smaller minds."

"See? You've answered your own question. This is why I'm safer in the closet. At least for the foreseeable future."

He had a point. "An' now I get why Caleb stayed away. Why would he keep comin' back to a place where he could never be himself? He could never've brought Liam here, right? 'Cause let's be honest here. Liam would've been on the receivin' end of a double whammy, an' we both know it."

"Liam seems like a nice guy," Taylor mused. "He was obviously lookin' out for ya in Atlanta, an' he seems to care about ya too."

Jake regarded him in surprise. "Really?"

Taylor laughed. "What—did you miss the way he came over to me in that restaurant? Talk about protective. An' I think that's a good thing. He's right, too, about us havin' each other. I meant it when I gave you my number last time. You can call me anytime you need me. An' that goes for when you wanna talk about things we're both goin' through, too."

Jake snickered. "Not sure I could tell you *everythin'*."

Taylor's eyes gleamed. "Oh, Lord. What have you been up to now?"

Jake hesitated. "This is... kinda personal."

"I see." Taylor folded his arms. "Okay, how 'bout if you share somethin', an' then I share? 'Cause believe me, I can probably tell just as embarrassin' a tale."

That did it. Jake related going to Brushstrokes and buying the toys. Taylor's eyes widened. "There's a gay bookstore in Atlanta that sells sex toys? Why didn't I know this?"

Jake guffawed. "Does that mean you haven't been to the bathhouse either? It was pretty cool."

Taylor's jaw dropped. "*You've* been to a bathhouse? *How long ago did you come out?*"

He exploded into laughter. "Hold on a second there. I didn't get up to anythin', I swear. Unlike Liam's friends."

Taylor shook his head. "I'm clearly hangin' out with the wrong comp'ny." Then he looked Jake in the eye. "Wait a minute.

Truth & Betrayal

I'm not hangin' out with *any* comp'ny, but it doesn't have to stay that way." He gave Jake a smile that lit up his face. "How'd you like a *new* friend in LaFollette? One whose idea of a good time *isn't* hangin' out in a quarry, smokin' dope an' getting' out of your gourd? How 'bout a friend who likes burgers, an' movies, an' bowlin'?"

Jake liked that idea a whole lot. He also thought his Mama would be a lot happier about him hanging out with a cop, than with three guys who did as little as possible. But right then an idea occurred to him. "Shouldn't you have checked in or somethin' by now?" They'd been sat talking for an awful long while.

"Holy shit." Taylor touched his chin to the radio mic on his shoulder. "444 to Dispatch." Jake stared at him.

"Go ahead, 444."

"Area all clear. I'll be 10-8."

"10-4."

He clicked off the mic. "An' that's the end of this conversation." His eyes sparkled. "For the time bein'. Now I'd better get you home."

"An' about my parents…"

Taylor smiled. "They don't need to know. Besides, this is the last time it's gonna happen. Right?"

"Right." Jake wasn't sure whether he wanted to hug Taylor or dance on the spot.

Three thoughts came to mind as Taylor drove him through the dark streets toward his home. The first was that maybe Taylor was a little lonely, and the idea that Jake could do something about that made him feel ten feet tall.

The second was that he had a friend he could trust.

And the final thought was that Taylor was right. Liam *was* a nice guy. A good-lookin', protective, caring guy.

If I ever find myself a guy, I want him to be jus' like Liam.

Chapter Twenty-One

The first thing Jake noticed when he woke up the following morning, was that his head felt like lead. That could have been down to mixing weed and booze. He was aware of noises beyond his bedroom: Mama humming one of her favorite hymns; Daddy whistling in the yard; and the tweeting birds in the trees who seemed to have turned up their volume.

Maybe Taylor has a point. Every time Jake got together with those three, he ended up off his gourd. *Jus' how many brain cells am I killin' off?* Maybe it *was* time for a change.

A rap on his door made him start like a frightened rabbit. "Jacob? Are you awake?"

"Yes, ma'am," he mumbled.

"Well, are you comin' to church or aren't ya?"

Gotta give Mama her due. She sure is persistent. "No, Mama. You an' Daddy go on without me."

He didn't miss the clucks of disappointment, even through a solid wooden door. "Don't lay in bed all mornin' then. Make yourself useful, an' put the laundry in the dryer when it's done."

"Yes, Mama." He could do that much.

"I'll give Sarah your best wishes."

Sure, you do that. Jake didn't trust himself to say *that* out loud. He waited until he heard her footsteps dying away, focusing on the one sound that spoke of freedom.

Daddy's truck fired up, then faded away, and Jake let out a sigh.

The laundry could wait.

It took him a second or two to realize he could smell the flowers in the yard. A glance toward the ceiling told him why. Apparently, the previous night he hadn't switched on the ceiling fan, but had opened the window instead. *Yeah, figures. I wasn't exactly firin' on all eight.*

He threw off the sheet, baring himself to the morning breeze that drifted in through the open window, wafting over his bed-warmed skin and cooling it a little. His nipples stiffened, and he rubbed one with the pad of his thumb, enjoying the resultant shudder of pleasure that trickled its way through him. Jake inched his hand down his torso, until his fingers encountered the waistband of his shorts. He proceeded lower, meeting the swell of his dick beneath the fabric. Jake kept both hands in motion: fingers flicked his nipples, sending shockwaves through him, while he stroked and squeezed his cock, not ready to reach into his shorts just yet. He spread his legs wide and moved lower, tracing a path with his fingertips, skating lightly over his balls, pausing to squeeze them gently, before heading for his ultimate destination.

It hadn't taken Jake long to discover that he loved playing with his ass. And while he couldn't be bothered right that second to get out of bed and grab his toys, he was more than happy to enjoy some quality time fingering his asshole. He pressed hard against the seam of his shorts, moving his hips as he imagined it was someone *else's* finger wanting in there, someone *else* who was lying beside him, stroking, stroking, stroking, while Jake got hotter, and hotter, and hotter…

He closed his eyes and finally slid his hand into the shorts, rubbing the hard flesh, bringing his other hand into play as he reached inside and cupped his balls, before edging lower, lower, until his finger came into contact with the tight pucker. *Oh yeah.* He circled it, delaying the moment when he'd press inside to feel hot silk wrapped around his finger. Quickly, he withdrew his hand, got one finger good an' wet, then went right back to it, only this time he dipped the tip of his finger into his tight hole.

Jake wanted to enjoy every second of time he got to

himself, and his shorts were a fucking nuisance, but at least they promised delayed gratification. He poked his dick through the flap, curled his hand around it, and set up a delicious cycle of pull, slide back, squeeze, pull, slide back, squeeze... Add to that his finger as he explored the sensation of penetration to its fullest, and Jake didn't want to wait anymore.

He pushed down his shorts, kicking them off the bed, and yanked open his nightstand drawer. The lube was all the way at the back, hidden from (his mama's) sight, and he had to scrabble around until he found it. Then it was a case of slicking up fingers on both hands, and Jake was officially in heaven. He closed his eyes again, hands working in tandem, one tugging on his cock while sinking the middle finger of the other into his ass.

Fuck. That always felt so good. And if *fingers* felt so amazing, he couldn't imagine how the dildo was going to feel. Maybe so good that he'd explode. With his eyes closed, it was easier to imagine someone else on the bed with him, caressing his chest with a dark brown hand...

Holy hell. Yeah.

Jake squeezed his eyes tight shut for fear of destroying the illusion. "Yeah, Liam. Touch me," he whispered.

"You like that?" Liam's happy chuckle reverberated against his skin as he kissed Jake's chest, tongue flicking his hard little nipple, while he slid slick fingers over Jake's balls.

Oh yeah, Jake liked that a *lot*.

"In me, in me," he pleaded, pushing his finger in until it was up to the first knuckle.

It wasn't enough.

Jake got onto his knees, grabbed the headboard, arched to tilt his ass, reached back between his cheeks, and sank his index finger as deep as it would go. *Better.* His breathing quickened as he imagined the blunt head of Liam's dick against his asshole, the sting as Liam slid languidly inside him...

"That feel good?" Liam asked breathlessly. "You want it harder?" He gave a quick thrust, and Jake groaned, his shivers multiplying, tripping up and down his spine, skin erupting in a carpet of goosebumps.

"Oh fuck, just like that." It didn't matter that he had no idea how a dick would feel as it stretched him. In that moment, *God*, it felt so *real*. He could almost feel Liam's hand gripping his shoulder as he buried his shaft inside Jake's body, feel his hot breath on Jake's back as he fucked him faster, deeper, harder… Jake added his middle finger, then played with his hole, alternating between fingers, using one finger, then two, pushing back onto them, his cock rigid and leaking precome onto the sheet below.

Whoa, too close. Jake went back to one finger, pumping it deep, while his mind conjured up images of Liam, his body curved around Jake's, his ass cheeks hollowing as he filled Jake to the hilt, hips rocking as he drove his dick all the way home.

"Oh my God, Jake. Gonna shoot inside ya, fill you up."

That did it. Jake knelt up, tugged on his aching cock, and shot his load all over the headboard. He braced himself against the wall above his bed, his body trembling with the force of his orgasm. His cock pulsed out its last drops of come onto his pillow. *Jesus, Mary an' Joseph…*

He collapsed onto the bed, panting, content to lie there and enjoy the sensations. The thought occurred to him to try out the Fleshjack while he was assured of no interruptions, but he was too damn melted to get up off the bed and fetch it. It wasn't until his heartbeat had returned to normal that the first pangs of guilt sliced their way into him.

That was wrong. Okay, so it had been hot, but Liam had been Caleb's *boyfriend*, for chrissakes. Usually when Jake jacked off, it was over way too fast, normally because he didn't want his parents to hear him. Fantasizing about someone being there with him? That was new. The fact that he'd chosen Liam to fantasize about? That was….disturbing.

His phone vibrated against the nightstand, and Jake almost had palpitations. It had to be his mama. She'd used her freaky intuition and—

A little paranoid, don'tcha think? That made him snicker, but when he picked up the phone and glanced at the screen, he gaped. Liam. *What the fuck?* He took a moment to even out his breathing, then read the text.

Can we talk?

His heartbeat racing a little, Jake called him. "Hey," he said, trying to sound laid back. *Hey, Liam. No, I* don't *sound like I jus' jerked off to thoughts of you fuckin' me.*

"Hey. Sure this isn't a bad time?"

Lord, the irony…

"Nope. Mama an' Daddy have gone to church. 'S jus' me." *An' my hot fantasies.* There went those claws of guilt again, only this time they dug a little deeper.

"How are you? Recovered from your stay with Dev an' Pauli?" Liam chuckled. "They *are* somethin', aren't they?"

Christ, was that only a week ago? "I really liked 'em. An' I had a lotta fun."

"I'm glad about that." Liam's voice was warm. "It was good spendin' time with ya. After all these years of hearin' that 'Jake did this', or 'Chuck did that', finally gettin' to see ya was… not what I expected."

"Oh?" Jake wasn't sure how to take that.

"What I mean is… I had this picture in my head of this little scrawny kid."

"Geez, I'm flattered."

Liam laughed. "Hush. I'm tryin' to say that I expected a kid, an' then this *man* turned up. A guy who was nothin' like his brother."

"Is that a bad thing?"

"Not at all," Liam said emphatically.

Damn. For some reason, that made Jake feel good. "I'm glad 'bout that."

"Anyhow, I called to see if you're doin' anythin' the last weekend in July. It's my Mom's birthday, an' we're havin' a big meal for her at home, seein' as it's a big birthday an' all. And… I thought you might like to come stay with us for the weekend."

That came from out of left field. Not to mention being a huge coincidence. "Did you know it's my birthday too?"

"What? When?" Judging from his tone, Liam hadn't had a clue.

"Monday July 31st."

"Wow. It's Mom's on Sunday." Liam laughed. "Oh, that's perfect. Now you *have* to come." A pause. "Wait a sec. I'm not thinkin' right, am I? Your folks'll want you home to celebrate. I can't ask you to come spend a weekend with us, not when it's your birthday too."

Jake huffed. "What makes you think there'll be any celebratin' goin' on? It's not like when I was a kid, an' Mama threw a birthday party, right? I'm gonna be *twenty*, for chrissakes. I'll prob'ly just get a card or somethin'." He didn't say what lay heaviest on his heart—that he had a feeling the day would be just awful, because their family had a hole in it, and no amount of birthday cake was gonna fill *that* up.

Then he reconsidered. "It's not that I don't appreciate the invitation, but… don't ya think it's a bit weird askin' me to visit? I mean, birthdays are for family, and yours don't know me from Adam. An' then there's the whole 'I'm Caleb's brother' thing."

Silence fell for a moment. "Caleb didn't come home much, did he?"

Jake's throat tightened. "You know he didn't."

"Okay, well… all those times when he wasn't in Tennessee or Atlanta? He was here. With us. Man, he came home with me so often, it was like he was one of the family. An' he talked about you. A lot."

In the quiet that followed, it occurred to Jake that here was yet another chance to see a part of Caleb's life. He couldn't deny it intrigued him.

"Jake? They'll love ya. Trust me, one weekend with this crazy family, an' you'll feel like you've known 'em all your life."

Jake liked the sound of that. "I'll ask them when they come

home, how's that? An' whatever happens, I'll let you know." He liked the idea, he surely did, especially if it meant spending more time with Liam.

"Fine." A slight pause. "Are you sure you're okay? You sound kinda…distracted."

No, he was *not* okay. Distracted? Hell yeah. There was come all over his headboard, and Lord knew, he'd have to clean *that* up before Mama and Daddy got home, not to mention cleaning himself. Jake forced calm into his voice. "Yeah, I'm okay. Jus' got some chores to do 'round here before they get back, so I'd best be gettin' on with 'em."

"Sure. I look forward to hearin' from you later. With good news, I hope." Liam disconnected.

I look forward to hearing from you too. Hearing Liam's voice, even if he *had* imagined it, had made jacking off that much hotter. Jake dropped the phone onto his chest, glancing along his body to where his cock lay soft, a puddle of come beneath it. He sighed. More laundry.

The bodily heaviness he'd awoken with had fled, driven away by an amazing climax. For some reason, what came to mind was the previous night, and Taylor.

He could've booked us. He knew we'd been smokin' weed. But he didn't.

Jake pulled Taylor's scribbled number from inside the sleeve of his phone case, and sent a text.

Got a sec?

Taylor's reply was immediate. *Sure. It's my day off. Text or talk?*

Jake smiled and hit Call. When Taylor answered, Jake dove right in there. "Thanks again for last night."

"Which part? The bit where I *didn't* arrest y'all? The bit where I drove you home an' we talked so much, I forgot I was on duty? Or the part when I threw myself at ya as your new BFF?"

Jake laughed. "Wow. We were busy last night."

"So that was it? You called to thank me?"

He could've ended the call right there, but something prodded him. "Well, there *was* somethin'… You know how I started to tell you somethin', an' then I didn't, 'cause you had to drive me home?" Jake felt awkward as hell about this, but damn it, he had no one else to talk to, not about shit like this. And there was no way on God's green Earth that he could talk to Liam….

"Something botherin' ya?" When Jake didn't respond, Taylor sighed. "Jus' tell me, Jake. It'll be okay, whatever it is."

"When you… jerk off, do you ever have… fantasies while you're doin' it?" Lord, his face was on fire.

Crickets.

"Taylor? You still there?"

Taylor cleared his throat. "Well, I did say 'Tell me', didn't I? Sure. I fantasize. Why'd you ask?"

Nope. Nope. Not sharin' that. "I… I've never done that before, an'…I was thinkin' 'bout someone I know."

Another rough cough filled his ear. "Jake, honest, it's normal. Trust me."

Relief flooded through him in a slow tide. "Oh, great. Thanks."

"I'm not gonna ask who you were picturin', but… I just wanna make sure it wasn't…"

In a burst of clarity, Jake knew. "Oh Lord. No, Taylor, I was *not* jackin' off thinkin' 'bout ya, okay?"

A sigh shuddered through the phone. "Oh, thank Christ for that. I mean, you're a great guy, an' you're cute an' all, but you are *so* not my type. I like 'em a little older."

Well, *there* was a coincidence. "You can relax. Me too."

"So we're good?"

"We're good," Jake assured him. "An' I'm sorry if I embarrassed ya."

"Hey, no. You listen to me. If you need to talk about *anything*, you go right ahead an' call. I mean that, Jake. After all, what are best friends for?" Taylor snickered. "An' while I got you on the line, how 'bout we go see a movie next week? I finish early on Wednesday—which means I get to go home at a reasonable hour. What do you say? There's the Ritz over in Clinton. That's not too far."

Aw wow. The last time Jake could recall going to a movie, he'd been eight years old, and his parents had taken him and Caleb to see The Incredibles. "I'd really like that."

"Cool. I'll see what's showin', an' message you. Jus' one thing. Nothin' too gory or scary, alright?"

Jake tried not to laugh. "So the big bad cop is a fraidy cat?"

"Before you breathe a word of this, jus' remember one thing. I have a gun. An' handcuffs."

Okay, he had to laugh at that. "Ooh, kinky. Okay, not a word, I swear." He sat up and glanced at his headboard. *Hoo boy.* "Sorry, Taylor. I gotta go. I got somethin' to take care of."

Taylor snorted. "Well, it can't be the first thing that came to mind, 'cause you already took care of that, didn't ya?" Another snicker. "Talk soon." The call ended.

Jake put down his phone and sighed. His list of chores had grown a little. Then it struck him that he hadn't been this happy in a long while.

Chapter Twenty-Two

Jake threw his bag into the truck and closed the passenger door. Daddy had already left for work, with only a muttered goodbye, so no change there. He'd been pissed ever since Jake had brought up the Wilmington trip, and although Jake understood why, he thought his daddy was being unreasonable. They'd worked together since the day Jake had graduated, and in all that time, Jake hadn't taken a single vacation. Okay, so Mama and Daddy didn't take vacations either, but that was their choice, right? He was gonna be *twenty*, for chrissakes. All work an' no play? Made for a very dissatisfied Jake. *An' it's one freakin' day!*

Mama stood by the front door, clutching a brown paper bag and a flask. "You make sure you take regular stops, y'hear? Don't you go tryin' to drive the whole way without at least a couple of breaks."

Jake walked over to her. "Mama, I'll be fine. An' can you really see me drivin' all that way without hittin' a few restrooms?" He grinned. "'Specially when you've made me up a flask of tea." He leaned in and kissed her cheek, before taking the flask from her. "I'll text you as soon as I get there, but it's gonna be nearly eight hours without stops, dependin' on traffic."

"Still don't know why you're goin' all that way to spend a weekend with people you don't even know," she murmured.

"We talked about this," he said patiently. "Caleb used to visit Liam's family regularly. They were kind enough to invite me. An' Liam's promised we can go surfin'. There's a couple of beaches near there that are great for paddleboardin', kayakin'…" Liam had sent him pictures during the last week, and Jake had to admit, he loved the idea of seeing the ocean.

"Sounds like you'll have fun."

Jake arched his eyebrows at her flat tone. "You say that like it's a bad thing. I thought you'd be happy for me. Lord knows, there's been little fun in *any* of our lives recently."

She sighed, then held herself upright. "You're right. You need to let your hair down a little." Mama smiled and ran her hand over his head. "Not that you have much of that nowadays. I think I like it. Caleb always wore his hair too long. I was forever tellin' him—" She swallowed. "Enough of that. You'd better git goin' or you're gonna hit all kinds of traffic." She kissed his cheek, before handing him the bag of snacks. "Safe trip."

He returned her kiss. "Thanks, Mama. An' thank you for whatever's waitin' for me in this bag. I know it'll be delicious."

Mama swatted his arm. "Flatterer. Now git."

He laughed and got into the truck. As he drove away from the house, he raised his hand in a wave, watching her in the rear-view mirror. Guilt lanced through him.

I jus' don't wanna be here right now.

Wilmington beckoned, and Jake couldn't wait to see it. And Liam.

Mom tapped Liam on the shoulder. "You ever heard the phrase about a watched pot? You've been looking out that window for the past hour. He'll get here when he gets here." She chuckled. "And it's not like you don't know where he is. He's been sending you texts, hasn't he?"

She had a point. "Yeah." He tore himself away from the window and walked through the house into the kitchen, Mom following. In the den, Dad had been busy putting up a banner emblazoned with the words, 'Happy 50th Birthday', and Rachel and Will had hung brightly colored balloons from the ceiling, over the fireplace, and anywhere they could find a spot.

Mom shuddered as she stared at the banner. "Did he have to choose *that* one?"

Liam put his arm around her. "Hush now. You don't look your age an' you know it. You certainly don't look old enough to have a son who's—"

Mom reached up and covered his mouth with her hand. "Don't you go saying it, y'hear?" She gazed at him, shaking her head. "Why is it that all my children ended up with their dad's height?"

Liam took hold of her hand and kissed it. "Yeah, but we inherited other things from you."

Mom regarded him with interest. "Such as?"

"Your kindness. Your way of gettin' along with everyone you meet. Your generosity. Not that Dad doesn't have those things too, but when the good Lord made *you*, I think He gave you double the usual quantity."

Mom caught her breath. "Sometimes you say the sweetest things." She grinned. "And then you usually go and spoil it by being snarky." She shook her head. "Last time I had a medical, the nurse measured me at five feet four inches. I'd lost an inch in a year!" She glanced around the room. "Somewhere around here, there's a whole inch of mine, and I want it back."

He laughed, before pulling out his phone to check for any more messages from Jake. Nothing. "I'd thought he'd be here by now."

Mom gave him a hard stare. "What time is it? Just past five o'clock? You know how traffic gets during rush hour. He's probably caught up in it." She smiled. "Anyone would think you're looking forward to seeing him. It's only been a few weeks since you saw him in Atlanta, right?"

"Yeah, I know. I jus' want him to have a good time, seein' as it's his birthday too. Except he'll be gone by then." Liam wished Jake could stay longer. One full day there didn't seem enough to his way of thinking.

"Does he have to go home Sunday?"

Truth & Betrayal

Liam gave her a speculative glance. "I know that tone. What're you up to?"

Mom widened her eyes. Yeah, like he bought *that*. "Nothing. I just thought, if he could stay until Monday, we could make Sunday night a joint celebration. But I get that he needs to go home. He has a job, after all." She grinned. "Just like you."

"Don't go getting too excited," he admonished her. "I haven't started yet." His first day would be Tuesday.

"You'll be just fine." Mom frowned. "Okay, where is everyone? I couldn't move in here this morning, for people organizing stuff, and now it's like a graveyard."

Liam chuckled. "Dad went to meet a client. He said to tell you, yes, he *did* sneak in one appointment, even though it *is* his day off, but the guy was only gonna be in town today, so it was kinda urgent."

"Yeah, okay," she muttered.

"An' *you* sent Will an' Rach to Food Lion with a list of things you needed, remember?"

"So I forgot!" she said indignantly.

Liam snickered. "Must be your age gettin' to ya. After all, you *are* gonna be—"

Mom narrowed her gaze. "Say another word, Liam Miller, and *you* will be sleeping in the tool shed with the spiders this weekend." She tilted her head to one side. "I hear cars. Someone's here."

Liam dashed over to the back door, in time to see his dad pull up in front of the garage door. Damn it. Where was Jake? He peered down the driveway, just as his sister turned onto it. Then he sighed with relief when a truck followed her. *Finally*.

He strode past Rachel as she was getting out of her car. She chuckled. "Yeah, missed you too." Will cackled as he got out.

Liam ignored her. He stood to one side of the driveway while Jake parked neatly behind Rachel's car. Liam had put his Ford in the garage, along with Mom's car.

Jake got out, smiling when he saw Liam. "I made it," he

said with a grin. He walked around to the passenger door and opened it. "Sorry if I'm a little late. I stopped to get these." From the cab, he carefully removed a large bunch of flowers, a vibrant mix of colors with a fragrance that was heavenly. "I saw this place on the way over—Verzaal's, I think it was? —an' I suddenly thought I hadn't brought anythin' for your mama. Almost didn't make it, neither. They were about to close for the day." He gazed hopefully at Liam. "D'you think she'll like 'em?"

Liam thought that just might be the understatement of the year. "She will *love* them." He wished Jake wasn't holding them right then, because all Liam wanted to do was hug him. "Let's get them into some water. I'll bring your things." He reached around Jake to get his backpack from the cab, and brushed against him. The brief contact brought his arms out in goosebumps, and he didn't miss Jake's slight shiver. Liam straightened and closed the passenger door, before giving Jake a wide smile. "I'm glad you're here."

Jake flushed. "Yeah, so am I, 'cept I *am* still nervous 'bout meetin' your folks."

"Don't be. I told ya, they're gonna love you." What was there not to love? Jake was a sweet, kind soul. Lord, his mom would probably want to adopt him, given half a chance. She'd even love it when he showed a little sass. Liam certainly did.

It was then that he realized he really had been looking forward to Jake's visit. Not only that—starting a new job meant an end to long weekends in Atlanta, so they'd have few opportunities to meet.

That's why he has to feel comfortable here. That's why this weekend has to be a success. Because Liam wanted him to come back again.

Jake took a deep breath, then stepped inside the back door. The kitchen was a hive of activity. A young man and woman were in the midst of emptying shopping bags onto the countertops, laughing and joking with a woman who had to be Liam's mama. She had an air about her, kind of… efficient, and for a moment Jake's nerves doubled. Then she looked up and saw him, and her smile reached her dark brown eyes. She walked over, arms wide.

"Welcome, Jake. We're so happy you could join us." She stopped short when she caught sight of the flowers. "Oh my, they're beautiful."

Jake held them out, his heart pounding. "For you, ma'am."

She took them, her eyes wide. "Aw, thank you." She inhaled deeply. "Oh, they smell divine. I love lilies. I never hold with those folks who say lilies are only for funerals."

Jake swallowed. "Oh. I didn't mean—"

She chuckled. "Stop right there. These are beautiful."

"Why don't I put those in water, Mom, while you say hi to Jake?" The young woman flashed him a smile. "I'm Rachel, an' that nuisance over there is my little brother, Will."

"Hey!" Will gave her an indignant scowl, which she completely ignored.

"We can get acquainted later. Right now, I'll take care of these." She took the flowers from him.

"Thank you." Jake turned to Liam. "I can see where you get your looks from now."

Liam blinked. "Thanks. I think."

Jake hastened to reassure him. "No, I mean… Your mama is beautiful." He couldn't miss the hitch in his mama's breathing, and Jake's face was suddenly on fire. "Can I go out an' come in again?"

Liam's mama laughed. "Sweetheart, you are doing just fine. And thank you for the compliment." She addressed Liam. "Why don't you take Jake to your room? He can leave his things there. And he can share your bathroom." She turned back to Jake with a smile. "Thank goodness for three baths, that's all I can say."

Jake rolled his eyes. "Hel—heck, yeah. We have one at home, an' I have to fight my daddy for who gets the shower first." *Shoot.* "Well, I don't mean we *fight*, exactly…"

She laid a gentle hand on his arm. "Jake." Her voice was soft. "Try to relax, please? You have no idea how pleased we really are to have you here. We just want you to feel at home, okay?"

Jake's heartbeat climbed down a notch, and he breathed more evenly. "Thank you, ma'am."

She bit her lip. "I love your manners, but I will *not* cope with an entire weekend being addressed as ma'am. Call me Sharon?" She chuckled. "Having said that, it took your brother months to be able to come out with that." Beside him, Liam snickered.

The reference to Caleb eased Jake's nerves a little more. "I'll do my best to remember… Sharon."

"And when you get to meet him, my husband is Anthony, but everyone calls him Tony." She glanced at her wristwatch. "We'll be having dinner in about an hour, so you've got time to take a shower and freshen up before then. You've had a long trip to get here."

Jake was acutely aware of his T-Shirt clinging to his back, and he didn't want to know how he smelled after nine hours in the truck. Then he was relieved Sharon hadn't given him a hug after all. "That would be wonderful."

"Come on, I'll show you where the bathroom is." Liam led him out of the kitchen.

Jake followed, still apprehensive, but determined to quash his nerves. His first impression was that Liam had a lovely family, and the fact that they'd known Caleb went a long way to making him feel like this was a safe place.

Truth & Betrayal

Chapter Twenty-Three

Liam knocked on the bedroom door. "You decent?"

From inside, he caught Jake's snicker and muttered response. "Well, I wouldn't go *that* far." Liam laughed quietly. It seemed like a shower had restored Jake's usual wit. The door opened, and Jake stood there, a towel wrapped around him. "C'mon in. It's your room, after all." He walked over to the bed, where he'd arranged his clothing.

Liam stepped into the room, pushing the door shut behind him. "You got everything you need?" He tried not to stare at Jake, but his lean body was beautiful to see, with slim hips and a smooth back, not to mention his chest with the slightest dusting of hair.

He was even more beautiful than he'd been in Atlanta. *Hey, whaddaya know? Absence does make the heart grow fonder.*

Jake nodded absently. "Hey, you sure I'm not in your way?"

Liam shook his head. "This used to be my room, before I moved to Atlanta. As you can see, it's my mom's study these days. If anythin', I'm in *her* way." He shrugged. "Won't be forever, mind you. Now that I'm workin', won't be long before I start lookin' for my own place."

"Workin'?" Jake's face broke into a huge smile. "You got a new job?"

Such delight was infectious. Liam returned his smile. "Yeah. I start work at a bank here in Wilmington next Tuesday."

"That's great news." Jake peered at him. "Then why aren't you singin' an' dancin' about it?"

Liam sighed heavily. "Because a drawback of havin' a Monday-to-Friday job is I can't take long weekends... in Atlanta..." He let that sink in.

Jake's face fell. "Oh. I see."

"Yeah, that was how I felt too. I kinda liked visitin' Dev an' Pauli, showin' you around... But it's a six-hour trip, an' that's a lot for jus' one night away. Unless I drive through Friday night, of course. I could be there by midnight, in theory, except we both know that's not gonna happen. Bein' stuck in traffic can be a bitch." This was just getting depressing as hell. "So, why're you starin' at your clothes?"

"Because I have no clue what to wear?"

Liam snickered. "Well, anythin' would be better than the towel, unless you really wanna create an entrance."

Jake narrowed his gaze. "You're s'pposed to help me."

Laughing, Liam glanced at the clothing. "Okay, so what's wrong with jeans an' a T-shirt?"

Jake made an unhappy noise. "Too casual. I mean, your mama an' your sister dress real smart. I'd feel... shabby beside 'em."

There was no way Liam could let Jake think like that. "There is *nothin'* shabby 'bout the way you dress, y'hear? Believe me, you shoulda seen how *Caleb*—" He broke off. He didn't need to be forever comparing Jake with Caleb. Lord knew, Jake was—

Different. And Liam was starting to appreciate the differences.

He pointed to a plain white shirt. "That's fine. An' as for Mom an' Rachel bein' smart? I hate to shatter your illusions, but *you* haven't seen them sprawled on the couch on a Saturday night in their onesies, chuggin' white wine an' emptyin' a crate of popcorn between them." Jake giggled, and that was just the effect Liam wanted. "Okay, so maybe not a crate, but you get the idea."

Jake laughed. "Okay, the white T-shirt it is." He picked up a pair of faded jeans, and glanced at Liam, his cheeks flushed. "I was gonna ask if you wanted to leave while I got dressed, 'til I realized you've already seen what I got, in that locker room at Flex." And before Liam could say a word, Jake turned away from him and dropped his towel, bending slightly to step into his jeans.

Holy Mother of God, he's goin' commando. And Liam couldn't help but look.

Fuck, that is a beautiful ass. Now he knew why guys referred to peaches, because *Lord*, those globes were round, firm, and pink, with a light covering of hair, and—

Down boy. That is Jake's *ass you're droolin' over. You remember? Caleb's brother?*

He didn't want to think like that about Jake, but Liam couldn't deny how much he yearned to caress that gorgeous ass. Except he didn't want to stop at caressing it…

"Are you okay?"

Jake's question yanked him back into the moment. "'Scuse me?"

Jake pointed to the desk, where Liam had placed his deodorant, cologne, and several other items. "Are you takin' meds?"

Puzzled, Liam followed the direction of his finger. *Hoo boy.*

It was a cinch Jake wouldn't know what PrEP was.

Liam decided to go with the simplest explanation. "Caleb and I were negative, an' we wanted to stay that way. Well, with us sharin' guys occasionally, an' neither of us likin' condoms, we both took what you see there. It's called PrEP, an' it prevents the transmission of HIV." He shrugged. "It keeps you safe." He knew there was a lot more he could say, and he was damn sure Jake would have a ton of questions, but that would be for another time.

Right now Mom was making dinner.

"O-*kay*," Jake said slowly.

Liam held up his hands. "We can continue this conversation another time, I promise. Then I'll answer your questions."

Jake smiled. "Because you *know* I have 'em, right? I mean, they don't exactly teach this sorta thing in school, an' I have to be real careful what I look up on my phone, 'cause my mama loves to pry. So yeah, you can bet this conversation isn't over." He pulled the T-shirt over his head.

"Fair enough. You ready to meet everyone properly?"

Jake grinned. "Now that I don't smell like—to quote my mama—twenty pounds of shit in a ten-pound bag, sure. I have to tell ya, I'm so hungry, I could eat the south end of a northbound polecat."

Liam bit his lip. "That's… graphic. I'm not so sure you didn't just make that up."

Jake chuckled. "You know what I meant, so it worked. An' don't tell me Caleb didn't come out with much worse, because then I'd *know* you were a liar for sure." His eyes sparkled.

Liam wasn't about to say any such thing. "He loved yanking my chain."

"There's iced tea if you want it," Rachel called out. "An' dinner's nearly ready."

Jake's eyes gleamed. "Well, what are we waitin' for? I could eat a—"

Liam stopped his words with a hand across Jake's mouth. "I get it. You're hungry. So let's eat." He removed his hand, and Jake snickered.

Liam followed him out of the bedroom and into the kitchen, doing his damnedest not to think about how that gorgeous ass filled out those jeans.

Maybe it's time I checked out that gay bar in town, because man, *I need to get laid.*

He realized it was the first time such a thought had occurred to him since Caleb's death. Part of him rebelled against that. He shouldn't be thinking about sex when Caleb had only been gone *three months*, for God's sake. Then another thought flitted through his mind.

Maybe it was just a reminder that life goes on, and that he needed to meet his body's needs.

"More potato salad, Jake?" Rachel held out the bowl. "You seem to like it." She smirked.

Jake took it from her and helped himself to another spoonful. "Okay, never thought I'd say this, but… Sharon, your potato salad beats my mama's, hands down." It was the best he'd ever tasted. And as for the chicken, the spicy sweet potato wedges… It was all perfect.

Sharon beamed. "Aw, thank you, sweetheart." She glanced across the table at Liam. "I got déjà vu here."

Liam smiled, and nudged Jake with his arm. "Caleb said the very same thing. Only thing was, he looked so guilty after he said it, we all felt sorry for him."

"I can understand that," Sharon said. "It's only natural to take pride in your momma's cooking. I expect he felt like he was betraying her. Of course, he *wasn't*, but…" She held out the bowl of bread rolls. "Would you like another?"

Jake stared at it for a second, debating internally. Finally, he nodded and took one. Lord, the *smell* when he opened it up. Heaven.

"Caleb always said you were good with your hands," Will commented. Jake liked the look of Will, who resembled Liam very strongly. *Mind you, all of Liam's family are so good-lookin'.* His mom was a brunette, shoulder length, the tips of her hair curling under just enough to give the strands life when she moved. Jake loved the hint of sun-kissed red that shone through when the sunlight hit it just right. Rachel had her mom's facial bone structure, but she wore her hair in long box braids, pulled together to one side at the top, while the rest cascaded down her back and over her shoulders. The style showed off her face, and made her appear taller, not that she needed it: not one of the kids was under five feet ten. And as for Tony, their dad? Lord, he had to be six feet tall, starting to thin out on top, but with graying stubble along his jawline. His eyes reminded Jake of Liam's: they had that same warmth.

More than the way they looked, Jake liked their manners, their easy-going attitude, the way they interacted with each other, and the care they took to make sure he was happy.

Jake could see why Caleb had liked spending time with them. They were good people.

"Jake?"

With a start, Jake blinked. "Sorry. I must've zoned out there for a sec. What were you sayin'?"

"I said Caleb always mentioned how good you were with your hands."

Jake narrowed his gaze. "Tell me he didn't show you a photo of me with a plastic saw." When Will bit his lip, Jake rolled his eyes. "Good Lord. Why did he have to go an' do that?"

"He was proud of you," Tony said simply. "He said he didn't have a creative bone in his body, but he reckoned that was okay, because while *you'd* gotten all the creative bits…" He paused, his eyes twinkling.

Jake sensed there was a punchline coming. "Yeah? What did he get?"

"All the good looks."

Jake's jaw dropped. "Say what? Why, that… vain little *turd*!" He didn't doubt for a second that Caleb had said those exact words: it was *so* him.

There was silence for a moment, and then everyone around the table started laughing, until there wasn't a dry eye, and Jake was laughing along with them. When they finally stopped, Liam leaned in close and whispered, "For what it's worth? I think Caleb was talkin' out of his ass."

For some reason, Liam's words sent a shiver through Jake that was kinda…pleasurable. *He's been lookin' at me.* Then Jake gave himself a mental shake. *Of course he's been lookin' at me.* But Liam's words implied more than that. Jake couldn't look at him right then, not when all he saw in his head was the Liam he'd encountered in his fantasy. *Can't think about that, damn it.*

"Jake, can I ask you something?" Sharon's voice broke through his tortured musings. "I've been thinking about my party. Is there any way you could stay until Monday? That way, we could have a joint celebration on Sunday. No pressure. It was just an idea. I know you have work commitments."

Daddy's face flashed across Jake's mind. *I should say no. I'm already on his shit list for takin' off today.* Then he reconsidered. *Why the hell not?* If Sharon was kind enough to do this, why should he refuse? And it wasn't as if they'd be doing anything special for his birthday at home, right?

"Can I call my mama after supper? Then I'll decide?" He gave a half-smile. "I do like the idea."

Sharon beamed. "Of course you can. And please don't worry. I'll understand if your momma wants you home for your birthday."

Jake resolved then and there to help Mama come to the right decision.

"Of course you can't say no. You're the guest, Jacob. An' we'll get to see you when you get home, right?"

Jake gave an internal sigh of relief. "Thanks, Mama. I'll try not to be home too late." He spun lazily in the tire swing, enjoying the scent of flowers carried on the evening breeze. The Millers' back yard was beautiful, a large open space with a huge tree at the bottom, and a wide bench set under a dark wood pergola, covered with climbing roses and honeysuckle. Solar lights provided a colorful glow.

"Jus' don't you go drivin' like a maniac, y'hear?"

He chuckled. "I promise I won't go above the speed limit."

"Then that's fine. I'm glad you're havin' a good time so far."

Jake had a good feeling about the weekend. How could he feel otherwise, spending time with a family who had no issue with their son being gay, and had welcomed Caleb as one of their own?

"I am." He tried to stifle his yawn, but it crept out.

"I think I know someone who needs to go to bed." Mama chuckled. "You've had a long day."

"Not gonna argue with ya." Jake wished her good night, then disconnected. He pocketed his phone, then recommenced his slow spin.

"I see you've found my favorite spot."

Jake glanced up as Liam approached, strolling leisurely across the grass. Jake stilled himself, feet on the ground, and smiled. "I could never resist a swing. Caleb an' me, we'd fall out all the time when I was little, over who got to play on it. In the end Daddy put up another one."

Liam laughed. "Oh wow. He didn't change then. Caleb was like a big kid when it came to this swing." He regarded Jake closely. "Well? What did your mom say?" Jake simply beamed, and Liam broke into a wide smile. "That's awesome. I'll let Mom know."

Jake nodded, fighting another yawn.

"Okay, you need to sleep. An' before you start arguin', you're taking the bedroom. I'll be on the couch in the den."

"Er, no. I'm not kickin' you out of your room." Jake set his jaw.

Liam walked up to him, grabbed hold of the rope, and stared at him. "You're not gonna win this one. I let you have your own way in Atlanta, but not this time. Now you're in *my* home, an' what I say goes." He let go and folded his arms.

Jake snickered. "Wow. I had no idea you were this bossy."

"Yeah, well, suck it up. Jus' means I'm gettin' used to bein' around ya."

He liked that. "Oh Lord, does that mean you might get worse?"

Liam's eyes glittered. "Probably. Now get inside before the

mosquitos discover how tasty a Tennessee boy can be."

Jake laughed. He climbed out of the tire and followed Liam across the grass. He had two full days to look forward to.

Things had just gotten a whole lot better.

Truth & Betrayal

Chapter Twenty-Four

Liam leaned on the pier railings and stared out at the ocean. "Y'know, this is what I missed most when I lived in Atlanta. When I was just a kid, I wanted a house right on the beach." He inhaled deeply. "Wow. That smell. I could never describe it to Caleb. I couldn't say it was salty, because what the hell does salt smell like? Then of course, Caleb had to go an' spoil it all."

Jake frowned. "How?"

Liam could recall the conversation like it was yesterday. "Well, there *I* was, trying to describe this scent that clings to your hair an' skin, something so… evocative it brings back memories of childhood, an' Caleb looks me in the eye, an' says what I'm smellin' is death, sex an' fish food."

Jake blinked, then guffawed. "What 'n the hell was he talkin' 'bout?"

Liam laughed. "I'll give the short version, but you know what? He was right! Apparently, what we're smellin' right this minute is the bacteria that feeds off dyin' microscopic organisms, the sex pheromones of seaweed, an' chemical compounds produced by the bottom feeders that fish live off."

Jake pulled a face. "Ew. Thanks for that." He gazed glumly into the blue water that lapped Kure beach. "You had to go an' tell me that, didn'tcha? That's the last time I breathe in that smell an' think, 'Wow, that smells good.' Talk about burstin' a bubble."

"Now you know how *I* felt." And right that minute, Liam was feeling good. He'd woken up that morning refreshed, and had found Jake sitting on the bench in the yard, watching the sun come up. Liam had joined him, and they'd sat in silence, listening to the birds, and observing the sky go through its color changes as the sun climbed higher.

When Mom had suggested he take Jake to the beach, Jake's face lit up, and it was a done deal.

"This is great," Jake said with a sigh, turning his face toward the sun. "An' as much as I really like your family, it's good to get some quiet time with ya."

His words echoed what was in Liam's mind so perfectly, it was uncanny. "Quiet is always good." Liam didn't know how else to respond, not until he had a clue to the meaning underlying Jake's comment.

Jake straightened, and walked unhurriedly toward the end of the pier.

Something was in the air. Liam could feel it.

He caught up with Jake and touched his arm lightly. "You got somethin' on your mind?"

Jake stared down at the wooden planks beneath their feet. "Can we talk about…" When he dried up, Liam's intuition kicked in big time.

"You wanna know about PrEP, don'tcha?" Jake gave him a grateful smile. "That's okay. I said we could talk about this, right? Well, what do you wanna know?"

"You an' Caleb… you took this stuff…so you could fool around with other guys an' be safe, right? Without condoms? So what I guess I'm askin' is… should I be on it too?" Jake flushed. "Not that I'm doin' anythin' with anybody right now, but I'm kinda assumin' I'm goin' to. One day."

Liam came to a halt. "Okay, this is where a lot of gay guys have issues." He leaned on the railings, and Jake followed suit. "There's a whole lotta shamin' goin' on about this. Some people think PrEP is basically a license to fuck anything that moves, but I swear, that is *not* the case. AIDS has not gone away. HIV has not gone away. An' if you're sexually active, then yeah, it makes sense to keep yourself safe. But…." He paused, thinking how best to frame his thoughts. "I get tested every three months. So did Caleb. Any guy we fucked, we asked about his status. An' here's the important stuff. PrEP does *not* protect you against STDs. You still need condoms for that. Caleb an' me, we just hated the feel of sex with a rubber."

"I see." Jake's facial expression gave away no clue as to what was going on in his head.

"An' as for whether you should take it? I can't answer that for ya. That's your decision. I can tell you it's expensive, but you don't need to take it if you stop havin' sex." Liam shook his head. "That bottle has stood there untouched since I moved back home."

"I don't think I'm any clearer," Jake said with a sigh.

Liam placed his hand on Jake's shoulder. "Listen. Here's what's important. We'll call 'em Liam's Top Three. One. Before you decide to bump uglies with a guy, you both talk. Two. There is nothin' wrong with usin' condoms. An' three. If someone wants to go bareback an' *doesn't* wanna share their status? Well, you tell them to fuck the hell right off. Sex is about trust, okay?"

To his relief, Jake nodded slowly, his expression lightening. "Thank you. I got no one else I can ask 'bout these things. Well, I *could* ask Taylor, I suppose, but I get the feelin' he's pretty much in the same boat as me."

"I'm glad he's your friend."

Jake smiled. "Yeah, me too. You should've seen Mama's face when I told her I was goin' to a movie with him. Taylor's a couple of steps up from Pete an' his little gang of haters."

Liam's stomach clenched. "Wait a sec. These the friends you called hateful assholes?"

"That's them. I haven't seen 'em in a few weeks, an' you know what? That's jus' fine."

Liam nudged Jake's hand with his. "Anytime you need to get away from home, from that town, you jus' call, y'hear? So what if I'll be workin'? There's always the weekend. An' if it gives you a little space to… I don't know, decompress? Then you don't hesitate, okay?"

Jake's face glowed. "Okay. I got the message. An' at least I have a friend now back home that I can trust."

"D'you think you an' Taylor might be more than friends?" It wasn't an outlandish suggestion—Liam didn't think they were all that far apart in age—but Liam found himself hoping Jake wasn't interested. Fucked if he knew why.

Jake smirked. "Oh Lord. Yeah, we both cleared that up pretty fast. He said I'm cute an' all, but he's into older guys, which is okay by me, 'cause he ain't my type neither."

Liam regarded him with interest. "So you have a type already? You don't waste any time, do ya?"

Jake's mouth fell open, he blinked a few times, and his face went through several different shades of red before settling on a deep rose color. It was an intriguing reaction, not to mention absolutely adorable.

Liam chuckled. "Taylor's right about one thing though. You *are* kinda cute, 'specially when you blush." He couldn't resist just a little teasing.

Jake widened his eyes. "I don't blush."

"Yeah right. You could warm a small New Hanover town with the heat your face is generatin' right now." Then Liam relented. "Sorry. That was mean. How 'bout I make it up to ya, an' hire us a paddleboard so we can get out an' enjoy these waves?"

Jake glanced down at his shorts. "'M not exactly dressed for goin' in the ocean."

"Well, you can take 'em off, and jus' wear your boxers, or whatever."

Oh hell. Jake's flush deepened. "That would be great—if I was wearin' any."

Liam had to resist the urge to glance down. "Oh. Then how 'bout we go for a stroll on the beach instead? An' there's ice cream. They got so many flavors, it'll make your head spin."

Jake laughed. "You had me at beach. Sure, let's do it."

They walked in a leisurely manner along the pier, Liam regaling him with stories about Will and Rachel, who really were like chalk and cheese. Jake seemed completely relaxed, and that was just fine by Liam. He tried not to think about Monday, when Jake would leave.

Just enjoy his comp'ny while he's here.

Except to Liam's mind, it was beginning to feel like he wouldn't be there long enough.

Jake was as full as a tick on an old coon dog, not to mention muzzy-headed on account of the champagne Tony had poured for everyone once dinner was over. Except Jake was starting to think the meal would never come to an end, especially when Rachel brought out the most delicious cookies he'd ever encountered, to accompany the coffee.

"Good Lord above, where d'you folks put it all?" Not that it stopped him from sneaking three off the plate.

Sharon laughed. "I could say the same thing about you, mister. For a skinny guy, you sure can put it away too." She sagged into her chair, a glass of champagne in her hand. "Rachel, that was awesome."

Rachel snickered. "Just 'cause you didn't have to cook any of it."

Sharon beamed. "Exactly. That's why it was awesome." She winked at Jake, before peering at his empty glass. "Tony? Jake needs more champagne."

More? He'd already had three glasses.

Tony was filling his glass before Jake could stop him. "We can't have that. It's your birthday too, remember?"

Jake let out a slightly drunken giggle. "Thass' not 'til tomorrow, an' if you keep refillin' my glass like this, by the time my birthday gets here, I'll be in no state to enjoy it."

Liam leaned in and whispered, "Forget about tomorrow. That's gonna be mostly the drive home. Enjoy tonight."

There was something about Liam's voice that sent ribbons of pleasure unfurling in the pit of Jake's belly, conjuring up images in his head that made him wish he was alone to enjoy them to their fullest. Of course, that *might* have been the alcohol talking, but Jake doubted it. All the booze did was chase away Jake's inhibitions.

It apparently loosened his tongue too.

"I can see why my brother wanted to be with you," he whispered, his fingers aching to trace a path along Liam's forearm to his wrist.

Liam's eyes seemed to go that little bit darker. "Oh yeah?"

"Bathroom break!" Will announced cheerily. "You've got five minutes while we set up Mom's birthday present in the den."

That was the cue for everyone to get in motion, scurrying off in all directions.

Jake didn't need a bathroom. He needed air.

"'Scuse me." He got up off the chair and hurried, a little off-balance, to the kitchen and out into the yard. Once there, he sank onto the bench and inhaled deeply, forcing the cool night air into his lungs.

What the fuck? He did *not* mean to let that slip, and especially to Liam. *Goddammit, brain! What 'n the hell are you playin' at?* He put his head in his hands and closed his eyes. Fantasizing about Liam was bad enough, right?

When he caught the hushed sound of feet on grass, he kept his eyes shut, hoping whoever it was would take the hint.

No such luck. And just to prove God had a real twisted sense of humor, Jake knew immediately that the figure now sitting beside him was Liam.

Well fuck.

Jake opened his eyes and straightened. "Just wanted some air."

Liam gazed at him steadily. "Mm-hmm."

"All that champagne went straight to my head."

"Mm-hmm."

Jake groaned. "What? What do you want from me?"

Liam's eyes never shifted their focus. "Tell me what you meant back there. About why you thought Caleb wanted to be with me."

Say nothin'. Keep your fat mouth shut. Say nothin'. You're only diggin' a hole for yourself.

"Because you're sexy as fuck," Jake blurted out.

Liam stilled. "I see. Whereas *you* are fuckin' adorable." He smiled. "Thank you. I'm flattered."

All Jake wanted in that instant was a time machine. "Look, forget I said that, alright? It was jus' the boo—"

To his shock, Liam pressed a couple of fingers to Jake's lips, momentarily silencing him. "Now, don't go an' spoil it by tellin' me it's 'cause you're drunk. Leave it there, where you've made me feel good." He removed his fingers and rose to his feet. "Time to give Mom her present. I think you might like it too." Liam extended a hand to him. "Need some help?"

The way Jake was feeling right then? All he could get. "Yeah," he said, grasping Liam's hand and hauling himself to an upright position. He hoped to God no one else had heard him.

Liam released his hand, and they walked toward the back door. Liam stopped him as they reached the threshold. "An' jus' for the record? You're pretty sexy yourself." Then he pushed open the door and stepped inside.

Jake almost stumbled over the step as he entered the house.
He did not jus' say that.
He's jus' tryin' to make me feel good.

Warmth flooded through him, spreading all the way to the ends of his fingers.

He thinks I'm sexy.

Will stood beside the wide screen TV mounted on the wall,

a laptop connected to it by cables. "Mom, we thought long and hard about what to give you for your birthday. I have to admit, we were stumped." He counted off on his fingers. "You don't collect anythin'. You hate it when we buy you clothes. You don't eat chocolates. You don't 'do' spa days. You only ever wear one perfume. In fact, pretty much every idea we came up with, we crossed out."

Sharon gave him a sweet smile. "Hey, I don't like to make things too easy for you. Where's the fun in that?"

Jake had to smile. It sounded like Christmas and birthdays were a real bitch in their house. Mama was a walkover by comparison. A bottle of her favorite perfume, and a bunch of flowers, and she was happy.

Will glanced at Liam, who got up off the couch and joined him. "So instead, we thought we'd give you something you'd value." He clicked on the mouse pad. "Like, the past fifty years."

Rachel clicked off the lights, and the TV burst into life, revealing a screen entitled *Sharon Miller - This Is Your Life*.

"Lord, *now* I'm scared," Sharon muttered.

Jake stared, fascinated, as the screen morphed into photos. Baby photos. Sharon as a little girl, playing in the back yard. Singing in the church choir. Performing on a stage. So many memories.

"Where the *hell* did you get all these?" Sharon gasped.

"Grandpa was real helpful," Rachel said with a snicker.

Jake couldn't tear his eyes away. There were videos too, of Sharon and Tony's wedding day, of when the kids were just babies, all of it blending seamlessly into a photographic representation of Sharon's life. He snuck a glance across at her. Sharon stared at the screen, mesmerized.

"Aw, kids, this is amazing."

"Hey, look, there's Caleb," Will called out to him.

Sure enough, there was Caleb, standing beneath a sprig of mistletoe, grinning, and beckoning with his finger. Liam joined him, and they kissed briefly under it, while the others applauded.

There were more photos too, similar to the ones he'd seen on Caleb's laptop, and as the images passed before him, tears pricked Jake's eyes.

Mama doesn't have any videos of us as kids. Sure, there was photos albums stuffed onto bookshelves, but it wasn't the same. Here was Caleb, living and breathing again, happy, laughing, always smiling, surrounded by people who clearly cared for him.

It was too much. Tears trickled down Jake's cheeks, and he hiccupped, fighting to control the sobs that begged to be freed.

Liam was beside him in an instant, reaching for him, and Jake clung to him, feeling Liam's own tears hot against his cheek. "I'm sorry. I should've warned you. I know, baby. Let it out. I gotcha."

Jake took Liam at his word, and for the second time in his life, Jake held onto him while he cried out the tears he'd thought had finished.

Liam whispered into his ear. "I'm not cryin' for me, Jake, but for you. I'm cryin' because you're hurtin', an' I caused that." He rubbed a hand over Jake's head, the action almost soothing.

Little by little, Jake regained control of himself. The tears subsided, and he released Liam. He wiped a hand across his damp eyes. "Sorry, folks. I didn't mean to spoil the party."

To his surprise, Sharon joined him and held her arms wide. "You've spoiled nothing, sweetheart." She hugged him tightly, and he breathed in her scent, a floral smell that comforted him somehow. "We're just glad to have you here." After a moment, she let him go, and glanced over at Tony. "I think some more coffee might be a good idea. And I'll watch the rest of my present later." Sharon cupped Jake's cheek, staring intently into his eyes. "Are you okay?"

Jake gave a brief nod, not trusting himself to speak right then.

She didn't look away but continued her study of him. Finally, she lowered her hand. "I think for the rest of the evening, we'll watch a movie. Something to make us smile."

A chorus of groans greeted her words, and Jake looked at her family, surprised by the reaction. Liam laughed. "It's okay. When Mom says that, we know what's comin', right, guys?" He mouthed a silent countdown from three, and everyone yelled, "Men in Black!"

Sharon huffed. "My birthday, my movie."

Tony chuckled as he pulled up Netflix. "Except she knows we all love it too." He peered at Jake. "How about you?"

Jake had seen it once at a movie theater. It wasn't Mama's or Daddy's kinda movie. "I think that sounds great. Jus' one thing? No one suggest makin' popcorn? 'Cause if I eat one more mouthful, I'll burst." He was calmer now, if a little ashamed of his emotional display.

Liam laughed again. "Okay. No popcorn." He gestured to the couch. "C'mon. Squeeze up an' make room for me."

Jake decided watching a movie with Liam's family had to be the nicest way to end the day. He settled back against the cushions, his head on Liam's shoulder.

No one batted an eyelid, like it was totally natural.

Jake could deal with that.

Chapter Twenty-Five

"That everything?" Liam asked, coming alongside the truck.

Jake nodded. "I've checked your room three times." He chuckled. "I think I've said goodbye to your mama three times too." Sharon was a sweet lady, and Jake hoped to see her– and the rest of her wonderful family—again real soon. Not that he had any clue as to when that might be.

Life sure was getting complicated.

Liam handed him a large brown paper bag. "I made ya a couple of sandwiches with yesterday's meatloaf, seein' as how you liked it so much. An' there's a banana, apples, an' a couple of snack bars." He snickered. "I don't know 'bout you, but I always gets the munchies when I'm drivin'."

"Aw, you didn't have to do that. But thank you." Jake took the bag and put it in the truck. He closed the door with a heavy *thunk*. "About last night…"

Liam shook his head. "Please, don't say another word. I still blame myself for not thinkin' it through."

"What do you mean?"

Liam leaned against the truck, his hands in the pockets of his jeans, his white T-Shirt hugging the contours of his torso and biceps. "When Will first came up with the idea, he asked me if I'd be okay with it… with seein' Caleb again. I knew I'd cope, so I gave him the go-ahead. But I should've realized. Of *course* I could cope. What were *my* few years of knowin' him, compared with you knowin' him all your life?"

His obvious pain touched Jake. Awkwardly, he laid a hand on Liam's upper arm. "You know what? I didn't think I had any tears left. Last night kinda surprised me. But you need to stop kickin' yourself, okay?" Jake squeezed his arm. "I'm fine, honest. An' it did make me think. Caleb's always gonna be here. He'll be right up there on that screen whenever your mama watches her birthday present. He's in all those photos." He removed his hand and placed it over Liam's chest, covering his own heart. "An' he's right here too."

Liam glanced down at Jake's hands, and Jake pulled them away. "Anyhoo, I'd best be on my way. Gotta long drive home." Jake smiled. "Thank you again. I had a great time. An' if I ever need to get away, I'll take you up on that offer, I promise."

He went to get into the truck, but Liam caught him in a tight hug. "Happy birthday, Chuck."

Okay, that brought him close to the edge again. Jake closed his eyes and stood there, Liam's strong arms around him. *Oh Lord, that feels good.* When Liam released him, Jake thanked him, and climbed into the truck.

His last view as he turned onto the street was Liam standing on the driveway, waving.

Jake put on the radio and headed home.

Liam went into the house and closed the door, feeling unexpectedly heavy in both heart and body. From the kitchen came the sound of singing: Will was clearing up after lunch and belting out Run by the Foo Fighters. Rachel was at the law office in town where she worked part-time, and Dad was in the room above the garage that served as his office, working on his designs.

Back to normality. Except that the following day, everything would change with Liam's new job.

"Is that what the younger generation calls music these

days?" Mom came into the hallway and grimaced. "Now, in *my* day, we had *real* music." Her eyes sparkled with good humor.

Liam rolled his eyes. "You gonna give me another lecture on how the Seventies produced the best music there's ever been?"

Mom chuckled. "I don't need to. It appears you already know it." She looked out through the wide front window. "Jake gone?"

Liam nodded. "Just now. At least there'll be some of his birthday left by the time he gets home." Saying goodbye had left him feeling oddly deflated.

Mom sat on the leather couch and patted the cushion beside her. "Come sit with me."

Oh God. Liam knew that voice. "What have I gone an' done now?" He perched on the edge of the seat.

Mom laughed. "Nothing I know of. No, I just wanted to talk with you a while." She paused, her hands clasped in her lap. "I like Jake."

"Yeah, he's alright, huh?" He was more than that in Liam's mind.

"I think he has a few of Caleb's mannerisms."

He laughed. "Like how he uses his hands when he's talkin'? Yeah, I noticed that one too. He runs his hand over his head when he's thinkin' hard 'bout something too. 'Course, Caleb had more hair, but he used to do that too, an' he had this habit of brushin' his hair out of his eyes all the time."

"Apart from that, they're not really alike, are they?"

"No." Jake was a whole different ball of wax.

Liam was suddenly aware of the silence. He glanced at his mom, who was regarding him closely. "You like him, don't you?"

Liam blinked. "Of course I like him. What's not to like?"

Mom arched her eyebrows. "Seriously? You want to take that line with me?" Her lips twitched.

Yeah, when she put it like that…

Liam sagged into the couch. "Is it… wrong that I like him?"

Mom tilted her head to one side. "I understand why you're

asking the question. To be honest, I'd been wondering when you'd ask it. Why should it be wrong?"

"I guess it's the whole guilt thing. I mean, I dated his brother. An' it's only three months since Caleb passed."

Mom nodded. "I remember something someone told your grandpa when my mom died. She'd been gone about two months, an' he wanted to know if he'd ever feel… normal again. Anyhow, they told him to think of it in terms of one month for every year they'd spent together, as a rough guide."

Liam snorted. "So I'll be right by Halloween then? I'll mark it on my calendar."

Mom patted his knee. "Baby, everyone's different. It takes as long as it takes."

His chest tightened, and his throat thickened. *What if… I'm already there?* It wasn't like she didn't know the score between him and Caleb. But the way he saw Jake—the *intimate* way he saw Jake—only deepened his guilt.

"Liam, you didn't die with him. You still have a life to live. And if you're interested in someone, there's nothing wrong with that."

Liam stared at her. "Y'know, in olden days, you'd have been burned as a witch."

Mom widened her gaze. "Just because I know how you think does *not* make me a witch." She smiled. "It just makes me a mom." Then her eyes sparkled. "Isn't there a gay nightclub over on Market Street? Maybe you should go take a look. You know, get your mojo back."

Liam snorted. "Yeah, I had you nailed right the first time. Definitely a witch." He couldn't deny he liked the idea.

"You think he'll come back here?"

Liam certainly hoped so.

Jake finished the meal his mama had prepared for him, trying to pinpoint what had felt wrong since he'd stepped through the door. On the surface, nothing had changed, and yet… he gazed at the kitchen, the faded lemon walls, the window blind covered in corn cobs…

Then it hit him.

This doesn't feel like home anymore.

What did he expect when he was living a lie every damn day? Home was the place where you felt safest, right? Well, he didn't feel that. How could he, when he was conscious of hiding anything that might betray the difference in him?

I could jus'… tell 'em. I could have 'em all wrong.

Except he knew in his heart that wasn't the case. Hadn't he heard the words from his daddy's own lips?

What's the worst that could happen?

He already knew the answer to that one. He could find himself out on the street, shoved there by parents who couldn't stomach the idea of having a gay son. And then there was his job to consider. He couldn't set up on his own. He didn't have the capital, the work space…

Anyway he looked at it, the situation didn't improve by telling them.

Then there's only one option. Say nothin'.

Jake knew once he got back into his routine, he wouldn't have time to think about such things. He could always take a leaf out of his daddy's book and work all the hours God sent. The only bright spot on the horizon was Taylor.

Thank God for that.

"You alright, sugah?" Mama stroked his head.

What came to mind was Liam's gentle hand there, the night of the homemade movie.

Jake turned his face up to look at her. "I'm fine, Mama. Jus' fine."

Except for the day Taylor and his partner had turned up to bring Jake's whole world to a grinding halt, he'd never been so far

Truth & Betrayal

from fine in his life.

Chapter Twenty-Six

By the time Jake got out of the shower, he felt almost human again. It had been an overly long, hot day. The temperature hadn't dropped below ninety degrees, and the house where they were working was like an airtight box. Jake's shirt had been soaked with sweat by the end of the day, and his daddy's was no better. Once they'd gotten in the house, it was a race for who made it to the shower first.

Jake won.

His phone warbled, and Jake peered at the screen. Taylor. That brought him a smile.

"Hey. What's up?"

"I've had a crap day. Wanna go bowling?"

Jake laughed. He was getting used to Taylor's manner. "Sure, why not? Only, I haven't had supper yet. I jus' got outta the shower."

"So what? We can eat there. Unless a burger an' fries doesn't do it for ya?"

Jake's belly rumbled. Supper was cold chicken and salad, so he didn't think Mama would mind so much if he skipped it.

"Not forgettin' *the* most important part," Taylor added.

"What's that?"

"Damn good AC."

"Oh, *now* you're talkin'." Hillcrest Lanes was the only bowling alley for miles, about half an hour to the west in Harrogate. Apart from the bowling, there were slot machines, pool tables, vending machines, everything to keep a person entertained

Truth & Betrayal

for hours. Then he considered the time. "It's almost seven now. We won't get much time to play."

Taylor snickered. "Well, isn't it a good thing that *someone* checked their closin' times? It's Friday. They close at midnight."

Yup, Jake's evening was definitely looking better. "I'll talk to Mama. It should be fine."

"I'll pick you up in fifteen minutes if it's a go. That gives you time to dry your hair. That'll take, what, all of ten seconds?" Taylor chuckled.

"Well you should know, Mr. Buzz Cut." Jake retorted. "Now git off this phone so's I can talk to Mama. I'll text ya." He disconnected the call, in a better mood than when he'd answered it.

Two weeks since Wilmington, and it felt like the days were crawling by. A distraction was exactly what Jake needed.

"You sneaky son of a bitch. How 'n the hell did you do that?" Jake marked off Taylor's score. "Splits are just evil."

Taylor buffed his nails on his polo shirt. "What can I say? It's all about approach an' rotation. Watch an' learn, boy. Watch an' learn from the master."

Jake nearly snorted soda all over the score card. "Is that the same master who stepped over the foul line at least twice this evenin'?"

Taylor narrowed his gaze. "I was warmin' up."

"Sure you were. Master, my ass."

Taylor reached into his pocket. "I can arrest ya, y'know, for insultin' a police officer." His eyes gleamed. "So don't push me."

Jake remained silent, his lips pressed tightly together in an effort not to laugh. He got off his seat and strolled over to pick up a bowling ball.

"My my, isn't this cozy?"

He froze at the familiar voice and straightened. Pete, Dan,

Mike, and another guy he recognized from their high school days stood at the next table. *Aw crap.* Jake had done a real good job of avoiding them since the quarry episode. It wasn't just that Taylor was a whole lot more fun to be with, it was the fact that Pete had gotten awful close to the mark, right before Taylor had made his well-timed entrance.

Pete stood there, his arms folded, his familiar smirk pasted all over his smug face. "I had wondered why we'd not seen so much of ya lately. Well, now I know." He glanced over his shoulder at the others, grinning. "Looks like Jake done found himself a boyfriend." They snickered and snorted. Pete gave them a simpering smile. "Ain't that sweet? Jake an' the officer, sittin' in a tree. K-I-S-S—"

"Do you always talk outta your ass?" Taylor asked mildly, appearing a damn sight calmer than Jake felt. Inside he was a mess.

"You gonna 'rrest me for speakin' my mind, Mr. Officer sir? 'Cause it looks to me like you're not on duty right now." Pete locked gazes with Taylor. "Does the Chief know he's got a fag on his police force?" That smirk hadn't shifted an inch.

Jake's stomach roiled. This was bad, *so* bad.

Taylor arched his eyebrows. "Oh, so goin' bowlin' with another guy makes me gay? I see. So what does that make your little gang over there? A foursome?" He smiled, but it didn't reach his eyes, and just for a second, Jake felt a chill spread through him. "That how you're gonna spend *your* evenin', Mr. Delaney? A couple of games, then off to fuck each other's brains out?"

Pete's face turned a shade of purple. "You can't say shit like that."

Taylor appeared surprised. "Why not? You jus' said I was gay. What's the difference?"

"Yeah, but—"

Taylor pointed a finger at him. "I did you a favor, remember?"

Pete's eyes bulged. "I walked your damn stupid line!"

Taylor gave him a cool glance. "An' I didn't search any of

ya. Remember that too. Next time, my approach won't be so lax." He glanced over to their table. "Maybe I should take a closer look at those sodas of yours. Seems to me, guys like you who like a drink or two wouldn't see anything wrong with spikin' their Coke."

All the color slid from Pete's face, and the others were just as ashen.

Taylor's cool smile disappeared. "I think you boys had better choose another lane. Maybe at the far end. An' a word to the wise, Mr. Delaney. Slander. Think about that, because I don't think you wanna open up that particular can of worms, do ya?"

Pete swallowed. "Let's find ourselves another table, guys." He stumbled over to the table and picked up his soda cup, the others doing the same. Jake watched them slope off to the farthest lane, before sinking onto his chair, his knees shaking.

"How could you jus' stand there so freakin' *calm*? An' what if he decides to press charges 'gainst you for what you said about him?"

"He won't. I've met his kind before. An' we both know what he said is a load of bullshit."

"The part about us datin', sure. But..." Jake lowered his voice. "What about you bein'...? Not to mention me."

Taylor smiled, only this time it was a whole lot warmer. "I'd like to see him prove it, seein' as there's no evidence." He tapped his temple. "Not when it's all in here. It's not like I've ever dated a guy, right? There are no skeletons in *my* closet." He snickered. "They wouldn't fit anyhow. I'm already in there, an' I've got no plans to come out of it anytime soon."

Despite his apprehension, Jake had to laugh at that.

Taylor laughed too. "That's better. Now how 'bout we finish this game, an' then maybe after I can teach you a thing or two 'bout pool?" He flexed his fingers.

Jake snorted. "You can try." Taylor's calm manner went a long way to quelling his nerves. He picked up his bowling ball and grinned. "'Course, first I'm gonna wipe the floor with ya."

As he approached the line, he caught Taylor's murmured

remark. "You can try."

Trying to bowl accurately while laughing your ass off? Never gonna happen.

The music was loud, the AC was a waste of time, and the lights were bright.

Liam loved it.

Ibiza turned out to be a fun place. There was a pretty decent drag show, but Liam had been spoiled by Lips in Atlanta, where all the servers were queens, and the shows were a riot. The clientele wasn't overwhelmingly comprised of gay men: there was a healthy mix of men and women. The drinks weren't overpriced, and the music was good.

He was having a great time.

What had surprised him was the fact that he was nervous.

When was the last time I went to a gay club on my own? He couldn't remember. Maybe not since he was first out. He couldn't help remembering the times he'd gone out clubbing with Caleb, when they'd danced all night long. He knew he didn't need a partner to lose himself in the music, but making that first step toward the dance floor alone felt strange.

"Hey."

Liam looked up from his glass. A blond guy in a tight-fitting pink shirt and even tighter jeans stood beside him, leaning against the bar. Big blue eyes, cute as hell. "Hey."

"Not seen you here before, have I?"

Liam shook his head. "I've only recently moved back to Wilmington." Those times he'd visited with Caleb, they'd spent them with his family, which was more important than going to a club. That would wait for when they were back in Atlanta.

"So… wanna dance?"

Lord, those were pretty eyes. "Sure." Liam smiled. "I'm Liam, by the way."

The cutie returned his smile. "I'm Paul."

Liam drained his beer, then slid off his stool to follow Paul onto the dance floor, where they were soon swallowed up by the crowd, lost in a heap of bodies gyrating to the rhythm that pulsed through the air and the floor. Liam moved to the music, hardly noticing Paul who faced him.

It was glorious.

When Paul signaled he wanted a drink, Liam nodded, and they eased their way through the dancers toward the bar. "What can I get ya?"

Liam waved his hand. "Let me. I wouldn't have gotten out there if you hadn't asked."

"Oh. Okay. A vodka an' Coke, thanks." The bartender set about fixing their drinks. Paul gazed at Liam. "You're a good dancer."

"I'm outta practice. It's been a while."

"I couldn't tell, the way you move out there."

Liam couldn't miss the way Paul looked him up and down, nor the gleam of interest in those baby blues. "Thanks for the compliment." He couldn't return it: he had no clue as to how good a dancer Paul was, and he didn't want to give him the wrong idea. He'd enjoyed the dancing, and for right then, that was enough for him.

"You must get a lot of those." Liam regarded him quizzically, and Paul flushed. "Seeing as you're such a gorgeous guy."

Oh.

Liam took a deep breath. "I'm glad you asked me to dance. I'd been sittin' here, thinkin' 'bout how long it's been since I came to a club on my own. We're talkin' more than five years. I'm only recently single again, an' this feels a little… weird."

"Glad I could help." Paul cocked his head to one side. "This is you givin' me a gentle brush-off, isn't it?"

Relief shuddered through him. "Yeah. Sorry if I gave you the wrong idea."

"You didn't," Paul assured him. "I jus' thought I'd try my luck." He grinned. "Obviously not my lucky night. I've been where you are, by the way. Getting back to datin' when you've been in a relationship is difficult. Maybe you're just not ready."

Liam wasn't so sure about that part. It wasn't even as if his mom would react badly if he brought someone home for the night, not that he'd ever do that.

Maybe it's just that the wrong person asked me to dance. Only, the right one is about five hundred miles away.

The second the thought flashed through his mind, Liam knew it to be more than just maybe. He didn't *want* a one-night stand. He didn't want to start something with someone, not when he knew there was a strong chance it wouldn't amount to anything.

Not when he was already thinking about Jake.

"Wanna dance again?"

There was that sense of relief again. Liam grinned. "I thought you'd never ask."

Laughing, Paul led him to the dance floor.

Truth & Betrayal

Chapter Twenty-Seven

August had apparently decided it was going out on a hot and sticky end, and Jake was longing for fall. September's arrival was bittersweet, however, bringing with it an event that had always brought him pleasure in the past, but that only promised to bring an ache in his heart this time.

Saturday, September 3rd. Caleb would have been twenty-seven.

A couple of times during the week leading up to that day, Jake had retreated to his room, got comfortable on the bed, and opened up Caleb's laptop to look at his photos again. Only now, he could put names to faces. There were Dev and Pauli at a New Year's Eve party, wearing silly hats and blowing noisemakers at each other. And Lord have mercy, there was Caleb in drag, looking… well, he had to confess, Caleb looked *amazing*. He really rocked those high heels, and appeared to be having a wonderful time.

Jake avoided the US folder. He didn't need to see those. It felt too much like prying into something that was definitely not his business. Except he knew that was only the half of it. Looking at Liam in those unguarded moments sent all kinds of feelings skittering through him, the main one being a longing that he did his best to push aside. Sure, there'd been moments back in Wilmington where Jake had deluded himself that something might come of those feelings, but he knew better than to dwell on them. So what if Liam thought he was pretty sexy? Jake wasn't about to read more into that.

Truth & Betrayal

Along that path lay only hurt. Rejection.

The day before Caleb's birthday, before breakfast, Jake paused at the bedroom door that had remained shut since he'd brought back Caleb's possessions from Atlanta. A yearning filled him. That room was *full* of Caleb. How better to celebrate his life than be surrounded by him? Jake opened the door and went inside.

Drapes covered the window, giving the room a drab feel. Jake flung them open, letting the sunlight spill into it, watching the motes of dust dancing in the air. Boxes were stacked up in one corner. Clothes sat in neat piles, ironed and folded. The old peach satin comforter on the bed lay straight, its surface smooth.

Jake stared at it, suddenly seeing Caleb teaching him to do tumbles across it when he was four years' old, until Jake's shrieks of joy had brought Mama. Her admonishment that 'Beds are for sleepin' in' had brought a premature end to their fun.

The dresser was as Caleb had left it, only... A row of framed photos had been added, standing in a long line, all of them depicting Caleb growing up. For some reason, the sight sent an uneasy shiver down Jake's spine.

"What are you doin' in here?"

Mama's shrill cry gave him a start. "Lord above, Mama, you just 'bout gave me a heart attack."

She stood in the doorway, her hands gripping its wooden frame. "What are you doin' in here? You have no reason to be here."

Jake stilled, his heartbeat racing. "No reason? Since when do I need a reason to be in my brother's bedroom?" He gazed around the room in confusion. *Am I missin' something?*

Then he got it. The neatness, the dark, the photos... *Oh, Mama, no.*

Deliberately, Jake faced her, trying to push down on a rising tide of anger tinged with sympathy. "Mama, you're turnin' his room into a shrine, an' you can't do that."

Mama's eyes widened, her mouth opened, and then she snapped it shut.

Jake shook his head. "There's no point keepin' it as he left it, because he's not comin' back. An' if we can't come in here an' remember him, then what in the *hell* is the point of keepin' his room as it was?"

Mama's face was so pale, Jake thought she was about to faint.

He softened his voice. "Look, tomorrow is—"

"I know what tomorrow is," she snapped.

Jake held up his hands in a peaceful gesture. "Fine, an' how are ya gonna spend it? At church? 'Cause let's be honest, Mama, you spend so much time there nowadays, you might as well live there. Daddy will work, because that's all *he* does nowadays, an' it bein' a Saturday will make no difference anyhow. That leaves me, an' I'm sorry, Mama, but I have to do somethin'." In that moment he knew exactly what. His heart hammered. "So I'm gonna spend the weekend with Caleb's… friends, people who wanna celebrate his life." Not that he thought of the Millers as friends. They were more like Caleb's second family.

Mama stared at him in silence for a moment, her face flushed red. Then she seemed to just… crumple. "Fine. Go. Leave us. Obviously, we're not important."

Oh, great. Jake walked over to her and placed his hands gently on her upper arms. "That's not what I said, an' you know it. You *are* important, Mama, you *and* Daddy, but right now we need… different things."

For a second, he swore he saw a flash of something in her eyes that looked almost like… fear. Then she sighed. "When will you leave? Are you gonna work today? I know your daddy was sayin' how much work there is to do—"

Jake squeezed her arm. "I wouldn't do that to Daddy, not when he needs me. No, I'll go tonight, right after we finish. I'll grab a bite to eat on the way, an' I'll drive through the night if I have to."

Mama's eyes flashed again, only this time he knew why. "Like I'd let you eat from some fast food place, when I can make you somethin' miles better."

Jake chuckled. He leaned in and kissed her cheek. "That's 'cause you're the best mama ever."

She rolled her eyes. "Quit flatterin' an' git in that kitchen. You'll need a good breakfast inside ya for today."

"I will. I jus' have to make a phone call first." He left Caleb's room and went into his own, closing the door behind him. It was only seven thirty. Liam might still be asleep. Then he reconsidered. Liam was a working boy now.

Jake quickly composed a text. *Can we talk?*

Liam's response was equally fast. Moments later, the phone rang. "Hey. What's up?"

"I know you're gettin' ready to go to work, so I'll make this fast. I wanna come see ya. Tonight. It'll be late when I get there, after midnight." He paused, his pulse racing. "Is that gonna be a problem?"

"Not at all," Liam replied instantly. "I thought I might hear from ya this weekend, seein' as it's… Yeah, sure. I'll stay up 'til you get here. An' Mom will be happy to see ya too. Jus' one thing though?"

"Yeah?"

Liam's voice quietened. "Drive careful, Jake?"

"I will, I promise." He disconnected, then set about packing his bag. He wouldn't need much, not for two nights, but at least he'd be ready to go once work was done for the day.

The thought of spending Caleb's birthday with the Millers made his heart glad.

The thought of spending it with Liam created a whole other set of emotions.

Liam awoke with a start, unsure for a moment of his surroundings. Light splashed across his face, and he realized it came from headlights outside, coming up the driveway.

He's here. Liam peered groggily at his phone. It was almost three in the morning. He went through the house to the kitchen, and carefully opened the back door. The security light was already on, triggered by movement. Jake was locking the truck, a backpack over his shoulder.

Lord, he looks tired. There was tension in the way he stood, the way he held himself.

That decided Liam. Talk could wait until the morning… well, later in the morning. Jake needed to sleep.

Jake gave him a weary smile as he approached the door. "Sorry it's so late," he whispered. "We didn't finish 'til gone six, an' I hit traffic a couple times." He sighed. "You should've gone to bed. I'd have found a couch to sleep on."

Liam ignored him and pulled him into a hug. "I'm jus' happy to see you," he whispered back. Jake's head rested on his shoulder, and it was as if all the tension melted out of him. "Now, you're goin' straight to bed. We can talk later."

Jake straightened. "Right now, a bed sounds awesome." Liam released him, and he stepped into the cool interior. Liam locked up behind them, then guided Jake to the study/bedroom. He'd set up the bed as soon as he got home from work. Mom had been delighted, although he caught her giving him an inquiring glance now and then after dinner. Her questions could wait.

What mattered then was Jake.

Once he was inside the room, Jake dropped his bag onto a chair, shucked off his sneakers, pulled off his T-shirt, jeans and socks, then crawled between the sheets and sank his head into the pillows.

Liam smiled to himself. *He'll be asleep before I leave the room.*

Then Jake rolled onto his side. "Don't go jus' yet." Fatigue laced his entreaty.

Liam joined him on the bed, reminded of that night in Atlanta. "Hey," he said softly, stroking Jake's head. "You need to sleep." He yawned and covered his mouth with his hand.

Jake gave a drowsy chuckle. "You too." Just for a moment, he appeared more alert. "Hey, whadda y'know? It's officially Caleb's birthday."

Liam nodded. After a few seconds' thought, he stretched out beside Jake on top of the sheet and held his arms wide. "C'me'ere."

Jake didn't hesitate. He cuddled up to Liam, his smooth head against Liam's chest, his arm around Liam's waist, his hand resting lightly against Liam's back.

"We'll do somethin' Saturday night, alright? To celebrate his birthday." Liam already had an idea.

"Sounds good," Jake said sleepily. "You feel good."

Liam caught his breath. It was such an innocent statement. "So do you." He lay there, Jake in his arms, listening to his breathing as he slipped deeper into sleep.

Unsurprisingly, Liam followed him.

Jake blinked. Daylight. Wilmington. He was back in Liam's bed.

And Liam was in bed with him, lying on his side, facing him. Fast asleep.

Jake peeked beneath the white sheet. Neither of them was naked. He had to check, seeing as he had no memory of undressing however many hours ago it was. Liam wore jeans, but his chest was bare, and Jake stared at the smooth, dark skin, his nipples a shade darker, pebbled circles with proud little nubs that begged to feel a mouth around them. Over Liam's sternum lay a trail of black fuzz, petering out to nothing, until it dipped past his navel and disappeared beneath the waistband of his jeans.

Fuck, he was beautiful.

"Did you take off my T-shirt?"

Shit. Liam was looking right at him.

Jake shook his head, and Liam huffed. "Must've been me then. Not that I remember." He glanced down at their bodies. "At least I kept my jeans on."

Lord, the temptation to tell him Jake wouldn't have minded in the slightest if he'd taken them off. "I guess we were both pretty tired. I mean, you waited up for me."

Liam peered at the clock on the table beside the pullout couch. "Damn, it's already past ten. You want some breakfast? Okay, brunch."

Jake's stomach growled out a reply, and Jake didn't know where to look.

Liam snickered. "I'm guessin' that's a big yes. I'll rustle up some pancakes, an' if we're real lucky, there's bacon in the refrigerator. You've got time for a shower if you need one."

Jake decided that hunger beat hygiene this time. "I'll help with the breakfast. Jus' tell me what to do."

"Great." Liam threw back the sheet and found his T-shirt that had been tossed to the foot of the bed. He squirmed into it. "I'll see ya in the kitchen." And with that, he was out the door.

Jake stared at it. *What the hell?* Then he figured his questions would have to wait. Sharon would be wondering where he was. He had to admit, that was one helluva way to wake up.

An' at least this time I know it was no dream. Liam had really been there, gorgeous against the white sheets, smelling of cotton and something else, a spicy scent that Jake could've inhaled all day long.

Breakfast. Enough with the torture. Liam hadn't appeared perturbed at all to find himself in Jake's bed, and Jake wasn't sure whether he felt relieved or disappointed by that reaction.

Liam knew Mama was watching him. He felt her eyes boring into his back. "C'mon, say whatever it is you're dyin' to say," he said, pouring the pancake mix into a jug, next to the griddle. The bacon was already laid out in strips on the foil-covered baking sheet, ready to go into the oven.

"Oh, I was just standing here, thinking how well I taught my children to fend for themselves. Of course, if they'd been awake at a reasonable hour, *I* would've made 'em breakfast. Except when I got up, one of my kids wasn't where he was supposed to be. Now, why was that?"

She didn't sound pissed, more amused.

Liam put down the jug of pancake mix and turned to face her. "Jake didn't get in 'til gone three. I dozed off waitin' for him. I guess we both fell asleep."

"I didn't peek in on him, just in case."

Liam blinked. "In case what?" When she didn't respond, Liam lowered his voice. "What did you think you might see?"

She shrugged. "I wasn't sure, to be honest." When Liam stared at her, she stared right back. "What? You think I'm blind? You think I don't see what's happening? And before you say another word, if it is what I *think* it is, that's okay, baby."

Liam covered his eyes with his hand. Fuck, this was getting complicated.

Mom put her arms around him. "What is it, sweetheart?"

How could he tell her, when he wasn't sure himself?

Liam took a breath. "Waking up with him like that felt… good. Like he had every right to be in that bed with me. But that only made me feel like…."

"Like you were betraying Caleb's memory," she concluded. When Liam nodded, she sighed and kissed his cheek. "We've talked about this. If it's time to move on, then it's time to move on."

"Yeah, but with Jake?"

"Why not with Jake?" She let him go and stared into his eyes. "Just because of who he is? Liam, honey, you got to listen to your heart, not your head. Now, I'm not saying do anything right now about how you're feeling, but at least accept this is a possibility. Don't push it away because you think it's somehow… wrong. Because it isn't, believe me." She turned her head slightly toward the door. "And now you'd better sit down and entertain your guest. *I'll* take care of breakfast."

"I was doin' it!" he huffed.

"Mm-hmm," she said, pouring the pancake mix back into its bottle. "This is for your Dad when he's at home working, I'm not around, and he wants pancakes. No child of mine is going to eat ready mix pancakes while *I'm* alive. Now sit your ass down and let me do my thing."

He gave her a tight hug. "I love your thing," he whispered.

She giggled, then pushed him away. "You can make coffee, but that's all. Leave the rest to me."

"Yes, ma'am."

Mom narrowed her gaze, then broke into a smile. "Morning, Jake. Food'll be ready soon. Meanwhile, there'll be coffee as soon as Liam gets his ass in gear. First though, where's my hug?"

Liam watched the way they embraced, how Jake seemed real happy to see his mom.

He looks like he belongs here.

Liam couldn't argue with that.

Truth & Betrayal

Chapter Twenty-Eight

Jake had to admit, this was a great way to celebrate Caleb's birthday. *He'd have loved this.* The nightclub was packed, everyone around him was having a good time, and better yet, you only had to be eighteen to get in.

"Havin' fun?" Liam yelled over the music. Jake gave him the thumbs up. He couldn't imagine telling his parents he was going to a nightclub back home. Mama would likely explode. Okay, so maybe explode was an exaggeration, but the overall effect would be the same.

She wouldn't like it.

The music changed to a number with a heavy bass beat, and Jake fucking *loved* it. He threw back his head and gave a shout of joy, surprised when those around him joined him. It was an awesome atmosphere, all those people moving to the heady rhythm… It was something primal.

It was also hotter 'n hell. All those lights, those bodies…

Liam's shirt was already clinging to his skin, and Jake watched, mesmerized by the bead of sweat that trickled down his neck and disappeared beneath the layer of cotton. *Fuck*, that was sexy. Jake danced closer, until their bodies were almost touching, the colored lights above their heads reflecting on Liam's glistening chest, visible where he'd left his shirt unbuttoned.

Jake couldn't resist. He reached out, and casually undid another button.

Liam's eyes widened, but he said nothing.

Emboldened, Jake did it again, and again, until Liam's shirt was open to the waist. "That's better," he murmured, before letting his fingertips skate over Liam's damp flesh. Liam's chest rose and fell more rapidly, and he swallowed hard.

"I think... I need a drink."

Jake grinned. "Gotta keep hydrated, right?" If he didn't know better, he'd have sworn he'd just made Liam nervous. "Let's go to the bar."

Liam nodded and edged his way through the crowd, Jake following close behind.

Jake had just discovered something about himself.

He liked flirting with Liam.

Okay, what the hell just happened?

Stupid question. Liam knew *exactly* what had happened. What shocked him to the core was that he liked it. Not only that, he wanted more of the same.

What had him running for the bar, however, was the fact that they were in that nightclub because of Caleb. He connected them. *Take that link away and...*

It felt like he'd be taking advantage of Jake. It didn't matter what Mom said, what Mom thought. He couldn't take another step on this road until he convinced himself Jake wanted this as much as he did. That if he removed Caleb from the equation, they were just two gay guys, attracted to each other.

At least, he *hoped* Jake was attracted to him, and that this whole... sensual episode wasn't just him flexing his newly discovered gay muscle. Because Liam didn't think he could stand that.

Liam reached the bar, then turned to Jake. "Another bottle of water?"

Jake nodded. He stared at the dance floor. "Y'know, when we were out there, the music didn't seem so loud, but now? I can hardly hear myself think."

"There's a room upstairs, with a pool table. Might be better if you wanna rest from dancin' for a while. This place stays open until two, after all." Liam grinned. "Plenty of time to dance your feet off."

Jake nodded enthusiastically. "Yeah, let's give our eardrums time to stop bleedin'."

Liam laughed. He collected the two bottles and led Jake over to the stairs.

The second floor had windows front and rear that opened out onto small balconies, where clubbers called out to the passerby on the street below. The music was definitely a little quieter, and there was seating if you wanted to hang out and chat. In the corner was a pool table, and a crowd of people surrounded it, watching two guys play.

Jake sank onto a couch by the wall, and drained half his bottle of water. He wiped his mouth and gave Liam a speculative glance. "Okay. Is it jus' me, or are there not that many gay guys down there? Because so far, I've seen a helluva lotta girls. An' they look kinda… straight."

Liam snickered. "Welcome to the real world of gay bars an' clubs. The girls come with their gay BFFs. Havin' said that, it obviously depends on the night. I read a review of this place that basically said, 'where are all the girls?' But this is pretty much the only gay club worth anythin' here in Wilmington."

"It has some good points." Jake waggled his eyebrows. "Some of the bartenders downstairs were hot as fuck."

That sent Liam's heart sinking into his boots. *I hate being right.* Liam didn't respond but took a long drink of water.

"By the way…" Jake gestured to his still open shirt. "That's a good look on you."

Liam gave him a hard stare. "Well, you obviously thought so."

"Well, I don't see you butt'nin' it up, so I guess you must too," Jake retorted, his eyes sparkling with good humor. He took another drink. "Seriously though, this place is amazing. The music is awesome, an' the bartenders are real polite." He got to his feet. "Okay, enough rest. I wanna dance some more."

Liam laughed and joined him. "That *is* why we're here, isn't it?" He followed Jake downstairs, where the even bigger crowd swallowed them up.

Jus' dance. Have a good time. An' try not to think about Jake as anything other than a friend, because you'll only wind up gettin' hurt.

Only problem was, Liam didn't want to be Jake's friend. He wanted more.

It was almost two in the morning, and the day was catching up with Jake real fast.

He'd had a wonderful time, but there'd been this vague sense of something missing. For one thing, he was disappointed in Liam. That part with the shirt, for instance. It might have started out as flirting, but seeing Liam's reaction lit a fire in Jake, and he wanted more.

Only thing was, Liam apparently didn't.

That upstairs room was another for instance. Quieter, more relaxed, perfect for…

What, exactly? What the hell was I lookin' for? Because he hadn't found it.

Yet.

He gazed at Liam, his arms held high above his head, lifting his shirt, his abs visible. Clearly not someone who worked out all the time, but definitely took care of himself. A beautiful man, one Jake wanted to get closer to, but there was something in the way.

It has to be Caleb. Has to be. Liam saw him as Caleb's brother, not as a gay man who was attracted to him. That part, Jake wasn't even gonna *begin* denying. Liam had shown himself time and time again to be a good person, kind and thoughtful, caring and sensitive. All good qualities. But it was only in their recent encounters that Jake had begun to see him in a new light.

Sexy. As. Fuck.

Jake stared at him, mentally yelling. *Can't you see I'm interested? What was me unbutt'nin' your shirt, if not me showin' you I'm fuckin' interested?*

There was only one thing for it. Jake had made the first move, and Liam apparently hadn't seen it for what it was.

Time to make things really obvious.

Jake moved closer, until he couldn't have slipped a piece of paper between them.

Liam stilled, right there in the middle of the dance floor, all around them a constant flow of movement. "Jake?"

He smiled. "You know what? You're beautiful, inside *and* out." And before Liam could respond, Jake leaned in and kissed him lightly on the lips.

Liam kept so still. Like… no movement whatsoever.

Jake's heart pounded, the blood rushed past his ears, and his legs trembled. *Please, see me? See me, Liam?*

Mentally taking hold of his courage with both hands, Jake leaned in again and repeated the kiss, brushing his lips against Liam's. This time, however, Liam pulled free, before placing his hands gently on either side of Jake's face.

"If you're gonna kiss me, Jake," he said, his voice husky, barely audible above the music, "then *really* kiss me." And with that, he closed the gap between them, taking Jake's mouth in a kiss that *wasn't* light, *wasn't* subtle, that was nothing short of claiming him, their lips fused while his fingers stroked Jake's cheeks.

Holy fuckin' hell.

Jake was dizzy from it all, his head spinning, lost in sensation, from the music pulsing through him, to the ticklish rasp of Liam's mustache against his lips, to the feel of his fingertips exploring Jake's face like he was learning the touch of him by heart.

He didn't want it to end.

Liam broke the kiss, and Jake could've howled with

frustration. But then Liam focused those dark eyes on him, and leaned forward to brush his lips against Jake's ear. "D'ya wanna keep dancin'? Or do you wanna go home?"

Talk about a no-brainer.

Jake made sure Liam was looking him in the eye. "Take me home."

Liam nodded slowly. "Then let's get outta here." He held out his hand, and Jake took it, his heart still racing.

Holy fuck, this is real.

Chapter Twenty-Nine

Neither of them said a word the entire time Liam drove them home, but that was fine. Jake kept reliving that kiss over and over in his head, still reeling from it. Butterflies danced in his stomach every time he thought about Liam's hands on his face, so gentle, like Jake was something precious.

When he thought about what might be coming his way, the butterflies multiplied. Because for all his fantasies? Jake was as nervous as a cat in a room full of rocking chairs.

Liam switched off the engine, and Jake realized with a start that they were back already. The house was in darkness as it had been twenty-four hours previous when he'd first arrived.

"We're gonna have to be quiet."

A shiver slid down Jake's spine, because there was more than one way to take Liam's words, and he wasn't entirely sure how he felt about that. He got out of the car, and waited while Liam locked it, then followed him toward the back door. Once inside, Liam locked the door, then paused.

"You wanna take up where we left off?"

Jake swallowed. "If that means you kissin' me again, hell yeah."

Liam took hold of Jake's hand and led him to the bedroom. He closed the door softly behind them. Jake stood beside the fold-out couch, hands by his sides, his body quivering with anticipation. Liam switched on the lamp beside the bed, climbed onto it, then crooked his finger, beckoning Jake to join him. Jake swore his heart missed a beat. Haltingly, he got onto the bed and lay on his back, head supported by the pile of pillows.

Liam shifted onto his side, snuggled up against Jake's body, his hand resting lightly on Jake's thigh. "So, I think we were about… here." Then he leaned over and their lips met in a tender kiss.

Yeah, fucking perfect. Jake liked the way Liam kissed, like he could do this all night long. He liked the way Liam squeezed his thigh, not venturing higher.

Then Liam stopped. His eyes sparkled. "You *can* touch me, y'know."

Jake's heart did that skipping a beat thing again. Hesitantly, he placed his hand on Liam's chest, feeling the damp cotton beneath his fingertips. A firm chest lay hidden beneath the fabric, and Jake rubbed over it, not missing Liam's sharp intake of breath when Jake encountered his nipple. Encouraged, Jake mimicked Liam's movements, squeezing the pec, before sliding his hand higher to Liam's broad shoulder, then to his neck.

"That's it." Liam kissed him again, only this time his tongue flicked Jake's lips, and on instinct Jake opened for him, moaning softly when Liam's tongue met his. The kiss deepened, and Jake's pulse quickened at the touch of Liam's hand on his thigh, his hip, his belly. When Liam slid his hand beneath Jake's T-shirt, his fingers warm against Jake's skin, Jake moaned again. Liam reached higher, rubbing over Jake's nipples, and Jake gave a shudder.

"You like that?" Liam did it again, only this time his tongue plunged deep, and Jake was carried away on a wave of intense pleasure like he'd never known before.

He broke the kiss, gasping. "Jus' need to breathe."

Liam chuckled. "So I take your breath away, huh?"

Jake locked gazes with him. "Like you didn't know that." His fingers sought the buttons on Liam's shirt. "Wanna see you."

Lord, he could swear Liam's eyes were so dark, they were black. "Me too."

Swiftly, both their hands were in motion, lifting T-shirts,

undoing buttons, until they were both bare above the waist. Jake's heart pounded as Liam took up his original position, gazing down at him. "Fuck, you're beautiful."

Jake stared at him incredulously. "Have you looked in a mirror lately? I wasn't lyin', back there at the club."

Liam's eyes glittered, and Jake's heartbeat sped up. He caught his breath as Liam leaned over and flicked Jake's nipple with his tongue. "Jesus fuckin' Christ, do that again."

Liam chuckled, before enclosing the nipple in his warm, wet mouth, sucking on it, teasing it with his teeth. Jake couldn't stop touching him, rubbing over Liam's firm shoulders and back, feeling the muscles move beneath his fingers. Then breathing became a real chore when Liam languidly rubbed over Jake's crotch.

Holy fuck.

Liam's mouth was on his, while his hand gently squeezed and fondled Jake's erect dick that pushed against his zipper. Jake's heart hammered, and he moaned into Liam's kiss, desire coursing through him, mixed with a good ol' dose of panic. He couldn't think straight, couldn't get enough air into his lungs...

And then Liam nudged his fingertips under the waistband of his jeans.

Jake broke free of Liam's kiss and gasped out, "Wait!"

Liam froze immediately, withdrawing his hand. "You okay?"

He was *not* okay, but he didn't have a fuckin' clue as to why. "Can... can we slow things down a bit?"

"Of course." Liam rubbed over Jake's hip, and it was sort of comforting. He didn't say anything, and Jake appreciated that. Liam was giving him some space to breathe, to think, and he surely needed the latter.

I don't get it. I wanted this, right? Lord, how he'd wanted it.

"I'm sorry," he blurted out.

Liam's eyes widened. "Hey, wait a sec. You have *nothing*

to be sorry for, y'hear? The bottom line is, if you don't wanna do somethin', then we don't do it. Simple as that." He leaned in and kissed Jake lightly on the lips. "Seein' as it's real late—or early, dependin' on how you look at it—why don't we get some sleep?"

Jake nodded. "Yeah, we should." When the thought occurred to him, he hesitated to share it, but he'd gotten this far. "Would you mind if we… didn't sleep together? I mean, I know we fell asleep here last night, but… this is… different." He couldn't tell Liam exactly how the situation differed. He only knew it did. "I feel real bad 'bout askin' you to sleep in the den, 'specially after—"

Liam silenced him with a finger to his lips. "Jake, it's okay, alright? I understand." After kissing him once more, Liam got up off the bed and collected his shirt from where it had fallen to the floor. "Get some sleep. We can talk in the mornin'."

Jake nodded. Liam gave him a quick smile before leaving the room, closing the door quietly behind him.

Jake shucked off his jeans and crawled under the sheet. Suddenly he didn't feel so sleepy after all.

By the time Liam had glanced at the clock on the wall three times, he figured it was a waste of time just lying there. He might as well get up: the sun was already in the sky, had been for an hour or so.

He got up off the couch and folded the sheet he'd thrown there a few hours earlier: unfolding the bed would've made too much noise. He padded barefoot over to the kitchen area and set up the coffee machine. *Christ, I bet I look like hell.* He studiously avoided the stainless-steel hood above the stove. He did *not* need to see his reflection.

By the time the coffee had finished dripping into the pot, he knew he wasn't the only one awake. What surprised him was that it was Jake. He walked into the kitchen, rubbing his eyes, dressed in his jeans and a clean T-Shirt.

Liam didn't bother asking. He poured out two mugs of coffee and handed one to Jake. "Creamer in the refrigerator if you want it."

Jake grimaced. "I think takin' it black's a better idea right now."

Liam was suddenly conscious of his state of undress. "Why don't you go an' sit on the bench? I'll join ya when I've put on some clothes." He was *not* about to go into the yard in just his shorts.

Jake nodded, bleary-eyed, and headed for the back door. Liam quickly pulled on his jeans, deciding against the shirt he'd removed. His clean clothes were in Jake's room. He walked shirtless into the back yard, coming to a halt when he saw Jake. He was sitting on the bench, leaning forward, elbows on his knees, hands wrapped around his mug, his head bowed.

Jake looked like he carried the weight of the world on his shoulders. *An' it's my fault.*

Liam sat beside him, leaning back against the comfortable wooden slats. He sighed. "About last night. I'm sorry. I shouldn't have moved so fast."

Jake jerked his head to stare at him. "Hey, this is *not* your fault, alright?" His sigh echoed Liam's. "Look, I'm not sure if I can explain what happened. Lord knows, I've been thinkin' 'bout it enough since you left me."

Liam stared into his coffee. "Do you regret kissin' me?"

"Fuck no!" When Liam stared at him, Jake flushed. "No, I don't," he said a moment later, clearly in an effort to speak more calmly. "I wanted to kiss ya. Sweet *Jesus*, you have no idea how much I wanted to kiss ya. An' I wanted to do more than kiss ya." He bit his lip. "At least, I *thought* I did." Jake let out a wry chuckle. "It's like this. I thought I was ready for… you know… an' trust me, my imagination was doin' a fuckin' good job of lettin' me know that."

Okay, *that* was intriguing.

"All the time you were kissin' me, touchin' me, I was thinkin', 'I'm ready for this! I'm ready for this!' Then when you reached into my jeans, it was like my brain screamed, 'I'm *so* not ready for this!'"

Liam laughed softly. "There's nothin' wrong with list'nin' to what goes on in your head." A wave of relief washed through him. *He jus' got cold feet, that's all.* Liam didn't have a problem with that whatsoever. *Then maybe I'd better tell him that.*

Liam put his mug on the ground, then reached across to take Jake's hand. "It's okay to be nervous. You should've seen me, my first time. I was so hyped up, I came in less than a minute. I tell ya, I was so disappointed. So was the guy I was with. An' I didn't get a second chance either." He squeezed Jake's hand. "I guess what I'm sayin' is…when you're ready, you'll know. An' then we'll take things nice an' slow."

Jake's breathing hitched. "We? So… this isn't the end?"

God, Liam hoped not. He took the mug from Jake's other hand, and pulled Jake onto his lap, his arms around him. "Oh, baby, this is *so* not the end. This is jus' the beginnin'."

Then Jake made the moment perfect by looping his arms around Liam's neck, and kissing him like it was about to be outlawed. Liam stroked his hands over Jake's waist, moving them leisurely around to his back, loving the feel of Jake's hand on the back of his head, pulling him deeper into the kiss.

I wanted this too. Liam did his best to ignore his racing heartbeat, pushing aside his own fears and doubts. Everything had changed in the blink of an eye, leaving so many questions, they made his head spin. *Where do we go from here?*

Liam didn't have a fucking clue.

When they parted, Jake's eyes shone, and his face glowed. "Wow. Now *that's* the way to start a day."

Liam snickered. "Kisses may satisfy *your* belly, but they don't fill mine. An' right now, I could do with Mom's chicken fried steak, eggs, biscuits, an' sausage gravy."

Jake groaned. "Did ya *have* to put that idea into my head?"

Liam stroked his cheek. "We'll work on her once she's up an' around. But until then…" He brushed his lips over Jake's, and Jake let out the tiniest moan of pleasure. "We'll just keep on kissin'," Liam murmured against Jake's lips.

Judging by the soft sigh that escaped him, Jake really liked that idea.

Jake did *not* want to leave.

His bag was packed, sitting in the hallway beside the couch, and the slow, steady tick of the clock in the corner was a reminder that time was slipping away from him, that he had to make a move sooner or later.

Jake voted for later, but he knew that wasn't an option.

He had to go home.

"Jake, you okay?" Rachel was in the dining room, laying the table for lunch.

He pasted on a bright smile. "I'm fine."

Rachel snorted. "Wow, you're as bad a liar as my brother. Liam can't lie for shit either." She finished putting the plates on the table and walked over to him. "Is there anything I can do?"

Jake reminded himself for the umpteenth time how lucky he was to have met this family.

"Not really." *Not unless you can find a way to lose the five hundred or more miles that lie between LaFollette an' Wilmington.* Any way he looked at it, putting distance between two guys who were just finding out they might have something going on, was a bad idea. Never mind 'distance makes the heart grow fonder', an' all that crap.

Jake wanted to make this work. He just didn't know how. And he got the feeling Liam didn't know either.

"It's been real good getting to know you, and I hope we're gonna see a lot more of you." Rachel's eyes twinkled. "I know Liam certainly wants to see more of you."

Oh Lord, are we that *obvious?*

He'd tried his best not to keep staring at Liam throughout the morning, but it was as if part of him needed constant reassuring that he hadn't dreamed the whole thing. As for Liam, he seemed to have the same issue. Jake would look up, and find Liam watching him.

Can *we make this work?* God, he hoped so.

"Lunch is ready!" Sharon yelled from the kitchen.

Rachel tugged on Jake's arm. "Come on, let's feed ya before you have to leave. Mom's pot roast is amazing."

"*All* your mama's cookin' is amazin'," Jake corrected her.

"I heard that!" Sharon stepped into the dining room, carrying a large covered dish. She placed it in the center of the table, then inclined her head toward the kitchen. "And Will, I've counted those roast potatoes, before you get any ideas."

"Mom, really?"

Jake laughed at Will's plaintive tone, and Sharon winked at him. "Good thing I know what my kids are capable of, right?"

"What's Liam's favorite?"

Sharon grinned. "My roast chicken. He can't keep his fingers off. The number of times I go into the kitchen, and find him picking bits of the carcass. Of course, he'd deny it, but there's no getting around grease marks. Especially if you're dumb enough to wipe your fingers on your pants."

"It's all lies," Liam said as he entered the room, smiling. "Don't believe a word she says."

Jake held up his hands. "Hey, don't you make me have to choose between you an' your mama." He sat at the table, and Liam took the chair next to his.

He leaned in close. "I thought you'd be on my side," he said in a low voice.

Jake arched his eyebrows. "Well, sure, but if I take *your* side, I don't get fed."

Everyone around the table laughed, Liam too.

Sharon snickered. "Looks like you picked a wise one,

Liam."

It took Jake a second or two to realize no one batted an eyelid at her statement.

Either they missed it, or...

The implications in the word *or* left him feeling grateful beyond imagining.

Jake snuck a peek toward the house. "Okay, the coast is clear."

"I think that ship has sailed," Liam said, smirking. "Because if you think for *one second* that no one saw us in the yard this mornin', me with my tongue halfway down your throat? Think again. My mom sees *everythin'*, even when I'm sure she's nowhere in sight."

Jake blinked. "But... no one said a goddamn word!"

Liam smiled. "An' they won't, not until we kinda make it official. They *can* be discreet... when they choose to."

Jake took a deep breath. "Okay, this is your last chance."

"To do what?"

"Back out. Tell me you don't want this."

Okay, where in the hell did that come from? "An' why would I do that?"

Jake snickered. "Because I caught you in a weak moment? I jumped on your bones in that nightclub? I blinded you with my expert kissin'?" His eyes sparkled.

Liam snorted, lifting his eyebrows. "'Jumped on my bones?' 'Expert kissin''? Babe, I hate to disillusion ya, but—"

Jake covered Liam's mouth with his hand. "Stop right there, or you'll have me cryin'." When he pulled away, he sighed. "Y'know, that's the third time you've said that, an' I like it better each time I hear it."

"Hear what?"

"You callin' me babe. Or baby."

Liam frowned. "When did I call you baby?" He had no recollection.

"Jus' now, this mornin'… and the night we watched that movie for your mama. Y'know, when I got real upset, an' ya held me?" Jake's expression softened. "You said, 'I know, baby. I gotcha.'"

Liam didn't remember. "I guess it just slipped out."

"I'm glad it did."

"An' jus' for the record, but specifically 'cause you asked me?" Liam moved in closer, until he had Jake pinned against the side of the truck. He bent to whisper, "Yes, I want this."

Jake swallowed. "Someone'll see."

"Let 'em. It's not like they haven't seen two guys kissin' before. Now how about you give me a kiss for me to remember, an' for you to think about all the way home."

Jake locked his arms around Liam's neck, and Liam lost himself in a kiss that promised so much. A kiss that sent blood surging where it really shouldn't have been going right that minute.

Jake's eyes widened, and he gasped. "Oh my."

Liam grabbed Jake's hands and gently removed them from around his neck. He took a step backward. "An' now you've really gotta go. Before I change my mind an' decide to keep you here." He resisted the urge to adjust himself.

Jake nodded. He climbed into the truck and fired up the engine. He leaned on the sill. "I don't know when I'll see you next. It might be a while."

Liam was trying not to think about that part. "I know, but it's not like we're not gonna talk or text, right? You'll hear somethin' from me every day." He smiled. "Can't have you forgettin' 'bout me, can I?"

Suddenly, Jake's eyes glistened. "Like I could ever do that." Before Liam could respond, he put the truck into gear, and headed for the street.

Liam stood there until he could no longer hear the truck. Then he turned, his heart heavy, and walked up to the house.

He hoped to God they could make this work, because Lord knew, the odds were already stacking up against them.

Truth & Betrayal

Chapter Thirty

September appeared to be in some big damn hurry to change places with October, or at least that was how it felt to Jake. The weeks just flew by, and he was grateful for that. Every week brought him one step closer to another chance to visit Liam.

He could've just told his parents he was going, and that was that, but…

Since he'd returned home that weekend, the atmosphere had been a little… frosty, and the last thing he wanted was to make matters worse. Jake had ended up stuck between a rock and a hard place. Staying home and working hard kept the peace with his folks, but all these weeks apart from Liam was not good. Jake wasn't stupid. Any relationship in its early days had to be a pretty fragile thing, right? That was the time to lay foundations, to bond…

Hard to lay anything when you were five hundred miles apart. And as for it being a relationship? Jake didn't know what the definition was. Did it mean you both came out with the L word? Because Jake didn't know if he'd call it that yet. He couldn't forget Liam's revelation, that he'd loved Caleb, but hadn't been in love with him.

Liam clearly thought there was a difference. Jake didn't know *anything* anymore.

That first day home had been the most difficult. Jake couldn't get over the fact that what was happening somehow didn't feel real. He'd lain awake Sunday night, going over the events of that weekend, telling himself he hadn't just thrown himself at the first available gay guy. Taylor was available, wasn't he? And Jake certainly wasn't into *him*.

Then he analyzed every little thing. *What did we actually do, when it came down to it? We kissed.* Quite a lot, but hey, Jake wasn't complaining. Liam made it clear he wanted things to continue. So what, they were dating now? They were a couple?

The more Jake thought about it, the more time he spent combing through the minutes and seconds of every encounter, the less he felt he knew. And just when he had reached the point of thinking it was never gonna work between them...

Liam emailed.

From: lemiller
To: jgreenwood97

September 5

Hey. I'm sitting at my desk at work, thinking about you. Don't worry, it's my lunch break. They're not gonna fire me.

*What was I thinking about specifically? You unbuttoning my shirt. Dirty boy. *grin emoji**

Seriously... This whole last weekend just blew my mind.

You said I had no idea how much you wanted to kiss me. Think again. I wanted that just as much, only...I didn't see it happening this weekend. You blindsided me.

That's not a bad thing, by the way. I needed you to shake up my world.

You also said how no one mentioned what was going on? Mom kinda did, and there's a reason for that. We talked about you, about how it was time to move on... That's the hardest part for me. Well, she was trying to get me to see that it was okay to have feelings for someone else.

That brings me to you.

*Yeah, I have feelings for you. I think that was sort of obvious *grin emoji* What I <u>didn't</u> know, was how you felt about me. I guess I do now, right?*

So yeah, this weekend kind of turned my world upside down, but in a good way.

I'll be honest. Right now? I have no idea how we're going to make this work. We'll sort that out as we go along.

So here's what's important. (Revising my list - now Liam's Top Four lol)

No change in #1 - #3

#4 Nothing is going to take away what happened between us Saturday night/Sunday morning, so hang on to that, okay? Don't forget it. Burn it into your memory. Because I will.

Okay, ran out of time here. More later.
Your Liam.

That last part had sent a warm glow through him. *Your Liam.* What warmed him even more was the knowledge that he wasn't on his own. Liam was working through this too.

Monday night after supper, Jake had retreated to his room and gotten out Caleb's laptop, grateful that his daddy was up with the times enough to have internet for his business.

From: jgreenwood97
To: lemiller

September 5

You have the best timing. Seriously. Not gonna tell you what the last 24 hours have been like. Talk about self-doubt. Getting your email turned my day around. Seems like we're both over-thinking this.

So your mama knows? She's okay with it? Wow.

You didn't know how I felt about you? Cue eye roll. I dropped enough hints. That kiss was sort of a last resort.

Don't worry about me forgetting Saturday. Not gonna happen, no way Jose.

By the way, I like this. Emails, I mean. Talking on the phone isn't always easy.

I know what you mean about not seeing where things are heading. Too many obstacles. The distance. My folks. This town. Did I mention my folks? LOL

I just don't see how we can get past this. But I want this, same as you, so I guess we find a way, right?

Can we do this again?

And two can play that game.

Your Jake.

Jake smiled as he hit Send. *Right back atcha.*
The response had come within a couple of minutes.

From: lemiller
To: jgreenwood97

How about I send an email every night? Something to look forward to.

Even if it's just a few lines. You'll know I'm thinking about you.

Your Liam

Jake really liked that idea. He was about to send an email in reply, when he had a better idea. He stripped off his T-shirt, lay on the bed, and grabbed his phone to take a selfie. Him, staring up at the camera, from the waist up, smiling. Then he sent it to Liam, with the caption:

Love that idea. Here's something to look at. As you can see, I'm thinking of you too.

He clicked Send, grinning.

Back pinged the reply.

Hey, no fair. Where's the rest of you? And are you naked? I can't tell.

Jake chuckled. *Gotta keep my mystery, right? Don't worry. You'll get to see it all.*

When Liam's response flew back, he laughed out loud. *Fucking tease.* Then he caught his breath when a photo came through. It was Liam, standing by the window in his room. He'd obviously taken it on a timer. *Oh my God.* He was facing the window, looking back over his shoulder—naked as a jaybird. He stood with his legs apart, his hands on his ass. That look on his face was hot.

Then the message came through.

This is yours whenever you're ready.

Jake's jaw dropped. *Holy fucking hell. Look at him.* Tall, lean, with a totally gorgeous butt that Jake longed to reach into the photo and touch. Long, toned legs, with just the right amount of muscles. His fingers trembled as he typed his reply.

Thanks for that. And you know what I'm gonna be doing later, right?

Seconds later. *LMAO. Start your own spank bank.*

Now there was an idea. After he'd changed the password to one even his mama couldn't guess. And he knew just what to choose.

myliam2017

Reluctantly, Jake turned off his phone and put his shirt back on. Liam's beautiful butt would have to wait until bedtime.

And so September became the month of exchanging emails. Liam's were the highpoint of Jake's day. Sometimes they were short, just a few lines where he shared about his day, but always with a line to let Jake know he was in Liam's thoughts. The photos kept coming too, nothing too graphic, but enough to get Jake real hot an' bothered. The one that always made him lock the door and reach for his lube, was just an image of Liam's crotch, encased in his jeans. *Lord, he must've been so fuckin' hard when he took it.* The way the denim molded around his dick…. What made it over-the-top hot was the caption.

Thinking of you.

Yeah, Jake's life sure had gotten interesting. But by the time September was on the way out, Jake knew in his heart that emails and texts and photos weren't enough. He wanted the real thing.

He wanted his man.

Jake finished putting away the dishes. It was a beautiful evening, and the thought crossed his mind to walk down to the creek. It was his favorite place to sit and think, listening to the water trickling over rocks. As to what—or who—he'd be thinking about, that was a no-brainer.

"Jacob? You got a minute?" Mama stood by the kitchen table, her hands gripping the chair frame.

"You okay, Mama?" The quaver in her voice alarmed him.

She gestured to the chair opposite. "Sit down. I need to talk to ya."

That was all it took to have Jake's heartbeat racing. *Oh Lord.* He tried hard to think of anything that might have revealed his secret. Hell, it could be any number of things. *Please, Lord, don't tell me she's been on my phone.* "Sure, Mama." He sat, his heart quaking, his knees trembling out of sight under the table.

"I've bin thinking 'bout what you said, about Caleb's room." She cleared her throat. "I still think you were wrong to speak to me the way you did, but… you were right."

"I was?" Okay, this was the last thing he'd expected to hear. His heartbeat climbed down a little.

She nodded. "These past few days, while you an' your daddy were out workin', I went in there, jus' to sit a spell an' think. I took a good, long look at the room, an' yeah, I had to agree, it does feel like a shrine. An' then I got to thinkin' 'bout Caleb. I asked myself, what would he think about it?" She shook her head. "I think he'd hate it." Her gaze met Jake's. "Do *you* think he'd hate it?"

Jake had to take a moment to breathe. "I told his roommate once that as long as we have Caleb in photos, in our heads an' in our hearts, he's never gonna go 'way. We don't need a place to go that's full of him. This house is already full of him. From the lines on the door frame where you started markin' off his height as soon as he was old enough to stand by himself, to the holes he made in the hall rug when he set off a firecracker one Fourth." He paused. "An' yeah, I think he'd hate it."

Mama sighed. "Thank you for bein' honest. So what I've decided is to go through all his clothes, an' those that are in a good state, I'll give to the Goodwill. Same goes for all his books. But before I do that, I want you to pick out anythin' you'd like to keep, somethin' that'll remind you of your brother."

Jake swallowed hard. "I… I could do that."

That seemed to satisfy her. "Fine. You tell me when you're done, then we can make a start." She got up, walked around to where he sat, and bent over to kiss the top of his head. "You're a good boy." Then she left the room.

Jake fished out his phone and composed a text.

Hey. Mama's finally gonna go through Caleb's stuff. Is there anything you'd like, that I can keep for you? Maybe something that has good memories?

Liam's response was almost instantaneous. *Would love that. Let me think about it.*

Jake put away his phone, his mind already thinking about something else. Going through Caleb's things afforded a great opportunity—to find wherever he'd stashed his gay mags and move them before Mama got the chance to see them.

Because the thought of her coming across them didn't bear thinking about.

Mama's voice changed, and the hairs stood up on Jake's arms. "Oh my. No, you can't do that. Let me talk to Hank first…. Just don't do anythin' until I call, alright?" She disconnected the call, her brow wrinkled, her hand at her throat.

Daddy peered at her. "Maggie? What's up?"

"That was Clara. Seems like she has to have an operation. They're gonna remove…" She glanced at Jake and flushed. "Something. Anyhow, she was talkin' 'bout goin' to some nursing place after, so they can take care of her, 'cause she can't do nothin' for a while, not even lift an iron."

Daddy smiled. "An' you wanna go an' stay with your sister, to look after her, don'tcha?"

Her eyes widened, and she gasped. "Why, how did you—"

He chuckled. "Lord, woman, we've bin married for nigh on thirty years. You think I don't know by now how that mind of yours works? When is her op?"

"Next week. They're takin' her in Sunday, an' operatin' first thing Monday. Seems like they need to do it in a hurry."

"Fine. Call her back. Tell her I'll be drivin' you to Knoxville first thing tomorrow mornin', an' I'll put you on the first bus outta there. You can stay as long as she needs ya."

Mama gaped. "But… what about you an' Jacob?"

Daddy gave her a mild stare. "I think two grown men are more 'n' capable of takin' care of themselves for a while, don't you? Now, why don't you go an' pack a suitcase? Then we'll call it a night. We'll need to be up awful early in the mornin'."

Mama got up from her armchair, crossed the room to where Daddy sat, and gave him a kiss. "I married a good man."

He gave her a playful swat on the butt. "Pack, woman." Mama chuckled and left the room. Daddy regarded Jake steadily. "You an' me can take care of ourselves, right?"

"Sure. Long as you know right now, I can *not* cook like Mama."

Daddy smiled. "What we choose to eat while she's away? Ain't nobody's business but ours." Then he tapped the side of his nose. "It'll be our secret."

Jake laughed, but inside he gave a sigh. *Like I haven't got enough of those already.*

Jake heard the sound of his daddy's truck, and hurried to put on some coffee. Ever since he and Mama had left that morning, he'd been doing some serious thinking. Now all he had to do was convince his daddy.

"Coffee's on!" he called out as the front door opened.

"Great. I could do with a cup." Daddy came into the kitchen and sat at the table. "She's on her way." He shook his head. "We won't starve, that's for damn sure. There's still enough mac an' cheese an' casseroles in that freezer to last for a month."

Jake poured out the coffee. "Got something I wanna talk to you about."

Daddy arched his eyebrows. "What a coincidence. So do I." He took the cup and inhaled its aroma.

Jake's stomach clenched. "Why don't you go first?"

Daddy took a sip, then stared at Jake. "What's goin' on, Jacob?"

Shit. Jake forced a chuckle. "This is gettin' to be a habit. Seems like we keep havin' the same conversation where you ask me what's goin' on."

"Don't give me that. I gotta be honest, son. Lately it jus' feels like… we're growin' apart."

Fuck. No one ever said his daddy wasn't observant. It was true, of course. Not being able to be honest with either of them had put up a wall between them, and Jake didn't know if they'd ever get over that.

"Nothin's goin' on, Daddy," he lied. "I just… got some things on my mind that I need to work through. Nothin' you can help with."

"I see." Daddy took another drink. "I had to ask. Your mama's bin worryin' too. She mentioned it on the way to the bus this mornin'." He peered at Jake. "Y'know, your mama would sure be happy if you' an' Sarah started datin'."

Aw fuck. "Datin'?"

"Sure, why not? She's a nice girl. You could do a lot worse." He sighed. "Can't be a bachelor all your life, son. Man needs a woman. A man ain't…complete without a woman. He needs someone to share his joys an' woes with. A soulmate."

"I agree." At least on the last part. Where they'd differ would be the sex of said soulmate.

Daddy blinked. "You do?"

Jake nodded. Then he sighed. "But I gotta say, I hate bein' pushed. An' every time I see Sarah, or hear Mama mention her—which she does, often—it's like I can feel Mama breathin' down my neck, feel her hands on my back."

Daddy chuckled. "Okay, so she might've been a little… heavy-handed. All I'm askin' is that you think about it."

"I got somethin' I'd like *you* to think about." Jake recounted the conversation with Mama about Caleb's room. "I got an idea. While she's gone, why don't we clear out the room, then fit it out with shelves, an' make it into a real nice sewin' room for her, as a surprise for when she comes home? That way, we can move all her bolts of cloth, her sewin' machine, her dress form, an' all her old paper patterns out of the dinin' room, an' give Mama her own space."

Daddy beamed. "That's a great idea. We could work on it together. I'd like that."

Jake laughed. "You work with me every damn day."

"Yeah, but this would be different. This would be me an' you, doin' somethin' for your mama."

That made Jake smile.

"Somethin' else I've bin meanin' to talk to ya about." Daddy's expression grew serious. "I know I'm only fifty-one, but I don't intend workin' 'til I'm about to drop. A man needs to plan for his retirement, an' I was thinkin'… How would you feel 'bout takin' over the business one day?"

Jake stared at him. "Seriously?"

Daddy snickered. "Why in the hell d'ya think I've bin teachin' ya everythin' I know? So's you can earn a livin' from it. I mean, you're a natural, son. An' you seem to enjoy it."

"I do," Jake assured him. He loved working with wood, taking a property in need of some TLC, and making it sparkle again.

"I'd take a cut from the business, nothin' too big, you understand. I mean, I got my pension all sorted out, so there's no worries on *that* score. But yeah, just a little to make life a bit more comfortable for your mama an' me. An' you can do what you like with the business. If you wanna expand, take on someone to work with ya…" He shrugged. "Like I said, somethin' to think about."

Wow. Jake didn't know how to react. It was easy when you were a kid to think of your parents as immortal. To hear his daddy talk about such things gave him a shiver.

Daddy cleared his throat. "Anyhoo, back to your plan. How you wanna do this? Seein' as you're in charge."

Jake liked the sound of that. "Tell you what. Why don't you start thinkin' 'bout supplies? I'll make a start on clearin' out Caleb's stuff. We can go through it all in the evenin' after supper." And if Daddy was off buying supplies, that gave Jake a window to search for Caleb's hidey hole.

Daddy nodded enthusiastically. "I'll make a list. Get thinkin' 'bout what kind of wood you'd like for the shelves."

They discussed the different varieties of wood while they finished their coffee. Jake had to admit, talking like this gave him a warm feeling. He was actually looking forward to working with his daddy. And what with work during the daytime, and refitting the room in the evenings, he wouldn't have time to miss Liam.

Yeah right.

Truth & Betrayal

Chapter Thirty-One

By the time Liam finished reading Jake's email, he was laughing his ass off.

Jake had written about the renovations he and his dad were making to Caleb's old room, and it sounded like they were having a good ol' bonding session. Not to mention a few hiccups along the way. Of course, Jake hitting his dad's thumb instead of the nail wasn't *really* funny, but the way he recounted his dad hopping around, holding his injured thumb and swearing enough to turn the air blue sure was.

Liam reached for his phone. *Any luck finding Caleb's porn stash?*

The response was swift. *Nope. I looked everywhere. Wherever he put them, it was not in here.*

That had to be the silver lining, right? *That's good. No fear of your parents coming across them.*

Hey. NOT good. Because if they're not here, where in the world are they?

Liam didn't have an answer to that one.

When's your mom home? It had been nearly three weeks.

Must be soon. LOL. We're gonna need a MAJOR clean-up before that happens.

That made him smile. *You mice been slobbing out while the cat's away?*

Jake's reply wasn't instant, and then Liam saw why. He gasped at the photo of the kitchen sink. *Oh my.* Liam chuckled. *I'd say that's a big yes. Better get busy, boys. That might take a while.*

A scowling, red-faced emoji popped up on his screen. *You are enjoying this way too much.*

Liam laughed out loud. Then he had an idea. *Tell you what. To make up for it, I'll send you a little video tonight.* He'd make sure to film right before he came, and it would be with Jake's name on his lips.

Hell yeah. Make it a good one.

Liam intended to.

Just remembered a question that occurred to me. You never did tell me, you know. What the letters stood for in Caleb's password.

Liam smiled. *It was a song by Jack Johnson. It's Always Better When We're Together. And you already know why he chose 2011.* A moment later, he sent another message. *You know what's strange? When I gave that to you, I couldn't even listen to that song without tearing up. I heard it on the radio last week, and... I was fine.*

Really?

Liam sent a grin emoji. *Really. And now if you'll stop messaging me, I'll get off here and get...busy.*

That was it. Jake was gone.

And Liam had a video to make.

They'd just finished breakfast when the phone rang. Daddy answered it with a smile. "Hey, sugah. How's Clara doin'?" Jake's belly did a little flipflop when his daddy paled. "Tonight? Hey, that's great. What time is your bus due in?" He turned panicked eyes on Jake.

Oh Lord. Jake glanced at the kitchen. He knew how *he'd* be spending the rest of the day. Then he reconsidered. How *they* would be spending it, because half of this mess was his daddy's. He tried not to laugh as he watched his daddy's flustered facial expression, while he tried to sound cheerful on the phone. When the call finished, Daddy put down the phone and glared at him.

"We've got 'til six to make this place look less of a hog trough. No work today. We're gonna be too busy here."

Jake sighed. "Right now I'll bet you're regretting sayin' no every time Mama asked for a dishwasher."

Daddy narrowed his gaze. "That is *not* helpful." Then he widened his eyes. "You know what though? That's a great idea. If I get my ass in gear, I could have one installed before I have to leave to go pick her up in Knoxville." He got up from the table. "Where's the Yellow Pages?"

"Somewhere under all your magazines that are piled up by the side of the couch." Jake got up too. "I'll make a start in here." *This is gonna take all freakin' day.* At least he'd have something funny to tell Liam in their nightly email session. It was his favorite time of the day.

Then a thought occurred to him. "Daddy? Where in the wide world are you gonna put a dishwasher in here?"

Daddy froze. He scanned the cabinets, and Jake could almost hear the cogs clicking in his brain. "Aw, shoot. I'm gonna have to do a little shufflin', ain't I? Lemme work this out on paper." He went out of the room.

Jake shook his head. It was going to be a *very* long day.

At the sound of his daddy's truck, Jake took one last look around the place. Perfect. The door opened, and Mama came in, Daddy behind her with her suitcase. Jake gave her a huge hug.

"Welcome home, Mama."

She hugged him tight. "Oh, it's good to be home." She released him and shook her head. "I never knew my sister had become so slovenly. That house was a disgrace! While she was in the hospital, I cleaned it from the basement up to the attic. Took me four days." She gazed around the room, beaming. "Well, this looks nice. You boys have obviously been takin' care of the house."

Jake arched his eyebrows. "Did you think we wouldn't?" Behind Mama, Daddy smirked.

Mama bit her lip. "I'll be honest. I had visions of comin' back to find everywhere knee deep in takeout cartons, pizza boxes an' beer cans."

"Aw, Maggie." Daddy did his best to look wounded, and Jake had to turn around quickly before he started laughing.

"Don't you *Maggie* me. I know what you're like. Your mother warned me 'bout you before I married ya."

Jake swung around and stared at them, smothering his laughter.

"Say what?" Daddy gaped at her.

Mama's eyes sparkled. "She told me you were a slob, but that all you needed was firm handlin' to keep you on the straight an' narrow." She glanced around the room again, looking smug. "Guess I trained you real good, 'cause this place sure looks immaculate."

"We got a surprise for ya, Mama." Jake took her hand and led her to the kitchen. She surveyed the room, then suddenly froze, her mouth open.

"Is that a–"

Daddy came up behind her. "Well, don't look so shocked. You've only bin askin' for one for the last *decade* or more."

She spun around and flung her arms around him. "You wonderful man." Mama planted exuberant kisses on his mouth, and Daddy went bright red. Then she released him and dashed over to the dishwasher, opening and closing it, running her fingers over it, and cooing with delight.

Jake glanced at his daddy and gave him the thumbs up. Daddy returned it, grinning. *We done good,* he mouthed. Then he cleared his throat. "When you've finished pettin' the damn thing, you ready for your next surprise?"

Mama's eyes bugged out on stalks. "Another?"

Jake chuckled. "Follow me." He led the way to Caleb's old

room, pausing at the threshold and gesturing to the door. "Go on in, Mama."

Almost hesitantly, she pushed it open and stepped inside. When Jake caught her low cry of joyous surprise, he met his daddy's gaze. *We done good again.*

Daddy surprised the hell out of Jake by putting his arm around his shoulders. "You're a good boy." He rubbed the top of Jake's head, like he used to do when Jake was little.

Jake had to admit, it had been a fantastic idea. Mama gained a sewing room, and he and daddy closed the gap that had opened up between them. Except he knew in his heart it was only temporary. He couldn't hide forever, and when the day came to tell them, as he knew it had to, that gap was gonna bust right open.

Not yet. Let me enjoy this while it lasts.

Jake settled back against the pillows, his phone in his hands. *You should have seen her face.*

I'm glad it all turned out so well.

Yeah, so was Jake. *I don't know which was the bigger surprise - the sewing room or the dishwasher.*

Liam's message pinged back. *Sounds like your dad scored some major brownie points with your mom. So… you think you're in their good books right now?*

Jake knew Liam by now. *Why do you ask?* Because he knew *something* lay behind that innocent-sounding question.

Got an email today from Dev and Pauli. They're having a Halloween party, and we're invited.

A party? Jake hadn't been to a party in… forever. A question arose in his mind. *We? Would I be going as Caleb's brother and their friend, or as…?* He left it like that, because, to speak the plain truth, he had no idea what he was.

They don't know about us, if that's what you're asking.

Aha. So there *is* an us.

Liam's response was swift. *Ass. You know it. And if they don't know now, they surely will by Halloween. Does that mean you wanna go? The party's on Halloween itself, which is a Tuesday, so it would mean missing work.*

Now Jake got it about being in their good books. *I'll ask, okay? All I can say for the moment.* Not that he didn't love the idea. His heart was racing at the thought of seeing Liam again.

One thing? If it's a yes? Think about where you'll be sleeping.

Oh. *OH.*

Jake didn't have to think. *With you. Wanna sleep with you.* His pulse raced at the thought.

That did it. One way or another, he was going to that party. He was gonna have a good time, get drunk, but not *too* drunk–and get his cherry popped.

His phone vibrated. *I'm glad. Can't wait to see you. Hold you. Kiss you.*

Lord, he wanted all that too. Then another thought occurred to him. *What about you? Can you take the time off?*

Already put in for a few days' vacation. I'd have to be back here Thursday. I was thinking of getting into Atlanta on the weekend.

Good to know. God, that sounded awesome. Five days with Liam. Awesome? That sounded like heaven.

Let me work on the olds. I'll let you know.

He smiled when he saw Liam's reply. *Keeping my fingers crossed. Because right now? Want you so bad.* A moment later another message appeared. *So hard for you.*

Yeah, Liam had the same idea. *Ditto. You know it.* Jake's was a rock.

It was clear neither of them wanted to finish the conversation, and Jake knew he had a long day coming. *Hey. I need to sleep. Talk tomorrow?*

Sure. *grin emoji* Want another video?

Jake laughed. *Evil man. And DUH.* Liam's first video had

been just an image of his head and shoulders on the bed. He'd lain on his side, staring into the camera, but it was obvious things were going on out of view. He hadn't said a word, and that had been so fucking *hot*, nothing but that focus on Jake while his hand moved unseen, his breathing growing harsher and less regular. Jake had been right there with him, tugging his dick with slick fingers, trying to keep pace. And when Liam came, he uttered the only word of the entire video—Jake's name.

That was all it had taken for Jake to shoot his load. Because there was this beautiful man coming before his eyes—for him.

Do I get to see your dick this time?

Liam's reply was instant. *Uh uh. Saving that for when I got you in my bed. To quote you - gotta keep my mystery, right? LOL*

Jake shook his head. *I repeat. Evil man.* With that, he switched off his phone, clicked off the lamp, and pulled the comforter over him. The temptation to jack off was huge, but his parents hadn't been in bed that long, and besides, keeping it quiet was damn near impossible for him.

It would have to wait until Sunday when they went to church. He'd put up with blue balls until then.

Either that, or they'd burst.

By the time Daddy's truck had pulled out onto the road, Jake was reaching for his box of toys. He gazed thoughtfully at the dildo. He'd used it a couple of times, but had come to the conclusion that he wasn't getting the most out of it. He had an idea how to change that, however. And as for the Fleshjack, it felt amazing, and if that was what fucking felt like, he couldn't wait to try the real thing. The last time he'd used it, his phone had sat on the bed beside him, showing the photo of Liam, displaying that gorgeous ass. It didn't take much imagination to put two and two together, and it had been an awesome load.

What he had planned was either going to be epic, or an epic fail.

He slipped out of his shorts and grabbed the dildo. Wetting his finger liberally, he slicked up the sucker at its base, and slammed it down on the hardwood floor. That fucker wasn't going *anywhere*. Then he used a couple of lube-slick fingers to get himself ready.

He gazed down at the dildo, debating whether to crouch or kneel. Crouching had way too much potential for falling on his ass. Kneeling, then. When his phone vibrated on the nightstand, he groaned out loud. "For fuck's sake!" He went to switch it onto silent, until he saw it was Liam.

"Your timin' is lousy," he said with a chuckle.

"Why? You busy? I only called to ask what your parents said. I know, I should've waited for you to message me, but I got impatient."

"You? What a surprise." Jake gazed at the dildo, its pink, veined surface glistening with lube. *Talk about a distraction.* "I was gonna text ya later. They said yes." Not right away. Mama had been the first to say yes, and that meant Daddy went along with her. Still, Jake wasn't going to argue with a positive result.

"Aw, great! So why is my timin' lousy?"

Jake sighed. "Because they've gone to church, an' I've got this narrow little window where I can… enjoy myself."

"I see." Liam's voice dropped lower. "What did you have in mind? An' can I help?"

Ohhh. Okay, that added a totally new dimension. "Possibly." Practicalities first. "Lemme put you on speaker." He clicked on the icon.

Liam's laughter rang out. "Oh. We talkin' hands free?"

"For what I have in mind? Hell yeah." He picked up the Fleshjack and dribbled lube into it, then stood it within reach. *Ready.* He knelt on the floor, positioning himself just right so that the head of the dildo slid between his ass cheeks.

"Tell me what you're doin'," Liam demanded. Jake heard

the metallic click of a belt being undone, and grinned.

"I've got the dildo stuck to the floor, I'm kneelin' over it, an' I'm gonna lower myself onto it slowly." Jake caught his breath as the wide head popped inside his hole, then groaned as he sank down onto it, until it was buried all the way inside him. "Oh, fuck."

"Is it inside ya?"

"Oh yeah." Jake raised himself up a little, keeping the movement unhurried, then let it fill him again. "Feels real good. I can make believe I'm ridin' a dick."

"Pretend it's my dick," Liam said, a raw edge to his voice. "You're sittin' astride me, an' I'm balls deep inside ya. Bare."

Jake moaned. "Don't. You say stuff like that, an' I am gonna shoot my load right now." He recommenced his slow up-and-down motion, picking up a little speed as his body grew accustomed to the intrusion. "Damn. Feels so good." He caught slick sounds that told him exactly what Liam was doing.

"Go faster. Slam down on it."

Jake snorted. "I do that, I'll hurt my ass. These floors are damn hard." He picked up Part #2 of his plan. "Okay. I'm slidin' my dick into the Fleshjack."

"At the same time? Lord, but you're ambitious."

Jake snickered. "You're just jealous 'cause you can't multitask for shit." Having said that, it was a little awkward, trying to ride the dildo, *and* jack off into the Fleshjack.

"God, I wish I could see ya." The slick sounds sped up.

Jake threw back his head and laughed. "Yeah, right. I am *not* makin' this a video call. I got enough to cope with." Okay, this was getting silly. He couldn't coordinate his ass and his hands.

"How does it feel?"

Jake had no words to adequately describe the sensations. "Oh, fuck." He began to rock back and forth, trying to keep time with his hand, but it wasn't happening. In frustration, he yanked off the Fleshjack and threw it at the bed.

"What's hap'nin'?"

"Goddamn it! It's like tryin' to rub your belly an' pat your head at the same time."

"Just ride it, baby." Liam's voice was calm. "Forget about the Fleshjack, an' just feel that hard dick slidin' in 'an out of your ass. I love how that feels. Love gettin' fucked."

"Yeah?"

"God, yes. The joys of bein' vers."

"Vers?" Jake was having a hard time keeping up. Fucking himself on a dildo, jerking off *and* carrying on a phone conversation... Maybe *he* wasn't such a hot multitasker either.

Liam snickered. "Versatile. Top *and* bottom. Fucker an' fuckee."

Lord, he liked the sound of that. "Sounds like... the best of both worlds."

"You know it."

Jake wrapped slick fingers around his dick, and let the rocking motion force his cock through them. "Oh fuck."

"You want that? Wanna slide your dick inside me?" Liam sounded breathless.

Holy hell. Jake could see it clear as day, his reddened cock splitting those gorgeous dark brown globes, Liam's wide back damp with sweat, Jake's hands spreading his cheeks wide as he plunged deep...

He shuddered and came all over the floor. "Oh, my fuckin' God."

Liam's breathing grew harsh and loud. "Oh fuck, Jake."

Jake knelt there, his body tight around the dildo, his dick still pulsing out its last drops, sweat covering his chest that rose and fell sharply, his breathing as rapid as Liam's. "Well, that... was an experience."

Liam's wry chuckle met his ears. "An' how do *you* rate at mutlitaskin', Mr. Ambitious?"

"Yeah, yeah, alright." Jake knew he'd never hear the last of this.

"Here's a thought to cheer you up. In just a short while, you'll get to experience the real thing. With me. If you think you're ready. Your choice, baby."

Jake was more than ready. "Can't wait." Gently, he lifted himself off the dildo and got to his feet, his legs a little unsteady. He gazed at the come-spattered floor, lube trickling out of the Fleshjack, and the dildo that had somehow managed to remain upright. "I think I have some cleanin' to do before they get home."

Liam snorted. "I can imagine. That's okay. I have some laundry to do here." He paused. "Not long now."

Thank God for that. "You know what I've missed most?"

"What?"

"Sittin' in your back yard early in the mornin', talkin' an' kissin', watchin' the colors change."

Liam sighed. "Yeah. Me too. We'll have that again." He paused, and Jake wondered for one brief moment if Those words would fall from his lips. Because they hovered on *his* tongue, not that he had enough nerve to say them. "Talk soon?"

Jake closed his eyes. Apparently neither of them were quite ready for that yet. "Sure." He disconnected the call, then proceeded with Operation Clean-Up.

He should've felt good. Blissed out. *That's how orgasms were supposed to make you feel, right?*

What he felt was… deflated.

Truth & Betrayal

Chapter Thirty-Two

Jake spotted Liam's Ford in the parking space, and pulled the truck into the adjacent one. He switched off the engine and sat there for a moment, enjoying the birdsong audible through his open window. The day had warmed a little since he'd left LaFollette early that morning, and had reached 72 degrees according to his phone. The sun was shining, and the air was heavy with the scent of magnolia, which grew on either side of the apartments. Jake closed his eyes and inhaled their perfume.

He was finally back in Atlanta.

He had to admit, the city had a special place in his heart. He'd loved seeing where Caleb had lived, but now he had his own memories, and was keen to make more.

Starting with this weekend.

A tap on the window made him yelp. He opened his eyes to find Liam grinning at him.

"Just makin' sure you weren't sleepin'." Liam's dark eyes were warm. "Hey, you," he said softly.

Jake was out of that truck in a heartbeat. He went straight for the hug he knew was coming, and Liam held him close. "Missed ya."

"So good to see ya," Jake whispered. He tilted his head up, and Liam took his mouth in a tender kiss. *Lord, yes.* Jake gave back as good as he got, and Liam sighed into the kiss. When it broke, Jake cupped Liam's cheek and smiled. "I drove two hundred fifty miles for that."

Liam chuckled. "Lucky for you, I got plenty of 'em, so I'll

make it worth the trip." He peered into the truck. "That your bag? Well, grab it, an' let's get inside. Dev an' Pauli have started this weekend the way they mean it to continue."

"Should I be worried?"

Liam snorted. "Oh yeah. Pauli makes a vicious Long Island Iced Tea."

Jake arched his eyebrows. "Cocktails? At this hour? It's only just past noon."

"Hey, it's already six pm in London, an' it's seven in Paris. Cocktail hour." Liam laughed. "You don't have to have one if you don't want one." He started to walk toward the main door, but Jake grabbed his arm.

"So, how're we playin' this?" He'd been thinking about this on the way there. "Are we gonna say anythin'?"

"That kinda depends on you, Chuck." Liam regarded him steadily. "I mean, what are your thoughts?"

Jake bit his lip. "This is ours. Mine. An' I don't wanna share it with anyone jus' now. I like how this feels, when it's only us."

"You haven't said anythin' to Taylor?"

"Nope."

Liam nodded. "Then we say nothin'." His eyes sparkled. "'Course, you *know* it's not gonna stay secret for long, right?"

Jake gave a shrug. "Then I'll deal with that when it happens." Part of him was nervous about the prospect, and he knew why. Caleb. He knew how this looked. Caleb's ex, dating Caleb's brother. Just because Dev and Pauli were their friends, didn't mean they might hold back on saying something about that.

Like I said, I'll deal with it when it happens.

"Gotcha." Liam curved his hand around Jake's cheek. "In that case, I'll have a kiss to be goin' on with."

Jake was only too happy to go along with that.

By the time they reached the apartment, Jake could hear singing from inside. He grinned. "Born This Way?" He recognized the singer as Dev.

Liam shook his head and sighed dramatically. "I know. I mean, that's jus' so… gay." He snickered, then pushed open the door. "Look what I found out on the street."

Dev paused in mid-flow and beamed. "Hey, Jakey-boy!" He seized Jake in a hug, before kissing him loudly on each cheek, his full beard itching Jake's face like crazy.

"Jake isn't a what, he's a who," Pauli commented. He pushed Dev aside impatiently. "Hey, my turn for a hug." He gave Jake a quick squeeze. "Good to see you again."

Liam laughed. "Guys, he's here for a few days. Plenty of time for hugs."

Pauli's eyes glittered. "Yeah, because *now* is the time for… cocktails!"

Jake rolled his eyes. "You two are unreal."

"Nothing unreal about cocktails, Jake." Pauli poured him a tall glass from a pitcher, then added a cherry and a slice of orange. "Perfect." He handed it to Jake. "Have you ever had a Long Island before?"

"Nope." Jake sniffed its contents. "What's in it?"

Dev snorted. "It's more a case of what *isn't* in it."

Liam counted off on his fingers. "Vodka, tequila, rum, triple sec, gin…"

"Don't forget the splash of Coke," Dev added with a grin. "Everythin' a growin' boy needs."

Jake took a cautious sip, and grimaced. "Tell you what. I'll jus' have the Coke."

Pauli laughed and took the glass from him. "How can you not like Long Islands? They'll take away your gay card for that." He kissed Jake's cheek. "I'll get you a Coke, honey."

"Speaking of gay cards…" Dev put his hands on his hips. "Has a certain small town in Tennessee recently gained a newly out gay man? Or are you still lurkin' in that closet?" He snickered.

Jake didn't see the funny side of that remark. Neither, apparently, did Liam.

"So Jake should jus' come out, regardless of the

consequences?"

Dev blinked. "I didn't say that." Beside him, Pauli stilled, his gaze going from Dev to Liam, and back to Dev.

"No, but 'lurkin' kinda said it for ya. It's Jake's decision, okay? He doesn't *have* to come out, an' no one should force his hand neither." Liam set his jaw, his eyes glinting.

Jake took one look at Dev's pallor, and held up his hands. "Alright. Dev, I know you didn't mean anythin' by it, but yeah, 'lurkin' was a bad choice of words. Liam…" Jake smiled. "Thanks for steppin' in, but I can fight my own battles."

Liam gazed at him for a moment, then nodded.

"Yeah, remember he's twenty now," Pauli added with a wicked gleam in his eye. The others laughed, and just like that, the tension in the room dissipated.

Jake groaned. "You're never gonna let me forget that, are ya?"

"Nope," Pauli replied promptly. "Now, if you need a nap after lunch—which is ready, by the way—then take it, because we're gonna keep you up late tonight."

Uh oh. Jake recognized that look. "Where are we goin'?"

Pauli waggled his eyebrows. "To stuff singles in the armbands of gorgeous naked guys, watch them jiggle their cute little asses, and do their helicopter dick trick."

Jake stared at him. "Really?"

Liam nudged his arm. "I can't wait to watch you stuffin' some guy's… armband. An' the best part is, you'll remember it all, 'cause you'll be sober."

Jake had every intention of staying sober that night. He was determined to remember everything that happened.

Everything.

Liam was having a great time. More importantly, so was Jake.

They had a table right in the middle, next to the stage, a prime location if ever there was one. Pauli had made sure Jake had plenty of singles, and every guy who came to their table, left with a tip. That went double for the cutie who sat on Jake's lap and writhed his ass off. Lord, the look on Jake's face…

"Wanna go up to the stage?" Liam asked him. "Because you haven't left your seat once, apart from goin' to the restroom."

Jake stared at him. "There are girls in here."

Liam chuckled. "And? Girls can come in, as long as they're accompanied by a guy. But still, it *is* a gay strip club. An' the purpose of bringin' all those singles was to get rid of 'em. So…?" He pointed to the stage, where guys and girls lined up, staring up at the dancers.

Jake bit his lip, a gesture Liam found freakin' adorable. "Okay, but only if you come with me."

"I had every intention of doin' jus' that." He leaned in and whispered. "Can't run the risk of one of those cute guys stealin' my Jake."

Lord, Jake just *glowed*.

As soon as Jake reached the railing that ran around the stage, a beautiful Latino guy sauntered over, wearing a pair of black satin shorts. "Hey, hot stuff." Jake blinked, and the guy laughed. "Yeah, you. God, you've got beautiful eyes." He got down on all fours, until his head was level with Jake's, then arched his back sinuously, moving languidly like someone was fucking him doggy style. "Want me to dance for ya?"

Jake nodded, apparently unable to get a word out.

What he got was a performance clearly aimed at him. Jake appeared mesmerized, if a little shocked when the guy dangled his dick in Jake's face. When he got bopped on the nose by it, the guy laughed. "I was aimin' lower."

That was when Jake relaxed. He laughed and beckoned for the guy to come closer. The dancer knelt in front of him, cock dangling, his hands on his hips, and Jake shoved a handful of singles into his armband.

Truth & Betrayal

"Thanks, gorgeous." The guy leaned in and kissed him lightly on the mouth, before getting to his feet and moving off to another part of the stage.

Jake shook his head. "Well, that was a new one."

Liam grabbed his arm. "I'm takin' you back to the table, where I can keep my eye on you."

Jake locked gazes with him. "I'd prefer it if you took me back to the apartment," he said in a low voice that Liam just about caught.

Holy hell. "You've not changed your mind then?" Liam's throat just about dried up.

Jake shook his head again. "Nope. So what's the plan? I go to bed on the fold-out couch like last time, but when the coast is clear…?"

It was Liam's turn to swallow. "Come find me. I'll be waitin'."

Jake sighed. "If you knew how much I wanna kiss you right this second."

"It'll have to wait. Later." He glanced over at their table, where Dev was gesturing for him to go to the bar. "Better get back there, before they start wonderin' what in the world we're standin' here talkin' about."

Jake snickered. "Then let's get over there, so I can tell 'em how I jus' got bopped on the nose by a guy's dick." He led the way, Liam following, his heartbeat just that little bit faster.

This is gonna be a first.

For all Liam's experience, he'd never been with a virgin before. And to his mind, that meant only one thing.

Making it perfect for Jake.

Jake lay in the semi darkness, listening intently. All was quiet, outside as well as in. Not all that surprising, seeing as they'd gotten back to the apartment at two in the morning. He caught the faint rumble of snores coming from Dev and Pauli's room. *Finally.*

He got out of bed and crept along the hallway, past their room, to the guest bedroom. The door was ajar.

I guess that's my cue to come on in.

Jake took a deep breath, then deliberately pushed open the door.

Truth & Betrayal

Chapter Thirty-Three

The lamp beside the bed cast a warm glow around the room. The first thing Jake noticed, however, was the wide mirror just above the bed, taking the place of a headboard.

Oh my.

Liam lay on his side beneath the sheets, regarding him. He obviously noticed Jake's stare, and his gaze flickered to the mirror. "Yeah," he said quietly. "This is kind of a two-edged sword. Not so good when you wake up first thing, because who wants to see themselves like that? But when you're jerkin' off, or better yet, fuckin', seein' it all in the mirror takes things to a whole new level of hot."

Just *looking* at it got Jake hot. "I waited 'til I was sure they were asleep."

"Wasn't sure if you were still comin'." Liam smirked. "If you get my meanin'."

Okay, that might have been intended as a joke, but the state Jake's nerves were in? It definitely didn't help.

He walked over to the foot of the bed, which had wooden posts at each corner, elegant, twisting columns that almost reached the ceiling. He reached out and stroked one. "This is nice. Big, too." Butterflies fluttered in his stomach.

"Jake."

He stopped examining the bed post and met Liam's gaze.

"Why don'tcha get in here with me, so I can hold ya?"

His heart pounding, Jake slowly walked around the side of the bed to where Liam threw back the sheets. Seeing he still wore shorts gave Jake a moment of relief. *I've done this, right? It's jus' like that last time we were together.*

Only, he knew it wasn't.

"Jake?" Liam's eyes danced with amusement. "It's three in the mornin'. At this rate, by the time you get in, it'll be time to get up. An' I was hopin' to fall asleep with you in my arms before that."

Jake breathed a little easier. "We gonna be sleepin'? Just… sleepin'?" He didn't want to blow hot and cold, but he couldn't seem to control it. *I am such a mess.*

Liam regarded him warmly. "We can do whatever you want. Whatever you're comfortable doin'. You're in charge."

Jake shuddered out a sigh of relief. "I think you jus' said the magic words." He climbed onto the high bed, and Liam covered him with the sheets. Liam lay on his back, his arm wide, and Jake snuggled up to him, his head on Liam's chest, his arm snaking across Liam's waist. "You must think I'm—"

Liam stopped his words with a gentle kiss. "I don't think anythin'. I've been where you're lyin', so to speak. I remember. One minute I was so horny, I could've cut glass with my dick. The next, my heart was hammerin' fit to bust." Another soft kiss. "All totally normal reactions."

Thank God for that.

"An' if all you wanna do is sleep in my arms, then that's what we'll do."

Sure, he wanted that… but only after they'd done something else first.

Jake tilted his head and gazed into Liam's eyes. "What I want… is for you to kiss me."

Liam's eyes sparkled in the lamplight. "I think I can manage that." He held Jake's face tenderly in his hand, then moved in to claim Jake's lips in a kiss that sent warmth pulsing through him.

God, yes. *This* was what Jake had dreamed of most nights since that weekend. He murmured softly against Liam's lips, nonsensical noises, his hand on Liam's chest, exploring the smooth skin and those tight little nipples. Liam moaned weakly when he teased one between his finger and thumb, and a wave of confidence flowed through him. Jake opened for him, his moan echoing Liam's when their tongues met. The kiss deepened, and Jake couldn't get enough of Liam's lips, his skin, that familiar spicy scent that seemed to cling to him…

He wanted more.

Then he glanced up and saw the mirror. Liam's words came back to him, and a shiver ran through him. *He's been in here before. With Caleb.*

Jake wasn't sure how that made him feel.

"Hey. Where'd you go?"

Jake blinked. Liam was regarding him with concern. "Sorry, I kinda zoned out there for a sec. I…" He had to say something. "The mirror. I was just thinkin' that when you talked about fuckin', you had to mean…."

Liam became so still. "Oh Lord." He took a breath. "Okay. I'm gonna be honest here. When I got into bed this evenin', knowin' you were gonna join me? Yeah, I thought it might be a little… strange. I didn't know how I was gonna feel when you walked through that door." He sighed. "Almost like I was expectin' Caleb's ghost to be here too, sittin' in the corner, watching us. But then…."

Jake's heart pounded as he waited.

Liam stroked his face. "You came into the room, an' all I could think about, all I could feel in this room, was you. All I wanted… was you."

"It still feels like that?"

Liam smiled. "Fuck, yeah." And then he kissed Jake, softly, so softly, and Jake lost himself in the kiss, swept away on the rising tide of arousal that pushed all his fears and doubts aside. *Yeah, I want more.*

Jake broke the kiss, his breathing a little fast. "Okay, so I know what your ass looks like, but… I want to see *you*. All of ya."

Liam's eyes never left Jake's. He threw back the sheet, and Jake propped himself up on one elbow, gazing at the beautiful dark man, so stark against the pale sheets. Then Liam's blue shorts twitched, and Jake snickered.

"Looks like somethin' wants to see me too."

"Then you'd better let him out," Liam suggested, his voice husky.

Jake grinned. He knelt up beside Liam, grasped the waistband of his shorts, and slowly, gently, pulled them down over Liam's hips. Liam obligingly kicked them off the rest of the way, and then Jake was face-to-face with another guy's dick. It was long and cut, with a nice girth to it. The head was the same color as the rest of Liam, maybe a little darker, but the shaft was almost black, its root disappearing into a tight triangle of jet black pubes. His balls were low, kinda soft-looking, covered with fuzz. As Jake stared, Liam's cock jerked up off his belly, like it had a life of its own.

He snickered. "Mine does that when I lie in bed, thinkin' 'bout you."

Liam chuckled. "Nice to know you think about me in bed." His hand caressed Jake's shoulder. "An' what goes through your head?"

Jake tore his gaze away from Liam's thickening dick and smiled. "What it would feel like to touch you all over."

Liam's breathing hitched. "Funny. I think about the same thing." He beckoned with his finger. "Come an' kneel here."

His heartbeat racing, Jake shuffled up the bed and knelt by Liam's pillow. He let out a low gasp when Liam lowered his shorts, and Jake's cock sprang up. Liam ignored it and pushed the shorts down to his knees. "Take 'em off, then come an' lie here with me."

Jake hurriedly kicked them off, before retaking his place next to Liam. He lay on his back, his dick standing upright, his belly quivering. Liam lay on his side, his rigid cock against Jake's thigh. He leaned over and kissed him, murmuring approval when

Jake stroked his arms and shoulders, before reaching around him to caress his back. Liam hooked his leg over Jake's, and Jake felt the heat of his shaft. Liam smiled against Jake's lips as he took hold of Jake's hand and guided it to his ass.

Jake chuckled, breaking the kiss. "How did you know?"

Liam laughed softly. "I figured, I was dyin' to touch your ass, so there was a good probability you wanted to touch mine." He locked gazes with Jake. "Touch. Squeeze. Whatever you want. Learn how I feel. Learn what makes me feel good, 'cause I'll be doin' the same thing." And with that, he pulled Jake onto his side, slid his hand over Jake's hip, and stroked his ass, his fingers light as a feather, softer than silk.

Jake shivered. "Feels good."

Liam nodded. "See? I'm learnin' 'bout you too." Then all talk ceased as he kissed Jake again, only this time it was less gentle, with a hungry edge to it that made Jake's heartbeat speed up. Lips fused as they touched, stroked and caressed each other, first on their sides, then rolling, in constant motion, their hands never still. Jake gave a low cry when Liam slid a single finger between his ass cheeks, and he responded by pulling Liam half on top of him, exploring those firm globes he'd fantasized about. Liam's low gasps and moans were music to his ears.

Then he realized they'd reach someone else's ears too. "Less moaning," Jake hissed.

Liam's eyes widened. "Then stop doin' things that make me wanna moan!" He grinned. "You wanna stop?"

"Hell no." And then they were in motion again, only now Liam played with Jake's nipples, flicking them with his tongue, and Jake kissed Liam's neck, sucking at the skin, listening to Liam's soft noises. Liam's hands seemed to be everywhere, on Jake's belly, his back, his thighs.

Everywhere but one *pretty vital fucking place*, in Jake's mind.

"Fuck, will you jus' *touch* me, for chrissakes?"

Liam's breathing quickened as he leisurely slid his hand

over Jake's belly, until finally, *Praise Jesus*, Liam's fingers curled around his dick. "You mean, like this?"

"Thank fuck for that." Then his own breathing grew ragged as Liam grabbed Jake's hand and brought it to his heavy cock, so hot beneath Jake's fingers, the skin so soft, he didn't want to stop touching it. He wrapped his hand around the firm length, feeling the throb that pulsed briefly through it.

Liam chuckled. "Oh my God, Jake. 'Go slow'. 'Go fast.' 'Touch me.'" He grinned as he began a deliciously slow pump of Jake's shaft. "You need to tell me what you want."

"That," Jake gasped. "More of that. An' don't fuckin' stop."

Liam covered Jake's hand with his own, and mimicked the speed of his fingers around Jake's dick. "Together, okay, baby?"

"Lube?" Jake rolled his eyes back as Liam settled them both into a sensual rhythm. "Oh fuck, that feels amazing." He let out a growl when Liam stopped.

"Hey, you wanted lube, remember?" Liam reached into the nightstand and tossed a tube onto the bed. "An' less noise, unless you really *do* wanna wake 'em up."

That shut him up real fast.

Liam squeezed out the liquid onto both their fingers, snapped the tube shut, and then they were back where they'd left off, lying on their sides, facing each other, slick hands working increasingly slicker shafts. Liam didn't look down once, but kept his focus on Jake.

Fuck, that was hot.

"Feel my dick slidin' through your fingers?"

Jake moaned, his own hand moving that bit faster, hips rocking as he thrust into Liam's tight fist. Liam covered Jake's mouth with his other hand. "No moanin', remember?"

Jake widened his eyes. *Fuck.* The heat level in the room went sky-high.

Liam slowly removed his hand. "Not gonna be long now."

Jake couldn't look away from those gorgeous eyes. "Me too," he whispered.

Liam inclined his head toward the mirror. "Wanna look?" There was a wicked gleam in his eyes.

"Lord no. I'd come in a heartbeat if I did that."

"Another time then." Liam reached lower to pull gently on Jake's balls.

Another time? Fuck. "Lemme concentrate on *this* time for the moment?" Thinking was turning into a chore. Jake wanted to close his eyes, but staring into Liam's was almost mesmerizing. All he heard was their breathing, and the slick, wet sounds that brought him closer to the edge.

Fuck, it's like his video all over again, but way better. This time he got to feel Liam come.

Liam grinned, his hand speeding up. "So… you make a noise when you come, baby? You gonna moan for me? 'Cause I sure wanna make you moan."

"You said… no moaning…." Jake's balls tightened, and his skin tingled all over.

"You're jus' gonna have to moan quietly." Faster now. "Gonna make you come, Jake, all over my hand. Is your cum sweet, like you?"

Holy fucking Christ. "So close." He so was. He could feel it, like he was about to fall into the sweetest ecstasy any second now.

Liam's breath quickened. "You gonna say my name when you come?"

"Yes," Jake whispered, hips rocking faster, his hand keeping time with them.

"Yeah? Gonna call out my name?"

"Yes!" Louder this time.

"Tell me when, baby. Let me know." Liam's hips were in motion too.

"Now, now, Liam, fuckin' *now!*" Jake buried his face in Liam's neck, stifling his cry by biting into Liam's shoulder, Liam's flesh muffling the moan that he couldn't keep inside. He stiffened as he shot his load, harder than ever before, his whole body shaking.

"Oh fuck." Liam shuddered, and Jake's hand was covered with warmth. Then Liam pulled him close, and they were kissing, both still trembling with the force of it all, Jake stroking sticky hands over Liam's back, clinging to him. Liam's hands were on his back, his ass, moving unhurriedly, while their kisses grew less urgent, more tender, until at last they were at peace, the tremors gone.

Neither of them spoke for a few minutes, and that was just perfect. Jake wanted to lie there, wrapped in Liam's arms, an indescribable feeling of serenity flowing through him.

Finally, Liam broke the silence. "You still with me?"

Jake chuckled. "Where else would I be?"

Liam kissed his forehead. "Well, we made a mess of the sheets, *and* ourselves, an' neither of us can stay like this. So… we're gonna creep into the bathroom like mice for a lightnin' quick clean-up, then we're gonna make the best we can of the bed, an' get some sleep."

Jake bit his lip. "We weren't all that quiet. D'ya think they heard?" Then he realized it was a stupid question. No way could they have slept through that. But if they weren't banging on Liam's door, demanding quiet, then he guessed later that morning would be 'face the music' time.

Oh Lord.

Liam kissed him on the lips. "I guess we'll find out." Gingerly, he pulled away from Jake. "Oh Lord, we're stuck." Jake snickered, and Liam gave him a mock glare. "Hey, half of this is yours."

Jake glanced down at their bodies. "I don't think that matters."

Liam climbed off the bed and held out a hand to him. "Mice, remember?"

Jake took it, cocking his head to one side. "The snorin' has stopped. Is that good or bad?" It seemed to be his night for stupid questions.

"Never mind them. They don't matter." Liam gazed at him

intently. "What *does* matter is if you enjoyed it."

Jake gave his sticky torso a wry glance. "What do *you* think?" He smirked. "An' you're wrong. What *really* matters is when we get to do it again." He grinned.

Liam grinned back. "Yeah, but next time, I'm gonna use a gag."

Jake stilled. "You wouldn't."

One look at Liam's innocent smile told him yeah, of course he would.

Liam curved his body around Jake's back, inhaling the smell of Pauli's jasmine soap that he always kept in the bathroom.

"You smell clean," he murmured.

Jake gave a sleepy chuckle. "Thass' better than smellin' of cum." He pulled Liam's arm right around him. "Like this."

Liam kissed his neck. "Good. Now go to sleep." He closed his eyes, breathing Jake in, aware of every part of his body relaxing into that blissful, warm state just before sleep.

"Actually? I love this." The words were barely audible, but Liam caught them, and for a moment his heart skipped a beat, until he realized he'd misheard. It took a moment for him to regain his previous calm. The thought occurred to him that he had three more nights of Jake.

I could get used to this.

Liam brought his lips to Jake's ear. "I love this too," he whispered. Jake's response was to lace his fingers through Liam's. Seconds later he was asleep.

Liam lay there in the darkness, focusing on one thought that followed him down into the depths of velvet oblivion.

I think I could fall in love with him.

Truth & Betrayal

Chapter Thirty-Four

Liam opened his eyes, aware that something felt… different. Then he remembered.

Something *was* different. There was a beautiful, dark brown-haired man in his arms, his head tucked in against Liam's chest, hand resting on Liam's waist, sleeping peacefully.

Okay, this was heaven.

Then he realized something else had changed. What had taken place all those hours ago had been because he'd wanted to make *Jake* feel good, to satisfy *his* needs, not Liam's. Sure, it hadn't been an entirely selfless act—c'mon, he hadn't had sex for six months—but he'd gotten more pleasure watching Jake unravel, than from his own climax.

An' if I'd just wanted to get laid, Blue Eyes in Ibiza would've been more than happy to oblige, right? No, something had held him back—or should he say some*one*?

The same someone who shared his bed.

Jake stirred in his arms, warm and smelling of clean cotton sheets and the faintest whiff of soap. He gradually opened his eyes, his brow furrowed slightly, and then he blinked when his gaze met Liam's. "Hey." It was a happy sound, and the smile that accompanied it lit Liam up on the inside.

Lord, jus' lookin' at him makes me happy.

Liam pulled him gently until Jake lay on top of him, their mouth inches apart. "Mornin'," he said, before taking those warm, soft lips in a tender kiss. Jake caught his breath, then just plain *melted*. He shifted his weight onto his elbows, on either side of

Liam's head, then it was back to the important business of kissing. It was amazing how a chaste kiss could be such a sensual experience, and for the moments that followed, Liam lost himself in the joy of it all.

When they parted, Jake's eyes shone. "Wow."

Liam sighed happily. It wasn't just him then. "Did ya sleep well?"

Jake's lazy smile was answer enough. "Like I haven't slept in ages. I wondered if I'd get all claustrophobic, y'know, but I guess I fell right asleep. Don't think I woke up once."

Liam glanced at the bedside clock. "Hate to break it to ya, but we've only slept five hours." It was eight o'clock, and the apartment was still quiet. "Doesn't sound like they're up yet."

Jake huffed. "They might not be but *I* sure am."

Liam was suddenly aware of the hard length sandwiched between them. "Lord, you ain't kiddin'." He slid his hand between them, his fingertips meeting the smooth head of Jake's dick.

Jake shivered, raising himself up slightly to give Liam better access, his shudders increasing when Liam wrapped his hand around the hot shaft. "It's always like a flag post first thing in the mornin'."

"Want me to take care of that? Jus' to put ya out of your misery, of course." He stifled a chuckle.

Jake's breathing hitched, and just like that, the atmosphere in the bedroom changed. "Fuck, yeah," he whispered.

"On your back then. Get comfortable." As an afterthought, Liam retrieved the lube from where he'd left it. Jake shifted on the bed, until he was lying across it, pillows shoved under his head. Liam gave him an inquiring glance, and Jake flushed.

"Wanna watch you in the mirror."

Okay, *now* he was going to chuckle. Then Jake's words sank in, and he recalled their conversation those few hours ago. An internal sigh of relief rolled through him. *I didn't screw this up. It's gonna be okay.*

Liam crawled over to where Jake's head rested, and bent

over him to kiss him again, only this time he stroked Jake's chest, making sure to pay special attention to his nipples, because he knew they were a hot spot. Jake fed him a low, guttural noise that went straight to Liam's dick, but this wasn't about him.

"Spread for me, baby," Liam said in a low voice.

Jake's eyes widened, and he spread his thighs haltingly, his cock rising from his belly, stiff and dark in comparison to his pale skin. Liam lay between his legs on his belly, one hand holding Jake's shaft steady while he leisurely stroked Jake's torso with the other. Jake's breathing stuttered as Liam's breath warmed the head of his dick. "Fuck," he said weakly.

Liam smiled. "Relax. You're gonna love this." Then he took Jake's cock into his mouth, and Jake arched up off the bed, a stream of soft moans falling from his lips. Liam rubbed his belly with a firm hand while he gradually took more and more of Jake's dick into his mouth. By the time he reached the root, Jake was writhing, low cries pouring out of him.

"Oh, f-fuck."

Liam unhurriedly slid Jake's cock from his mouth. "Is that a good 'Oh fuck' or a bad 'oh fuck'?"

Jake craned his neck up off the pillows and gaped at him. "You didn't have to stop!"

Liam chuckled. "Guess I got my answer." He went right back to enjoying that dick, alternating between sucking on the head, sliding his lips up and down the shaft, and licking it from root to slit. Judging by the noises that poured out of Jake, his first blow job was *not* gonna last all that long. Jake seemed unable to lie still, pushing up with his hips, both hands on Liam's head as he held him there, until he was steadily fucking Liam's mouth, gasping with each thrust.

Then he glanced toward the mirror. "Oh, my God. Fuck, lookit you."

Liam chuckled, his mouth full of hard dick. He pulled free again, ignoring Jake's low whine of frustration. "Then you're *really* gonna love this. Bend your knees."

Jake did as instructed, his gaze focused on Liam, his breathing ragged, his cock standing proud.

Liam beamed. "Look at that dick. So hard for me." As unobtrusively as possible, he opened the tube of lube and slicked up a finger. When he was ready, he placed one hand flat to Jake's belly, while he slid a finger between Jake's ass cheeks to circle his hole. "Ready for more?"

Jake nodded, his eyes locked on Liam's mouth as it neared his cock, his chest rising and falling rapidly. Liam took him deep, and at the same time languidly pushed his middle finger into tight heat.

"Holy fuck." Jake's eyes rolled back in his head. Liam bobbed up and down on his shaft, while he crooked his finger, gently exploring Jake's channel, his other hand still rubbing Jake's belly, keeping the motion soothing. He pulled free of Jake's dick, and stroked his leg.

"That's it, baby. You like playin' with your ass, don'tcha? Don't it feel even better when someone else plays with it? You like my finger inside ya?"

A shiver ran the length of Jake's body. "God, yeah."

Liam stayed that way for a while, letting Jake become accustomed to it. When he was ready to take him further, he waited until Jake was focused on him, then began a slow in-and-out motion, making sure to keep it in time with each slide of his lips down Jake's shaft.

Jake went wild. One minute he was chasing Liam's finger, pushing down hard onto it, the next, he was thrusting up into Liam's mouth, his body trembling. Liam set the pace, his mouth and finger maintaining the same rhythm, until Jake was almost sobbing, unable to lie still. Every time he nudged Jake's prostate, Jake's shivers multiplied, until he was moaning nonstop, and his dick swelled on Liam's tongue. *C'mon, baby. Give it to me.*

Jake might not have heard Liam's thought, but he obviously got the hint. Liam slid his finger as deep as it would go, and gave the head a hard suck. Jake gave a low cry and creamed in Liam's mouth, his back arched, body shaking, one arm across his eyes as he rode the wave.

Liam swallowed every drop, before cleaning Jake's cock with his tongue, taking his time. Jake watched him, lips parted, totally blissed out, and that was just fine. Liam's own dick was like a rock, but that could wait. He'd have to take care of it before he took a leak, because peeing with a hard-on was just *not* gonna happen.

Jake let out a happy but tired little sigh. "Okay, that was awesome." He held his arms wide. "C'mere." Liam crawled up his body and went for the kiss he knew Jake wanted. Jake locked his arms around Liam's neck and gave himself up to Liam's embrace, eyes closed, his breathing more even. Then it was Liam's turn to catch his breath when Jake opened his eyes, reached between their bodies, and curled his fingers around Liam's heavy cock, slow-pumping the shaft. "Wanna feel your cum on me," he murmured, his hand working faster.

Liam didn't even have time to give him a warning before he shot all over Jake's belly and chest, leaving creamy trails over his skin, his orgasm juddering through him. Jake's nostrils flared, and he ran a finger through a puddle of cum, before bringing it to his own lips and lapping at it almost experimentally with his tongue. He grinned at Liam. "Oh, c'mon, I had to taste it, right?"

Liam laughed quietly. "Of course." He rolled off Jake and onto his side, gazing down at the mess he'd left on Jake's body. "I'd grab the bathroom now if I was you, while the coast is clear."

"You could always come in the shower with me." Jake flushed. "I didn't mean it to come out like that." He did an eye roll. "Lord, seems like every other word outta my mouth is come."

Liam snorted. "I had noticed. An' no, I will *not* be gettin' in the shower with ya. You're way too distractin'."

Jake pulled a face. "Spoilsport." He sat up in bed, glancing at his torso. "Seemed like a good idea, seein' as this is your mess." His eyes gleamed. "I guess now you have your answer."

Liam frowned, momentarily lost. "To what?"

Jake gave a wicked grin. "Whether my cum is sweet or not." He trailed his hand lightly down Liam's arm.

Liam grabbed him firmly by the wrist. "In the shower, dirty boy." Jake got to his feet with a sigh of resignation, but before he headed for the door, Liam got up too and kissed him unhurriedly. "An' for your information, it was delicious." Then he swatted Jake's butt.

Jake let out the cutest little yelp, before walking toward the door, his ass jiggling.

"Er, baby?" Jake glanced back at him, and Liam pointed to the towel hung on a hook on the back of the door. "You might wanna cover up. Unless you really want the boys to see your junk."

"Shit." Jake grabbed the towel. "Thass' your fault. You mess with my head." He wrapped the towel around him and left the room.

Liam stripped the bed, ready to sneak the sheets into the laundry. He smiled. *Well, he messes with* my *head, so it's only fair.* He pulled on a pair of shorts, bundled up the sheets, and left the bedroom to head down to the laundry in the basement. With any luck, he could have them washed, dried, and back on the bed before the guys noticed.

Apparently, this wasn't his lucky day. Dev was in the kitchen, making coffee.

What hit Liam like a punch to his gut was the fact that he wasn't smiling.

Liam came to a halt, a sudden chill lifting the hairs on the back of his neck. "Mornin'," he said tentatively. He placed the sheets on the floor. Then Pauli came out of their room, and walked past him to the sink. He placed a glass there, then turned to face Liam, his brow furrowed.

"What the hell do you think you're doing?" His voice was low.

Liam blinked. "Excuse me?"

Pauli widened his gaze. "You're going to play dumb? Fine. Tell me you two weren't fucking last night and this morning." He folded his arms across his chest, his eyes glinting.

Liam's pulse sped up, his body tensing. "Whatever went on in that room is none of your fuckin' business."

Dev snorted. "We're not thinkin' 'bout you gettin' your rocks off, we're more concerned about Jake right now."

Liam could not believe this. "Jake is fine an' dandy, I can assure y'all of that. Now d'ya wanna tell me *why* you're so all-fired concerned?"

"You're gonna hurt him, that's why!" Dev kept his voice low too. "I mean, c'*mon*, Liam. Would you be fuckin' him if he wasn't Caleb's brother?"

What the fuck? Liam was lost for words.

"I suppose I get it," Pauli added. "You've kinda got Caleb back, right? Or at least a part of him. But that doesn't make this right."

"Now wait a minute." Liam had to take a moment to breathe. He balled his hands into tight fists at his sides. "You think that's what's really goin' on here? That I've got myself a Caleb 2.0? That it?" Another deep breath. "Fuck. You could *not* be more wrong. This is *nothin'* to do with Caleb, an' *everythin'* to do with that beautiful man in your bathroom. Did you ever *once* stop an' wonder if I might have feelin's for him? Well? That I might be *fallin'* for him? An' those feelin's have *nothin'* to do with Caleb."

Dev's mouth fell open. "Oh Lord."

Pauli swallowed. "You're not shitting us, are ya?"

Liam glared at them. "Right now, I don't know whether to be thankful you're lookin' out for Jake, or so pissed that I wanna rip your heads off." He was *so* close to packing up and walking out of there, and taking Jake with him.

Dev paled. "Can I vote for the former?"

Pauli nudged him in the ribs. "Hush." He unfolded his arms and took a step toward Liam. "How long have you felt this way about him?"

Liam finally got his temper under control. "I guess since Mom's birthday at the end of July. That was the start of it."

Pauli's breathing hitched. "Three months?"

Lima nodded slowly. "Then things kinda sped up a bit last month. I do understand where you're comin' from though, 'cause I struggled with this too. Only, I was more concerned about how it might look, so soon after Caleb's passin'. Mom put me straight on that one."

"Your mom knows?" Dev's eyes were huge.

Liam snickered. "Like I could ever get anythin' past her." He pulled himself up to his full height. "So, I gotta know. Is this gonna be a problem, us bein' here an'…bein' together? 'Cause Jake wasn't ready to share with y'all."

Pauli glanced at Dev. "Well?"

Dev sighed. "We fucked up, didn't we?"

"Yup." Liam wasn't about to make them feel better, not after what they'd just put him through. "Although I'm kinda comin' round to the 'not pullin' your heads off just yet' side of the fence. I guess you only spoke up 'cause you care for him."

"For you too," Pauli added. "And as to your question, no, I don't think it's going to be a problem. For either of us." He smirked. "Although I might have to invest in some ear plugs." Dev snickered.

"Promise me you won't make Jake feel bad? This is all so new." The last thing Liam wanted was for Jake to feel self-conscious. "I mean, no jokes about noise, or anythin' like that. An' no offerin' him advice on sex neither."

Pauli gave him a wide-eyed innocent look. "Us?"

Liam guffawed. "Yes, you. An' you know exactly what I'm talkin' 'bout, so don't try bein' coy." Just then, he heard the shower click off. "We good?"

Dev nodded. "We're good. An' sorry for jumpin' off the deep end like that."

Liam waved his hand. "Your hearts were in the right place, I guess." Thank God they'd had the good sense not to say any of that in front of Jake. Liam could only imagine how confused he'd have been.

At least one good thing came out of it. They didn't have to hide anymore.

Now to see how long it took Jake to notice.

Chapter Thirty-Five

By lunch time Sunday, Jake knew something had happened, although he wasn't sure what exactly. The atmosphere in the apartment was subtly different. Dev and Pauli's manner had changed: there were fewer jokes, and they seemed quieter. Liam was a little subdued too, and Jake got to worrying.

Have I done somethin'?

He put up with it until after lunch, but by that time, the suspense was killing him. He waited until they were sitting on the couches before speaking his mind.

"Okay, what's goin' on?"

That was when he knew he'd nailed it. Everyone fell silent. Next to him, Liam stared into his glass of sweet tea.

"I guess things might have felt a little… strange around here this morning," Pauli began.

Jake cut him off right there. "Ya think? You guys are weirdin' me out."

"It's just that we didn't know how to put it without—"

"Put *what*, for chrissakes?" Jesus, it was getting worse, not better.

Dev grinned. "Congratulations?"

Jake blinked. "Say what?"

"How about, 'we're glad you're an item'? Or 'you've got great taste in men'? Or even 'congrats on handing in your V card'?" Pauli suggested with a sweet smile.

"You promised," Liam growled.

Pauli rolled his eyes. "Ah, c'mon. I kept my mouth shut all

morning. I think that was a minor miracle, don't you?" Beside him on the couch, Dev guffawed.

Aw crap. Jake turned to Liam. "I take it they know 'bout us?"

Before Liam could reply, Dev snorted. "Honey, this is a small apartment. A mouse farts in here, an' everyone knows about it."

"Oh Lord."

Liam took his hand. "Think of it this way. You don't have to worry 'bout bein' quiet anymore."

Jake gave him a hard stare. "Sure. *Now* I'm jus' gonna be waitin' for the applause to break out when we finish."

There was silence for a moment, and then the three men burst out laughing. Jake saw the funny side too. What he didn't expect was to find himself on the receiving end of hugs from Dev and Pauli.

Pauli kissed his cheek. "Liam's like family, so I guess that means you are too."

"An' you're always welcome here, whenever you need to be 'round folks who care for ya, to feel safe," Dev added.

Tears pricked his eyes. It already felt like he'd gained another family in Wilmington, but Jake figured there was always room for more. "Thank you, guys." He glanced at Liam. "Did ya really make 'em promise not to say anythin'?"

Pauli snickered. "No, what Liam wanted was for us not to tease you about... certain things."

Jake snorted. "Really? I haven't known you two all that long, but even *I* know that's askin' for too much."

Liam retook his hand, placing it on his thigh. "I jus' didn't want you to be embarrassed."

That touched him. "Thanks for the thought, but that's like pissin' in the wind where these two are concerned."

"Yeah, but I had to try, right?" Then Liam leaned in and kissed him on the lips, not bothering to keep it short. The gesture made his heart swell.

No hidin' anymore. It was a great feeling. Then he thought about his parents, about if he would ever feel brave enough to take Liam home. Just for a moment, his elation ebbed away, and he chased after it, pushing such thoughts from his mind. *Can't think about that now.*

This was a special place, a special time.

"There's a whole lotta guys gettin' dressed up in costumes this evenin', an' goin' round the bars. Wanna join us?" Dev asked.

Liam said nothing, and Jake knew he was leaving the choice up to him.

"Sounds like fun," he said brightly. "Why don't you guys go an' have a great time?" He squeezed Liam's thigh. "We might jus' hang out here an' watch TV or somethin'." He kept his tone as natural as he could manage.

Pauli bit his lip. "Oh honey, you are so *cute*. Sure, you two stay here and enjoy your 'something'." His eyes gleamed, and Jake knew he wasn't fooling them. Then Liam's gaze met his, and Jake forgot all about being embarrassed.

Yeah, he hadn't fooled Liam either. Not for a second. Better still, judging by the way Liam was looking at him, it seemed they were both on the same page.

Thank God.

Liam glanced at the clock beside the bed. Jake had been in the bathroom for the past twenty minutes. He smiled to himself. *Too cute.* He left the bedroom and knocked lightly on the door. "Everythin' okay in there?"

"Sure." The word came out like a squeak. The sound of a throat clearing. "Yeah, sure. I'll be out in a second."

Liam left him to it, still smiling. The first time he'd gotten laid, he'd spent half an hour in the bathroom, desperately trying to make sure there'd be no surprises later on. *Lord, talk about nervous.* He hadn't had a clue, and the guy fucking him had been no help. All he'd wanted was to pop Liam's cherry.

Well, it's not gonna be like that for Jake. Liam would see to that.

The bathroom door opened, and then Jake appeared in the doorway, a rainbow beach towel wrapped around him, covering him from the chest down. Liam chuckled. "That was the towel they gave ya?"

Jake nodded. "Pauli said somethin' 'bout all the rest of the towels bein' in the laundry, but you know what? I think this is his idea of a joke."

"It does kinda bury ya." Liam grinned. "Why don'tcha take it off?"

Jake smirked. "Subtle. Very subtle." But he casually removed it, revealing his hard dick that bobbed up.

"Nothin' subtle 'bout that, is there? At least I know what you were thinkin' 'bout in the shower, an' why it took so long." Liam smiled. "Lord, you have a pretty cock."

"Not too short?" Jake peered down at it.

Liam walked over and curled his fingers around the shaft, tugging gently on it. "Jus' right," he said in a low voice. Jake's breathing hitched, then grew more ragged with each leisurely pull.

"Don't I get to touch ya?" Jake's voice was hoarse.

Liam pushed his shorts past his hips, kicking them off as they dropped to his ankles. "All yours."

Jake took a step closer, his hands on Liam's chest, and kissed him, close enough that Liam caught the tremor that rippled through him. Liam cupped Jake's head and deepened the kiss, stroking his tongue between Jake's lips until Jake was feeding him soft moans of pleasure.

That's it, Jakey-boy. Liam wanted him lost in a fog of arousal, aching for Liam's cock.

Jake reached down and grasped Liam's dick, his fingers gentle as he worked the shaft. Liam nodded, his hand matching Jake's, tug for tug, slide for slide. "Yeah, that's it. Perfect." When Jake started to lower himself to his knees, Liam stopped him.

"Let's do this on the bed, alright?" He took Jake's hand and led him over there, both of them climbing onto it and shifting into the center. Liam got on his back, his cock standing upright, as if it was begging for those soft-looking lips. He spread his legs, making room for Jake, who knelt between them, his own dick pointing toward Liam like an arrow.

Jake leaned over him and kissed Liam's neck, moving lower until he reached his nipple. Liam held his breath as Jake gave it a hesitant lick. "Flick it with your tongue. Suck on it. Tug on it gently with your teeth."

Jake lowered his head. "Like this?" Liam groaned as Jake played with the little nub, alternating between flicking and sucking, before tugging it, sending exquisite pleasure shooting through him, all the way to his cock.

"Fuck, yeah, jus' like that."

Jake made a happy little noise, giving his nipple one good, hard suck before moving lower, kissing his abs, his belly, until he reached the head of Liam's dick, his hot breath wafting over it.

"Lick the underside," Liam demanded. "A long, slow lick all the way from the root to the head."

Jake dipped his head and did as instructed, pausing when he reached the head, before taking it in his mouth, his hand wrapped around the base.

Liam shivered. "Oh, Jake, that's so good."

Jake moaned around it, taking him a little deeper but not venturing too far, which was perfect as far as Liam was concerned. His gaze flickered toward Liam, and Liam nodded.

"Let your mouth slide down it, then suck hard on your way back up. Keep doin' that."

Jake pulled free and grinned. "What's this? Liam's Cock 101?" Before Liam could think of a suitable reply, Jake proved he was a damn good student, bobbing his head up and down on Liam's shaft, concentrating on the head, until Liam was shaking all over.

He laid a hand on Jake's head. "Fuck, stop, or I'm gonna

come in your mouth."

Jake knelt up, his breathing rapid, chest rising and falling. "Uh uh. I want you inside me when you come."

Liam let loose a low moan. "Somethin' you'd better learn right now. You talkin' like that turns me on."

Jake grinned. "Well, that works out jus' fine, 'cause you were doin' the same to me this mornin'."

Liam chuckled. "So you wanna play? Fine. Let's play. Get on your hands an' knees, an' face the mirror."

Jake's breathing sped up, but he did as he was told. Liam gazed at that ripe little ass, creamy skin, a light covering of down, and that cleft hiding Jake's pretty little hole. "Legs wide apart," he said quickly. "That's it, show me that ass." He ran his hands over the firm flesh, making sure to rub a finger through Jake's crack. Jake shuddered. "Yeah, you know where I'm goin, don'tcha?" He paused, his hands on those round cheeks. "Look in the mirror, Jake."

Jake raised his head, and Liam locked gazes with him. "You're gonna love this, baby." He gently pulled Jake's ass cheeks apart, and there it was, that tight little pucker, just waiting for him. Taking his time, Liam rubbed his face through Jake's crevice, his nose skimming over Jake's hole that tightened on contact. Liam flicked it with his tongue, and Jake gasped. Another flick, and another, and another, until Jake was panting. Liam made sure Jake was focused on his reflection, before giving Jake's hole a slow, lingering lick.

"Oh my God."

Jake couldn't look away. All he could see of Liam were those dark eyes, focused on him, Liam's face buried in his crack. And holy fuck, the *sounds,* noises that left him in no doubt that Liam was enjoying every second of this.

Jake reached under his body to palm his cock, balanced on one hand, his gaze locked on that view. The lower half of Liam's head was out of sight, the top only visible from the eyes up, his hands on Jake's ass, his hips, his back, stroking and rubbing while—holy fucking *hell*—he pushed his tongue against Jake's hole.

"Oh, *GOD*." The cry was torn from him, and Jake caught sight of his own stark face in the mirror, his wide eyes, mouth open… He dropped his head to the mattress and reached back to where Liam licked, probed and sucked. His fingers came into contact with the soft coarseness of Liam's hair, and Jake pushed his head deeper, wanting more, his whole body quivering, swimming in sensation. He wanted to *move*, goddamn it, to push back, but Liam held him steady, arms across his lower back while he fucked Jake with his tongue, until Jake couldn't stop shaking.

"Please," he begged. "Please…Oh God, please, Liam…" Jake collapsed onto the bed, incapable of holding himself up any longer.

Liam halted, covering Jake with his body, his breath warm on Jake's back and shoulders as he laid a trail of kisses, moving higher, higher, until his lips brushed Jake's ear. "What do you want?" he whispered.

"Fuck me." The words shuddered out of him, and Jake twisted to look Liam in the eye. "Fuck me, please."

Liam took his mouth in a fervent kiss, and Jake felt the weight and heat of Liam's cock on his back. "You want me inside ya?"

"Lord, yes," Jake moaned.

Liam pulled away from him and Jake scrambled to his knees. Liam sat with his back to the mirror, a pillow hastily shoved behind him, and reached into the nightstand drawer. When he dropped lube and condoms onto the bed, Jake grabbed his wrist.

"You said it was my choice, remember?"

Liam frowned for a moment, then his brow cleared. "An' we also talked about protectin' yourself."

Jake's heartbeat raced. "I don't have an STD, do I? 'Cause I'm a virgin, remember?"

Liam's eyes were so dark, they were black. "Like I could forget that."

"An' you haven't got anythin' floatin' around inside ya, do ya?"

Liam raised his eyebrows at that. "No. Got my latest test results just last week. An' I haven't been with anyone since…" He cleared his throat. "I've not had sex for six months."

Jake nodded slowly. "Then it's still my choice. You said sex is all about trust, an' I trust ya. An' all the while we're talkin', we're losin' out on time when we could be doin' somethin' a damn sight more enjoyable, if you get my meanin'?" He straddled Liam's lap, reached back and pressed Liam's dick into his crease. "So why don't we jus' stop talkin' so you can fuck me?"

Liam grabbed Jake's wrist and pulled his hand forward. "An' why don't you jus' slow down so we can really enjoy this?" He snapped open the lube, squeezed the tube over Jake's rigid cock, and began a gentle up-and-down motion. "Like that, yeah?"

Jake rocked his hips, pushing his dick through Liam's slick fingers. "Yeah, jus' like that."

"Now lemme make it even better. Sit back a little."

Jake did as requested, then let out a long sigh when Liam wrapped his hand around both their shafts.

"Doesn't that feel good, your dick slidin' against mine?"

Jake nodded, rocking a little faster.

"You're gettin' harder, baby. Look down."

Jake glanced down and moaned at the sight, the heads of their cocks emerging through Liam's fingers, glistening. "Oh fuck," he whispered.

"Looks fuckin' hot, doesn't it?"

"Lord, yes." Rocking faster now, Liam moving with him.

"Gonna be hotter in a minute, when I slide my bare cock into your hole."

"Liam… please…." Jake gripped Liam's shoulders, his

gaze fixed on their slick shafts, the friction dancing a fine line between 'Fuck, don't stop' and 'Fuck me now'.

"Hold out your hand." Liam dripped lube onto Jake's fingers. "You know what to do. Get yourself ready."

Jake reached back between his cheeks and sank first one finger, then two, into his loosened hole, rocking between them and Liam's hand.

"That's it. Get that hole ready for my cock."

Jake nodded, breathless, fucking himself on his fingers, hips bucking. Then Liam stilled his hand. "Now, baby. You're gonna ride me."

Jake pulled his fingers free, and shifted forward, pushing out a soft cry when the head of Liam's dick pressed against his hole. It felt hot—and so very big.

"Look at me."

Jake looked him in the eye, trying to breathe.

"Now ease down onto it, as slow as you like. You set the pace. You're in charge, remember?"

Jake let out a whoosh of air. "Thanks for the reminder." He reached back once more, his fingers skating lightly over Liam's bare cock, feeling how it nestled between his cheeks. Jake curled his fingers around the shaft and held it steady while he lowered himself so very gradually, gasping when the head finally made it through the ring of muscle. "Oh Lord, I feel that."

"Fuck, yeah. Holy hell, you're tight." Liam breathed deeply. His hands were on Jake's hips, like he was holding Jake steady, and Lord knew, Jake appreciated that.

Jake kept one hand wrapped around Liam's dick, the other cupping Liam's nape. He leaned forward, their foreheads touching. "That is one huge cock." Down, down he sank, inch by inch, until at last his ass was cradled against Liam's body. "Gimme a sec?"

Liam kissed him, a slow-burning kiss that set him on fire. "Take your time. We got all night."

"Thank God for that." Jake gave a leisurely pull on his own dick. "'Cause once we're done… it's my turn." He gasped. "You feel way better than the dildo. Thicker, for one thing."

Liam chuckled. "That's gratifyin'." He stroked Jake's thighs. "You wanna try movin' a little? Jus' rock on it, nice an' gentle."

Jake gave an experimental rock forward, sighing as Liam's length eased out of him. "Feels just as good, you slidin' out as you slidin' in."

Liam nodded. "An' once you're used to it, I'll take over an' do all the work."

"Don't know 'bout that. Makes me… sound kinda lazy." He rocked a little faster, and Liam slid in and out a little easier. "Oh yeah… Lord… yeah, that's good." Jake placed one hand on Liam's chest and squeezed his pec, his other hand working his shaft while he kept up that delicious rocking, heat spreading through him. "Think I'm about ready for more."

"Then lean back. Put your weight on my thighs."

Jake balanced himself, and Liam started to thrust into him, sending sparks of electricity arcing through him. "Fuck, that feels amazing." He shuddered. "God, Liam, it's like… every time you slide into me… makes me wanna come…."

"Not yet." Liam hauled himself into a sitting position, his dick still buried in Jake's ass. "Put your arms around me." Jake clung to him, shifting his legs onto either side of Liam's body, one arm taking his weight while they kissed, Jake unable to keep still, almost bouncing on Liam's cock, his own dick slapping against his belly.

Lord, it was glorious.

Liam's mouth fused with his, a demanding kiss that made his toes curl, and Jake just wanted more. "Fuck me," he murmured against Liam's lips. "C'mon, fuck me."

Liam eased out of him, shifting him onto his back, and then he was right there where Jake wanted him, spearing his cock deep inside Jake's body, his arms hooked under Jake's legs, spreading him wide.

Holy fuck. This was… different.

Liam's face was inches from Jake's, those beautiful dark eyes focused on him. Suddenly, it had gone from fucking to something more intimate. Liam slowed right down, moving sinuously above him, not once breaking eye contact. Each time he slid deep, Liam made a small noise of pleasure, like he couldn't get enough of Jake.

"Lord, how you feel," Liam whispered, before kissing him, first on the mouth, then his neck, sending shivers convulsing through him.

Jake held onto Liam's broad shoulders, moving with him, a sensual dance where Liam led and Jake mirrored his steps. "So good, love." The endearment slipped out, and Liam's eyes widened.

"Then let me make it even better."

No more talk, only the harsh sound of their mingled breaths as Liam buried his face in Jake's neck and proceeded to fuck him with short thrusts, moving faster now. Jake held onto Liam, his arms locked around Liam's neck, the heat inside him almost unbearable as Liam pushed him closer and closer to the edge. Added to their gasps and sighs was the sound of Liam's body slapping against Jake's, quick and sharp, and Jake knew he was about to come.

He tugged on his cock, once, twice, three times, and warmth spattered his torso. Liam groaned, but kept fucking him, until he cried out and leaned forward to kiss Jake, his body trembling. Jake gasped at the throb of Liam's dick inside him, clinging to him while they kissed, not severing the connection between them. He wrapped his legs around Liam, caging him while the last waves of pleasures crashed over them, leaving him weak, yet elated.

Liam kissed his forehead, cheeks, nose, and chin, finally claiming Jake's mouth in a lingering, tender kiss that was the perfect ending, an unhurried exploration that left him at peace. Jake stroked Liam's head and neck, all the fire burned out of him, replaced with a sense of calm.

"Thank you," he said, feeling almost serene, cradling Liam's nape in his hands.

Liam stilled. "I think that was a joint effort, don'tcha?"

Jake smiled. "Yeah, I guess." He sighed. "You're still inside me."

"Not for long."

He knew it had to end, but he wanted to hold on to that feeling for as long as possible.

Liam awoke to soft kisses on his chest, his neck, his face, and finally his lips. He gave a shiver. "Your mustache is ticklin' me. What time is it?"

Jake gave a soft chuckle. "Too early o'clock."

Something hard and hot nudged Liam's hip, and he responded with a chuckle of his own. "I think I know what time it is."

"Yeah?" More kisses, this time moving down his body.

Oh yeah. "Guess it's your turn then."

Another chuckle, then a wet mouth closed over the head of his cock, while gentle hands rubbed his belly and thighs.

"If this is a dream, I'll be real upset."

When Jake finally entered him with a sigh, Liam knew it was no dream, and as the sun came up, they wrapped their arms around each other, moving as one, in no hurry to reach the end.

Getting there was the best part.

Chapter Thirty-Six

Jake lay there in the early morning light, trying to ignore the heaviness that pervaded the room, but he knew it was no use.

He had to go home.

I don't wanna lose this. Four nights of lying in Liam's arms, falling asleep to the soothing rhythm of Liam's heart beating against his ear, feeling safe, feeling… loved. Not that either of them had said the word yet. Jake wasn't worried though. He knew it was coming, knew it with every beat of his heart.

The question was whether it would stand up to five hundred miles of separation, and an uncertain future. *That* had given him a few moments of stomach-churning anxiety during recent days. But even then, it was as if Liam had somehow known what was going on inside Jake's head, because those were the moments Liam had taken him by the hand, led him to their bedroom, and proceeded to obliterate all such fears with his hands, his lips, his tongue, his cock…

Yeah, Jake had *floated* through the last two days, carried along on a tide of pleasure and joy, not caring that they'd spent most of those days in bed, as if both of them were determined to make every second of their time together count. Dev and Pauli, to his surprise, had said nothing, not even the previous night when they snuck out of the party early and took refuge in their room. No one would have heard a thing with the music blaring, and that was just fine. It was almost as good as having the apartment to themselves.

Almost.

Liam's arm tightened around his waist. "You're thinkin' again." His breath warmed Jake's shoulder, and Jake sighed with pleasure when Liam planted a row of soft kisses there.

"What gave me away?"

"You're always thinkin'." Liam shifted in the bed, until he was lying between Jake's legs, his face hovering inches above Jake's. "I know, baby." His voice was soft. "I don't want this to end any more 'n you do."

Jake drew in a deep breath. "Then let's make it last a bit longer?" He stretched out his arm, reached onto the nightstand where they'd left the lube, and squeezed liquid from the tube onto Liam's dick.

Liam smiled. "I was hopin' you'd fuck me again."

Jake grinned. "Who says I'm not gonna? You're jus' gettin' first bite at the apple. Then it's my turn."

Liam laughed. "I love the way you think." He took the tube from him and placed it on the nightstand. Jake wrapped his legs around Liam's waist and his arms around Liam's neck, both of them catching their breath when Liam guided his dick to Jake's hole and slid home in one slow glide. Liam buried his face in Jake's neck, and began the leisurely, exquisite rocking that Jake had come to love, their arms tight around each other, holding on for dear life.

"That's it, love," Jake sighed. "Take me home."

Because home *was* Liam, his voice, his smile, his body, his scent, his touch…

God sure had a lousy sense of timing.

Jake had only just found his true home, and he was about to lose it.

Liam closed the door of the truck and stepped closer, leaning in with his elbows on the window sill. "Drive safe, take a break if you need one, an' text me when you get there."

"You gonna email me tonight?"

Liam's heart ached to see the hopeful look in Jake's eyes. "You know it."

"Then I guess I'd better go." He didn't switch on the engine, however.

Impulsively, Liam reached into the cab, his hands on Jake's nape, and pulled him into a kiss that he hoped said more than words. Jake moaned softly, his tongue parting Liam's lips, and Liam lost himself for a moment in its sensual sweetness. When they parted, he pulled back a little and locked gazes with Jake. "You know how I feel 'bout ya."

Jake swallowed. "I guess."

"You *guess*?" Fuck no. That wasn't good enough. And that was when Liam realized there *were* words after all. "Then let me spell it out for ya." He cupped Jake's cheek. "I love ya, Jake Greenwood."

Jake stilled, and his face lit up. "Love you too."

Liam snickered. "Well, I'm glad we got *that* cleared up." Inside he was buzzing. *He loves me.* "Make sure you remember that, 'specially those times when you're low, an' it feels like the world is kickin' your ass." He grinned, unable to resist. "Jus' think about me *lickin'* your ass instead."

Jake's eyes widened. "You are just *evil*." He bit back a smile.

Liam cackled. "An' we both know you wouldn't have me any other way."

"I'll have ya any which way I can," Jake said with a grin.

"An' you can stop right there. Time to get goin'." Liam knew a delaying tactic when he saw one, not that he blamed Jake for that, not for one second.

Jake nodded, and the truck's engine fired into life. Liam retreated from the cab and stood back, his hand raised. "'Bye for now, beautiful."

Jake mouthed *bye*, and backed the truck out of the parking space. Just before he turned the steering wheel, he stared at Liam,

Love ya.

Liam mouthed the words right back at him, his heart beating that bit faster. He watched as Jake drove out onto the street, until he was no longer in sight. Then it was time to get behind the wheel of his own car, and begin the trek back to North Carolina.

Guess Elvis nailed it when he sang that home is where the heart is. Because Liam's home was on its way back to Tennessee, and with all the obstacles in their way, it might as well have been a million miles away.

By Friday evening, it felt like Jake had never been away. Daddy had them starting a new job, and that had meant trips back and forth between home and Kash and Karry's building supplies, until both of them were exhausted, and Jake ached like a bastard. He knew he hadn't been all that talkative since his return, but keeping focused on work was the only thing getting him through the days right then. He lived for those moments when he could shut the bedroom door, snuggle under the comforter, and shut out the world.

Then it was just him, his laptop, and Liam.

Saturday morning dawned a bright, sunny day, the temperature dipping to 62 degrees. Jake got up, had breakfast with Mama and Daddy, and then Mama went off to clean the church, a new habit she'd acquired, and Daddy disappeared to do some more work on the new project.

Jake was having a second mug of coffee when his phone pinged, and he fished it out of his pocket eagerly. His heart sank a little when he saw the message was from Taylor, but then he recalled they hadn't spoken for over a week.

Jake smirked. *I was kinda... busy.* He pulled up the message.

Hey stranger. I'm on the late shift today. Wanna meet up for a coffee or something?

Now that was a great idea. Jake clicked on Call. "Hey," he said warmly.

"Oh, so you *are* alive."

Jake snickered. "I've been outta town. Got back Wednesday night. Been workin' my nuts off since then. Coffee sounds great. Where an' what time?"

"D'ya know the Common Ground coffee shop on Central Avenue? Next to Fast Cash?"

"Yeah, I know it."

"We could meet now if you jus' want coffee, or a bit later an' we can have a bite to eat. They got snacks an' shit."

"That sounds even better. How does noon sound?"

"Sounds good. See ya there. Looks like we've got some catchin' up to do." Taylor disconnected.

Jake smiled to himself. *You have* no *idea.*

Jake pushed open the glass door to Common Ground, and stepped into the aromatic interior. Heavy, square wooden tables stood on a hardwood floor, surrounded by red metal chairs. Taylor sat in the corner in civilian clothes, nursing a coffee. He stood as Jake approached.

"Good to see ya. I was startin' to think I'd said somethin'. Either that, or my body odor is worse than I thought." He winked.

Jake snorted. "Ass. Lemme grab a coffee, then we can decide what we're eatin'." He walked off to the counter, returning a couple of minutes later to sit in the chair facing Taylor. "I ordered a latte an' a couple of slices of that cake they've got on the counter." He leaned back in the chair, inhaling the wonderful smell that wafted through the air, the heady aroma of freshly brewed coffee.

"Yeah, smells good, don't it?" Taylor sat forward, his gaze focused on Jake. "You said you went outta town. Where did ya go?"

"Atlanta."

Truth & Betrayal

Taylor grinned. "Again? An' what were you gettin' up to in Atlanta?" He lowered his voice. "Makin' the most of the gay bars? That gay strip club you were tellin' me about?"

Jake took a deep breath and sat forward, his volume matching Taylor's. "Actually? I was there visitin' my… boyfriend." His heart hammered, and his palms grew clammy. *Fuck. I said it.*

Taylor's mouth fell open. "Boyfriend? Since when? Who? Gimme details," he whispered. He shook his head. "You sly bastard. You kept this quiet."

Jake chuckled. "If you shut up for more than one second, I'll tell ya." Just then the server brought over his coffee and cake, and both he and Taylor fell silent. He thanked her, then waited until she was back behind the counter. Half the tables were occupied, the air filled with lively chatter. That didn't matter none: Jake was still going to keep the conversation to a whisper.

He took a sip of his latte, then wiped the foam from his mustache. "Since when is kinda tricky. We've both been thinkin' 'bout each other for a couple of months, but we only really got together last weekend. An' as for who, you met him." He waited.

Taylor became very, very still. "Liam? Caleb's ex?"

Something quivered deep in Jake's belly, and his scalp prickled. "Yeah," he said slowly.

Taylor sat back in his chair, drawing his mouth into a straight line, his gaze focused on the table.

"Okay, you're startin' to freak me out a little." Jake tried to keep his tone light. "Wanna tell me what's wrong? You *met* Liam. You talked with him. 'Seems like a nice guy', you said. 'Obviously lookin' out for ya', you said. 'Seems to care about you', you said. 'Protective—"

"Okay, okay, *Jesus!*" Taylor snickered. "Ain't no one can say you have a bad memory, Jake."

He couldn't ignore that uneasy sensation in his belly. "Then tell me why you're reactin' the way you are." *Anyone would think I'd just told him I was datin' a serial killer, or somethin'.*

Taylor held up his hands. "Look, I'm sure Liam's a great guy. He sure seemed like it to me. But...."

"But what?" The hairs on his arms stood on end.

Taylor took a long drink from his coffee cup. "Okay. A couple of things... concern me."

"Like what?" Jake was trying not to panic, but Taylor's odd mood was getting to him. "Taylor, out with it."

"Okay, okay." Taylor raised his chin and looked Jake in the eye. "For one thing, this seems awful fast."

"I met him in May," Jake said, a little defensively.

"At Caleb's funeral," Taylor added. "You only got to *really* talk to him when? Early July? You've only *seen* him a couple of times. But that's not what I'm referrin' to." He paused for a moment, and Jake wondered what the hell was wrong with him. He'd never seen Taylor like this.

Same could be said for us, of course. We ain't been friends that long. How would I know what Taylor's really like?

Taylor sighed heavily. "Caleb has only been dead six months, Jake. Six months. An' now Liam's datin' *you*? I guess that's my real concern. Who does he see when he looks at ya? You—or Caleb? 'Cause he's got to be missin' Caleb like crazy. I mean, how long were they together? Six years?"

Holy hell. Panic gave way to anger, a slow bubbling that rose to the surface. Jake clenched his fists under the table. "You know nothin' 'bout their relationship," he said in a low voice. Not that he was about to share. That was Liam and Caleb's business, no one else's.

"Okay, so I don't," Taylor flung back at him. "What concerns me is that *you're* the one who's gonna get hurt in all this."

"How in the hell do you work *that* out?" Jake was torn between confusion and that bubbling rage he tried so desperately to keep a lid on.

Taylor sighed. "Jus'... listen to me, alright? Granted, I'm not that much older 'n you, but I've seen more of life than you have, okay? An' I'm tryin' to share what I've seen, so hear me out,

Truth & Betrayal

please."

The worry in his voice finally got through, and Jake eased back on his anger. "Okay."

"So… I'm sure Liam has told ya he cares for ya. Hell, he may have told ya he loves ya, an' I don't doubt for a minute that he feels *all* those things—now. But…what if he's just on the rebound?"

"Rebound?" Jake frowned. "I don't understand."

"I'll try to explain as best I can. Liam has just come out of a serious, long term relationship. Right now, he's a mess, emotionally speakin'. Now sometimes, after such a relationship, a person feels like they should move on, ya know? Start a new life, find a new partner… I've *known* people this has happened to, Jake. This ain't jus' hogwash."

"I'm still listenin'."

Taylor appeared relieved. "Okay then. Right now, Liam is very vulnerable. He's not capable of makin' solid decisions about startin' up with someone new. He's emotionally… needy. He prob'ly still has feelin's for Caleb. He might even be tryin' to… detach himself from the relationship with Caleb by datin' you. What I'm *tryin'* to say is… people who come out of such relationships should avoid serious datin' until they've got themselves—an' their emotions—under control again." Taylor's eyes were sad. "Add to that any similarities between you an' Caleb, an' this is a disaster waitin' to happen."

Jake felt numb. "These… rebound relationships. Do they ever last?"

Taylor shook his head. "Sorry, Jake, but no. You have to ask yourself, why is Liam attracted to you? Is it because of you—or because of Caleb?"

For several seconds, Jake couldn't respond. Cold hit him at his core, and he felt dizzy as fuck. He wanted to hide away—*run* away—from the scenario Taylor had painted, because it couldn't possibly be true.

Could it?

"Jake. Jake!"

It took a while for him to realize Taylor was talking to him. "Huh?"

"You zoned out for a minute there. You okay?"

It was on the tip of Jake's tongue. *How can I be okay, after what you jus' told me?* Instead, he rose to his feet. "Sorry. I gotta go." He couldn't stay there a second longer. He needed somewhere quiet to think.

"But you jus' got here!" Taylor gaped at him.

"Sure, an' now I gotta go, alright?" Jake gestured to the cake. "You can eat that. I've lost my appetite." He went to leave, but Taylor caught his arm.

"Are we okay?"

Jake gazed at him incredulously. "You jus' told me my boyfriend is basic'lly gonna dump me 'cause it's too soon after his ex—my brother—died, an' *then* you ask if we're *okay*? Whadda ya think, Taylor?" Christ, his head was still spinning from it all. One look at Taylor's pallor cooled his temper a smidge, however. "Tell you what. Ask me again when I've calmed down, an' pref'rably after I've talked to Liam, jus' to make sure you really *are* talkin' a load of hogwash."

"Trust me, if I'm wrong? It'll make my day." Taylor locked gazes with him. "Let me know how it goes? 'Cause you know I'll only worry 'bout ya if you don't."

"Sure." Jake patted Taylor's shoulder. "An' thanks. You could've kept your mouth shut, but ya didn't, an' I know that's 'cause you're a good friend." It came out more generous than he was feeling right then, but he couldn't let Taylor see how badly his comments had affected him.

He walked dejectedly out of the coffee shop, heading for his truck, his head still trying to deal with it all.

Tell me this ain't real, Liam. Tell me Taylor's talkin' outta his ass.

Because if he wasn't, the alternative didn't bear thinking about.

Truth & Betrayal

Chapter Thirty-Seven

Jake sat on the wishing seat, knees drawn up, arms hugging them, his mind in constant motion. A cold wind blew past him, not that he noticed it all that much. He'd been that way for the last hour, and he was still no clearer on what he wanted to do about Taylor's bombshell.

He can't be right. It doesn't make sense.

Except a small part of him thought it made perfect sense. Liam talked about Caleb all the time, right? He made comparisons between them. And despite him saying they hadn't been head-over-heels in love, you just didn't get up and walk away from six years of being with someone. It wasn't like switching off a faucet. There had to be memories. Feelings. *Lots* of 'em.

Jake sat there and replayed conversations over and over in his head, until he wasn't sure which way was up anymore. He analyzed everything Liam had said, searching for some indication that Taylor was wrong.

What he got was utter confusion.

This is gettin' me nowhere. There was only one way to solve this issue, and that was to talk with Liam. But not over the phone or via an email. No sir. Jake wanted to look him in the eye, because that was the only way to know for sure.

He got up off the hard rock, dusted off his jeans, and walked back home.

Guess I'm goin' on a trip. Jake knew he wasn't being entirely logical or clearheaded at that point, but he didn't care. All that mattered was getting to the bottom of this mess and working out what happened next.

The house was empty when he got there, but Jake wasn't about to wait. He grabbed his mama's writing paper, and scribbled a note.

Mama, I've got to go see someone. I probably won't be home tonight, but I'll be back tomorrow. Don't worry. I'll be fine. I know what I'm doing.
See ya.

Jacob

He regarded that last line. *Like fuck I know what I'm doin'.* Then he glanced at the clock over the fireplace. If he was going to make it to Wilmington by nightfall, he'd better get his ass in gear.

Jake grabbed a bottle of water, a couple of bags of chips, and his jacket.

Time to go.

Liam put away the last of the dishes. "I miss Will."

From the breakfast bar, his mom chuckled. "What you *really* mean is, you miss him doing the chores. Don't worry. He'll be home before you know it for the holidays." She peered at him. "Are you all right? You seem a little low."

Liam huffed. "Ignore me. It's nothin'."

"Aww, Liam's missin' his boyfriend," Rachel cooed as she came into the kitchen.

Liam wasn't going to stand for that. "Well, duh. Of *course* I'm missin' him. *You* try livin' five hundred miles away from the guy *you* love, an' see how it makes *you* feel. An' yeah, I know it's only been three days since I last saw him, but you know what? That don't make it any easier."

Rachel gave him a startled glance. "Yeah. Sorry. I didn't think." She stilled, her head inclined toward the back door. "Are we expectin' anyone? Because it sounds like someone just pulled into the driveway."

Mom frowned. "Not as far as I know."

Liam opened the door and peered out. "Oh my God, it's Jake." He grinned. "Talk about a surprise visit."

"You sure you didn't know about this?" Mom came up behind him.

"Not a clue. I was jus' gonna write him an email. Looks like he saved me the trouble." Outside, the exterior light burst into life, and Liam got a good look at Jake's face.

Shit. "Somethin's wrong," he murmured. Before he could work out what might have happened, Jake was at the door. "Hey." Liam kissed him on the cheek.

Jake's face was tight. "Hey." He stepped into the kitchen and waved at Mom and Rachel.

"Why didn't ya tell me you were comin'?" Liam murmured. "Not that I'm complainin', you understand. It's great to see ya." He peered intently at Jake. "Or it *would* be, if you didn't have that look on your face."

"Can we go somewhere an' talk?"

Liam swallowed. "Talk?" His heart was somewhere in his boots. *This is* not *gonna be good.*

"Somewhere... private."

"Why don't you take Jake to your room?" Mom suggested. "I'll bring you both some tea."

"Thank you, Sharon." Jake flashed her a smile that didn't fool Liam for an instant.

"C'mon," he said. Jake followed him in silence to Liam's room, and every step felt like his feet were made of lead. *What in the hell has happened?* Once they were inside, Liam left the door ajar. "Mom'll be here any second with the tea. We can talk when she's gone."

"Sure." Jake sat on the chair at the desk, his hands in his

lap, twisting them nervously.

When nothing else was forthcoming, Liam's skin erupted in goose bumps as if icy fingers had brushed over his body. *He came out to his parents. That's it. They threw him out.* It was the only explanation that made any sense.

Mom came into the room quietly, carrying two glasses. She placed them on the nightstand. "I'll leave you boys to talk." Then she left, closing the door behind her.

Liam sat on the bed, unable to tear his gaze away from Jake. This was nothing like the man who'd driven away from Dev and Pauli's only a few days before. His face was drawn, the skin tight around his mouth, and there was something in his eyes, some pain Liam couldn't guess at.

"What's happened?" Liam kept his voice low, doing his best to ignore the churning in his stomach.

"Why're you with me?" Jake blurted out.

"'Scuse me?" Liam gaped at him.

"Why're you attracted to me? Why're we datin'? Is it only 'cause I'm... Caleb's brother?"

"Whoa there." Liam lurched up off the bed. "What brought this on? And in answer to that last question...Hell no." He walked over to where Jake sat, and laid his hand on Jake's shoulder. "Tell me what's goin' on, baby."

Jake gazed up at him. "I told Taylor 'bout us. I figured he'd be pleased. I mean, why wouldn't he be, right? Two guys in love." He swallowed hard, his Adam's apple bobbing.

Liam went over to the nightstand and brought him his tea. "Here."

Jake took it gratefully and gulped down half of it, before setting the glass on the desk.

"I take it Taylor had somethin' to say 'bout us?" And judging by what he'd just heard, it had to be something pretty devastating, for Jake to drive all this way.

Jake nodded. "He said you're only with me 'cause you're still thinkin' 'bout Caleb, an' I'm the next best thing to havin' him back. He said we're not gonna last, 'cause you're on the rebound."

"I'm what?" Liam didn't believe what he was hearing. "An' how the everlovin' fuck would he know that? He doesn't even *know* me, for God's sake." He crouched beside Jake's chair. "Baby, you listen to me. I am *not* on the rebound." Liam covered Jake's hand with his own, but Jake pulled it away. He got up out of the chair and began pacing, rubbing his hand over his head.

"Look, I've done nothin' but think about this all the way here, so I jus' have to let it all out, alright?"

Liam nodded apprehensively. He had an awful idea about where this was going, and he didn't like it one bit.

"See, what Taylor said makes sense. What's happ'nin' between us is way too fast."

"Says who? Taylor?"

Jake held up a hand, and Liam fell silent. "You an' Caleb were together a while. You can't jus' switch off your feelin's for him, jus' like that. An' maybe Taylor's right. Maybe the fact that I remind ya of him is what drew us together."

Liam sighed. "No, babe. That's not what drew me to you, I promise."

"You *say* that, but how do I know if that's the truth?" Before Liam could respond, Jake plowed ahead. "Here's the thing. What if Taylor's right? What if, a few months down the line, you realize you've made a mistake? You suddenly see things more clearly, an' you realize you're not in love with me after all. You realize I'm not what you need. Sure, you care for me, but *love*?"

"But I *do* love ya," Liam protested.

Jake raised his eyebrows. "Like you loved Caleb? You weren't in love with him though, were ya? So what we gonna do, Liam? Meet up when we can, maybe get together at New Year an' hope we'll still be together for another year? That sound familiar?"

Liam's stomach clenched.

"One day, you're gonna know I'm not enough for ya. An' the way I see it, when that day comes, I'm gonna be… destroyed. I don't think I could stand to have you walk away, jus' 'cause you've come to your senses. An' let's be honest here. The longer we're together, the worse that pain is gonna be when… when it happens."

"What are you saying?" Liam choked out the words. It felt like his whole world was spiraling out of control.

Jake gave him a sad smile. "We've been together a week. One week. I'm not countin' all that time before. I'm talkin' 'bout us *physically* bein' together. You know what you're feelin', Liam. You've been there before. It's not like you're madly in love with me. So… maybe it would be better if we called it a day now. Okay, so it's gonna hurt, but if we let it go on, an' then break up a few weeks, maybe even a few months down the line, it'll hurt more, an' I don't want that."

Cold snaked its way through Liam's body. "You want us to break up now… because if we possibly break up in the future, it'll cause you more pain? Are you *list'nin'* to yourself? Baby, this makes no sense. Who in the hell says we'll break up anyway? Some fool statistics 'bout people on the rebound?"

"If it was just that, then maybe not. But think about it. Look at our situations. You have parents who accept you as you are. You think mine will? Well? Plus, we live hundred of miles apart. That's no basis for a relationship. That right there is a prime reason why this won't work. An' supposin' one day I finally get up enough nerve to bring you home. What am I gonna do, deliver a double whammy? 'Hey, Mama, Daddy, guess what? I'm gay, an' this is the guy I love.' You wanna think 'bout how they'll react? Because that is *all* I have thought about since I realized how I felt 'bout you." Jake's face was a picture of misery. "I'm sorry, Liam, but when you add it all up, we weren't meant to be together."

"An' what if I don't believe that?" Liam said softly. "Doesn't that matter?" Lord, this was just fucked up. It was like he was in the path of a freight train, and there was nothing he could do to get out of its path.

Jake shook his head with an air of sadness. "Nope, because I'm not comin' back here, an' you're sure as hell not comin' to LaFollette. If you were, you'd have made the trip at some point durin' the last six years. But you didn't, did ya? Because you knew what you'd find there. Caleb knew too. So stay here, Liam. Stay where you're loved. Find someone who can be everythin' you need."

"I thought I already had." Liam's world was slowing down, his heart feeling like it was about to break.

"I know." Jake went to the door.

Panic flooded through him. "You… you're not leavin', are ya?"

Jake gave him a half smile. "I can't stay here. Not now. So yeah, I'm goin' home. Don't worry. I'll drive real careful. An' if I get too tired, I promise I'll stop along the way an' find a bed, alright?" He sighed heavily. "I jus' wanna go home."

"Can we stay friends?" Liam clung to the fragile hope that they could find a way, one day, to make this work. They *had* to.

Jake blinked. "Really?"

He nodded. "We have somethin' in common after all. We have Caleb. That kinda makes us family." Right then he would've said anything to hold onto what they'd had. "I'm not sayin' we have to stay in touch like we have done. An email now an' then, texts." Liam took a deep breath. "I don't wanna lose ya completely."

Jake regarded him in silence for a moment. "Okay." He opened the door and walked through the house toward the kitchen. Mom and Rachel were still there, sitting at the breakfast bar, both of them with grave faces.

"Thank you for everythin'," Jake said to Mom. "It was such a pleasure meetin' ya."

Mom's gaze met Liam's, her brows knitted together.

"I'll walk ya to your truck." Liam followed Jake out of the house and along the driveway. He shook his head as Jake got behind the wheel. "I still think you're wrong 'bout this." Only, that was the fucking understatement of the year.

Jake shrugged. "We're never gonna know, are we?"

Liam gripped the sill of the door. "Please. Change your

mind? It's not too late."

He turned the engine on, and the overhead light in the cab flashed on, catching in Jake's glistening eyes. "Don't, okay? Jus'… don't." And with that, he backed out of the drive and onto the road.

Seconds later he was gone.

Liam stood there in the cool night air, his mind still scrambling to understand what had just taken place. He stared down at the concrete driveway, feeling lightheaded, like someone had just whacked him over the head with a lead baseball bat.

This makes no sense. He's barely out of his teens. He doesn't know what he's sayin'. As soon as the thought occurred to him, Liam knew it was a lie. Jake was no kid. Hell, if he had been, Liam wouldn't have started up this whole thing in the first place. No, Jake was a man. He'd come across as level-headed, like he'd reasoned it all out.

Except his reasoning was all wrong.

Liam walked dispiritedly back to the house, and into the kitchen. Rachel wasn't there, but Mom stood by the sink, her gaze focused on him as he entered the room.

"What's going on?"

Liam pushed out a bitter laugh. "You wouldn't believe me if I told ya. 'Cause right now I'm not sure I believe it myself."

"Liam? Has Jake really gone?"

"Not only has he really gone, he's gone for good."

Mom stared. "What the hell? Was this a joint decision?"

"Nope, he did all the talkin'."

"And you just stood there and *let* him?"

Liam was sure he could've said more, but he'd been blown away by the unexpectedness of it all. Too late now. The damage was done. "You know what? I don't wanna talk about this right now. I'm goin' to my room."

"Liam, please…."

He held up his hand. "Mom, right now I can't even think straight, let alone have a discussion. We can dissect this whole mess some other time, when I'm thinkin' more clearly. All I wanna

do is shut my door an' go hide under the comforter."
She nodded. "Okay, sweetheart. When you're ready."
He huffed. "Not sure I'll ever be that, but yeah, whatever."
Right then everything just *hurt*.

Chapter Thirty-Eight

By the time he crossed the town boundary into LaFollette, Jake was bone-tired. He'd stopped a couple of times along the way, just pulled over to the side of the road, switched off the engine, and closed his eyes.

Not that he'd slept. There was way too much going on inside his head for that.

The sun was just coming up as he turned into their driveway, the only sound the chirping of the birds in the trees. Jake climbed out of the truck and stretched. All he wanted was his bed, and the chance to switch off the voice in his head that had been shouting at him all the way home.

I did the right thing, didn't I?

He knew what Mama would've said. The number of times she'd told him to put his brain into gear before he put his mouth into action…

Except he knew every argument he'd put forward made sense.

Was I too quick to act?

Yeah, that was so like him, but he was certain thinking about it for days on end wouldn't have helped him arrive at a different conclusion. And right then, he was so tired, he *couldn't* think.

His bed was calling him, and Jake was only too happy to listen. Better than listening to that voice in his head.

The one that kept telling him he'd just fucked up.

Jake crept into the house, doing his best to avoid the

creaking floorboard outside his room, and tumbled into his bed.

All he wanted right then was… oblivion.

"Jacob. Jacob!"

"Whaa?" At first he thought the loud pounding was inside his head, until he realized it was Mama at his door. "Time is it?"

"We just got back from church." The door handle moved, and Jake stared at it in horror. "I'm comin' in."

Too late to stop her now.

Mama stood at the foot of his bed, her gaze narrowed. "Don't you *ever* do that again, you hear me? I was worried sick. How could you jus' go off like that, no word of where you were goin'…."

"I left ya a note!"

Mama arched her eyebrows. "An' what did that tell me? Nothin'." She gazed down at him, lips pressed together, her hands gripping the foot board. "I heard ya come in this mornin'. That's why I let ya sleep. I'm about to make lunch. You've got half an hour to get yourself lookin' human. We got comp'ny comin'."

"Mama, tell me you didn't invite Sarah again." She wouldn't.

Her eyes gleamed, and his heart sank. *Hell yeah, she would.* "Half an hour. An' wear your Sunday shirt." She walked out of the room and closed the door.

Jake wanted to scream. It didn't matter that at least this time he'd gotten a warning of Sarah's arrival. He didn't want her there at all, especially when she goddamn *knew* how he felt. Hell, he couldn't have made it any plainer the first time she visited.

When his phone pinged and Liam's text popped up, his heartbeat quickened, until he read it.

You got home alright?

Jake wasn't sure what he'd expected. Liam begging him to reconsider? Demanding to know why the hell he'd done such a fool thing? But just those four words?

Then he read them again. *He's thinkin' about me. An' he still cares.* Like Jake still cared for him. The thought only served to confirm his argument. *See? You can't jus' switch it off.*

This wasn't the time. Sarah was coming, and he had to look bright-eyed and bushy-tailed. Jake caught sight of his reflection and groaned.

Some hope of that.

Jake tried to stifle his yawn, but the third time there was no holding it back. He wasn't looking in Mama's direction, but he could feel her eyes on him.

"I'm sorry," he apologized to Sarah. "I had a long day yesterday, an' I jus' got back at dawn." He was only being civil to her because his mama and daddy were right there, but his manners were wearing awful thin.

Sarah's eyes widened. "Wow. Where did you go?" She dabbed her mouth with her napkin. "That was delicious, Mrs. Greenwood."

"I had to go see a friend." That was as far as Jake was willing to go. "He lives in North Carolina."

"Must be some friend, for you to drive all that way, just to see him."

Jake's throat tightened. Suddenly he didn't want to talk anymore.

"There was somethin' I've been meanin' to ask you." Sarah smiled. "It'll be the holidays soon, an' my daddy is talkin' 'bout organizin' a Christmas dance for the young people. I wondered if you'd like to come…as my guest."

Daddy coughed. "In my day, it was the boys who asked the girls out, not the other way 'round."

Sarah giggled. "But Mr. Greenwood, times are changin'.

Nowadays if you want somethin', why, you jus' have to go out an' get it."

He snorted. "An' if you waited for Jacob here to make the first move, you might still be waitin' 'til Rapture." He grinned at Sarah. "Nothin' wrong with a little initiative."

Christ, could this get any worse? Jake was still seething at her having the nerve to invite him. *What the fuck? Hell, she knows I'm not interested.* And asking him out like that in front of Mama and Daddy?

Jake hated being ambushed.

"Do you need an answer right this second?" he asked her. God, he hoped not. He didn't want to refuse her, not with Mama and Daddy hovering like buzzards. Because he doubted he could keep a civil tongue in his head for much longer.

Sarah shook her head. "They haven't even decided on a date for it yet. As soon as that happens, there'll be fliers all over town, lettin' folks know, as well as in the paper."

"Okay. Well, when they announce it, I'll give it some thought." *Like, all of one second before I say no.*

"When was the last time you went to a dance an' had some fun?" Mama piped up.

Jake couldn't stop the thought that flashed through his mind. Him and Liam in Ibiza, Jake grinding on him. Unbuttoning Liam's shirt. His face heated up. "I don't rightly know."

"Well, be sure you give this some thought."

And there were Mama's hands again, pushing firmly against Jake's back. It felt like her feet were getting in on the act too.

Jake bit his tongue for the remainder of the time Sarah was with them, only really relaxing when she said goodbye and walked out to meet the reverend who'd come to collect her. Jake made sure to stay out of the way for that. When he got indoors, Mama was beaming. "Wasn't that nice of Sarah to think of you like that?"

"Sure was," he lied. "So… even though we hardly know each other, she jus' decided to ask me."

Mama's eyes were large and round. "Why, of course."

"Hm. Did she have any help?"

Just for a second, the mask slipped, and Mama's lips thinned. "Excuse me?"

Yeah, he wasn't buying it. "Jus' seems funny she'd ask me, that's all. I wondered if maybe you'd suggested I might like to go."

Mama flushed. "I'm sure I don't know what you're talkin' 'bout."

Jake had had all the BS he could stomach for one day. "I'll see to the dishes," he said as he headed for the kitchen. One minute longer, and he'd say something he'd regret. He'd already stepped way over the mark.

"You don't have to. Not now I got my dishwasher," she said proudly.

Lord, he'd plum forgotten about that. Not that he'd wanted to do the damn dishes anyway, but keeping busy kept him out of her sight and gave him less time to think.

He suspected he was going to be doing a lot of that.

"Have you spoken to him this week?"

Liam glanced up from his book. "'Scuse me?" The house was peaceful. Rachel was in her room, talking to some friend on the phone. Dad was in his office, working on a new project.

And Mom was obviously on a mission. *Lord, not now, alright?*

Her eyes glinted dangerously. "Don't you give me that. You know exactly who I'm talking about."

Apparently, the Lord wasn't listening.

He marked the spot with a bookmark, then closed the book with a sigh. "I sent him a text three days ago."

"And?" Mom's hands were on her hips, always a bad sign.

"An' nothin'. He answered. He's fine. Keepin' busy." Liam didn't want to discuss this. Over a week since Jake's visit, and he was still hurting. He wasn't sleeping. His appetite was for shit. At work he couldn't keep his mind on the job.

He was a mess.

Mom narrowed her gaze. "And if there's any justice in this world, he's as miserable as you are." Liam gaped at her, and she bit her lip. "That was unkind. I'm sure he thought he was doing the right thing, whatever his reasons were. But look at you, sweetheart. You *are* miserable." She walked off into the kitchen, and he thought he'd been reprieved.

No such luck. Minutes later, she returned, carrying two glasses of wine. "Thought we deserved these." She handed one to him, then sat with him on the couch.

"Thank you." Liam sipped the cold white wine.

"Sometimes I forget you're not just my son, you're an adult."

Liam snickered. "Last time I looked, yeah."

Mom sighed. "This is just *wrong*, baby. You an' Jake are meant to be together."

Liam put down his glass on the small table beside the couch. "I've done a lot of thinkin' since he left."

"Good. Now tell me what you're gonna do to get him back."

He laughed. "Lord, woman, you don't give up, do ya?" He picked up his wine glass, then twisted on the couch until he was facing her. "When me an' Caleb were together, I wanted him to tell Jake the truth, but he wouldn't. So we never went to Tennessee, an' after a while, I didn't mind so much, because we were happy. We worked as a couple because we had our life in Atlanta. We were together. But me an' Jake?" He shook his head. "He's right. It was never gonna work. We're miles apart, an' were probably gonna be for the foreseeable future. Tellin' his parents is *not* an option, he's made that much clear. It don't exactly bode well for a future together, does it?" Liam stared into his wine. "We were jus' deludin' ourselves."

"Well, listen to you."

He jerked his head up at the sharp edge to her voice. "What?"

"Have you heard yourself? 'It was never gonna work'. With *that* attitude, I'm sure it wouldn't." Before Liam could come back with a reply, she speared him with a look. "Do you love that boy?"

"You heard what I said to Rachel, right? The day he showed up? 'Bout me missin' the guy I love? There's your answer."

She huffed. "Love's a word we throw around like it was confetti. Hell, before I met your dad, I'd told two guys I loved them. No, I'm talking about *loving* him, about needing him like you need air to breathe."

"It doesn't matter now, 'cause we're—"

"Just answer the goddamn question. Do you love Jake?"

Liam gaped at her open-mouthed, hearing her curse like that jerking him as much as if she'd slapped him. But he couldn't escape that question. He closed his eyes, and Jake's face was there. His laugh still rang in Liam's ears. His expressions. His touch. The feel of him in Liam's arms. Making love with him. Waking with him those few precious mornings. Christ, he'd relived those days over and over again.

"I love him so much, it makes my heart ache."

Mom's hand was gentle on his, and Liam opened his eyes. She smiled at him. "Then stop saying this is never gonna work, and start telling yourself you're gonna *make* this work. Whatever it takes. Because you can *not* lose that boy." She leaned forward and kissed his cheek. "Sweetheart, we're not on this Earth a whole heap of time. Life is short, so if you're not happy? Do something about it." She grinned. "And Liam? Sooner rather than later? Because I want to dance at my eldest son's wedding one of these days, and I'm not exactly a spring chicken anymore."

Her words lit a fire under him. *She's right. Why the fuck am I jus' takin' this?* Because Jake had knocked the stuffing right out of him, that was why. "I jus' need to work out how to get him to see sense."

Mom nodded. "Think carefully about what you're going to say. You only get one shot at this, so you need to get it right." She stroked his head. "All I'm saying is don't spend too long thinking. Get busy doing." She gestured toward his glass. "Now drink your wine."

"Yes, ma'am." He snickered. "I'm still kinda reelin', to be truthful."

She frowned. "About what?" He merely arched his eyebrows, and she bit her lip again. "Yeah, I suppose I did come on a little strong."

"A *little* strong?" Liam smirked. "Does my dad know you use language like that?"

She narrowed her gaze. "Well, I had to do *something* to get through to ya. Seems like I picked the right approach." She smiled smugly. "And what your dad doesn't hear, won't hurt him."

He laughed and went back to drinking his wine. Inside he was almost vibrating. For the first time since that awful day, he had hope.

You are not *gettin' rid of me that easily, Jake Greenwood.*
Liam was on a mission too.

Chapter Thirty-Nine

Jake had finally had enough.

They were more than halfway through November, and Sarah Hubbert had been to supper twice in the last two weeks. Lord knew, he loved his mama, but this was getting beyond a joke. There was no way he was about to tell Sarah girls didn't do it for him, or that she needed to lose that wedding band sparkle from her eyes, because Hell. No.

I gotta do this subtly. Except he thought he'd been subtle, and that sure as shit hadn't worked. Then he smiled as he imagined what Dev and Pauli's version of subtle would be. *Prob'ly to leave gay mags all over the place.* That made him laugh. God, he missed them, but not a fraction of the amount he missed Liam. The one thing he was grateful for? At least he'd left the door open a smidge, so there was still room to maneuver.

Ha. Maneuver my ass. He meant room to take back what he'd said, and ask—no, *beg*—Liam to let them start over. Jake wasn't proud. The way he saw it, if anything was to come of this, there was no room for pride.

That still left the thorny issue of Sarah.

"Jacob, would you drive Sarah home? Her daddy jus' called. He's had to go visit a sick member of the congregation."

"Sure, Mama." *Perfect. Time for a chat.* Jake grabbed his jacket and smiled at Sarah. "Ready?"

"Certainly."

They went out to his truck, and Jake made sure the seat wasn't covered in sawdust or empty chip bags before letting her get in. He pulled out of the driveway and headed along Shoreline Circle.

Sarah cleared her throat. "I almost forgot. Daddy said to ask ya to come to supper next Tuesday evenin'. He'd like to meet ya."

Jake snickered. "Whaddaya mean, meet me? He knows who I am." He'd been to the house often enough to find his way there blindfolded. Not that Jake had any intention of going for supper. And if he did this right, she wouldn't want him to neither.

"Silly." She giggled. "I mean, he'd like to get to know you better. Seein' as your mama keeps invitin' me to have supper. That is…."

Sarah didn't have to say another word. Jake got the message, and he didn't like it one bit.

Uh uh. No way Jose.

His mind set to work. Fuck subtle—there was no time for that shit.

As they joined Central Avenue and drove past the line of stores, she pointed to one of the lots at the far end. "Have you seen that place? It's only been open 'bout a week or so."

Jake squinted at it. Judging by the window, it was a bike shop. *Rainbow Racers*. What caught his eye immediately was the rainbow flag that hung above the gleaming motorcycles. Then he saw the sign next to it, and slowed down to make sure he wasn't seeing things.

Love is Love.

Holy Mother of God. Jake had to fight not to betray his excitement. "No, I hadn't seen that." How he kept his voice even, he never knew. Inside he wanted to yell.

A freakin' gay store in *LaFollette. What the fuck?*

"I think that's dangerous," Sarah said, her voice quiet.

He frowned, jerked out of his elation. "Why? You're not about to go ridin' one, are ya?"

"I'm not talkin' 'bout the bikes, I'm talkin' 'bout the guy who owns the store," she hissed.

"What's dangerous about him?" Jake was genuinely not

following this conversation.

"Well, accordin' to what everyone's sayin', he's… gay." She almost whispered the word.

Okay. Jake was not gonna keep quiet on *that*. "So what if he is? Ain't nobody's business but his."

He caught her light gasp. "The Bible says that's 'gainst God's law."

Jake could recite those verses by heart, but he no longer believed them to be true. He recollected Pauli going off on a guy who turned up at their apartment to talk about how Halloween was basically pagan, and God wasn't happy about it. Pauli had let it rip on that topic, plus he'd taken the opportunity to blast the guy for the Church's selective use of Bible quotes to condemn homosexuality. He'd kept him there half an hour while Pauli brought up his own verses to prove that pretty much everyone who wore mixed fibers, had tattoos, ate shrimp, and was divorced was going to hell, and that included the guy sitting on their couch. Jake thought the poor man probably went home early that day, in need of a stiff drink.

Pauli didn't pull any punches.

"I still don't see how that makes him dangerous."

"Seriously? Havin' one gay man in LaFollette might jus' prove to be the openin' wedge. We could get more of 'em wantin' to live here."

Jake couldn't resist. "What makes ya think they ain't here already? I mean, you don't know what goes on behind closed doors, do ya?"

Her gasp was louder that time. "Then maybe it's time for the good people of the town to do somethin'. Y'know, make it plain to this man that he's not welcome, before any more of his kind get the idea that this might be a suitable place to live."

Jake felt sick to his stomach. What saddened him was that she'd probably learned all that hogwash from her daddy 'The Reverend', while he was bouncing her on his knee. *We ain't born with thoughts like that. Someone* teaches *that shit.*

He pulled up outside her house and switched off the engine. "About your daddy's invitation to supper…"

She beamed. "Yes?"

"Thank him kindly, will ya, but tell him I won't be takin' him up on it. Not Tuesday. Not any day, if it comes down to it."

Sarah's face fell. "Oh."

Jake seized his courage. "An' while I've got ya on your own… I think it's time I laid my cards on the table. I told you the first time you came to supper that I wasn't interested, an' that hasn't changed. But I guess I should be honest with ya." He took a deep breath. "I'm in love with someone."

In the silence that followed, he realized the truth of his words. It was no line—he loved Liam, heart, body and soul.

"I had no idea. Does your mama know?"

Jake shook his head. "We were keepin' it quiet."

"Can I ask her name?"

His pulse raced. "Sorry. That's a confidence I won't betray. Not that I'd tell ya anyway, 'cause it's none of your business." *Let's see if* that *gets through to her.*

Sarah stiffened. "I see. I understand." She opened the door. "Will we see you in church in the mornin'?" She closed the door and leaned on the sill.

Hopeful to the last. If she can't have me, she'll save my soul. An' by now, she must be pretty much convinced my soul needs savin'.

"Sorry, but no. I don't think you'll be seein' me at church again."

She appeared horrified, her mouth open, then took a step backwards, as though his truck could contaminate her.

"G'bye, Sarah." Jake switched on the engine, and pulled away from the curb, his heart lighter. He didn't even bother looking in the rear-view mirror.

It wasn't until he was halfway home that he started shaking. The conversation had made one thing clear as crystal. He could *not* be out in that godforsaken town. And that left him with only one option—leaving LaFollette, which would break his daddy's heart, with all his plans for the business.

I sure picked a fine time to mess things up with Liam.
Right then Jake needed him more than ever.

Mama had one last try before they left for church. "Come with us, sugah. You don't have to sit with us if you don't want to." She smiled. "I can understand that. Most of the young people don't sit with their parents either. You could sit with Sarah."

He hated that look in her eyes, the one that begged him.

Jake shook his head emphatically. "No, Mama. You an' Daddy go on without me. I'll get the vegetables ready for lunch, how's that?"

Her sigh told him it wasn't much of a consolation.

He watched them leave, then closed the door and went into the kitchen to pour himself another cup of coffee. Another thought crossed his mind. He'd get a fire going before they got back. Mama always loved sitting by the fire when there was a nip in the air.

Jake had barely finished his coffee when there was a knock at the front door. He walked through the living room, his heartbeat speeding up when he glanced through the window and caught sight of a familiar car.

No. It can't be. He looked again.

It was Liam's car.

Oh my good Lord, he is here.

Jake flung open the door, to find Liam standing there in jeans, boots, a sweater and jacket, looking—

Damn, he looks tired.

"Come on in." He stepped aside to let Liam enter. "They're not here, by the way," he added.

"I know. I waited 'til I saw them leave." Even Liam's voice sounded weary.

Something clicked in Jake's head. "Have you driven all night to get here?"

Liam nodded. "Though the way I'm feelin' right now, I may not make it back there tonight. I'm exhausted. But there are things I need to say, an' I'm not leavin' 'til I've said 'em."

That sent a chill through Jake. Liam had never seemed so... serious, so determined.

"Kinda surprised to see ya, I have to admit." Except stunned was probably a better word. He still couldn't believe it. Liam, standing in his living room...

Liam snickered. "Well, I had to prove you wrong, didn't I?"

"'Scuse me?"

"You were so sure I'd never come here." He held up his hands, palms toward the ceiling. "Well, here I am."

Jake had never been happier to see anyone in his life. "You sure are." Despite his apprehension, he couldn't hold back his smile. "An' I'm real glad to see ya." What tempered his happiness was the fact that there was space between them, and Liam seemed to have no intention of closing the gap.

Looks like I got some fixin' to do.

Liam glanced around the room and sighed. "Look, I've spent over seven hours starin' at nothin' but the road ahead of me, an' the radio blastin' to keep me awake. Right now I need some air, maybe feel the wind on my face. Can we go for a walk or somethin'?"

"Sure. Lemme grab my jacket." Jake led him through the house, out the back door, and into the yard. "If we duck under the back fence, there's a path that leads down to the creek."

Liam gave a weary smile. "Lord, the times Caleb talked about that creek. Can't believe I'm finally gonna see it."

Jake made his way through the cool woodland, holding back the undergrowth for Liam where it strayed too far into the path, both of them silent. No traffic noise penetrated this far, and the only sounds were the birds, and the creatures rustling through the dead foliage on either side of them. When they reached the creek, Jake stopped.

"Ollis Creek. Ain't much to look at, but this is one of my favorite places to be." As an afterthought, he added, "Caleb's too, I think."

Liam gazed at the slow-moving water. "He used to talk 'bout comin' down here with ya when you were just a little kid. An' there was a seat too, if I remember rightly."

Jake smiled. "The Wishing Seat. I was gonna take you there." He turned to the right and they walked along the creek a while, until they reached the boulder. "That there dent in the rock is the seat," he said, pointing.

Liam didn't hesitate. He climbed up and sat on it, before beckoning Jake with his finger. "There's plenty of room for two. Get your ass up here." He patted the boulder beside him.

Jake joined him, and they sat in silence for a moment. Jake didn't feel it was his place to start the conversation, not when it was so clear Liam had stuff on his mind.

A heavy sigh rolled out of Liam. "All the way here, I was rehearsin' in my head, all the things I wanted to say to ya, but now I'm here? I'm not sure where to begin."

"I'm still gettin' over the fact that you're here at all." Jake stared out over the creek, unable to meet Liam's gaze. "I didn't think I'd see you again, not after everythin' I said."

"You can thank my mom for that."

Jake frowned. "Sharon? Why, what did she do?"

Liam chuckled. "Helped me get my head outta my ass, in a nutshell. But about those things you said..." He paused. "Look, I know you set great store by Taylor, but I have to say somethin'. He talked to you 'bout relationships, an' people on the rebound an' such, but I think he has even less experience of those things than you do. *You're* the one with a boyfriend, not him, alright? An' part of me wonders if he might be jus' the tiniest bit jealous of that." Liam held up his hands defensively. "That sounds harsh, I know, but he's only human. An' I'd understand that, believe me."

"Funny you should mention Taylor. He hasn't been in touch

since I got back from your place." Jake wondered if he was ashamed of stirring everything up the way he had.

"I know he was sorta tryin' to protect ya, but baby…" Liam took Jake's hands in his, and the tension in his belly uncoiled a little. "You can't live your life based on other people's fears, Jake. An' as for us breakin' up because you *might* get hurt one day?" Liam locked gazes with him. "If you're gonna worry 'bout everythin' that may or may *not* happen in the future, you might as well stop livin' right now."

Jake's throat seized, and he lowered his eyes, but Liam gently cupped his chin, lifting it. "You reminded me that while I loved Caleb, I wasn't *in* love with him. That was true. Who's to say how long we would've lasted? But as to how I feel about you?"

Jake's heart hammered, and his breathing quickened.

Liam removed his hand and took a deep breath. "These last two weeks, I've been fuckin' miserable. I haven't sleep for shit, my appetite is a joke, an' my head is a mess. When Mom finally made me look at myself, I had to ask why I was in such a state. Because you were right. We'd been together such a relatively short time, so why in hell was I so… devastated to lose you? An' then it hit me." He laughed weakly. "Lord, I have been so *blind*. That all-consumin' earth-shatterin' love I'd been lookin' for? It was *right there*, in front of me. Because I *love* ya, Jake Greenwood. I love the way you light up my days. I love the way your smile makes my soul wanna do a happy dance. I love goin' to sleep with you in my arms, an' wakin' up to see that light in your eyes when you see me there. I love the way you bite your lip when you're nervous. I love that you're a bossy little shit. I love how you give yourself *totally*, heart, body and soul, in everythin' you do. I love how you argue, but how you're always willin' to see the other person's point of view." Liam stroked Jake's cheek. "I love makin' love with you, feelin' connected to ya in a way that no other person has ever been—or will ever be, not if I have anythin' to do with it."

Something deep inside Jake gave a flutter, and his heart pounded harder than ever.

"An, just in case that didn't get through, lemme spell it out for ya." Both Liam's hands were on his face, Liam's gaze focused on him. "I'm not gonna waste time wonderin' if we'll be together in the future, because I *know*. You hear me, Jake? I *know*. My future is with you. An' jus' so we're real clear on this, yes, I'm talkin' white picket fences, a dog, an' wedding bands."

Lord, the light in Liam's eyes...

Then his words finally sank in. *Did he jus' say... wedding bands?*

Jake couldn't stay quiet any longer. "You're sittin' in the Wishing Seat, remember?"

Liam's smile lit up his face. "Then I'd best make a wish, hadn't I?" He closed his eyes.

There was no way Jake could hold back after that. He leaned forward and brushed his lips against Liam's. "I love you, Liam Miller. An' may all your wishes come true." Jake kissed him on the lips, looping his arms around Liam's neck, loving the soft noise that escaped Liam's mouth as he wound his arms around Jake, pulling him closer until he was in Liam's lap.

All the pain and anguish of the last two weeks gradually ebbed away as Liam held him, their lips meeting in kiss after kiss, his hands on Liam's neck, head, shoulders, back, making sure this was real, that Liam was truly there, telling Jake he loved him.

"I'm so sorry," Jake whispered between kisses. "I know I hurt ya."

"You did. Not gonna deny that. An' I'm to blame too. I obviously didn't tell you enough how I felt about ya. Not gonna make that mistake again. But all that's in the past."

Jake stroked Liam's jaw, smiling. "I love that you're tryin' to grow a beard."

Liam's eyes widened. "'Tryin'? Lord, you sure know how to wound a guy."

Jake chuckled. "Well, if you're gonna grow one, for God's sake, *grow* it. Don't stick with this... scruff."

"Scruff? Why, I oughta put you over my knee an' spank

your ass for that." He was laughing. "After I get me some coffee."

Jake smiled. "Then let's go back to the house, an' I'll make you some fresh."

"*Then* can I take a nap?"

He laughed. "Sure." Jake knew it wasn't gonna be that easy. For one thing, there was a storm on the horizon, in the shape of his parents. It wouldn't be that long before they'd be back.

Liam gave him another weary smile. "I know there's things we need to discuss. An' I know this isn't as simple as I made it sound. But we can deal with it, as long as we remember one thing." He squeezed Jake's hand. "We're in this together." Then he grimaced. "I think my ass jus' fell asleep."

Jake chuckled. "Let's go home." He helped Liam down off the rock, and they headed back to the house that wasn't home anymore.

Home was right beside him.

Chapter Forty

They stepped into the house, and Jake closed the back door. "Okay, coffee. Sit down, an' I'll have it ready as fast as I can."

"Jacob? Who you talkin' to?"

He stiffened, his gaze going immediately to the wall clock. "Shit. They're back. I lost all track of time." Just like that, his heartbeat sped up.

Liam sighed. "Want me to slip out the door? I could come back later."

Jake shook his head. "No, not gonna hide anymore. An' they might as well hear it all." He held out his hand. "You ready?" His legs shook at the thought of what was coming.

"Hell no." Liam chuckled. "But we're doin' it anyhow." He took Jake's hand and squeezed it. "Lead the way."

Jake took a deep breath and walked out of the kitchen, leading Liam by the hand. No way was he about to let go. "Hey, Mama, Daddy, got someone I'd like y'all to meet." They went into the living room, just as Mama was removing her hat, and Daddy was taking off his tie and jacket. Both froze at the sight of Liam, open-mouthed.

Daddy recovered first. He squinted at Liam and suddenly his nostrils flared. He jabbed a finger through the air at him. "You're that… fella from the funeral. You were drivin' the car that—"

"Don't say it, Daddy," Jake warned. "Liam had nothin' to do with Caleb's death, an' you know it. That was an accident. Ain't nothin' he could've done to prevent it."

His eyes bulged. "What the… Why, *you* were the one who went for him at the funeral. You lost your memory, or somethin'?"

Jake's cheeks burned. "Like I could ever forget that day. But things have changed. I learned some stuff."

"Liam," Mama said faintly. Her lips parted. "You were Caleb's roommate in Atlanta. The one Jacob has been visitin'." She pressed her lips together. "I see."

Daddy's gaze alighted on their joined hands. "What in tarnation?" His face was red, his cheeks mottled, his eyes wide, showing so much white, his hands clenching and unclenching at his sides.

Before he could get another word out, Jake plunged ahead. "Mama, Daddy, this is Liam Miller—my… boyfriend."

Time just… froze.

Daddy's jaw dropped. "No," he said firmly, his eyes like steel. "No. No, Jacob. No."

"You can say no all you want, Daddy. It's not gonna change a thing." Jake straightened. "I love him." He did his level best to keep his voice even, because inside he was shaking. Where he got the courage from, he would never know. Then Liam's hand tightened around his, and he knew alright.

Daddy took a step toward them, but Mama laid a hand on his arm. "Ain't no use fightin' this, Hank."

Daddy glared at her. "How can you say that? You're jus' gonna *stand* there an' let Jacob ruin his life with this…this…."

Mama shook her head. "It's been comin' a while, I reckon. Lord knows, I've done my best to turn him from this path, but I guess I didn't act quickly enough." She glanced at Liam. "An' some things I *definitely* didn't see comin'."

Jake gaped. "Wait a minute. Mama, you sayin' you *knew* I was gay?"

She regarded him with such an empty stare, it made his heart quake. "I feared it. I saw the signs. I found out too late to help your brother, but I—"

"What in the *hell*?" Jake let go of Liam's hand and sat down on the couch, his legs unable to hold him upright any longer. Liam sat beside him, so very still. "You… you *knew* Caleb was gay? How? How could you know that when *I* didn't?"

She pursed her lips. "I found some… magazines he'd hidden in the space behind the drawers in his room. It was then I realized why he'd stopped comin' home."

"When? When did you know?"

She took a breath before replying. "Before he died. I took those magazines an' burnt them in the yard, kinda takin' temptation outta his way." She swallowed. "Only, he never came home after that."

"Say what?" Daddy's face was almost purple. "Caleb too? An' you didn't tell *me*?"

Mama's eyes glistened. "What good would it have done? I didn't want you to think diff'rently of him. He was still our boy. He'd just… chosen the wrong path, that's all. Knowin' the truth would only have brought ya pain, an' you'd suffered enough of that with him passin'. We all had." She wiped her eyes and swallowed hard, her gaze alighting on Jake. "But you? I wasn't sure 'bout you, 'til I got the feelin' you were hidin' things from me. So then I had to do somethin'. I couldn't let you go the same way as your brother."

"What did you think you could do, Mama?" Jake was genuinely puzzled.

She sighed. "All a mother wants is for her kids to be happy, an' I knew that if you started down *that* road, you would never be happy. So… I invited Sarah Hubbert to supper."

Jake's world slipped a little on its axis. "So I wasn't imaginin' it. You really did wanna hear wedding bells, didn'tcha?"

"I figured bringin' the two of you together would serve two purposes. I'd know once an' for all if you were… like that or not, an' Sarah would help keep ya on the straight an' narrow."

A feeling of heaviness sank over him, and his head swam. "You think I could've been happy like that? Livin' a lie? Because that's what you would've condemned me to, if you'd had *your* way."

"You'd have grown together, gotten used to each other," she protested.

"Really?" Liam's hand covered his, a gentle pressure, but it cooled Jake's anger. Jake forced himself to breathe. "Well, here's a newsflash for ya. I *am* happy—with Liam."

Daddy let out an explosive snort of derision. "I'm not even gonna talk about this while... *he's* in this house."

Liam cleared his throat. "Maybe I should go. I don't wanna put a rift between you an' your parents."

Jake turned to look at him, taking in Liam's earnest expression, the love in those dark eyes.

Love for me.

"You're not doin' that," Jake insisted. "*They* are. An' if they wanna lose me altogether, they're goin' the right way about it."

Mama let out a startled gasp. "No. We don't want that." She glared at Daddy. "Not when we've already lost one son." He blinked, his mouth falling open, and she nodded. "Don't you go drivin' him away. I couldn't bear it."

"No one is drivin' me away," Jake said softly, his anger finally abating. "But it's clear you both need time to think about this. So... I'm gonna go away for a while." Right then he had no idea where he'd go. He was acting on sheer impulse.

"Away?" Mama's eyes were huge. "Where? For how long?"

"He can come home with me for a couple of weeks," Liam said quickly. "That won't be any problem for my family, an' it'll give you some space." His gaze met Jake's. "If that's alright with you."

Jake could have kissed him. "I like that. I like it a lot." He turned back to Mama. "We can talk when I get back." He rose to his feet, and Liam copied him. "So I'm gonna go pack a bag, then we'll be outta here. You know how to reach me." He gave Mama a half-smile. "This is for the best, Mama."

Daddy stared at him. "Jus' like that? You're gonna run away?"

Jake shook his head. "I'm not runnin' away, Daddy. But I need a little time to think about my future—our future—an' you need that too. Leave work alone for a while. Spend time with Mama. Talk. You never take time for yourself, an' maybe this is what you need."

And with that, he walked out of the room, Liam close behind him.

When he got into his bedroom, Jake sank onto the bed, flopping onto his back. "Holy fuck." Then he laughed weakly. "Maybe *not* the right thing to say in this situation, but it sure as shit sums it up."

Liam joined him. "You alright?"

"Just need to get my breath back."

Liam rubbed his belly and chest, the motion soothing. "You were amazing. I was so proud of you."

"Didn't feel amazin'. I think I'm still in shock. She *knew*, Liam. She knew about Caleb, she guessed about me... An' she would've been happy for me to chain myself to a woman I didn't want, in a marriage that would've been a sham, that would only have ended in heartache for both of us."

"Hey, wait a sec." Liam cupped his cheek. "You would never have married Sarah, an' she knew it. She jus' had to try."

Jake shivered. "Why do I feel all shaky an' dizzy?"

"That's adrenaline. It's your body's response to all the emotions you're goin' through." Liam rubbed his belly again. "It'll pass, baby. You've jus' been through a lot." He kept up the slow motion, until the sensation had passed, and Jake's breathing was back to normal. "I know I didn't say much in there, but—"

"What you said was jus' right. I needed a lifeline, an' you tossed one right in there. You sure your mama won't mind?"

Liam smiled. "When she hears what's been goin' on? Absolutely not. What I *might* have to fight her over, is the sleepin' arrangements, because we are *not* spendin' a single night apart, an' she'd better get used to the idea."

Jake snickered. "You might wanna phrase it more…diplomatically than that."

"You might be right." Then he too rolled onto his back. "Christ, I'm beyond exhausted. I can't drive back like this."

"I *can* drive, y'know," Jake said with a smirk.

"I know, baby. But it's more than that. I need sleep, an' I can't sleep in the car. Makes me throw up. Is there anywhere near here where I can get a bed? Because I'm not sleepin' here."

Jake smiled. "There's a Holiday Inn Express not that far from here. We could get a room there, an' drive tomorrow." His eyes widened. "But you got work in the mornin'."

Liam huffed. "I predict I'm gonna come down with a fever tonight that'll keep me in bed for twenty-four hours. I'll call in sick first thing." He pointed to Jake's closet. "You, pack. I'll call ahead an' book us a room." He pulled his phone from his pocket.

Jake snickered. "I see exhaustion has no effect on your bossy side."

Liam lunged for him, and pulled him down into a kiss. "You have *so* much to learn about me—an' lots of time to do it in."

Jake sighed. "As long as I have you, that's fine by me."

He'd set one foot inside the closet when Liam called out to him. "Er, Jake? You might wanna pack your toys?"

Jake stuck his head around the door. "You're kiddin', right? If your mom saw them, I'd die of embarrassment."

Liam smirked. "Ask yourself which is worse—*my* mom seein' 'em, or *yours*, if she decides to poke around in your closet while you're gone?"

Jake blinked. "Fair point." He ducked back into the closet and reached up for the box.

The whole situation felt surreal, and he guessed it would be a while before that feeling wore off.

At least the cat is out of the bag. Then he snickered. *Well and truly out.*

"Lemme sleep," Liam murmured. He was just the right temperature, soft cotton against his skin, a firm mattress beneath him, and a warm body curved around his back.

Bliss.

Jake's breath tickled his ear. "Fine. I'll eat your supper."

That woke him up. He hadn't eaten much since he'd left Wilmington, only a couple of Mom's snack bars. Liam shifted onto his back, Jake moving with him. "There's supper?"

Jake nodded. "They don't do room service here, so I ordered in. Food should be here in about twenty minutes. I'll go down to the lobby an' collect it." He grinned. "I ordered a lot, seein' as how we missed lunch."

Liam couldn't even remember his head hitting the pillow. "Did you sleep?"

"Yup. I was wiped out. Go figure."

Liam held his arm wide, and Jake snuggled like he usually did. "How are ya?"

His sigh stirred the hairs on Liam's chest. "Alright, I guess. It's kinda hard to take in. All that time I was so scared they'd find out, an' Mama knew, not only 'bout me but about Caleb too. An' as for Daddy? Part of me keeps wonderin' which was the biggest shock—finding out I was gay, seein' you, or findin' out Caleb was gay too."

"Maybe it's best not to think too much on that one." Liam had listened enough to Caleb's tales to know his ethnicity was always going to be a problem.

"There's one thing that's gonna stay in the grave with Caleb," Jake murmured. "They don't need to know 'bout you an' him."

"I totally agree." Although Liam had his suspicions. He kept seeing Jake's Mom, her lips pressed together, that quietly muttered 'I see.' *I wonder if she really did see?* Then he reconsidered. If she'd truly suspected, Liam doubted she'd have kept *that* quiet.

He kissed the top of Jake's head. "It amazes me how you an' Caleb grew up the way you did."

"Jus' lucky, I guess."

Liam smiled. "I'm the lucky one. I got to keep the fairy tale after all."

"Huh?"

Liam pulled Jake on top of him, spreading his legs to give him room. "Once upon a time, I thought I'd found what I was lookin' for, the dream I'd searched for. But you know what? Turned out it wasn't that at all, for either of us. So I gave up on findin' my happily ever after."

Jake's brow furrowed. "I don't understand."

Liam kissed his forehead. "You're my dream, baby. You're what I was lookin' for."

"An' what was that?"

He cupped Jake's cheek. "A love that would last the rest of my life."

Jake's face glowed. "That's beautiful."

"Says you, the beautiful man." Liam kissed him, taking his time, Jake moving like a slow wave on top of him, until Liam was moving right along with him, heat blossoming between them.

"Hey," he said a little breathlessly. "We got food coming, remember?"

"Damn it."

Liam chuckled. "Put some clothes on, so you don't scare the delivery boy. While you're gone, I'll ring Mom an' let her know what's goin' on. Then we'll eat."

"An' then?" There was a hopeful look in Jake's eyes.

Liam pulled him into another lingering kiss. When they parted, he brushed his finger over Jake's lips. "An' then we're gonna make love, all night long if we want to." He grinned. "An' before you ask, yes, we both get to top."

Jake sat up, grinned, and smacked Liam's belly with his

already hard dick. Then he scrambled off the bed to get dressed.

"Subtle, Jake. Very subtle."

"You wouldn't have me any other way, an' you know it."

Liam had to smile. *Ain't that the truth?*

Truth & Betrayal

Chapter Forty-One

Friday December 2nd

"Thanks again for last weekend. We had a great time."

Dev chuckled. "What you *really* mean is, thanks for the chance to fuck each other's brains out of earshot of your parents."

Liam snickered. "Okay, you got me."

"Oh, I feel ya, believe me. When we went to stay with Pauli's folks last time? Almost killed me. It isn't until you have to be quiet that you realize just how much noise you make." He cackled. "We couldn't wait to get home." He paused. "Except your lovin' is gonna be in short supply now, ain't it? If he's goin' back to Tennessee."

"Can we not talk about that? An' I don't mean the lovin' part." These past two weeks had gone by way too quickly.

"There was somethin' I meant to say to ya last weekend, only I never got the chance."

"What was that?"

Dev sighed. "I'm real sorry for what we said that time. After watchin' the pair of ya…"

A few seconds of silence elapsed. "Dev? You still there?"

"You an' Jake… you're so good together. God, the way you look at each other… Gotta be honest here, it made me tear up."

That stilled him. Dev wasn't one to get emotional. "Why?"

"Because I couldn't help comparin' you an' Jake, with you an' Caleb."

"I try not to do that." Intrigue got the better of him. "An' did ya come to any conclusions?"

"Don't get me wrong, you' an Caleb were a great team. Same sense of humor, both fun-lovin' guys… but you an' Jake? That's in a whole new league."

His words only confirmed what Liam already knew. "Never thought I'd feel this way about someone, y'know?" There were times when the depth of his feelings for Jake was almost overwhelming, and this both scared and elated him. "He's… he's everythin', Dev."

"Like I can't see that." A pause. "Although I do have an interestin' question for ya. Next time you're here, say the weather's warm enough an' we all go to Flex… D'ya think you'd ever go back to how things were?"

Liam had already considered this. "You know what? No, I don't think so. I know you an' Pauli are happy bein' open, an' that works for ya, but… no." He laughed. "Wow. Never thought I'd say this, but I'm likin' the idea of monogamy more an' more."

"An' that right there says it all." Dev chuckled. "Okay, be sure to send us an invite."

"'Scuse me?"

He laughed. "Like we don't all know where this is headin'. I wanna be there on the front row, watchin' him make an honest man of ya." There was a muffled conversation that Liam couldn't quite hear. "Hold on. Pauli wants a word. Take care, precious. An' look after that man of yours. He's special."

"Don't I know it." Liam intended to make the most of what time they got to spend together. The future seemed uncertain right then, but the one solid thing was the way Liam felt about Jake.

There's no mistakin' love, is there?

Jake glanced around their bedroom, checking he'd gotten everything.

"Have you looked under the bed?" Sharon suggested from

the door. "The other week, Liam complained long and hard about losing a pair of shoes, and they were under the bed the whole time. 'Course, if he folded the bed *up* occasionally…"

He chuckled. "You're gonna be *so* happy when Liam finds a place of his own an' you get your office back, aren't ya?"

The second the words left his lips, he knew he had her all wrong. Sharon's smile faded a little. "I don't suppose there's been any headway in that department?"

Jake shook his head. Liam's apartment-hunting plans had been moved onto the back burner, until they worked out how their life was going to look. Not that they'd made any decisions in *that* department either. A lot depended on what was waiting for them in Tennessee.

Sharon cleared her throat. "You might remember to check the desk drawer," she added with a casual air that made the skin prickle on Jake's neck. "Unless, of course, you want to leave them here? Which is perfectly fine, by the way. I can see why you might not want them at home."

Oh Lord. That drawer. Jake's cheeks were on fire, and it felt like his chest and neck were joining them. "Okay, about those…."

Sharon chuckled. "Sweetheart, I have two sons. There isn't much you can do that would shock me." She coughed. "Having said that…"

"Please, don't," Jake begged her, even though he knew she was teasing. *I'm never gonna live that down*. His second night there, they'd waited until the early hours before making love, when everyone was asleep.

Apparently *not* everyone.

The following morning, he'd gotten up before everyone else, and had found a copy of the Yellow Pages on the kitchen table, open to the page marked Soundproofing, marked with a Post-it bearing the words, 'Option #1' in Sharon's distinctive handwriting. *Oh dear Lord*. Jake had hastily closed it and replaced it back on its shelf. He'd gotten the message, however.

The incident did have its bright side, however. Fucking with one of Liam's ties as a gag was hotter 'n hell.

Sharon sighed. "Have they contacted you at all while you've been here?"

"Nope. So I guess we'll have to wait an' see if this time apart was a good idea."

Sharon walked over to him. "Okay, I know I've said this before, but I'm gonna say it again. Any time you need a break, you get in that truck and you come here, all right? Don't bother to call first, just get here. You are always welcome, Jake, you know that." She patted his shoulder. "We've loved having you these past two weeks. The place won't seem the same without you."

"It'll be quieter, that's for damn sure," he said with a chuckle.

She laughed, then hugged him. "Love you, sweetheart."

He returned the hug. These two weeks had given him just what he needed—time to think. The days had been quiet, what with Sharon, Liam and Rachel out at work. Tony might have worked from home, but Jake had rarely seen him around. Those times when they did meet, had been great. Tony was a calm, sensible man with a positive outlook on life, and he talked a lot of sense.

God, I am so lucky to have such special people in my life.

Sharon released him and smiled. "And now that we're finally in December, you two might want to think about holiday plans. We'd love to have both of you here, but we'll understand if your parents want you there."

Jake drew in a deep breath. "I'll be wherever Liam is, I'll tell you that now." Laughter drifted through the hallway, and he smiled. "He's on the phone with Dev an' Pauli." They'd invited him and Liam to Atlanta the previous weekend, and it had been a blast, spending time with them. What had been even better was not having Liam's parents nearby, and they'd made the most of every minute they got.

Liam came into the room, his phone to his ear. "Yeah, sure, I'll pass that on. Now lemme finish packin', will ya?" He laughed.

"Sure. We'll let you know." He disconnected the call, shaking his head. "Those two."

"What now?" Jake loved seeing Liam so relaxed and happy. He'd made sure that from the minute Liam walked through the door after work, he didn't have to worry about a thing.

Liam rolled his eyes. "Pauli wants to know when he needs to start plannin' for a weddin' shower."

Jake suddenly launched into a coughing fit, and Sharon patted his back. "Breathe, Jakey, breathe," she said, barely able to get the words out for laughing. When he stopped, she smirked. "The thought scared ya that much, huh?" She walked out of the room, her shoulders still shaking.

Jake glared at Liam. "Did ya *have* to say that while your mom was here? I mean, really?"

Liam chuckled and kissed him on the cheek. "Get used to it. One of these days, she's gonna be your mother-in-law."

"Can we not talk about that now? I mean, we got a long way to go before we can be thinkin' 'bout such things." Not that he didn't love the idea…

Liam's eyes sparkled. "You change your mind? Gettin' cold feet?"

Jake arched his eyebrows. "Hell no. But we gotta be practical, right?"

Liam sighed. "I guess." He looked around the room. "You done?"

"I jus' have to decide who gets custody of the sex toys, apparently."

Liam snickered. "Me. That way, I get to call ya late at night, an' tell ya what I'm doin' with 'em." He grinned. "Look at it this way. We both get to come, right?"

Jake didn't see the funny side. "Sorry, but all I can see is us bein' apart."

Liam walked over to him and wrapped his arms around him. "We will find a way, I promise. I don't want you goin' back there neither. Let's wait an' see if there've been any changes while you've been gone, okay? It might not be as bad as you think."

"No, it might be a lot, lot worse." Jake sighed heavily. "Ignore me. I've jus' got the 'leavin' Liam blues'." He glanced at the clock beside the bed. "We'd best be on our way. I'll take first shift at drivin'. We can change over when you stop to take a leak. Because you know you *will* stop, right?" He smirked.

Liam reached down and swatted his butt. "That's for sassin' me."

Jake grinned. "You love it, an' you know it." He tried to put on a brave face, but inside he was aching.

I jus' wanna be with him, Lord. Can't ya jus' work that into your plans somehow?

Then he remembered the Lord's lousy sense of humor, and doubted it.

Liam switched off the engine, then rested his hands on the steering wheel. "Wanna take a minute before we go inside?"

Jake shook his head. "Can't put it off forever. Besides, it'll be warmer in there. Mama'll have the fire going."

"I booked a room at the Holiday Inn. I don't expect for one second they'll be happy 'bout me stayin' here tonight, an' I'm not gonna drive here an' back in one day." Liam squeezed his thigh. "An' if you wanna join me, then you'd best be prepared to let them know that."

"Yeah, I know." Jake took a couple of deep, calming breaths. "Let's do this."

They got out of the car, and Liam popped the trunk so he could get his bags. No Mama at the front door gave him an uneasy feeling, but Jake pushed it down deep.

Time to face the music.

Jake opened the door and stepped into the warm interior, Liam behind him. "Mama? Daddy?" He'd sent Daddy a text before they'd left Wilmington, giving him an idea of when they'd arrive.

"In the kitchen," Mama called out. "I'll be right with ya."

Jake walked through the living room where as predicted, a fire blazed, sending its heat out into the room. They went into the toasty kitchen. The air was filled with the mouthwatering aroma of freshly baked bread, and he breathed it in. "Smells good."

Mama stood beside the stove, stirring a pan. She smiled when she saw Jake, then gave Liam a cautious nod. "Hey. I've jus' finished makin' a batch of sausage gravy." She turned off the heat under it and put a lid on top.

That was enough to have Jake's stomach making a comment. Beside him, Liam snickered.

Mama chuckled. "I swear, you're always hungry."

"Tell me about it," Liam muttered. "I still have no clue where he puts it all."

To Jake's surprise, Mama smiled at Liam. "I know! He's such a skinny thing. But *I* can eat a slice of cake an' gain three inches on my waistline." She flushed. "Sit down, both of ya. I'll go fetch your daddy. He's out back, choppin' logs for the fire." And before they could say a word, she was out of there.

"Okay, that was… not what I expected." Jake sat at the table and patted the empty chair beside him. "You sit here. I want you close."

"Like I'd be anywhere else." Liam pulled out the chair and sat. "Your mama seems in a good mood."

"Yeah, I noticed." He wasn't about to get his hopes up, however. She hadn't hugged him, so this wasn't gonna be plain sailing. Daddy presented more of a problem though.

The back door opened, and Daddy came in, bundled up in his thick winter jacket. He gave them a brief nod, his expression neutral, then removed his outerwear and peered at the coffee machine. "There coffee still goin'?"

"Made some fresh five minutes ago," Mama said from behind him. "Now, why don't you sit with Jake an' Liam while I pour some? You boys want coffee?"

"Please, Mama." Jake was aware of a rolling sensation in

his belly, and his mouth dried up.

Nothing was said until Mama sat down, after placing four mugs of coffee on the table, along with sugar and creamer.

"Good trip here?" Daddy asked, dumping two spoonfuls of sugar into his coffee.

"Yeah. It was a pretty straight run," Liam commented.

Daddy said nothing, but gave another brisk nod. Silence fell once more.

Jake's heart was pounding, and he was feeling jumpy as hell. He glanced at Liam, who seemed as puzzled as he was by his parents' behavior. *C'mon, Mama, Daddy, say somethin'!*

Daddy cleared his throat. "I guess before we talk about the two of you, we need to share some things that've happened since you've been gone. Pretty major changes."

Jake blinked. "What's happened?"

"Well, for one thing, we stopped goin' to the United Methodist."

What. The. Fuck? Jake gazed at his mama, stunned into silence.

She nodded. "After you left, I went to see Reverend Hubbert. I needed advice, 'cause I didn't know which way was up anymore. I mean, I know I'd been expectin' somethin' like this, but findin' out you already had a… boyfriend, well, that kinda blew me away." She drank a little coffee before continuing. "Anyhow, he made it clear you'd only be welcome in the church if you repented an' turned your back on… homosexuality. He also made it clear that if this didn't happen, I—we—should turn our backs on *you*, until such time as you saw the 'error of your ways' as he put it."

"Oh, Mama." Jake's heart ached for her. "So what did you say to him?"

Mama drew herself up straight. "I thanked him for his advice, then I told him I'd be findin' another church." Her brows knitted. "What kinda man expects a mama to turn her back on her own son? It jus' didn't feel right. More than that—it didn't feel Christian. That church talks about love an' acceptance, but I sorta

370

got the feelin' that only goes for people who ain't gay, or… black, or… just plain diff'rent." She took another sip of coffee. "So… your daddy went on the internet, an' we found us another church."

"Where?" Jake's head was spinning. Liam appeared equally dumbfounded.

"Church of the Savior in Knoxville. We went last Sunday," she said proudly. "They say everyone is welcome there." Then she gave Jake a shy smile. "There are… gay people in the congregation. The minister introduced me to a couple of 'em, after I told them 'bout you an' Liam, an' why we were there. They seemed like real nice people. An' he said we all worship the same God anyhow, so it don't matter where I worship Him, right?" Mama set her jaw. "I was *not* gonna lose my only child."

Jake was out of his chair in a second, wrapping his arms around her in a tight hug. "Love you, Mama," he whispered. She kissed his cheek, her hand curling around his nape, stroking his hair.

When they parted, she wiped her damp eyes and patted his cheek. Jake retook his chair. Mama held out a hand to Liam across the table. "As a good Christian, I'm to love *all* God's people."

Liam stared at her outstretched hand for a moment, then took it, and they shook. Jake felt like his heart was about to burst. He hadn't expected any of this, and he knew Mama's statement was her way of telling Liam he was okay in her book. Not exactly a 'welcome to the family' but it was a damn good start.

That still left Daddy.

Jake's hands shook a little as he picked up his mug. He badly wanted to hold Liam's hand, but he didn't dare.

"Okay, I gotta say somethin'," Daddy said, his voice gruff. "You can't jus' walk in here, drop that bomb, an' expect me to change views I've held all my life."

Oh.

"'Cause that jus' ain't gonna happen overnight, y'hear?"

Jake stilled. Under the table, Liam's hand crept onto his thigh, and Jake seized it.

Daddy sighed. "But I keep lookin' at the change in your mama. She's accepted the situation, an' found peace in that decision. An' then I saw what happened to Reverend Hubbert. That was a shocker. Made me think twice too."

"What?" Jake gaped. "What happened?"

"Seems the United Methodist Church didn't hold with his views. They removed him."

"But... how did they find out?"

"Word got to them 'bout some of the things he'd been sayin'," Mama said. "Seems they didn't like the spin he put on things, an' they certainly didn't hold with parents bein' told to disown a child."

"But... how did they find out what he'd said to ya?"

Mama's eyes flashed. "'Cause I told 'em. Called 'em up on the phone. That man thinks it's okay to tell me to cast you off? Hell no." She flushed. "If you get my meanin'."

Jake shook his head in wonder. *Way to go, Mama.* "When did all this happen?"

"A couple days ago. But I'm not goin' back there. I'm happy where I am." She gave Liam a hesitant smile. "Do *you* believe, Liam?"

He nodded. "My mom brought me up with the words God is Love." Liam shrugged. "But I didn't see much of that love in evidence in those who claimed to follow God's teachin's, so I stopped goin' to church."

"I'd be real happy if you an' Liam would come with me tomorrow mornin'." She paused. "You *are* gonna stay 'til tomorrow?"

The hopeful note in her voice was what finally got to Jake, and he swallowed hard, fighting back tears. *Oh Lord. This jus' might work out.*

Liam smiled. "Yes, ma'am. I got a room at the Holiday Inn for tonight, an' I was gonna leave early tomorrow, but yeah, I'll come with ya." He gave Jake an inquiring glance.

Jake nodded. "We both will." Then he brought their clasped

hands out from under the table, and placed them in plain sight.

Mama gazed at them and swallowed. Then she nodded. "It's almost supper time. I don't suppose you boys would like some of my freshly made biscuits an' gravy?"

Liam beamed. "I would love some. Jake always talks about your cookin', ma'am."

Mama's face lit up. "He's a good boy." She bit her lip. "Guess he's not a boy anymore." Her gaze met Jake's. "You're a good man, son."

Liam squeezed his hand, and Jake squeezed right back.

Jake snuck a glance at his daddy, who was staring at their joined hands, his expression unreadable. It felt like they'd won this battle, but not the war. At least hostilities had ceased for the moment, thank God. "You okay, Daddy?"

It took him a moment to respond. "Jus' gonna have to give me some time, alright?"

Jake could do that.

Liam shivered. "Tell me why we're out here in the freezin' night air, when we could be in my hotel room, all cozy under the covers." The stone was hard and cold beneath him.

Jake chuckled. "Hey, it's romantic. A walk by the creek in the moonlight."

"Sure, with flashlights so we don't fall head first into the creek 'cause we can't see a damn thing," Liam groused. Not that he really minded all that much.

"Shut up an' cuddle me," Jake said, snuggling closer, sitting in Liam's lap.

Liam sighed, his arms around Jake. "I suppose we had to come back here, right?"

"I wanted to make a wish," Jake protested. He laid his head on Liam's shoulder. "Still can't believe Mama didn't say a word when I said I wanted to go to the hotel with ya."

"You heard what she said. You're a man now." Liam snickered. "I have to say, I have never heard you be so diplomatic. Why, even the way you brought up the subject was respectful."

"You catch more flies with honey than with vinegar, or didn't you know that?"

Liam kissed his head. "You made your wish yet? 'Cause I'm freezin' my ass off out here."

"Gimme a minute. This is important."

Liam sat there in the cold night air, the moonlight sparkling on the water, casting its bluish light over the trees, giving everything a ghostly appearance. Despite the cold, Jake was warm in his arms.

"You take your time. I already got my wish." *Right here in my arms.*

Jake sighed. "I still have no clue where we'll end up livin'."

"It doesn't matter, long as we're together." Liam tightened his arms around Jake. "Do you wanna stay in LaFollette?"

"I don't know. I mean, you know what's it's like here."

"See, I'd have said the same thing a couple of months ago, but times are changin' here too. Because if an openly gay guy can open a business here, an' not get chased outta town by a mob wieldin' pitchforks, then maybe there's hope for LaFollette too."

"Give it time," Jake said darkly. "They're still stunned. They could be meetin' right now in secret, puttin' their plans together."

Liam snickered. "You have way too active an imagination."

"I thought you liked my imagination," Jake said with a chuckle, snaking a hand over Liam's crotch.

"Down, boy. Besides, not even your dirty talk could help me get it up right now. I'm freezin' my nuts off."

Jake's peal of bright laughter rang out, and Liam rejoiced to hear it.

"Okay, so we may have to spend some time apart until we decide on somethin' more permanent," Liam told him, "but that won't change how we feel 'bout each other." He grinned. "Jus' think about all those times to come when we get together." *Lord, we'll burn up the sheets.*

Jake tilted his head up, and Liam kissed him, a soft brushing of lips.

"Okay, I'm done. I've made my wish. Let's get the fuck out of here." Jake got to his feet and offered Liam a hand.

"It'd better come true, after bringin' me out here to freeze my buns off," Liam grumbled.

Jake cackled. "I'll get you warm again, don't you worry."

Liam had no doubt about that whatsoever.

Together, they clambered off the boulder, and carefully made their way back to the house.

It wasn't perfect, but it was a good start.

Truth & Betrayal

Epilogue

March 2018

"Food'll be here in thirty minutes," Jake shouted through the bathroom door.

He caught Liam's chuckle above the noise of the shower. "You *can* come in an' tell me that, instead of yellin'."

Jake stuck his head around the door. "Hell no. I know what happens. You charm me with your gorgeous bod, you wiggle that delicious ass, an' the next thing ya know, we're fuckin' in the shower."

Liam pulled aside the shower curtain, revealing his hand lazily pumping his dick. "Would that be a bad thing?" His eyes gleamed wickedly.

"When we got supper comin' any second? Yes!" *Lord, but he's beautiful.* Another thought sent happiness surging through him. *An' he's mine.*

Liam turned his back to Jake and jiggled his ass cheeks. "Yeah, but you *could* be comin' in this." He glanced over his shoulder and grinned, rubbing soapy hands over his ass and spreading it, revealing that dark, enticing cleft. Then Liam turned around and waved his cock at him, still grinning.

Jake let out a sound of exasperation and left him to it. *Goddamn tease.* He smiled to himself. Like he expected anything else.

The sound of running water stopped. "I meant to ask, seen much of Taylor lately?"

"We saw a movie last week." A pretty crap movie, as it

turned out, so bad it was hilarious.

"No change there? He still on his own?"

"He hasn't said anything, but you know what? There's somethin' he's not tellin' me. Not sure what, but he's been kinda quiet."

Liam emerged from the bathroom, a towel slung low around his hips, doing little to hide his hard-on. Not that Jake could blame him for that. Two weeks without seeing each other made for a *very* horny Liam, and an even hornier Jake.

"Everything *is* okay between you two?"

Jake nodded. It had taken a month after The Conversation as Liam liked to call it, for things to get back to normal between them. Taylor had been the first to break the ice, apologizing over and over for opening his mouth in the first place. His pain had been so genuine, Jake had taken pity on him, and let him know they were good again. And he'd been delighted to learn what had happened between Jake and Liam. He'd not asked to meet Liam on any of his weekend visits, and Jake knew that was because Taylor got it.

Weekends were precious.

Jake tried not to stare as Liam walked around the hotel room, that bulge still making his mouth water. "Did you hear Wendy callin' out to us when we came back this afternoon? You know you're spendin' way too much time in a hotel when housekeeping wave at you an' call you by your name, an' you know theirs."

Liam snickered. "What d'ya expect? We're gettin' to be part of the furniture 'round this place."

He had a point. They'd spent Christmas with Liam's family, but apart from that, every two weeks Liam made the trip from North Carolina to Tennessee, leaving Wilmington as soon as he finished work Friday, and driving through the night. Jake would be waiting in the hotel room for him, and it didn't matter what time it was when Liam walked through that door, or how tired he was—clothes got discarded, bodies slipped between soft sheets, and two lovers connected again. No words, only kisses and caresses, hands learning the feel of each other's body all over again, and then the only noises were their breathing and the slick sounds of mouths and dicks lost in exploration, until both of them came with soft cries of joy.

Jake lived for those weekends, and sometimes it felt like his heart would break when Liam drove away, always leaving it way too late because neither of them wanted to say goodbye. He knew it was hard on Liam, doing all the driving, but they both agreed this was how they wanted it. Two nights in a hotel, with all its privacy, beat staying with Liam's family hands down.

The downside was the money they were spending on hotels and gas bills.

Liam sat on the bed, pillows stuffed behind his head as usual. "Come an' lie here for a minute. I wanna talk to ya."

Jake joined him, stretching out beside him, his head on Liam's chest so he could feel his heart beating. "Love it when we're like this," Jake said softly.

"Me too." Liam kissed the top of his head. Jake loved it when he did that.

"I was pretty impressed with what your dad did, by the way."

Jake smiled. "Yeah. Pretty cool, huh?" Daddy had finally taken Jake's advice and turned the linen closet in the hallway into a shower. Granted, it wasn't huge, but having that extra shower was great. No more racing between him and daddy as to who got to clean up first.

"We had a talk while you were in the kitchen with your mom."

"You did?" Jake craned his neck to stare at Liam. "What did y'all talk about?" That was a first right there.

"He was askin' me how work was goin' at the bank. When I told him they were lookin' to promote me into management, he seemed impressed. Then he talked about you, tellin' me about the house y'all are workin' on right now." Liam smiled. "He is *so* proud of you, baby."

"I've missed that," Jake said with a sigh.

"What?"

"You callin' me baby."

Liam chuckled. "Not sure how. You get to hear it every night when we talk on the phone."

"Yeah, but it's not the same thing as havin' you here to say it." Jake gave himself a little mental kick. These weekends were too precious to spend one second of them complaining or whining. "Ignore me. What did ya wanna talk about?"

Liam stroked his hair, his fingers gently moving over Jake's scalp in a soothing motion. "I've been thinkin'."

"Should I be worried?"

Liam swatted his arm. "Ass. I'm bein' serious here. I've come to a decision, an' I want to share it with ya."

Jake sat up slowly, the hairs on his arms standing on end. "I'm list'nin'."

"I've decided to apply for a job at another bank. In fact, I've already got an application ready to go, an' from what I've heard, I'm in with a good chance of gettin' the job."

He stilled. "Ain'tcha happy at your place?" He had no idea Liam felt this way.

Liam's eyes widened. "Huh? Oh, *'course* I'm happy. But I was happy in Atlanta too. I'd be happy anywhere, 'cause I don't mind workin' hard."

"So where's this bank you wanna apply to?"

Liam locked gazes with him. "Peoples Bank of the South, Jacksboro Pike."

Oh Lord, my beatin' heart. "Here? In LaFollette?"

Liam nodded slowly. He peered intently at Jake. "I thought you'd be pleased. Hell, I thought you'd be swingin' from the chandeliers."

"Don't get me wrong," Jake said quickly. "I *love* the idea of you movin' here, but…" He tried to get his thoughts into some semblance of order. *Don't get too excited. He hasn't thought this through.* "You know what it's like here."

"Sure I do. I only have to walk down Central Avenue with ya, an' I get looks. Not from everyone, but yeah, from a few people. Half the time I'm not sure if they're starin' at me 'cause of the color of my skin, or 'cause I'm walkin' with you, an' they've heard all about 'that gay couple'." He air-quoted. "But we gotta be practical here. Your dad wants you to carry on the business when he retires, right?"

Jake nodded. He wanted that too.

"Then it makes sense for ya to stay here. An' as for the looks an' the comments, so what? I got a thick skin."

Jake smirked. "You're gonna need it." He didn't allow himself the luxury of hoping. Not yet at any rate.

Liam tugged him until he was straddling Liam's lap. "I can cope with anything—long as I have you."

Lord, if that didn't make him wanna melt into Liam's arms…

"You're serious 'bout this, ain'tcha?"

Liam nodded. "I've thought of nothin' else since I last saw ya. I don't know 'bout you, but I've had enough of drivin' back an' forth, bein' bone-tired Monday mornin's 'cause we've gotten so little sleep the previous two nights, jus' livin' for those precious days we get to spend together…" He sighed. "It's not enough. I want more. An' for me, that means bein' where you are."

"So… does this mean we can start lookin' for a place of our own?" It was finally sinking in.

Liam laughed. "Well, let me get the job first, but sure. An' we already have a deposit. Mom said she an' Dad wanted to contribute, sort of an early… weddin' present."

Jake's breath caught in his throat. "Seriously?"

Liam's eyes shone as he cupped Jake's cheek. "Like I said, white picket fences, a dog—an' wedding bands."

Jake didn't let him get any further. He leaned in and kissed him, pouring every ounce of his love into that kiss. Liam sighed contentedly, his hands on Jake's waist, back, and shoulders.

Then he broke the kiss and smiled, and it lit up his face. "Lord, the look on your mama's face when I go 'round there an' ask her an' your daddy for permission."

"You're not gonna do that." Jake gaped at him.

Liam chuckled. "I'm an old-fashioned Southern boy. You bet your ass I will."

Jake couldn't wait to see his daddy's face either. "Not jus' yet? Let 'em get used to ya bein' around before we drop that on 'em?"

Liam laughed. "Whatever you say. I can wait. I'm not goin' anywhere."

Thank the Lord for that.

Liam glanced at the clock on the TV. "How long we got 'til the food arrives?"

Jake did a quick guesstimate. "Maybe fifteen minutes?"

Liam grinned. "Great. I got the very thing to occupy us 'til then." He pushed the towel lower, revealing his heavy cock that pointed right at Jake. "Well, to occupy your mouth, more accurately."

Jake laughed. "Perfect. I forgot to order a starter." And with that, he shifted down the bed to give Liam's dick the attention it deserved.

Fifteen minutes my ass. Jake intended to have Liam calling out his name in five.

He paused, the head of Liam's cock right there, and smiled.

"Somethin' wrong?" Liam asked him.

"I was jus' thinkin'… our life is gonna work out jus' fine."

Liam stroked Jake's short hair. "No thinkin' allowed. We've got the next fifty years to work it all out. Now, get busy." And then he pushed Jake down onto his dick, and Jake smiled again, his mouth full.

There sure are gonna be a lot of ups an' downs in our future. Not that he was worried. Liam was right. They could cope with anything, as long as they had each other.

Then he lost himself to the task in hand.

Well… mouth.

The End

A note from K.C.

Let's talk barebacking.

Safe sex – using condoms – has been the message preached ever since the AIDS era began.
But times are changing, and that means the message is changing too. HIV is still a threat, but now there are new weapons in our arsenal, namely PrEP (Pre-exposure prophylaxis). We are in a new era, the era of U=U (Undetectable Equals Untransmittable)
In this story, Jake is negative, and so is Liam. They are in a committed relationship. And once they decide not to use condoms, it isn't worth it to continue using PrEP, which is there to reduce the risk of transmitting HIV.
PrEP does have one limitation. As mentioned in the book, it can't protect against STDs. That's where condoms come in.
But…
Some men choose not to use condoms, for a variety of reasons.
The excitement that comes from taking a risk.
The sensations of skin-to-skin sex.
The expression of complete trust in a partner, and the intimacy this creates.
So it comes – pun intended – down to making conscious, sex-positive decisions.
Unprotected sex requires communication, knowing a partner's status – and being truthful with each other.
I recently read an article that says all this much more eloquently than I could. You can find it here: https://bodymindsoul.org/articles/gay-sexuality/why-do-men-bareback/
One final word: if times are changing, then books should reflect that change too.

Need to talk to someone about this?
https://switchboard.lgbt/

By K.C. Wells

Find out more about PrEP and U=U here:
https://men.PrEPfacts.org/the-basics/
https://www.positivelyaware.com/articles/undetectable-equals-untransmittable

And if you've enjoyed this book, please consider leaving a review on Amazon or BookBub.

Thank you for your support, and keep reading!

Jake and Liam will be back!
Coming 2019.... Pride & Protection.

What happens when an out-and-proud bear moves to a small Tennessee town, and takes a shine to the closeted cop? Fireworks, that's what.

When Del Walters agrees to go into business with his brother, he has one condition. Since he's putting up the lion's share, they'll run the bike shop *his* way - and that means he gets to choose the name. And in a small Tennessee town, a business called Rainbow Racers, complete with a not-so-subtle sign, was always going to attract attention.
Unfortunately, it's the wrong kind of attention, and after a few incidents, Del is forced to call on the local police to deal with the culprits.
When Officer Taylor Cox walks into his shop, Del thinks Christmas has come early. There's only one problem - Taylor is in the closet, and there's no way Del is going back into his.

When Taylor lays eyes on the sexy bear who owns the bike shop, he knows he's walking into trouble. Not that he's about to let Del know he's interested: his view from the closet is just fine, thank you very much. But as time goes by, Taylor realizes how badly he is torn between protecting the persona he's created, and giving in to his desires. And Del making it obvious that he wants Taylor isn't helping matters.

Between an out-and-proud bear and a firmly closeted cop, something has to give. Problem is, it might be their hearts.

By K.C. Wells

Coming soon from Dreamspinner Press

August, 2018

Threepeat (Book #3 in the Secrets series, written with Parker Williams.)

Can two Doms open their hearts again for a young man desperately in need of their help?

Two years ago, Aaron Greene and Sam Thompson were devastated when their submissive broke the contract that bound the three of them together. They still wonder what happened and whether they can find a way to move forward. When Aaron finds a sick young man by the curbside, his protective instincts kick in, and after consulting Sam, he takes Tim home.

After being thrown out of his home, Tim Waterman finds himself on the street, doing whatever he needed to survive. Until a bear of a Good Samaritan scoops him up and saves him. Then one bear becomes two, and a chance discovery gets him thinking about what might be, if he's bold enough to make a move.

So what happens when Aaron and Sam wake up one morning to find Tim naked in their bed? Will they get a new chance at life, or will history Threepeat itself?

October, 2018.

Truth Will Out (A Merrychurch Mystery)

Jonathon de Mountford's visit to Merrychurch village to stay with his uncle Dominic gets off to a bad start when Dominic fails to appear at the railway station. But when Jonathon finds him dead in his study, apparently as the result of a fall, everything changes. For one thing, Jonathon is the next in line to inherit the manor house. For another, he's not so sure it was an accident, and with the help of Mike Tattersall, the owner of the village pub, Jonathon sets out to prove his theory—if he can concentrate long enough, without getting distracted by the handsome Mike.

They discover an increasingly long list of people who had reason to want Dominic dead. And when events take an unexpected turn, the amateur sleuths are left bewildered. It doesn't help that the police inspector brought in to solve the case is the last person Mike wants to see, especially when they are told to keep their noses out of police business.

In Jonathon's case, that's like a red rag to a bull....

By K.C. Wells

Segreti Personali
Strettamente personale

Es wird persönlich
Persönliche Veränderungen
Mehr als Persönliche
Persönliche Geheimnisse
Streng Persönlich

Confetti, Cake & Confessions
Confetti, Coriandoli e Confessioni

Conncctions
Connexion

Saving Jason
Per Salvare Jason
Jasons Befreiung
A Christmas Promise

Island Tales
Waiting for a Prince
September's Tide
Submitting to the Darkness

Le Maree di Settembre
In Attesa di un Principe
Piergarsei alle tenebre

Lightning Tales
Teach Me
Trust Me
See me
Love Me

Lehre Mich
Vertau Mir
Sieh Mich
Liebe Mich

Il Professore
Fidati di me

<u>A Material World</u>
Lace
Satin
Silk
Denim

Spitze
Satin
Seide

Pizzo
Satin

Double or Nothing
Back from the Edge
Switching it up
Scambio di ruoli

<u>Anthologies</u>

<u>Fifty Gays of Shade</u>
Winning Will's Heart

By K.C. Wells

About the author

K.C. Wells started writing in 2012, although the idea of writing a novel had been in her head since she was a child. But after reading that first gay romance in 2009, she was hooked.
She now writes full time, and the line of men in her head, clamouring to tell their story, is getting longer and longer. If the frequent visits by plot bunnies are anything to go by, that's not about to change anytime soon.

If you want to follow her exploits, you can sign up for her monthly newsletter: http://eepurl.com/cNKHlT

You can stalk – er, find – her in the following places:
Facebook: **https://www.facebook.com/KCWellsWorld**

https://www.facebook.com/kcwells.WildWickedWonderful/
Goodreads:
https://www.goodreads.com/author/show/6576876.K_C_Wells
Instagram: **https://www.instagram.com/k.c.wells/**
Twitter: **https://twitter.com/K_C_Wells**
Blog: **http://kcwellsworld.blogspot.co.uk/**
Website: **http://www.kcwellsworld.com/**
Amazon: **https://www.amazon.com/default/e/B00AECQ1LQ**

Alter Egos

Writing MF romance as Kathryn Greenway

Kathryn Greenway lives on the Isle of Wight, off the southern coast of the UK, in a typical English village where there are few secrets, and everyone knows everyone else.

She writes romance in different genres, and under different pen names, but her goal is always the same - to reach that Happily Ever After.

Pulled by a Dream is Kathryn's debut novel, although in a whole other life, she is K.C. Wells, a bestselling author of gay romance.

Website: **https://www.kathryngreenway.com/**
Facebook: **https://www.facebook.com/KathrynGreen...**
Twitter: **https://twitter.com/KGreenwayauthor**
Instagram: **https://www.instagram.com/kgreenwayau...**
Goodreads: **https://www.goodreads.com/author/show/17633635.Kathryn_Greenway**
Amazon: **https://www.amazon.com/-/e/B0795VY3TM**

You can find Pulled by a Dream here: **http://mybook.to/PBAD**

Who is Tantalus?

For those who like their stories intensely erotic, featuring hot men and even hotter sex….
Who don't mind breaking the odd taboo now and again….
Who want to read something that adds a little heat to their fantasies….
…there's Tantalus.

By K.C. Wells

Because we all need a little tantalizing.
Tantalus is the hotter, more risqué alter ego of K.C. Wells Amazon page:
https://www.amazon.com/Tantalus/e/B01IN33IZO

Playing with Fire (Damon & Pete)
A series of (so far) four short gay erotic stories:
Summer Heat
After
Consequences
Limits

(Hopefully) coming in 2018, the first Tantalus novel in a new series, Leather & Kink

Learning the Notes

Steven Torland is about to reach his fiftieth birthday, and to celebrate the occasion, his publicist decides it's time someone wrote a biography of the famous composer and musician. When writer Kyle Mann is approached with the idea, he's flattered and leaps at the chance. It will be his first biography. The idea of spending six months getting to know Steven and researching his history excites him, but there is the added frisson that Steven is sexy as hell. Kyle has always had a thing for older men, and it's no secret that Steven is gay. In his heart Kyle knows it's just a fantasy, but he can still dream, right?

It doesn't take Steven long to realize he wants Kyle in his bed, and Steven usually gets what he wants. But Kyle proves to be more than a convenient fuck. There's something about him that leads Steven to think maybe it's time to let Kyle see the real Steven Torland, the one who is no stranger to the leather community of San Francisco.

Steven aims to take things nice and slow, because he doesn't want this one to get away. He wants it all – a lover in his life and a boy in his bed – and he wants to see just how far he can push Kyle, and what Kyle is prepared to do to please him.

Kyle has no idea how much his life is about to change….

Printed in Poland
by Amazon Fulfillment
Poland Sp. z o.o., Wrocław